Hard Men

Hard Men

Patrick Califia

alyson books
los angeles

ALL CHARACTERS IN THIS BOOK ARE FICTITIOUS. ANY RESEMBLANCE TO REAL INDIVIDUALS—EITHER LIVING OR DEAD—IS STRICTLY COINCIDENTAL.

© 2004 BY PATRICK CALIFIA. ALL RIGHTS RESERVED.

MANUFACTURED IN THE UNITED STATES OF AMERICA.

THIS TRADE PAPERBACK ORIGINAL IS PUBLISHED BY ALYSON PUBLICATIONS,
P.O. BOX 4371, LOS ANGELES, CALIFORNIA 90078-4371.
DISTRIBUTION IN THE UNITED KINGDOM BY TURNAROUND PUBLISHER SERVICES LTD.,
UNIT 3, OLYMPIA TRADING ESTATE, COBURG ROAD, WOOD GREEN,
LONDON N22 6TZ ENGLAND.

FIRST EDITION: JULY 2004

04 05 06 07 08 a 10 9 8 7 6 5 4 3 2 1

ISBN 1-55583-646-1

LIBRARY OF CONGRESS CATALOGING-IN-PUBLICATION DATA
    CALIFIA-RICE, PATRICK, 1954–
        HARD MEN / PATRICK CALIFIA.—1ST ED.
        ISBN 1-55583-646-1 (PBK.)
        1. GAY MEN—FICTION. 2. EROTIC STORIES, AMERICAN. I. TITLE.
    PS3553.A3987H37 2004
    813'.54—DC22   2004046255

CREDITS
COVER PHOTOGRAPHY BY BODY IMAGE PRODUCTIONS.
COVER DESIGN BY LOUIS MANDRAPILIAS.

This book is dedicated to the memory of Stuart E. Denton of Plainfield, Conn., who killed himself on January 20, 2002, after being arrested and charged with the criminal misdemeanor of loitering for indecent purposes at the Amazing Video store in Johnston, R.I. Fifty-five years old, he was the former treasurer of the Plainfield Republican Committee, a graduate of the University of Massachusetts at Amherst, the chairman of the Planning and Zoning Commission in his hometown, and a divorced father of one son, and he served as an Air Force captain in the early 1970s. He was employed as the long-term supervisor of housekeeping and laundry at a New London nursing home.

Three of the men who were arrested with him pleaded no contest to disorderly conduct and paid $93.50 apiece for court costs. They had their cases filed for a year, with the possibility of having their convictions erased from their records. Two entered not guilty pleas, and it was likely at the time this was written that they would win acquittals. Denton hanged himself after the Providence Journal in Rhode Island and the Norwich Bulletin in Plainfield published his name, address, and photo along with the personal information of the men who were arrested with him.

Under the aegis of eradicating "public sex," the cops had to go into an adult bookstore and then pay $5 apiece to enter a separate section of the premises, a small adult movie theater. Denton may or may not have had his own or another man's dick in his hand when the cops busted him, but the police have blood on their hands. And so do the newspaper editors responsible for violating the privacy of men who had not been convicted of any crime, knowing full well that to publicize the accusations against them would leave their lives in ruin. If my life has any purpose it is to lift the shame from men like Stuart Denton and put it back on the heads of those to whom it truly belongs.

CONTENTS

Acknowledgments—ix
How Hard Can It Be? An Introduction—xi
Belonging—1
Swimmer's Body—17
The Hostage—37
The Spoiler—53
Prez Meets His Match—77
Unsafe Sex—87
The Wolf Is My Shepherd, I Shall Not Want—96
The Cop and His Choirboy (written with Matt Rice)—111
Skinned Alive—149
Parting Is Such Sweet Sorrow—166
Pussy Boy—193
Polar Bear Hunting—212
Hooked—232
Holes—242
Publication Credits—257

Acknowledgments

The following people provided invaluable assistance in the preparation of the material that appears in this book: Sasha Alyson, Scott Brassart (formerly at Alyson Publications), Drew Campbell, Stuart Kellogg, Carol Queen, Ian Philips, John Preston, Matthew D. Rice, and Martha Silverspring. I'm sure there are several other people I've "invited" (read: issued an ultimatum) to read these stories and comment on them. If I haven't named you specifically, it's because my memory fails me, not my gratitude. By the way, you didn't have to return that manuscript, especially if some of the pages were stuck together.

This book is for all of the men who have taught me (just by example or hands-on) what it means to be a man who desires other men and what to do about the need to slap somebody around and fuck them stupid or vice versa. My gratitude and passion go out to Jim, Steve McEachern, Tony, Mikal Shively, Fred Heromb, Sky Renfro, Mike Hernandez, Shadow Morton, John Mudd, Lou Sullivan, Jack Fertig, Marcus Wonacott, the marvelous Mister Marcus Hernandez, Steven Brown, Puma, Matthew Rice, Ian Philips, Gauge McCloud, DethGawd, Mark Pritchard, Jim Kane, Skip Aiken, Buzz Bense and Bob West, Peter Fiske, Robert McQueen, Louie Weingarden, John Osborne, Abe Dorland, Duncan, Rich Dockter, and many others who shall remain nameless but not forgotten.

This book goes out with my undying, heavy-breathin' love to the men who made me want to write about hard-ons, butt holes, and leather sex as well as they did and do: Derek Adams, Terry Andrews, Joseph Bean, William Carney, Justin Chin, M. Christian, Randy Conner (who has been an unflinching ally of telling the whole truth about the history of our sexuality and the spirituality of queer carnality), Tony De Blase (a.k.a. Fledermaus), Samuel Delany, Lars Eighner, Jack Fritscher, Geoff Mains, Boyd McDonald, Charles Nelson, Ian Philips, Mason Powell, John Preston, Mark Pritchard, Kirk Read, Wendell Ricketts, Thomas Roche, John Rowberry, Steven Saylor (a.k.a. Aaron Travis), Jay Shaffer, Simon Sheppard, Samuel Steward (a.k.a. Phil Andros), Mark Thompson, Larry Townsend, Dirk Vanden, Marco Vassi, Sparrow 13 Laughing Wand, Greg Wharton, Edmund White, James Williams, and many unsung wielders of the phallic pen who left their mark on a lot more pulp than glossy paper.

For bravery in the face of identity politics, I want to acknowledge the gay male erotica of Carol Queen, Laura Antoniou, and Poppy Z. Brite.

For his shining example of how to be a real gentleman in an era of scoundrels, blessings on James Green.

And my gratitude and tachycardia to Boy George, whom I adore from afar, because there is not nearly enough glamour and glitter in these pages. Despite facing challenges that would have broken many lesser men and women, you have been a strong advocate for being out, proud, and drop-dead gorgeous. No one could thank you enough for the inspiration and comfort you have given us by voicing so many of our hopes and fears.

Introduction: How Hard Can It Be?

This collection of rude queer porn is not like any of my other books of short stories. In the past, I've endeavored to include material that depicted characters of all sexual orientations. I wanted the reader to encounter a sexual narrative that did not necessarily match his or her own experience. This is partly because not all of us fantasize about the same things that we ourselves do and partly because I've always been interested in writing about how eroticism colors the lives of all sorts of different people. It's a challenge that has helped me to build new skills of expression and empathy that have made me a better writer and a better person. Besides, my sex life has never been easy to categorize. I'm usually attracted to masculinity, but the occasional over-18 girl (or boy) in a dress can also catch my eye. The presence of intelligence, a sense of humor, a smart mouth, and a certain level of masochism gets me going. Gender is a toy or a spice for me, not the piled-up stones of a pasture wall.

When Scott Brassart, then editor in chief at Alyson Publications, suggested that we pull together (as it were) my smut about men puttin' it to other men, I was dubious. But editors don't get to be editors unless they are good at talking writers into doing things. And I can't say it was entirely nonconsensual. (As is so often true when pleasure is mixed with pain, that is not an easy call to make.) What appealed to me about this assignment was the chance to take a more in-depth look at one aspect of my erotic fiction. Exactly what is it about men who are on the prowl or lying in wait for one another that gets me breathing hard? Rereading these stories has been a hot but sometimes funny stroll through my own

INTRODUCTION

horny obsessions—cops, men in leather, men who are tied up and getting fucked, big cocks, men who break the rules, tears, sex between two people who have vastly different amounts of social power or status, whipping, humiliation, blood, a few more cops, sex in public, jockstraps, sharp-tongued hustlers with blue eyes, and imagining the ways that gay male desire might play itself out in an entirely different world. (Where there will of course still be men dressed in what my friend Fergus calls "the black leather pants of moral ambiguity.")

Is it cheating to tell the reader how you feel about your own work? A short story ought to stand on its own. If the reader can't get all that he (or she) needs from the story itself, without the writer helping it along with explanations, surely it's a flop. Still, I can't resist the opportunity to gossip about myself. Unless you are the kind of person who never skips ahead in a book, you might want to pass over what follows and come back to it after you've perused the stories themselves without these annotations.

One of my first forays into gay male porn was "Belonging," a story that was quickly picked up by *Advocate Men*, then drafted by John Preston for the first volume in the prestigious *Flesh and the Word* series. The inspiration for this story was a desire to turn the tables on the stereotype of the fag who cruises tearooms all hot and bothered to suck straight-boy dick. (Not that there's anything wrong with that, thank you very much.) This is a no-holds-barred revenge story in which the most obnoxious straight boy I could possibly imagine gets kidnapped, railroaded, and rammed into queer sexual slavery. The gay academics who believe being gay is a matter of social learning rather than genetic predetermination probably never envisioned this sort of training program in how to become a submissive, cocksucking fuck toy for a top man who has never taken no for an answer.

"Swimmer's Body" was not nearly as successful. This is a pretty obscure little tale that appeared once in *Advocate Men* and generated so many irate letters that it was months before I got another assignment from then-editor Stuart Kellogg. The idea came

INTRODUCTION

from a line that appeared over and over again in personal ads of that era. Anybody who didn't go to the gym referred to himself as having a swimmer's body. This litany really annoyed me, probably because you will never find my bearish body in a gym or in a swimming pool, so I started playing with the many ways that it could be interpreted. Everybody knows what a mermaid looks like, but frankly, their reported preference for making love to dead sailors doesn't do a whole lot for me. (That's no way to show a man in uniform a good time!) What about their male counterparts, and what if they were queer? Apparently some of the readers of *A-Men* weren't ready to be taken on this little fantasy trip with me. One guy was incensed enough to write to the magazine and complain that it was silly. As someone who has edited many such magazines, I can tell you that it's extremely rare to get a letter from a reader that says anything other than, "How can I get that hot model's phone number?"

Whether we're talking about writing smut or having sex, I think we risk being labeled silly any time we use our imaginations instead of relying on old, tired stock images. The ability to be flexible and take a chance on something new keeps sex piquant. I've beefed up the story a lot so perhaps in its current incarnation it will be more pleasing. This story was written long before the AIDS epidemic, so it's eerie for me to see a foreshadowing in it of "safer sex" in Marens's refusal to come inside of Gary until the young swimmer understands the implications of merging their internal ecosystems. The transformative power of semen plays a key role in mythology the world over, and this young man has to decide whether to remain locked into a system that is robbing him of his joy and individuality or accept his lover's come and become an entirely new sort of man. How do any of us deal with the ways in which our lust for homosex has made us into a breed apart? What most people may see as monstrous or freakish looks entirely different through the eyes of erotic longing. Lust is the salvation of the despised, restoring humanity and value to what the world repudiates.

INTRODUCTION

"The Hostage" was the third piece of gay male S/M erotica I wrote, and it did not fare as well as "Belonging" or even "Swimmer's Body." Editors rejected it because they were afraid it might be interpreted as describing sex between a child and an adult (which was most definitely not my intention). Rather, it is a different take on one of my favorite themes: the interplay of real social power with sexual power. Is love or pleasure possible when coercion is present? The hostage in this story ransoms his religion and his body to guarantee the safety of his people, but finds that his sexual servitude may be a good deal more complicated than merely submitting to a hated enemy. "The Hostage" also examines the very real power of the bottom, even one who is suborned, to fascinate and subvert the codes by which other men live. Who is really more powerful—the men who battle each other to possess something alluring or the valuable prize who may have subtly instigated the fight?

Just about every bottom in my life has hated "The Spoiler," and a couple of them have accused me of creating a piece of anti-bottom propaganda. Nothing could be further from my heart's (or hard-on's) desire. Still, art does imitate life, and in my real sex life I am fascinated by and enamored of the sweet torture of coaxing another top to lay it down for me. Need I add that if the Spoiler himself turned up at my elbow in the Eagle, I would not shoot him down?

"Prez Meets His Match" is excerpted from my first novel, *Doc and Fluff*, which is set in a future in which the union of the American states has been shattered by disease, financial disaster, war, and ecological catastrophe. In this unpredictable and ruined landscape, the free enterprise system still has its loyal adherents, albeit mostly among the criminal element. Doc is a big mean butch dyke who hobnobs with motorcycle gangs, drug manufacturers, and just about anybody else who can help her turn enough of a profit to keep her bike running. When she rides away from a bikers' party with the old lady of the club's president, he declares war. But he has a dirty little secret: He wants to keep the girl because

INTRODUCTION

he's taught her how to torture him. But Prez's sergeant-at-arms, Anderson, has sniffed out his commanding officer's masochism and pounces on him at a vulnerable moment. What follows is something you probably shouldn't try at home.

Porn writers have a lot of different strategies for dealing with the AIDS epidemic. The most popular tactic to take is to simply ignore it. Describing an ejaculation never made anybody seroconvert, and we ought to be free to at least fantasize about doing potentially risky things. In "Unsafe Sex," I take a few potshots at the A-gays and prudish fags of New York City who rejoiced when the Mineshaft was closed by the city. This alley encounter between an African-American top and a precious guppie guy raises some troubling questions about what really makes sex dangerous and who exactly is an unsafe person with whom to grapple.

Two stories in this book, "The Wolf Is My Shepherd, I Shall Not Want" and "Parting is Such Sweet Sorrow," rely on the same main character, a vampire named Ulric who suffers from unbearable loneliness because the nightwalkers who live on the blood of men cannot tolerate one another's company. He has taken the forbidden step of seeking out mortal companionship, despite the pain it would cause him to watch his beloved grow old and die. These two stories relate his bittersweet love for a Cajun bartender in one of San Francisco's South of Market leather bars.

Writing is the closest I'll ever come to sucking my own dick. It just takes you inside yourself in such a compelling way that collaborating with another writer is not something I've done very often. But "The Cop and His Choirboy" was the brainchild of me and my then-lover, Matt Rice. Even though we both lived in the city about 15 minutes apart, we did it a lot on the Internet. Kinky, huh? The e-mail messages our personae shot at one another eventually gelled into this not-a-love-story. Patrick Kelly is one of the meanest people I never hope to meet, and yet the smell of gunpowder and sexual doom that surrounds him makes knees grow weak whenever he crooks his little finger. Davy is a siren of the streets, a boy without a childhood who has forgotten more about human depravity than you'll ever know. Who can say which one of them hates the other more, or what sort of infernal force it would take to tear them apart?

One of the magazines that helps me pay my rent and keeps my mental pencil sharp is *Poz*, which was the center of a raging controversy when it published some articles about barebacking that truthfully examined why so many of us were fucking without condoms. Singled out to be pilloried in the straight press and the more conservative gay media was Tony Valenzuela, who had been brave enough to speak out about what it meant to him to sleep with another man's come inside of himself. The slogan "Use a condom every time" has saved a lot of lives, but it has also made it damn hard for us to talk or even think about what we give up when we stop sharing come.

If the news about barebacking was like blood in shark-infested waters, the revelation that there were gay men who consciously sought infection with HIV or who were willing to pass this "gift" on to another man made every homophobic moral panic about the AIDS pandemic seem justified. I wrote "Skinned Alive" in a deep state of grief, trying to communicate what it has meant to me to be isolated from other men because of fear of infection. In the world where this story takes place, a time when human beings touched each other at all is a dim memory. I don't know if I achieved my admittedly lofty goal of trying to convey both the horror of deliberate infection with a terminal disease and the fetishization of it, or the anxiety and need for human contact that leads to a desire to control, if nothing else, at least the time and place of being seeded. If nothing else, I wanted to humanize Valenzuela, because the harsh truth is that a lot of us have made the same decisions that he made; we just don't admit to it in public. And public health workers are still far, far away from figuring out how to take this information into account when they try to do education and prevention.

I don't have any answers to that problem either. But I do know that we only make matters worse when we cannot hold one

INTRODUCTION

another in mutual respect and compassion, knowing that any decision we make involves a risk of one kind or another, and that alienation and self-denial can be every bit as killing as a virus. Do you know what straight people call barebacking? They call it "making love." Despite the escalating rate of new HIV infections among heterosexual women, especially women of color, the federal government has never funded a single educational program to get heterosexual men to "use a condom every time."

When I worked as a volunteer at San Francisco Sex Information, answering random questions from an even more random public about virtually every aspect of human sexuality, I was amazed by the number of calls that came in from men who wanted to be castrated. It was a perplexing but apparently common fantasy. I have a lot of trepidation about allowing "Pussy Boy" to see print, because it takes this already drastic fetish one step further. Edge play is most safely done in fantasy or fiction. The Shadow is impersonal. In my forays toward its ever-receding secrets, I often wonder what would happen if some of the things that come out of people's mouths when they are getting plowed were taken literally. I trust the reader to understand that this story is not motivated by a hatred of cocks or men's bodies. However, you may recall the comments that some people made about "The Spoiler" being a piece of anti-bottom propaganda. Well, if there is such a piece in *Hard Men,* I'm afraid this is it.

Some stories never seem to find their niche in a periodical, which is why writers put them away in a desk drawer and haul them out when they do book-length collections. "Hooked" has been rejected by every single magazine I've sent it to. Science fiction magazines don't like it because it's a combination of SF and horror and way too kinky; porn magazines don't like it because there's not enough action that the average reader would recognize as hard-core pole-in-hole sex. But whenever I've read this piece out loud, it seems to grab the audience by some vital part of their anatomy, so maybe it will pin you down as well. If you've never fantasized about having sex with an alien, you'll probably wish I had left "Hooked" in my desk drawer. But I'll bet your dreams take you closer to the cave of the Reticulated Pythia than your rational self refused to go.

"Polar Bear Hunting" is by way of an apology to someone I've long had a crush on. For one stupid reason after another, we've never been able to consummate our mutual infatuation. While a dirty story is no substitute for the real deal, this may jump-start something more tangible between me and my far-too-distant polar bear. I hope it hotwires your engine as well.

Hard Men ends with "Holes," a story that elucidates another way in which this book is unique. (If you don't know what "elucidates" means, go get your dictionary. You're going to need it again later on. Just don't spill any lube on it.)

This won't be a surprise to some of you, but other men who have picked up this gay male–targeted product may be startled to learn that I wasn't born male. Although we are used to seeing everything in our community described by the awkward acronym LGBT, most of us have no intention of admitting people who are represented by those other letters into our friendship networks, let alone our beds and sex clubs. The emergence of gay or bisexual FTMs (female-to-male transsexuals) has been controversial in the transgendered community, where homophobia is as common as it is among straight people in the Midwest. Unfortunately, transmen also have to struggle with some huge obstacles to entering fully into the communities and erotic lives of genetic men who have sex with other men.

This story is more memoir than fiction, because it describes, as accurately as I am able to recall it, a very important episode from my own life that delineated my gender conflicts and my status as an outsider vis-à-vis leathermen's culture in the late '70s. This story is also about the weird ways in which men who have sex with other men have reconstructed masculinity. Gay men have made powerful use of the gay definition of manliness as aphrodisiac and lure, but they are also subject to the tyranny of heterosexual mandates and so operate in defiance of masculinity. This dance of

INTRODUCTION

attraction, appropriation, reworking, resistance, triumph, and guilt contains much of what I both detest and dote upon in the postmodern gay male identity.

How hard can it be for me to claim this desire, this social niche, as my own? I'm lucky to possess a set of specialized sadomasochistic skills that are in demand regardless of what people think my beard and genitalia make me. I don't know that it's possible to erase a very public history of living as a leatherdyke for more than 20 years. Those experiences are so precious to me that I don't want to set them aside either. Can you be a bisexual man who has a lesbian history? Erections are more than a clear sign that somebody is having a good time (or has just woken up with a full bladder). They are the rudders that genetic men take hold of to sail through the stormy sea of masculine expectations and obligations. A veteran who has lost his dick to a land mine is "unmanned," and a guy with a three-inch dick is "not much of a man." Or so some people would say.

But has this gold standard of maleness served us well? A hard-on is also just plain hard on the one who wears it—and impossible to sustain through every waking moment. It's interesting that men who try to do this wind up being called dickheads. We all recognize the potential cruelty of letting a cock off the leash of conscience. But a cock spends most of its time in a soft and vulnerable state, curled close to the body, nestled there in need of protection. And it isn't necessarily the primary locus of a man's desire. The cock stands guard over the asshole, which may be even more vociferous. Isn't there something sad about the phrase "fuck you" being a curse instead of a blessing?

One of the most difficult tasks I have faced is to create a personal vision of manhood that feels so valid and strong to me that I can wear it on the street and control my anxiety when the T-shaped Sword of Damocles is dangled over my head. (In other words, when the person I'm dealing with knows I am a tranny.) Like many other men, nature has not endowed me with a porn star's equipment. But that doesn't mean I can't be a good fuck or a

INTRODUCTION

good man, capable of courtesy and gentleness as well as sexual aggression and the maintenance of my territory and other boundaries. When I top, my intentions are diamond-hard and bright in my mind and body. What other people think of me is none of my business. I am only interested in the opinion of the orifice du jour.

If you think I don't know enough about cocks (those tender weapons) or queer boys' mean and yielding butt holes to do anything for yours, well, just sample a couple of these stories and see if your body agrees with your brain. The terror and beauty of sex lie in its ability to simultaneously make us aware of no one else's pleasure but our own and imbue us with the vicarious experience of another man's physical and emotional gestalt as he loses control (or claims it). For whatever knowledge the bodies of the men I've loved has given me, I remain eternally grateful, and eternally curious about what bawdy wisdom remains to be undressed and taken for my own.

Belonging

"Bartender!" Jerry shouted, loud enough to be heard over the raucous country music and the buzz of a very drunk Saturday night crowd. He was a handsome kid but spoiled-looking. In his mid 20s, he still wore the brooding expression of an adolescent who perpetually feels fucked-over and misunderstood. His clothes were cheap synthetics, too flashy for what they had cost him, and they made him seem oddly sleazy for somebody so young: James Dean playing the part of a bookie or a gigolo. He slammed his glass on the counter, not once but three times, and the startled, portly man at the sink in the middle of the bar hurried over to him, wiping his hands on his apron.

The barkeep was too harassed to notice the details of his obnoxious customer's personal appearance. His tastes ran to plump redheads with balcony-like bosoms. But there was somebody else in the bar whose preferred sexual quarry was young men whose expectations far exceeded their willingness to exert themselves. He had tracked Jerry to this noisy lair, and he was enjoying the opportunity to observe that sulky mouth and laugh silently to himself about the rude and ridiculous things that inevitably came out of it. Much better for a mouth like that to be taught silence. Hidden within the sozzled crowd, this hunter stroked the tool he used to gag his attractive but lazy prey. It was in good working order.

"Yeah?" the bartender said, none too friendly. The loudmouth was bobbing and weaving, scowling at the mirror behind the bar, obviously close to losing it.

That bitch Caroline, Jerry thought, *the fucking bitch. She won't let me in, and she won't answer my phone calls. How can I get to her? If*

I could talk to her, I'd make her understand. It's that guy I saw at her place, I know it, it's him, I'll bet he's with her right now and they're screwing their brains out. Shit! What makes her think she can do this to me, the whore? "Scotch and soda," he blared. "On the double."

"Forget it! The only thing I'm serving you is a cup of coffee. Finish what you got and go home."

There was no arguing with that grim, jowly face. Jerry picked up what was left of his drink and jostled his way through the crowd to the other side of the bar. There was a place by the pinball machine where he could lean against the wall. It took him two tries to light a cigarette. *Fuck, I must be high,* he thought, and tried to focus his eyes on the tip of his nose. Ouch. Yes. It was definitely getting drunk in this here shit-kickers' bar. He'd met Caroline in a much classier joint than this.

I must have looked like a fool, he thought, barging around, describing the cunt who stood him up, asking everybody in the place if they had seen her. *Took me forever to figure out she wasn't going to show. Then this woman said, "Be quiet. Sit down and help me finish this champagne."* Caroline never said "please" or "thank you" or asked a question, she just told you what to do and you did it, but he couldn't say she was rude, just very sure of herself. Way too sure of herself. She was wearing a severely tailored, dark wool suit, and he would have sworn she was wearing a man's shirt and tie if not for the pearl stickpin that held the length of silk in place. Her short black hair was expensively styled. He remembered thinking, *I sure got lucky, this one's old enough to know what she wants and rich enough to pay the price.*

Drunk as he was, it finally occurred to him that one of the men over by the pool table was not part of the quiet, business-like game—a handsome bastard with a big hooked nose and a black beard that made him look grim as hell. He wasn't dressed very nice for a weekend, just faded jeans and a T-shirt, one of those wide garrison belts that cops wear, and a black leather jacket. His hands were so big, you could hardly see the beer can he gripped.

Jerry's bitter reverie recovered from this brief interruption and flowed on, well-rehearsed. *All I did was drop by one Friday night. Is that a crime, huh? If a guy's been making it pretty regular with a broad for a couple of weeks, you figure he can drop by without getting arrested, right? Especially if he brings something along, I mean it isn't like I went over there empty-handed, for chrissake, I had a six-pack.*

The guy by the pool table turned toward him, hooked his thumb far back between his legs, and scratched his balls. He had a contemptuous look on his face, a look that said, "Kiss my ass."

When I rang her bell she didn't even use the intercom to ask who it was, just hit the buzzer and let me in. The front door to her loft wasn't locked. I walked right into her living room. And there's this dude stretched out in the armchair, watching porno movies on the color TV! Boy, was I mad. Anybody else would have slugged her.

Now the big man crossed his arms on his chest and pushed his hips forward a little. By some accident or some genius of self-arrangement, the length of his cock was a visible tube down the inner seam of one leg of his jeans. Then he made it jump. Jerry began to lose the thread of his aggrieved monologue. His mouth was awfully dry. He took a sip from his glass and adjusted the waistband of his slacks. It had been a long time since he'd gotten any. Weeks. Ever since she'd thrown him out, in fact. She had wheeled around, white-faced, and said, "You were not asked to be here." Step by step she had backed him into the foyer, not seeming to hear him as he demanded angrily who that man was, what was going on, until finally he shouted, "Goddamn it, I need to know that you belong to me!"

Her face broke into the biggest smile. "Don't worry," she said softly. "I know exactly what you need. And I'm going to make sure you get it." Beguiled by that sweet face and the sweeter promise, he had let her put him out and gone his way, confused but expecting to hear from her any day, to collect his reward for being so patient and understanding.

"Instead, all I get is a goddamn runaround," Jerry told his warm, flat drink.

Thumbs hooked in his pockets, the dark man stroked himself

discreetly, fingertips fanning out on his buttoned fly. His eyes flicked toward the back of the bar, then back to Jerry, with a questioning (but still hostile) stare. Here was a promise of satisfaction that would not be withdrawn at the last minute. *Queers just can't get enough of a real man's dick,* Jerry thought. But it was funny, he could usually spot faggots, and this guy was such a bad-ass, he looked like a truck driver or even a biker, maybe. *I look more like a queer than he does,* he thought, smoothing back the short sides of his hair and checking that the long top of his D.A. was still combed back, perfectly moussed and in place. But that wasn't too funny, and the injustice of it, the implied accusation, made him determined to follow through with the cruise. Shit, he'd never come here again anyway, he just stopped here because it was close to her house and he needed a drink after being turned away from her door again. So he headed toward the john, giving a look over his shoulder to see if the other guy had noticed. Wouldn't the girls here just curl up and die if they knew what went on in the men's room?

The bathrooms were on opposite sides of a small hall. Jerry kicked open the door that said "Men" and inhaled the familiar, raunchy aroma. After two or three breaths you didn't notice the smell any more. He kinda missed it. There were urinals along one wall, and some stalls. He really did need to pee. Let the fag come in the door while he had his cock out already, it would probably be a real treat for him. No reason why he, Jerry, should be the only one to get any fun out of it. Not that he was going to reciprocate or anything. He wasn't in high school anymore, for God's sake.

Yeah, he really needed to piss all right, but as he took his cock out, the familiar touch made it semirigid. His hand traveled up and down a couple of times in a lazy, j-o gesture. Nothing was getting out of his bladder now. It almost hurt, being caught between two pleasures, anticipating both of them, not really able to enjoy either one.

Then somebody else kicked the door open, but this was different—it sounded like storm troopers. He turned, startled, and let go of his pants. They slipped down over his ass. The guy in the leather jacket was coming at him with a great big knife! Who did this mad fucker think he was, Rambo? He stumbled back, almost tripped on his pants, but the guy stepped on the loose end of a trouser leg, and Jerry pulled his feet free. His loafers went flying. Then a hand like a bear trap fastened on his shirt front. "Hold still, boy," growled the man-trapper in his ear. The knife went between his shirt and his chest, and Jerry pulled away, frantic to keep that cold edge away from his suddenly hot skin. Ten inches of steel severed his shirt with one yank. He tried to get away but was caught by the seat of his shorts—and those too were neatly severed and ripped off his body. He had long since lost his erection, and a sudden spurt of urine wet the rags that had been his underwear. He was completely naked. But before he could scream, a fistful of the shorts was stuffed in his mouth, and the knife was under his chin. One of his arms was bent and twisted behind his back, high enough to make him dance on tiptoe. "Spit that out and I'll cut your throat," the man said, and Jerry believed him.

He was turned around (amazing how quickly pain could make him obey) and quick-marched down the short, dark hallway (jeez, they ought to mop that floor), and into an unlit parking lot. The gravel hurt his feet as he was led to a black van with oversize tires, a CB antenna, and customized flames curling around the windows and wheel wells. The man let go of Jerry's arm (but the sharp edge of steel kept his chin up), and released the side door of the van. Then the knife was gone, and he was shoved facedown onto the floor. "Put your hands between your ankles, fuck-face," his captor snarled, and he complied, even though it put his ass up in the air. There was a straight steel bar with four manacles on it—two big ones on the outside, two little ones on the inside—and his feet and wrists were put in the appropriate holes and the ratchets snapped shut.

"We got a long drive ahead of us," sneered the stranger. "This oughta take your mind off it." Something pointed and greasy intruded between the cheeks of Jerry's ass, and made him cry out. The cry loosened his bowels enough for the plug to lodge home, deep inside. Then it started to buzz. It must have a battery. This startled him so much he barely noticed the van had started rolling.

Oh, fuck, this was the worst. He had never imagined anything like this ever happening to him. God, he had never been so scared or unhappy—until he realized the vibrating butt plug was giving him an erection. At that, Jerry cried. He hadn't cried since the first time he went to camp. The other guys had made him get out of his sleeping bag to join in a circle jerk. He was the last one in the tent to come, so he had to eat his own load in front of everybody.

He kept crying until his untouched, unloved cock pulsed and he shot all over his own chest and belly. It was humiliating to come that way, all alone, being made to come by an object he had no control over, worse even than jacking off after a date with some cock-teasing bitch who let him spend his money on her and then wouldn't put out. The only good part of it was that the contractions of his orgasm pushed the nasty rubber plug out of his ass. The come dried slowly, itching, shrinking, pulling his nipples in and making them hard.

They had stopped moving. The door of the van slid open, revealing a garage. The kidnapper clapped new irons on his wrists and ankles, then released him from the bar. As Jerry was yanked out of the van, his tortured shoulder and neck muscles cramped, and so did his calves. He screamed and almost fell. But the man just picked him up, threw him over his shoulder, unlocked a door, carried him down a flight of stairs, and thrust him into a small cell. What kind of maniac has a real jail cell, with real iron bars and a door that locks, in their basement? The intense physical pain and the sudden conviction that he was going to be killed made Jerry break away from the hand that steadied him. He began to shriek and stumble around the cell. If his hands had not been manacled behind his back, he would have beat them on the bars. He tried to kick over the cot. It was bolted to the floor.

"Good way to work the cramps out," said the stranger, who then stepped out of the cell, turned a key, and left him alone with nothing but a single lightbulb (situated outside the cell and protected with a strong wire cage) for company.

The rampage—such as it was—petered out pretty fast. In such

a small space, with nothing to turn over or bust up—in fact, there was nothing in his environment that he could have a significant effect upon—throwing a tantrum did not relieve Jerry's feelings. He gave up and huddled on the cot for a while, but it was chilly in the cell, so he got up and began to pace, trying to keep warm.

He thought briefly of suicide. But how? There was no mirror to break. He had no belt, no shoelaces—not even a button to swallow! There were no sheets on the cot—just a thin mattress with a cover he could not tear with his fingers. There wasn't even a toilet to drown in! The only methods available (strangling himself with his chains, perhaps, or banging his head in on the floor) would have required a force of character he simply did not possess.

His prowling led to only one major discovery—a drain in one corner of the cell. So he could piss without fouling his own nest. Good. But as soon as he had relieved this major discomfort, he became aware of two others—hunger and thirst. These torments kept him on his feet until he was so tired he fell onto the cot and slept.

He woke up terribly cold, stiff, with a bad headache and an even worse taste in his mouth. He heard steps. The flight of stairs down to the basement was fairly long, and the man coming down them was taking his time. Instead of just waiting, Jerry took a piss, but his urine was so concentrated that it burned. Since he was unable to point his dick at the drain or shake it off, at least half of the piss wound up on his own legs. What was this guy going to do, watch him die slowly of dehydration? When Jerry saw the big man standing outside his cell, one hand on his belt buckle, the other on a canteen slung over his shoulder, all the resentment turned into relief. Here, finally, was something new, some alternative to the boredom of his own companionship.

"Thirsty?"

"You know I am!"

"Want a drink, do you?"

"Yes!"

"Then ask for it with some manners, boy, and call me Sir."

"Wh—wh—I—I will not!"

The dark brown eyes, under brows so bushy they met in the middle of the forehead, regarded him without a trace of impatience or anger. But there was also no compassion or remorse in that gaze. "Don't be stupid," he was told. "I got you locked up tighter than the president's rear end. There's no food and water in that cell. If you want any it has to come from me. So you just call me Sir like a good boy and count yourself lucky I don't make you call me God. Because your life is in the palm of my hand."

"I—can't—"

The cap of the canteen was slowly unscrewed. It was tilted. Precious water was about to be poured, wasted, onto the floor—

"Please! Sir! Let me have some water, Sir."

The cap was put back on the canteen and the man moved menacingly toward the bars of his cell.

"But I said it, I said it, please, let me drink!"

"Oh, you'll get something to swallow, all right. Get down on your knees."

This was tricky to manage on a concrete floor, with no help from his hands, but Jerry did it without hurting himself. His face was inches from the bars when a piece of sex-meat as dark as his captor's sun- and wind-burned face flopped into view and hit him on the cheek. He cringed. It was so much bigger than his own, and it wasn't clipped. The long foreskin, gathered at the tip of the cock head in a soft pucker, made it seem even more alien. His captor skinned his dick, slowly, and Jerry felt goose flesh go up his neck.

"This is the first thing I'm gonna feed you," the big man said. "Before anything else goes into your mouth, this does. That's how you earn your groceries. You better get used to it now because around here we eat three times a day. C'mon, boy, say 'Thank you, Sir,' and kiss it."

Jerry's gorge rose, and he tried to back away, but his tender knees and short chains made him slow on the floor. A callused paw darted through the bars, found his throat, and squeezed it exactly the way it had squeezed a can of beer in the cowboy bar, so long ago.

"Whatsa matter, gorgeous?" (Squeeze, squeeze.) "You couldn't take your eyes off my basket in that breeder bar." (Stroke, squeeze.) "What did you think I was taking you back to the toilet for?" (Extra-hard grip, the edge of the hand felt like iron.) "You probably thought I was going to suck on your ding-dong, didn't ya, huh?" (A stroke hard enough to make him choke a little, a softer stroke.) "We just never know how things are going to turn out, do we?" (Both hands were around his neck, twisting in opposite directions.) "The universe just chews us up and spits us out." (Both hands, jacking off his throat.) "But you ain't going to spit this out." (Blunt, strong thumbs pressing in at the joints of his jaw, forced into the muscle until Jerry cried with pain and the cock head slid between his lips and left a salty smear across his mouth. The taste of it, at least, was familiar, just like his own.)

For one split second, the smartest part of him whispered, "Suck it! You can't help it any more than you can help kneeling on the floor or being cold and thirsty." But then pride and stupidity intervened (as was their habit) and he bit down on the deliciously resilient knob that was lodged in the hollow of his cheek. As soon as he had done it, he realized his mistake. It's the kind of thing you'd better do all the way or not at all. He had not anticipated how hard it would be to hurt another man's dick. His own ached with sympathy.

The cell door slammed open and suddenly Jerry had more company than he dreamed would fit in such a small place—mad company, bad company. In two shakes of a dog's tail (*or my tail*, he thought bitterly), he was facedown on the cot. His ankle chain had been padlocked to the frame at the foot of the narrow bed, and it did not give him enough room to roll over. "You damn fool punk," the stranger said wearily, and took off his belt.

Every single blow hurt worse than the last. Not only was this man energetic and strong, but his strokes fell on a rather limited area—Jerry's butt and thighs. The broad, long garrison came down so hard it felt like a solid object rather than a flexible piece of leather. Jerry very quickly realized that sucking cock was not nearly as bad as this. Each blow had him rapidly revising his opinion of the relative merits of the two experiences—giving head and getting beaten—until he thought he'd rather deep-throat this man than go to heaven, if only it would stop the beating. The worst part of it was that he seemed to be saying all of this out loud, with a lot of "Sirs" and "please" and "I'll do anything you say" thrown in for good measure.

Still, the walloping didn't stop until Jerry had lost his breath and couldn't plead for mercy or call himself any more bad names. When it did stop, he was astonished by how little time had really elapsed. The Master (he had somehow become that in the dialogue that had accompanied the belting) was not even winded. Jerry looked at the man and his belt and his arm with new respect. When he was unchained he knelt by the side of the cot. "Thank you, Sir," he said, and kissed the cock that was put to his dry lips. Then he opened his mouth. The hands were on his throat again, squeezing, and every time they eased their grip, the Master's cock went down the boy's throat another inch. It was difficult but not awful. He arched his thighs and came up to get more of the rod. Just opening his mouth was not enough. He had to provide friction, traction. But it was hard to suck it and keep his teeth out of the way.

Above him, the Master was hissing, and one big fist was twisted in Jerry's forelock, practically banging his forehead against the muscular stomach, hard now with excitement and need. When his Master came, it was like having a hose down his throat that someone had suddenly turned on. It jerked as if it wanted to escape and sprayed hot thick stuff down his gullet. Somewhere, far away, another hose spurted sticky stuff all over Jerry's thigh. When he came to and realized he had come himself, once again without being touched, the fragile equilibrium he had achieved as a result of being beaten vanished, and he retched. The Master watched him crawl to the drain and attempt to be sick.

"Don't feel bad, shit-head," he said, not unkindly. "You ain't the first piece of so-called trade I busted down to cocksucker. Knock that off and come rinse your mouth out."

BELONGING

The boy (as he was coming to think of himself) was not too far-gone to recognize common sense. He abandoned the stinking drain and crawled over to his Master, who shoved his big leg between Jerry's thighs and told him gruffly to lean against it. The first swallow of water was tipped delicately into his mouth. It was still cold and smelled deliciously of the metal canteen and its wet wool cover. After that, the water was poured from up higher, so he had to abandon the prop of his Master's thigh and open his mouth under it, like a dog drinking from a faucet.

Standing over the shackled body he had just possessed, the Master said, "You got a lot of vanity, and it's all misplaced, boy. Whyncha try t'be proud of something you really can do—like let a big, fat dick tickle your tonsils? You're real good at that."

Then he was left alone, and was glad, because he was tired. The room was not so cold now. He slept. When he woke up, he realized he must have slept very deeply, because he had not heard footsteps coming down the stairs. It was the smell of soup that woke him. There was a big bowl of it on the floor, in one of those fancy dog-dishes that are weighted so they can't be tipped over. "That's smart," he thought. "I won't get it all over the floor." It was not until he was halfway through bolting down the wonderful stuff that he realized how far gone he had to be to think there was anything admirable or practical about eating from a dog bowl. But that didn't keep him from licking both the bowl, and as much of his face as his tongue could reach, clean.

Then he realized he had a spectator. The Master wiped Jerry's face with a bandanna taken from his back pocket. "Good boy," he said. "You ready for another lesson?"

Jerry was dubious. But the belt was safe in its loops, buckled, and no other weapons were in the Master's hands. "Maybe, Sir," he said.

Sir laughed. "You don't have much choice, do you, boy?"

"I don't have any choice, Sir," Jerry said ruefully as he was once more stretched stomach down on his cot and the ankle chain used to padlock him to it.

"Want some more water, boy?" He looked at the source of the

offer. The Master had hung a bright red bag from the cell door and was offering him the nozzle. "Come on, it's clean, nothing but water," said the Master, and let a jet of it hit him in the face. Anything to delay the insertion of that nozzle where he knew it was meant to (and would) go. Jerry opened his mouth and accepted a few swallows. Then the bag was taken off the door and his Master stuck his big cock into it. There was the unmistakable sound of somebody taking a healthy piss. "The enema du jour is prepared fresh daily," said the Master, and hung the bag back up. Jerry managed a weak smile.

"Before we do this," the Master said, "I think you ought to know that I'm not going to stop until I have exactly what I want from you." He lit a match on the sole of his boot, then slowly turned a big cigar in the flame. The cell was soon full of fragrant tobacco fumes. "We're being all cutesy right now, but as soon as I do anything serious you're going to fight me again. I don't mind because I know I'll win. But it will make this easier on you if you know you're going to lose. Have you got any questions?"

"What are you going to do to me, Sir?"

"You're going to do anything I tell you to do, and before much longer I won't have to tell you, you'll know what I want. But before we can reach that stage, I want to know everything about your sordid and misspent, snot-nosed youth. We're going to flush the past right out of you, starting now."

The nozzle was greased and inserted. "Just be glad it ain't my cigar—or something bigger," the Master chuckled. Then he wiggled some of the plastic tubing into his captive's ass. Jerry squirmed. "Come t'think of it, you kinda like getting things shoved up your ass, don't you, piss-pot? In fact, you creamed all over the floor of my van, didn't you? Now, how do you suppose a straight boy learned how to do a trick like that, huh?"

There was a long, deadly silence. Jerry tentatively pulled on the ankle chain, but the pain was awful and the padlock was not going to pop open on his say-so. He would not answer the question. Not even to save himself a beating.

The Master sighed. "I think you ought to see some of my home movies," he said softly. From his cot, Jerry watched him leave the cell and click off the lights. There was the sound of another button being hit, a motor revving up—and film flashed on the back wall of the cell. The picture was large and grainy and so close Jerry could barely see it, but the subject was so familiar that he didn't really need to watch it.

No wonder Caroline had always insisted on balling in her living room, on that big sofa. He was such a chump he never thought it was odd that she wouldn't take him in her bedroom. He just thought she couldn't wait to get some, had to have it the minute they walked in the door. She must have had a hidden camera set up in there, filming the whole thing. And, of course, the Master was the man he had accidentally discovered in her apartment.

She had Jerry on her lap. She was spanking him. How had she ever talked him into that? He had done something to make her call him a "bad boy"—oh, yeah, he wouldn't go down on her—and she had teased his prick enough to get him over her lap. (She had also had him by the balls, and had let him know—giggling—that she would hurt them if he did not do as she said.) Now she was putting a plug up his ass, rolling him over onto his back and poising herself over his erect cock, sinking down on it, holding his hands up over his head, playing with his nipples. The film had no sound, but he could remember the dialogue. "Who's fucking who now, little boy, huh? Who's fucking who? Can't you feel it up your ass? When I sit on your cock it moves it around. I've turned on the vibrator, it's going to make you come, it's my cock that's going to make you come."

The Master released the clamp on the enema tube, and water started to flow into the captive. He was allowed to use a bedpan, then made to bend over for another dose of water-and-piss, all in the ghastly flickering light of these movies, made of the stuff of shame. He had been so stupid then. He had excused everything she did to him on the grounds that she was a horny, older woman who was so hot for him, she couldn't help but go overboard expressing her lust. Now he saw the truth. Caroline had picked him up, initiated him into a series of demeaning and subservient acts (the film showed her shoe in his face, the long and dangerous heel going in and out of his mouth), and he had not resisted or protested. In fact, it was the best sex he had ever had.

Another session on the bedpan, more water. Jerry was fascinated by the sight of her putting clips on his nipples, clips that were connected by a chain. Now she was tying his cock up. The long ends of the leather laces were brought up and secured to the tit clamps. And the harder she pulled, the harder he got. The Master's hands fastened on his teats, hauled on them—rougher, more comforting than Caroline's sharp nails. He was lying on his back on the cot now. He didn't know if he was still watching the movie or just replaying memories in his mind. Clamps (identical to those in the film) were fastened on his nipples. He felt leather lace being wound around his cock and balls. The inevitable duplication—lace tied around chain, both pulled until he came up off the bed, hard between the legs, his balls swollen to bursting point, aching for more pain if it meant more sex, more stimulation for his cock, more intense release. Release from that woman, that awful, wicked, vengeful woman who had gone to so much trouble to get him into permanent trouble.

Damn her, damn her. Jerry brought his knees up as his Master climbed onto the foot of the bed. Sir was wearing leather chaps, a leather jacket; nothing else. As the Master bent over him to unlock his wrist chains, Jerry kissed his chest, rubbed his face into the coarse fur, grateful for the lack of perfume, the presence of hard muscle instead of soft breasts. He barely noticed the weight that rested on his well-clamped tits as the Master reached for the head of the bed and refastened the boy's hands to it so they were no longer pinned underneath his body. He was too busy sucking on those nipples, nipples that were not in pain, it was his job to give them pleasure while his own suffered. It was his vocation.

The laces kept his cock out of the way as a hand full of lubricant spread him, speared him, went where the nozzle and warm water and piss had prepared a way. He was clean inside and smooth. He opened to the touch, but his asshole was always clinging, providing a snug fit for the fingers that stroked him, longing to retain them and love them and keep them inside, where they gave him so much pleasure that he gasped, choked on his desire as the fingers were withdrawn. Restlessly, he moved his slippery ass so the ring of muscle lodged against the head of the cock that was being pointed at it—and absorbed it. The whole length of the thing inside him throbbed. This was not a piece of plastic, it was flesh, man flesh like his own, only free, free to use him. (And once again it was his task, his calling, to pleasure a part of his Master while his own equivalent part was hurting.) There was a little pain around his opening, a feeling of something resisting, then being broken, and he wanted it to be broken so he could experience everything fully, without resistance, without pride, meet thrust with thrust and groan into the same mouth that covered his and groaned.

"Fuck me, Sir, please, fuck me harder," he begged, and got his wish. He could not come because of the binding around his cock, and he was glad, because he wanted to be just a vessel, just to receive. He had fucked everything up, made a mess of it all, couldn't control or manage or direct things, so it was better to get fucked, to be controlled, to be shown how his body responded automatically to this touch, this stroke, this degree of dilation and penetration. The feelings kept changing and growing. How could he feel so much and still feel more and not explode or be damaged or destroyed?

His torso was imprisoned between arms that bulged with the strain of holding up a big man's body during a full-out fuck. Jerry turned his head and kissed the arms, licked them, tried to get his fettered hands down far enough to caress them. "Tell me," Sir gritted, "what a little shit you are."

There was no time for a full confession; he knew Sir would extract all the details: the faggots he would entice and then roll (and what really happened between him and the men he did not rob); the jobs he had botched with petty thievery or laziness; the women who had treated him with almost as much contempt as he felt for them; the physique magazines and where he hid them and what he did in the stores where he bought them. For now it was enough to just say, "I am a piece of shit, this is all I'm good for, I have to have your cock in me, please, please, please, Sir, please."

The cock went in and in again, meeting no resistance, but the lining of his ass had been roughened somewhat, giving the fuck a new texture, a slight edge. "I belong to you!" he cried, and with a sharp jerk, the Master released the cock laces and let the slave's jism spill between them. "I belong to you!" he continued to cry, even after his cock ran dry. After all, his Master's tool was still at work, and that was the only thing that mattered. A wolf's grin split the Master's black beard. Little sister Caroline had kept her promise.

The projector ran out of film and the loose end of celluloid flapped like a scarecrow in the wind, but the two of them never noticed they were fucking in the pure white light of an empty screen.

Swimmer's Body

Time for morning laps, Surfer Boy, Gary told himself. *No dawdling. Well, maybe a few extra deep-knee bends, just to show our bronzed and God-like body to the stolid Swede in the far lane. Wonder if he can see the crack of my butt in this new suit—or do the leopard spots (which make Coach Bassett cluck his tongue) camouflage the dividing line between my buns, which have been unbuttered for far too long?* Gary did an imitation of Coach Bassett's cluck. "A young man, so much promise, so little—what? Let's just say he wouldn't marry the boss's daughter."

The outdoor pool was perfectly smooth turquoise Jell-O in a white, Olympic-size trough. Gary thought (peeking between his toes) that it might really be like diving into a thick gel, and he would simply flounder, unable to pull his smoothly shaved torso through it no matter how long his reach. It would be a fitting end to these deadly dull two months (and two still to go!) at the Little Dixie training camp.

As always, he was in the water before he knew his body had decided to throw him into it. It was a good dive, and the shock of pleasure he felt at his own skill made him lose consciousness of the need to time arm strokes, breathing, and kicks. Instead, it felt as if a wave flowed down the whole, single muscle that was his body, propelling him smoothly, without thought or strain. Then he rolled (toes brushing the electric eye that timed his laps) and kicked harder, suddenly furious to be done with it. He had hoped, when he sent in his deposit, that the heat and isolation would make it easier for him to stay in the water here, building his peak for the spring matches.

But he hated swimming when he was only training, hated it as much as someone who wasn't any good at it. It was his ticket to college, to something other than obscurity and a desk job in a medium-size city. He loved competing—the adrenaline rush, the knowledge that, win or lose, you didn't dare hold anything back. But everybody in the pool came ready to win. You had to train, and it never got easier for him, only harder, and he was so upset with himself that he took in a lungful of water instead of air and had to haul himself up on the rim of the pool, choking like a little kid in his first Red Cross swimming class.

The Swede finished before he did, and Gary passed him in the shower on his way to his locker. Larsen was bigger than Gary. His muscles looked like slabs of pale stone when he was in repose, but in the water he was a buoyant streak of speed. His impartial, careful hands applied soap evenly to his body, completely unaware of the beauty of what they touched. Gary made the clucking noise again. He couldn't imagine anybody snapping a wet towel at his ass in this locker room, much less waving anything more interesting around.

Back in the dorm, Gary saw a small stack of mail on his cot. He immediately cheered up. Under a letter from his mother and a letter from his "roommate" Aaron (the return address had only a discreet initial before the surname) was a thin plastic envelope. *The Advocate* had finally caught up with him. He had debated whether it was wise to notify the magazine about his temporary change of address, then figured he would go nuts without a little contact with gay life. Since nobody was in the dorm, he slit the package and skimmed the magazine. The letters (even Aaron's) would be safe to read at lunch in the cafeteria. This was not.

They had sent him the East Coast edition. He chuckled at the restaurant reviews for New York City and Washington, D.C. No excuse not to have a swinging weekend now! It would take him—what—only a full day of driving to get out of the Deep South? There was probably nothing in the classifieds either, but what the hell, he didn't want to read the opera review or a feature about gay

SWIMMER'S BODY

involvement in the anti-nuke movement. There were four whole columns of ads from California. Unbidden, his eye picked out Aaron's post office box and flipped up to read the ad ("Straight-appearing young executive looking for summer fun, no strings, no games, no fats, fems or downwardly mobile types"). Well, they had agreed there was no sense in Aaron coming home to an empty apartment every single night. Feeling a little pain behind his sternum anyway, Gary flipped to the end of the classifieds. Well, what do you know—there was actually one entire ad running under his state. "Fine mind in a swimmer's body seeks same. Let's make a big splash!"

Gary couldn't stop laughing. He ripped the ad out, stuffed the magazine back into its envelope, and on his way to the cafeteria, as he buried it under a bunch of trash in a big oil drum, he was still laughing.

Over lunch, Coach Bassett stopped and handed him a thick packet. "What're these?" Gary queried rudely, around a mouthful of despised salad.

"Publicity photos. Pick out the three you like the best. You can keep the rest or pitch 'em."

Gary had forgotten all about the photo session last week. Surely this was an omen. He fanned them out on the table and picked one of himself on a stand, with his arms up and tense (showing off the deep armpit, his beautifully proportioned lats). His quads stood out nicely. Unfortunately for the newspapers, so did his basket. But the anonymous advertiser (read "geek") would appreciate it. Before he went to the track to run his laps there ("Are you a man or a merry-go-round, Surfer Boy?"), he stopped at the dorm again for an envelope and stamps.

"This is a real swimmer's body," he wrote on the back of the photo, "and if you can match it, drop a pic c/o," and the address of the camp. "If not, don't bother."

Three days later (three days during which training seemed less arduous), he had a snapshot of a man (still young, but older than Gary, with a nose that looked like it had been broken) treading water. Even wet, his dark hair curled. His thickly furred chest was so broad that Gary wondered if it didn't churn up too much water resistance to make good time. But those biceps and forearms looked burly enough to drag the Titanic to safety. He reluctantly conceded that in this case, the phrase "swimmer's body" had not been just a euphemism for "90-pound weakling." He turned the picture over and read, "All this, and I have my hair," and a phone number. Gary ruefully rubbed his shaved skull. He was so used to other swimmers' faces, he had forgotten how odd his pale blond eyebrows and bare pate would look to anybody who wasn't in training. Cocky fucker. Where was the pay phone?

It was a brief call. Something wrong with the connection. He even had trouble making out the guy's name—Marvin? Martin? No—Marcus. But it turned out he lived just a bicycle ride away. Gary explained his situation at the training camp—so many days of working out, followed by a break day—and received a standing invitation to come over any time during his "off-day." Tomorrow, as it turned out.

That night, in his sleep, the lumpy cot turned into the chest and thighs of the well-built stud in the photograph. He lay facedown on him, his hands pinned between them, searching for the other man's cock. He knew it would be thick, the foreskin like folds of silk, the balls heavy in a sac covered with crinkly black hair. The whole flexible, flaccid shaft could be cupped in one hand until he began to squeeze and massage it, then it would slowly add inches until it protruded beyond his fist.

Instead, Gary woke up, and realized it was his own cock that was thrusting in his grip. He took a deep breath, listened. Nobody else was awake. Then the urge to come was so sharp, a pain in his lower stomach, that he said, "So what?" out loud and took himself over the edge. The splashes of come felt good on his knuckles, hot, and the tangy smell made him realize he had not jerked off since his first night here. When was the last time he had felt a pronounced need to spurt, instead of having to coax that good stuff out of his balls?

Aaron had been a real find, a business major he met in an economics class. It had been fun, in the beginning at least, to put the moves on somebody who pretended to be a little reluctant. Aaron turned out to be the oldest son of a Conservative rabbi, and his coyness was not just flirtatiousness; he still was not out to his family about being gay or even living with another man. While Gary enjoyed the new side of himself that Aaron brought out, a more toppy, aggressive persona than he'd realized even existed, after a while he began to wonder if Aaron really wanted to have sex with him. He didn't mind pushing Aaron in the direction of the bed most of the time, all the while gently insisting that he really was going to fuck his brains out (and the front door was locked, and the oven was off, and no important phone calls were expected). But once in a while, he wanted Aaron to be the one doing to the pushing and insisting.

Lying on his uncomfortable dormitory bed, Gary rubbed his hands over his own body, resenting the smoothness of his skin but needing the reassurance that he existed, he could feel, the envelope that contained his consciousness was still alive. He couldn't even remember what he looked like with his fur intact. There was something emasculating about shaving so often, as if he were stripping away any physical impulse that had nothing to do with swimming. He admitted that it wasn't just the training camp and the constant rejection of being surrounded by straight boys that made him feel extremely lonely. Didn't everybody need the passionate reassurance of a lover's uninhibited desire, the experience of being taken somewhere by someone else's touch? Maybe he wasn't attractive to Aaron. He could easily conjure up his lover's bespectacled, usually serious face and see his kissable lips move in the fond phrase he repeated several times a day: "I love you, Gary."

Wasn't it sophomoric to want something more, something else, something more dirty, perhaps, even dangerous? Gary conjured up the photograph of Marcus and realized that he wanted to see it again, to study it to see if he could glimpse some hints about the rest of the big man's body beneath the opaque water. Did he have a big thatch on his lower belly? Were his balls large enough to hang low, two separate eggs in a fuzzy, crinkled sac? And did his cock have a slight curve to it, with a tulip-shaped head? Gary wanted to run his tongue along the rim between the head and the shaft of that cock and lap at the little tangle of nerves at its base. He wanted to slip his tongue into the piss slit of that cock and savor the thin salty clear precome that would tell him the dark man lusted after his hungry mouth. He wanted two hands around his ears, to be lost inside another man's need, to be able to stop thinking and exist only as a tunnel for his cock, a hole that offered just enough resistance and response to give that cock the best ride of its life. Sucking and sucking as if he needed Marcus's come instead of air.

The intrusive memory of Aaron's cold little personal ad intruded on the building tension of a second erection. It was out of character for Aaron to take initiative like that, to put himself out there as a sexual actor. What kind of man would answer that ad? Would somebody else plow the tight, round little ass that Gary had marked off as his own? Would Aaron do things for the man (or men) who answered that ad that he refused to do for Gary? Would he swallow that shadowy stud's come? Or lick his asshole? Would Aaron get down on his knees and beg to be taken? Could it be that Aaron might be the one who told his trick to get up on all fours so that he could plow him from behind? And did the specter of Aaron with his cock in somebody else's butt or face make Gary feel better or worse than imagining his lover's face distorted with discomfort and pleasure as he was penetrated by a stranger?

When they saw each other again, could it be that the bond between them, for all its faults, would be changed or even damaged? The rational part of Gary forced him to admit that it might be good for Aaron to loosen up a little, but the concrete picture of his boyfriend actually being loosened up by somebody else's hard dick made him unbearably sad.

By answering Marcus's ad, wasn't Gary going to put Aaron through exactly the same sort of sorrow and uncertainty? *No*, Gary told himself, *I will not feel guilty about wanting to get laid.* They had talked this over. He had Aaron's permission to get lucky. It would be distinctly uncool to take such emotional baggage to his encounter with Marcus, but in his cold and rough sheets, Gary longed to put his head on Marcus's big chest and receive absolution and comfort. He wanted to feel those hands rolling his cock back and forth, giving him a sort of sexual blessing, drawing him into a world where he didn't have to ponder such difficult questions. Eventually his imagination conjured up such a clear image of Marcus's red nipples, surrounded by swirls of bearish fur, and the sensation of that eager, arching cock sliding into the crack of his ass that Gary's hard-on came back with a vengeance and demanded some wrist music.

Normally, Gary just needed to jack off and come once; it was easier to get it up again when another man was present to give him bad ideas and a raunchy second chance. He was curious about what this orgasm would feel like, and it was as ambivalent as he was. His second shot was smaller in volume, but the feeling was more intense, as if his urethra were on fire. Despite that, he wanted it to go on for longer than it did; he was abruptly dumped back into a damp, sweaty, soft-cocked state. How could you actually feel dissatisfied after coming twice? Gary fell asleep before he could answer this or any of the other big questions he had about the mysteries of Eros.

He made himself eat the next morning, made himself wait. He read a newspaper that was two days old and started a letter to Aaron that he knew he would not finish. But it was only 9:30 when he got his 10-speed out of the shed and pedaled away from the training camp, a note with directions he had already memorized tucked carefully into the pocket of his T-shirt. He was only on the macadam for 20 minutes before he peeled off and went down a dirt lane. A pheasant broke cover and beat frantically across his path. He swerved, then realized it was already safe in the brush at the other side of the road. The sweat between T-shirt and skin reminded him of the shape of his own body, how it had felt to rub his palm across his nipples last night and pinch one of them gently, to make himself come.

Gary heard the creek before he saw it. The bike bumped across a wooden bridge. Then the road took a turn to follow the creek. Even when the water was hidden from view by thick growths of willow, he could hear it, laughing to itself. This charming, bucolic stream would eventually become one of the tributaries of America's largest river. On either side of the river were marshlands that had been set aside as protected habitat, a bird sanctuary. He wondered briefly about the existence of a private residence in the middle of a federal park. It must have been there for a very long time. The wild land and the free-running water were a reminder of how close Gary was to the gulf, to the salty father of all waters. But that ocean was not the lovely blue Pacific where he had learned how to swim and surf, where he knew a dozen beaches like the palm of his own hand. This was a land where water meandered, became swamps and sandbars. The Gulf of Mexico seemed to Gary to be older than the Pacific Ocean, more corrupt, and the way to it was treacherous, full of false turns and snags, alligators and other strange fauna. It was a place for a bayou boy, poling his pirogue, low and slow, silently blending into the background of drowned trees and Spanish moss. Death to a boisterous mob of young guys with California tans and freshly waxed boards.

According to the odometer between the handlebars, he must be almost there. Yep, the road forked here, and there was a lightning-struck oak, so he took the right-hand branch, away from the water (twinge of disappointment), and there was the house, "set back from the road a piece," as Marcus had promised, under shady trees. The yard was overgrown and the house looked uncared for. He knocked on the front door, got no answer, and walked his bike around to the back. A note was pinned there. "Welcome, Gary, I'm down by the lake. Just follow the trail. Hope you left your Speedo at the camp. Marcus."

He grinned, leaned his bike against the steps, and loped down the trail. It was a few hundred yards down a slope, and there was the river again, feeding a medium-size lake. A homemade dock ran into the water. This must be where the snapshot had been taken. But he didn't see anybody. Oh, well, the water looked good. He skinned out of his cutoffs and T-shirt and strolled to the end of the dock.

"Dive in! It's deep enough," somebody called. There was his host, treading water 10 feet away. How had he gotten so close without making a sound? Gary shrugged and slipped into the lake. It felt good.

Marcus had been submerged when Gary arrived, but he felt the tremors in the water when his guest's feet hit the dock. He came up for air, and it took a few seconds for his eyes to adjust. Nevertheless, he got a clear and very appetizing glimpse of a tall young man who might have been blond if he wasn't completely shaved. The lack of body hair made his guest seem vulnerable despite his almost inhuman, peak physical condition. Gary had a face that was masculine but expressive. His features had not yet settled into the immobile and unreadable condition of an older, more disappointed and resigned man. He seemed enthusiastic, although Marcus was sure he had to be feeling some anxiety about meeting a stranger. Somebody who might be even stranger than you could guess.

Doubt surged in his chest. Had he been right to come here, to return to his childhood home? So much had changed since he left to enlist in the Navy; his parents were both dead, and his brothers had scattered to South Carolina, even Tennessee and Texas, and one sister in Seattle. It was truly unsettling to feel like such an alien in this familiar place, one whose smells and sights conjured up a wealth of nostalgia and regret. (For even a happy memory can bring sadness, since that moment of joy has vanished, one bright bubble in a flock of malicious crows.) And what was he to do with this Yankee boy, someone who came from such a different place and time? But Marcus wanted what he saw. Sex, as it so often does, overcame any qualms he might have had about the consequences. He was bigger and stronger than Gary and could control the encounter, keep his secret, just this once.

The silky, cool water caressed Gary, noticeably more friendly than the dead, chlorinated water in a man-made swimming pool. It seemed to leach any trace of tiredness or pain out of him; the energy it infused him with as he did a shallow breast stroke was clean and light. Then he suddenly felt even better. A hand that was a great deal warmer than the water had circled his shaft and was measuring him slowly, up and down. He was face-to-face with the man in the photograph, and the smell of his body hit Gary in the face like the first smack in a spanking. Marcus smelled like something good to eat, and never stop eating. Up close, he was even furrier than the photograph had shown. He was matted with hair, and Gary wanted to rub his face all over that big chest.

Taken aback by the lack of preliminaries, he tried to reach for the other man's body, but Marcus evaded him. "Let me take you out farther," he said, and had Gary in a towing hold before he could protest. Gary could have sworn they didn't stop until they were in the center of the lake. Marcus let him go, then began a weird game of sexual tag. He was swimming around Gary in amazingly quick, tight circles, and he would dart in just often enough to administer a caress (and keep Gary afloat). Sometimes it would be his mouth instead of his hand that would enclose Gary's cock. He trembled, trusting the hands under his buttocks to keep his head above water. It had been too long since he'd felt so good. He was eager to reciprocate, but no matter how hard he tried, he couldn't grab hold of Marcus's dick, although a couple of times he felt it brush his stomach or thigh, and knew it was as hard as his own.

"Let me touch you!" he finally cried, exasperated, near tears, and Marcus (behind him) pulled him close, wrapped his hands around Gary's aching, overstimulated rod, and thrust his own cock in between the muscular cheeks of the other swimmer's ass. He timed the hand strokes to his cock thrusts, giving Gary the giddy sensation of simultaneously fucking and being fucked, though he knew Marcus's cock remained outside his body. He did not realize they were still swimming until he saw swirls of semen lost behind them and the familiar piers of the dock. He was pushed toward the makeshift wooden ladder before he could turn and kiss Marcus, who had darted away, back to deeper water. "You go inside, lunch is on the table. Don't wait for me to eat. I want to swim a little more."

SWIMMER'S BODY

Gary felt like he would collapse if he stayed in the water. The intensity of his orgasm was making his limbs shake as if he had hypothermia. How often had he fantasized about sex in the water—weightless, streamlined sex—with another athlete whose stamina and physique equaled his own? He dragged himself into the house. Just as he entered the kitchen, he saw the back of a departing older black woman. She wasn't wearing a uniform, but something about her neatly pressed dress and apron made Gary feel sure she was a servant. The table had been set with enough food for five people. He ate a lot of cheese and fruit and drank a couple of pints of water. He even made himself a thick sandwich out of forbidden cold cuts. This morning had made him feel better than months of coaching, lectures on nutrition, sprints, and power lifting. When he was done eating, Marcus still had not come out of the water. Gary wandered into the living room and fell asleep on the couch.

His dreams were disturbing. He had read about Vietnam vets who had been injured by a particularly nasty kind of land mine, one that jumped to waist height before exploding. The men who survived usually lost their genitals as well as their legs. (In his sleep, Gary protectively cupped his drained, waterlogged and tender cock and balls.) These men had a powerful incentive to participate in a government experiment with human DNA that might restore the lost parts of their ruined bodies. While a carefully crafted virus went to work on their genes, the men sat patiently in vats of nutrient solution and antibiotics. Part of the experiment worked fine. With proper recombinant encouragement, their newly ambitious cells re-created perfectly operating cocks and balls. But from that point on, things went awry. Their leg bones fused, articulated like a spine. Where new legs were supposed to grow, large and powerful fish tails sprouted.

The military was not apologetic. The experimental subjects were reminded that they had known they were taking a huge risk. The men (mermen?) were relocated to a larger, common pool, where they began to forge a team identity—although the purpose of that team remained vague, at least in the beginning. Sexual conditioning was used to reinforce that bond, and some of the methods used to break down the men's resistance to homosexual conduct were cruel. The Pentagon's liaison to the research staff hinted at the possibility of them reenlisting, being formed into some kind of special services unit. The idea of being kept together, belonging somewhere (and the accompanying training in underwater communications, demolition, navigation, and biology) kept many of them from going into shock. But there were some men who could not live in such a drastically altered form. Gary woke up before one desperate man in his dream figured out how to commit suicide in a tank with smooth aluminum walls.

The house suddenly seemed threatening, and claustrophobia propelled Gary outside, back down the trail to the lake. Where the hell was his friendly swimming companion? The hot afternoon sun was soothing and made the goose bumps fade from his bare skin. Once more he scanned the lake and saw no one, until he went to the end of the dock. "Ready for another round?" leered the handsome face.

"I'm not sure. I had some pretty weird dreams."

"Come into the water and tell me about it."

Gary slipped nude into Marcus's element. But instead of talking they wound up sexing, even more frantically than before. Gary barely made it back to the camp by curfew. He left behind a thoughtful man who was far too captivated by the young swimmer. Had it been so long since Marcus had had really good sex with another man that he was a pushover for falling in love? Love had not been part of the plan. But maybe it would be OK to have a regular fuck buddy. Despite his skill at maneuvering in the water, Gary had spent less time in that element than Marcus, so perhaps there was less danger in meeting again than the older man feared. The sincerity in Gary's voice when he cried out, begging for the chance to touch Marcus was moving, more moving than Gary probably knew. And Marcus wanted to feel those hands and that mouth all over his body. But it couldn't happen. Ironically, to allow Gary to do the things that Marcus ached to have him do would ruin everything. The sex could only keep happening if it was strictly limited.

There was such a difference between having sex with a man who knew that he was gay and accepted it than a forced encounter with a heterosexual who knew he had no other outlet than to make use of male flesh. Marcus knew that many a straight man had a far greater capacity to enjoy gay sex than he knew. But still, in an institutional environment, such revelations were unwelcome. When a man like that got his rocks off, there was an undercurrent of regret, shame, and anger that set Marcus's teeth on edge. He wanted the man he embraced to be thinking of *his* body, infused with desire for all of his virile attributes, not pining for breasts and the entryway between a woman's thighs. Gary's grace in the water, his quick intake of breath when Marcus supported his weight and almost fucked him, his hunger for more—these things were so seductive that Marcus put his face in his hands and tugged on his hair to try to get them out of his mind. He realized he would have a hard time waiting until Gary's next day off. A very hard time. Such a hard time that a cold shower (or a bath, of course) would not be much of an antidote.

The next off-day found Gary back at the old, empty house. The week of training had flown by. He had done better than ever before at meeting his goals and didn't give a shit when Coach Bassett told him so. The troublesome images of Aaron's—adventures? Not infidelity!—lost their sting. When he wasn't with Marcus, he was still with him in the spirit, reliving each precious moment of contact, moving in his arms, panting to be put upon his cock, and coming even though it was denied him.

He was there the next week as well. And the next.

The sex was *so* good, but Marcus would not allow Gary to touch him, nor would he engage in any kind of penetration. Gary accepted it after a while, assuming that since Marcus was calling the shots, he could change things if he wasn't satisfied. The brief heat of Marcus's semen jetting between the cheeks of his ass before lake water washed it away became an erotic trigger that always made him come too.

Then Gary would get out of the water, go inside and eat, take a nap (always marred by more weird dreams), and eventually come back outside for more sex. When he left, Marcus would still be in the water. Gary would cycle back to the camp, alternatively mulling over his sensory impressions of Marcus's body and the dreams.

His nightmarish visions of the military medical experiment were supplemented by dreamy visions of a blue, underwater world where silvery-scaled people cavorted in their strange cities, playing dolphin games with each other all day long, offering each other gifts of necklaces and sex and food. Their behavior with one another was so sensual that it was difficult to tell where sex began and ended. There seemed to be no restrictions on who or how they embraced. There was no obvious work being done, yet their playfulness was also creative. There were buildings, ornaments, art, and all of these things had a quality of buoyancy, with no sharp edges or corners. Gary loved these dreams. He sometimes found a trace of tears in his eyes when he woke up, exiled from that idyllic setting and those gentle, beautiful beings.

Over time, the underwater sex with Marcus was interspersed with more and more conversation. What little Marcus revealed of his personality fascinated Gary. He was a man who was apparently capable of violence in the appropriate context but was also burdened with a delicate conscience and a sense of compassion for human frailty. Gary had never encountered anyone like him before. Growing up in Southern California, with its emphasis on youth, novelty, and pretty surfaces, had not prepared him for the complexity of a Southern gentleman's melancholy character. Marcus had been nurtured in an atmosphere where there was no escape from a tragic sense of history and abundant evidence of man's capacity for evil as well as good. Nobody would ever guess from looking at Marcus or listening to him that he was gay. But he accepted his own desire for other men as naturally as he accepted all of his other basic needs. There could be no sexual shame in his presence, only permission and—even better—skill. Despite Marcus's insistence on controlling their encounters, Gary sensed that he would respond to an equally assertive partner. The fact that he could not find the trigger that would allow Marcus to bring down that wall tormented and teased Gary into a frenzy. How could he turn kissing somebody into a sexual fantasy? Who jacked off to thoughts of doing nothing but kissing another man? It was weird, being this crushed out, but the elation of the crush sped Gary through the tedium of rehearsing for races.

One fateful day, the strangeness of the repetitive dreams made it impossible for him to respond to Marcus's light, familiar, but still achingly arousing touch. Gary was also feeling a growing anxiety about the approaching end of his incarceration in the training camp. As the lusty grin on his friend's face was replaced with genuine concern, Gary knew he was falling in love with this man, and instead of making a joke about not being able to get it up underwater, he haltingly described the dark visions that troubled him. Eventually even Gary's muscles tired of treading water, and he relaxed into Marcus's tattooed arms, wondering how he could keep both of them afloat so effortlessly. Then he happened to look down, but off to one side, the way his father had taught him to look for fish in a brook. And he saw the lower half of Marcus's body for the first time. The two-fluked tail was muscular, dappled brown like a rainbow trout and undeniably masculine.

"It's true, then," Gary said thoughtfully, and wondered why he was relieved. Probably because he had known the truth for a long time, but had not let himself acknowledge it. Marcus was a mer.

"Yes. Do you want to hear the rest of the story?"

He did. Gary's body signaled urgently that he wanted something else, too, now that his tension and anxiety were gone, but he made himself wait.

"One of their own scientists betrayed them. She had spent years developing a way to communicate with dolphins, killer whales, and other intelligent ocean mammals. The military had gotten wind of it, taken over her project, and taught the pinnipeds to carry explosives and conduct underwater sabotage. A lot of the animals were injured or killed during carelessly conducted exercises. None of the stupid lifers in charge of this very hush-hush project could understand why this would traumatize her or anticipate that she might turn against them because of it. She was supposed to teach each of us how to work with a dolphin partner. A weird variation on the K-9 corps. Somehow, she found out that the Navy intended to use us to staff underwater nuclear missile silos. She also found out how they intended to replace us. The mer-virus is in our semen. Theoretically, we can make any man into a mer. But they never got far enough in the experiment to actually offer us a victim to see if that transformation would really take place. I think the woman who let us go was actually more upset about the prospect of the dolphins getting killed than she was about the way we had been treated. But one night she sneaked out to our tank, told us what the score was, and gave us the location of the underwater base they had already built for us. Then she let us loose, on the condition that we take our dolphins with us. We found it and moved in."

Gary postponed dealing with the full import of this by quibbling about details. "How do you live under water? You still breathe air, don't you?"

"I'm breathing with my lungs now, but in the water my gills keep the oxygen coming." Marcus took Gary's hand and ran his palm over his chest, then farther down, to his hips. The skin began to change there, acquiring a slightly abrasive texture, the triangular pattern of large, hard scales. Marine armor for a new kind of warrior. Gary could barely feel the frilled edges of raised half-circles, rhythmically fluttering open and closed. "I'm a deserter. I left when I found out that there was another, hidden agenda to our creation that even the scientists didn't know about.

"Being a mer is really hard on your mind and soul, Gary. I can't ever go back to the land again, and I never stop grieving about that, the fact that I can be so close to the shore but never really return home. They wanted to exterminate those people you saw in your dream. After the worldwide boycott of the tuna industry, which happened because of all that graphic publicity about dead dolphins, they are running scared about what would happen if school children and little old ladies and all the members of the Sierra Club knew there were people down there. I don't know why they think they need a war to do it, though, because we're killing them already. All the poison that we pour into the ocean has already endangered them."

Gary was so excited to learn that his idealistic nap-time visions had a basis in reality that he couldn't stop himself from interrupting. "But you and your buddies, you could put a stop to that. You could fight back! You could save them!"

"Gary, you don't understand. How can you when you haven't been there? When we found these people, they were so different from us. I never thought I would encounter such innocence unless I was dealing with a child. But they're not children, and yet they don't know the meaning of violence. I don't think they even know how to get angry. Even when they knew we came from the same people who had hurt them, they still took us in and helped us, made it much easier for us to survive. They don't even know what it means to be dishonest, Gary. They can't even tell a lie. And by teaching them to fight back, we're already changing them. And I don't think it's a good change. I just couldn't stand to watch it. So I left. I decided to come back here, to this house that my mother and father had left me, and…I don't know what."

"Stop. You don't need to tell me any more." Gary felt like his head was going to explode. He could get away! Away from Old Mother Bassett and his satchel of vitamin pills. Away from Aaron, who might be relieved, although he would never admit it. A series of tricks would be much easier to conceal from his parents than a boyfriend. Away from his own stifling closet, the racing circuit. Away from the boredom of staying in peak physical condition for no good reason. He would never have to come out of the water, and he could be surrounded by gorgeous, available men all the time—and it would mean something besides a trophy or a scholarship. But was he ready to be a soldier in an underwater world?

"Give me that seafood," Gary snarled, laughing, and dove for Marcus's rigid cock.

Marcus tried to fend him off, but Gary had acquired a strength born of a drive to join the strange new world that had opened up before him. He ran his tongue up and down the fat vein on the underside of Marcus's cock, which was indeed shaped exactly as he had imagined. Marcus's hands found his face under water and urged him to take the heart-shaped head into his mouth. He licked around, inside the piss slit, his lips rolling back and forth across the coronal ridge. Marcus's grasp on his head grew tighter, and Gary's teasing was soon rewarded with a thick, slick dick opening his throat. Just as he was about to run out of air, Marcus rolled onto his back, his wet erection glistening in the failing sun, and one of his arms closed around Gary, holding him above water so that he could complete his mission. The first dose of semen spurted into Gary's mouth almost immediately, and he swallowed every drop of the salty, sticky cream. Lost in the crisis of his own orgasm, Marcus let go of him, and Gary was unexpectedly dunked into the lake.

"All I can say is, I hope we have to do this a lot to change me," Gary sputtered, surfacing.

Marcus shook his head at the two-legged swimmer's giggling face. How could he joke about something so dire? How could he be so eager to abandon the dry world—wildflowers, museums, movies, music, crowds in shopping malls and bars? "I told you, man, I have no way of knowing if their crazy theories are going to work. We shouldn't have done even this much. What if the way that they fucked me up messes you up in a bad way? I don't want to be responsible for screwing up your body or your life. You need to really think this through. Even if you do change and become like me, I don't know if I can go back there. I love the sea-people, Gary, but by the time I returned, they wouldn't be the way that I remember them anyway. I don't think I can stand to witness any more suffering or death."

"But how can you refuse to help them? Look, you and the guys in your outfit, you didn't choose this war. It came to you. Fighting back is better than just giving up. How often do you get a chance in your life to do something really good? To be a hero?"

Marcus shook his head. "Listen to you, child. 'The guys in your outfit.' You haven't even been to basic training, and you're trying to talk like an old soldier. Have you even been on a hunting trip and had to shoot a deer, youngster? Yeah, I didn't think so. War is not some happy adventure, Gary, even if you honestly believe you are on the right side. Terrible things still happen. Things that you can't ever get out of your mind. I'm sick of it. I'm sick of killing and death. And I'm tired of being a pawn in somebody else's game. They want us back, and I never want to be their prisoner again. I don't imagine the punishment for escaping is going to be very pleasant, do you? And I just don't think we can pull it off, honey. How can a few dozen ex-Seabees and thousands of pacifistic, day-dreamin' mermen and mermaids who can't stop having sex long enough to finish looking at a map bring the entire U.S. military to its knees?"

"Well, we didn't exactly win in Vietnam, did we?" Gary challenged. "Guerrilla warfare is very damn difficult to defeat. And you have the advantage of dealing with an enemy who is entirely out of his element."

"They don't need to put on diving gear and come down to fight with us hand-to-hand," Marcus said wearily. "They can shoot us down with missiles. They can stay up on top of the water and beat us to death with huge sound waves. They can use chemical warfare or germ warfare. They prefer to kill at a distance."

"Yeah, well, they also don't want anybody to know this is going on," Gary said. "And I know who could tell on them. The two of us, right here. With you here to show them that it's no joke, no story out of *The National Enquirer*, we'd be on every news program from here to Sunday."

Marcus laughed. "I can't argue with you any more, honey. I'm tired of talking. Why don't you go inside and get something to eat?"

"OK," Gary said. "But then I'm going back to the training camp, and I'm going to pack up my stuff and come back here. I'm going to stay with you. After all you've been through, you shouldn't have to be alone. And you won't be. Never again. Whatever we decide, we can do it together."

Marcus looked at him thoughtfully, nodded once, and then swam away. Gary wondered if he ever got to stop swimming. Did he sleep? With those gills, he supposed it would be possible for Marcus to simply drift off underwater. *I want to sleep with this man*, he thought. He realized, with his heart so full of feeling that it was about to burst, that this was no euphemism for "fuck him to pieces" but was instead a softer desire for contact with his body, for affection and intimacy.

Someday I will, he resolved. *When I have a real swimmer's body.*

The Hostage

It was that time just before daybreak called "thieves' dawn"—the sun was not up, but there was enough light to warn adulterous lovers and other robbers that dawn was imminent. The Captain of Archers took his restive mount a little way off from his troop and galloped back, trying to calm it with a short, strenuous run. It flicked its big ears (full of stiff, protective hairs) at his shouted admonitions. As they picked up speed, those ears folded almost in half, the way they would in a sandstorm—a sure sign of tension and distress. The captain took the reins in his teeth and patted (pounded, almost, with both hands) the saddlebags of flesh where the swaybacked animal stored water. As they slowed to a walk, his mount twisted its flexible neck and presented its intelligent, very hard head for more rough punches of affection. Its nictating membranes closed with pleasure when he obliged.

Some of his men had fished pipes from the sleeves of their burnooses and smoked as they watched the village below. One had extracted a small scroll of scripture from his waist-scarf and studied it intently, his mustached lips moving with the flowing characters. Another man was twisting war-tassels out of heavy, thick gold thread, silent ornaments that would replace the bells on his harness the next time he rode into battle. Two others shared a flask of water and argued about the odds for a race to be run in 10 days' time. Since the animals these men rode were prized for their sure-footedness, their stamina, their ability to find water and kill poisonous reptiles, but not their speed, competitions resembled a combination obstacle course and survival test. Each of them scoffed at the other's favorite. "He would rather eat grain than raw meat!" one guffawed. "His ancestors are more distinguished than your own!" was the retort.

As the light increased, the sand dunes became a pale copper color. In the distance the black mountains turned to purple; their snowy caps acquired a faint tinge of blue. The dome of air above gradually darkened, from white to cobalt, and the few wispy, scarlet clouds were burned charcoal-gray, then melted away, until nothing stood between the world and the sun. Distracting pastimes were put away, and all conversation (except the constant communion a sanctified man has with God) ceased.

Finally, a ragged cortege trailed out of the despised and impoverished village below. The body in a winding-sheet, borne by several men, led the procession. The women sang a dirge, but the men were enjoined to be silent, which was fortunate, because the body was heavy, and it was hard work to carry it so far across loose sand. Seif law forbid the men of this people, the Jen, to ride. "Veiled for the dead man," the Captain grunted, gesturing at the keening females. "Would that those ugly bitches were kinder to living men!" It was a common prayer among the Seif, whose women covered their faces perpetually, and his men either laughed or tapped their breasts in agreement.

The villagers placed the body at the foot of the hill where the armed company waited and dispersed immediately without acknowledging it. No one stayed to guard the corpse or report on its fate. Even the singing ceased. The only sound was the weeping of one old man, the oldest man there, and he was led away by two young boys, barely more than children, his remaining sons.

With a curt order, the Captain held back his men until the Jen had returned to their noisome little town. Not for the first time, he wondered how men could feel like men, cooped up in hovels, bound to fields they tilled like women, unable to follow the wind or a war. Then he waved his troop forward, and they rode en masse down the hill, whooping like beasts of prey. The Captain (leaning off his horse, disdaining to dismount) slit the winding-sheet open with a pretty gesture of his strong right arm and a very sharp, hooked gutting dagger.

THE HOSTAGE

There, exposed in a cradle of rags, was a young man, so heavily drugged that he did not seem to breathe. The troop wheeled about, and two of the men hoisted the boy by his arms and threw him across the front of the Captain's mount, where he stayed, not waking, during the short ride back to the Royal Tent. The Captain's hand rested possessively in the small of the boy's back, keeping watch over his equilibrium and breathing.

If the boy had been awake, he would surely have been killed, because his terror would have made him violent. He expected these men to murder him. Rumor in his village had it that his predecessor had been compelled to kill himself (an unimaginable sin) or had been poisoned upon the death of his master, the old King. If someone had told the boy that this man had chosen to burn with his dead lord rather than live without him—well, he would have been too shocked by the blasphemy to even consider that it might be true. It was true that if these men had hated their new King, or if their King had hated the Jen, the Captain would not have brought him forth from his unnatural womb, unscathed. He was a hostage, given as a pledge of good conduct by his people. Without him, the Jen had no right to a home on Seif soil. This treaty was older than thought or memory.

The Captain did not know that this was the eldest son of the Jen's Teacher, and a devout boy, pale because he had been kept indoors, studying holy books, instead of laboring in the fields. The Captain would have felt only contempt for this learning, as he felt contempt for all of the pacifistic Jen. Imagine a leader who was not a general! He only knew that the white, naked buttocks were beautiful, lightly furred, neither slack nor overly muscular. The fine gold hairs that lined the Hostage's downy crack reflected the sunlight and made it seem especially deep and succulent. This sight made the Captain tighten his thighs around the powerful male animal coursing beneath him. Then, out of deference to the boy's pallor, he drew off one of his own headscarves and covered the inviting curves.

The archers had also noted the quality of those curves—but

they made no jests about the Hostage between themselves, until they should see how close the King intended to keep this new proof of his royalty. Nor did they mock their Captain for his solicitude. All of them had boys they treated tenderly.

The troop had to pass through stout, well-watched gates to enter the Royal Tent. This place was actually a city; the only tents remaining were pleasure-pavilions pitched in the palace gardens to catch the breeze during the height of summer. But the Seif had descended from nomads who lived in tents, and it would have been treason to say their monarch lived in a fixed, though luxurious, abode.

At the Oasis of the Queen (a palace, albeit one built over an artesian well), the boy was handed over to eunuchs, who undertook to prepare him for his audience with the King. The first thing they did was put a cactus button under his tongue to wake him up. The stimulant heightened his perceptions unpleasantly. The light seemed harsh, people loomed over him before he expected it, the sound of speech was exaggerated, but its meaning was muffled. The multicolored hair, dangling ornaments, bright clothing, keloid-marked faces, and musical voices of the eunuchs were like blows to his stomach. And everything they did to him seemed designed to violate cherished precepts his father had solemnly urged him to obey, lest he lose the right to sing to his Maker in the afterlife. A venal man, a man of sloth, was not even fit to hold the hymn books of the angels.

First he was bathed by other hands—and he was used to washing himself only once a week, underneath a voluminous robe, so he would not be subjected to the shameful sight of his own flesh. These hands were scrupulously chaste, but their softness betrayed carnal knowledge. Even the unveiled Jen women did not use paint or perfume. But now his face was made up—his eyes outlined with kohl, his mouth rouged—and he was perfumed in places he had been taught never to think of or name. They even poured a little scented oil into him, with an old, brass clyster. Its narrow neck was cold and evilly tarnished. Then the eunuchs shaved him to make his skin smooth and ensure that he took no unclean, tiny cattle to the King. They even shaved his head, something he had seen done only to people caught violating the dietary laws. Then he was fed wine, and wine should be administered only on sacred occasions, in small sips, to seal a prayer.

Yet he must be obedient, or his people would be exiled. So he endured it all and realized his father had been right to read the ritual for the dead over him while the other men wound him in strips of gauze and wept. He no longer had a people and thus was not, in this world of warring tribes, a person at all. He was property, a gift the King might decide to toss away.

They threw a transparent cotton robe around him, belted tightly, so the loose stuff revealed his shoulders and fell off his thighs but showed off his small waist and the swelling cheeks of his ass. They led him to the audience, fanning him, switching flies off of him, making dozens of solicitous gestures, but chattering only to each other. He was too upset to notice the present that one of the eunuchs gave him, a small, embroidered pouch worn on the belt. It contained a few cosmetics, a tiny pipe, and a real treasure, a palm-size, polished metal mirror. It would take only a few months for the Hostage to recognize this gift for what it was, a genuine act of generosity from someone who had more kindness than wealth, a small comfort sent from one prisoner of fate to another. There would be many gifts of another sort, expensive baubles that nonetheless caused no pain to those who parted with them, for they came from men who had far more wealth than real generosity.

The King's chamber seemed huge to the boy, who was used to tiny, two-room huts. It was also dark, lit only by candles in the back corner. It took him several minutes to see the King behind the candles, sitting at a low table. He could not feel his own feet walking forward but knew he had come closer because now he could see that the table was loaded down with more wine and platters of strange food—cubes of vegetables and meat on little spears; marinated chunks of fruit and raw, peppery fish; chilled curds; tiny bowls of spices and flagons of oil, vinegar, and fermented sauces.

The Hostage could not bear to see what manner of man now

owned him. But that was where he must focus for the rest of his life. The King had replaced his father and his God. So he looked up, unwilling, but unable to stop himself. The King stood, having nothing to fear from this examination. He was a big man, heavy with the muscle needed to walk miles in full armor, throw a spear a foot again as tall as himself, draw a longbow, control the head of a wounded steed, bear his share of a battering ram, hold up his own flag in battle if the standard-bearer should fall, or break the body of a man over his knee. He wore his dark, curly hair long, and his eyes were dark also but lit with an appreciation of this boy's comeliness and grace. Yet the Hostage shrank from this admiration, finding it more frightening than an openly expressed intention to garrote him.

"Leave us," said the King, and the eunuchs departed to make their own evening meal, gamble, practice new dances, and slip out to meet ardent (but anonymous) lovers. "Come here." The boy moved toward him and discovered then (in the silent chamber) that his clothing made a sibilant noise, like a slender tree disturbed by a strong wind. The King patted, once, the pillow beside him. "If we are not to be enemies, we must be brothers. And brothers must love each other. It is written, 'I will put my beloved under my arm, and place my heart between his enemy and the heart of my beloved.'"

The boy swayed on his feet. It was hot in this room; he felt faint. "You do not recognize the verse? It is from the oldest scriptures, shared by your people and mine, though in a slightly different form. You know, do you not, that this is the only reason the Jen share our land? The Prophet himself told us that God spoke also to your first Teacher. For reasons known only to Himself, he told your people to go in one direction and mine to go in another. May all glory be to His mysteries. All this was done so that we might have a sacred origin and become a pure people, unprofaned."

The King's tone gentled. "I see that there is much you do not know. Come to me, then, and be instructed." Again he showed the young man where he must sit, and the Hostage finally took the offered pillow, knowing if he did not, the King would fetch him and need not be gentle about it. Besides, it went against his nature and his upbringing to repay courtesy with insolence.

It seemed the verse was to be taken literally, for the King tucked his head into the space between his arm and his shoulder, and with his other hand laid skewers on a small charcoal brazier in the center of the table. As the food cooked, he turned them, then steadily regarded the boy in his embrace, silently praising him for not flinching or babbling. When the meat was brown and dripping with sweet juice, he lifted it from the grill, cooled it with his own breath, and fed the boy before he fed himself. Even though the meat was from an unclean animal and spiced in a forbidden manner, the boy could not reject this royal courtesy. It tasted better than anything his mother gave him to eat, and did that not make him an abominable traitor? (*Or*, he thought, in his first spate of rebellion, *am I an orphan, betrayed, abandoned? Who can blame me if I do what I must to survive?*)

The King gave him wine out of his own cup, which comforted him, then offered it out of his mouth, which outraged him. The King simply clamped his hands upon the reluctant face and forced wine and kisses upon it. With his head caught between those big rough hands, the Hostage drank blindly and felt the King's glossy black beard and mustache scrape his cheeks and chin. That harshness made the soft lips and slippery tongue seem doubly pleasant. He wondered if he was perhaps becoming a bit drunk. "You are delicious," a deep voice said, someone else's voice reverberating in his throat. Then the kiss was gone.

The steady pressure of the King's arm against his shoulder and side made him turn toward him, and he felt pleasantly warm and drowsy, like a small child who has just been suckled. The room was lit only by a few candles and the charcoal brazier, so he could see very little but the King's face and chest, which was rising and falling as quickly as his own. He felt awe, to think that perhaps some passion for his person could disturb that mighty breast. He laid his hand there, why he did not know, and the King was quick to seize it and turn the palm up, where he could lick and suck at it, then take almost the whole hand into his mouth, pleasuring it with his tongue and teeth.

The youth was already feeling pleasure in his groin without being touched, and the first caress below his waist was so light that he did not know when it began. The pleasure quickened and urged him to come after it, prolong it, so he actually thrust himself against the hand that circled his virginal manhood. "Yes," said the King, and put his hand further into the boy's robe, to feel his stomach and backside, his thighs, and heft his sac and stroke his shaft. "I will take your innocence before I give you wisdom," he threatened as he stroked the boy's nipples with his thumbs and plucked at them until they were hard as the pits in ripe fruit. "Look," said the King, showing him his own phallus, erect in that huge hand, a hand that could easily sunder that precious part from the Hostage's body but fondled him instead. "The Hand of God has brought us here," the King chuckled in his ear, making a joke—the King himself was called "God's right hand." By making reference to his own divinity, the King also warned the Hostage that something new and not so easy to give was about to be demanded from him. He could not look away as those hands, the size of small hams, every finger bearing one or two priceless rings, parted the King's robes and urged him to come close and see what was exposed.

It was a royal scepter, thick and tipped with a large ruby, and the rosy skin on it was whole, rolling under the Hostage's hand to expose a white-pink shaft. He had never seen a man's organ with its foreskin intact. "Kiss me, beloved, drink from me, since I have given you wine from my own mouth." More poetry with the authority of scripture. The boy hesitated, and the King seized his eggs and wrung them. When he cried out with pain, the King held his mouth open with both of his thumbs and showed the Hostage what he must do. The egg-shaped gem turned out to be a spongy bud, covered with slightly crinkled skin. The taste of it was not unpleasant, and the King took care to make his first thrusts shallow, not wanting to have to punish the boy for taking fright and biting down. But as his passion quickened—"This is the plow that will open the fields to receive my seed," the monarch hissed. "This is my charger whose strong legs devour the miles, bringing me to a new place, a place to conquer, a place where all my enemies will fall beneath me. This is the battering ram at the gates of the besieged city, receive me, I ride you, make my way easy, open for me, open for me, open for me!"—the chanting ceased as he completely lost control, but by then the boy was more ready to be plowed and plundered, and he swallowed everything poured into him, without thinking, then was ashamed of himself for being so compliant, and rolled away and hid his face and wept.

For a long time there was no speech. Then he heard the King rearrange his garments and pour himself more wine. After clearing his throat, the King said to him, "You think you are unmanned by me. You resent my power over you. But think of this, beloved, think what chains bind me." The boy was sullen and did not answer, or think of it either. Still the King continued: "Each man knows in his secret heart that he would do anything to live, and cannot believe (unless he is a fool) that anything done to preserve life is dishonorable. And that is all I have to hold you with—your life—and the life of your people. Which makes you an innocent sacrifice. But me? I am held in this net by my love of power. Power is more jealous than any lover. To possess it, you must love nothing else more, not even God, not even yourself. The Seif are an old people, very proud, and anyone who would rule them must shoulder a burden of history, customs and rituals which weighs more than all the wealth of this land, and never complain.

"When I would bed one of my wives, she is brought to me secretly, at night, by the other Royal Women. They choose for me. I may choose only youths for myself. And I never know which of my wives has conceived or how many children I have or which of my sons will succeed me. I only know if I fail as a commander of armies or as a stud-bull in the Royal Women's plans for their own bloodline, they will emerge from the harem and slay me, make me a sacrifice to the fertility of their fields, the way they murdered my father and his father and the King before him who was not kin to me. The women can do this because they are the only ones who know where to find the water between the land of each tribe and guide the merchant caravans to it, how to breed children that are free of wasting diseases. Even this palace is not mine, since a free man may own only what can be carried away on the back of his destrier and pack-mares.

"If my women have this hold over me, who are the least in my kingdom, can you imagine the rivalry and etiquette, hereditary honors and titles, blood feuds and boundary disputes, and royal debts which must be balanced and weighed each time I deal with that tribe or this one, with the elders, the priests, the scribes, the shepherds, the well-diggers, the tanners, the potters, the weavers, even the perfumers and the gardeners?"

Then because the boy made no answer, the King was filled with wrath, and used the Hostage's mouth again, to teach him it was wise to speak if he was given that opportunity. His great phallus plundered that delicate opening and took its pleasure, not from slow surrender or teasing strokes of the tongue, but from choking and tears and the forced swallowing of the thick rod put down the boy's throat again and again until he could not see for tears and his ears rang and the sea itself battered the back of his gorge, until he yielded and drowned and swallowed the whole ocean, bitter salt, and found himself lying on the floor in a pool of his own making, his thighs polluted by evidence of pleasure as copious as what now lay in his belly against his will.

"It is impious for a man to resent his Fate," the King said blandly, skimming the pitch off a new jar of wine. "All of us are in the hands of God. We live and die, suffer or know joy, as His will commands. According to His own design, He makes us rich or poor, slave-merchant or eunuch, saint or assassin. We must behave accordingly, and play the role He gives us. The only sin is to struggle against His will."

The boy knew this was heresy. He had been taught to strive to keep a body of commands and prohibitions so intimate, weighty, and intricate that a moment of carelessness or forgetfulness could undo a lifetime of obedience with an unforgivable sin. How much easier this new way seemed to him, how much more suitable to his present status. He knew he must yield to it sooner or later, but not yet—not yet.

The King picked him up and turned him over in his lap so that his limp-lolling cock rested against royal brocade and a thick, hairy thigh. The big hands with their calloused tips stroked between his cheeks. "You come from an immodest race," said the King. "Even your penis has no covering for his shame, because when you were an infant, your father cut off the veil God gives every man, to protect his pride. I will force you to have some modesty, since I cannot expect you to possess it naturally. So you will wear a veil, but not for the same reason our women wear veils. Since all their doings are secret, and no man knows if they speak the truth or a lie, it profits a man nothing to be able to see what passes across their faces. A woman's veil is a warning to take hold of your wallet with one hand and your nuts with the other. But you will wear only a half-veil, to cover your mouth, the only part of you I reserve for my own use."

The buttocks, covered with the goose flesh of barely perceptible pleasure, tightened beneath his hands. The King laughed. "What—did you think I was going to spread your legs? That is something I do to get children or to punish my vanquished enemies on the field of battle. If I ever made use of you that way, it would be a sign that I loved you too much to rule myself, and soon my army would not follow me, nor my people obey any law I made. But you are ready to be used like a woman or a defeated warrior, are you not, my beloved?" With that, he thrust his fingers inside the boy, enough of them to equal the thickness of his phallus, and made the Hostage moan with dread. Now he was not even fit to linger outside the doorway to the celestial realm and hear echoes of God's choral praise.

"Of course, with others, you may do whatever you like," the King said thoughtfully, continuing to rock four thick fingers in and out of his new possession. "As long as you do not let them lift your veil. I expect you will have many suitors, and I prefer that, because it will keep you out of mischief and off my hands." The boy writhed in his lap, uttering a heartfelt prayer to escape those hands. The lecture (and the penetration) continued. "But I warn you, take no bribes for my favors. Instead, set a high price on your own. Make them teach you the art of war, because I will have you with me wherever I go. I will not have you slaughtered because you falsely believe God is pleased at the sight of a coward. I will do what I like with you, I say, and if I cannot put my scepter in you, for fear of losing it, I will still have you here so that any other lover who takes you from behind will only remind you of me." The fingers found a certain place and stroked harder, pushed, commanded. The King's touch released odors of cinnamon and musk, made the perfumed oil burn inside the boy. The touch of his lord was painful but also created a wonderful feeling of urgency, of helplessness. Then two heavy blows, one on each cheek, from a hand that weighed as much as a brick, told him he was indeed helpless and had no choice, no control over what was done to him. He spurted, crying like a bereaved woman. "There is so much juice in you," the King said, self-satisfied, and rubbed the Hostage's jism across his own belly, and used it to make his rampant rod more slippery in his fist.

Once more, he let his Hostage slip to the floor. There, on his belly in the dust, it occurred to the boy that even if he were to come to his knees, he would still be holding his head higher than it was now. So he rose to his knees and went on them between the outspread thighs of his lord, and put out his hand as if he were begging or in the dark. What he found was erect to bursting, even the testicles swollen in their sac, riding high and tight against the shaft above them, eager to spurt. Instead, he pulled them down into his fist, gently closing the ducts, and took one of them in his mouth, sucking on the ball that moved within the skin, trying to peel it with his tongue. Because he was not thinking, he was not surprised when its brother joined his twin in his mouth, but the King was astonished, and only the whites of his eyes showed. His hands trembled upon the Hostage's shoulders.

When his bulging cheeks grew weary, the kneeling youth gently extruded one egg, then the other, but did not open his hand. Instead, he tugged down again, to bring the bobbing shaft within reach of his mouth. It was too rigid to come to him, so he used his other hand to make it bow a little, and returned its bow to put it in his mouth whole, as if it were a comb full of honey. It might torment his throat, but would give his cheeks a rest. There was already a copious leaking fluid, which ran in a silver trail across his tongue, lubricating its own path down his gullet. He sucked, drew back still sucking hard, then returned blowing hot, wet air all over it, fastened his lips about the base and twisted his head slowly from side to side, both hands now busy holding the foreskin back, tongue working beneath, his lips always trying to kiss, kissing but never able to close around that thick taproot. It was too much, it was not enough, the King tried again and again to seize him and fuck his throat, but a strange weakness would always overcome him so that he was only able to caress the boy's ears and scalp. It was of his own accord that the boy began to administer deep, plunging sucks. At the same time, he released the captive scrotum. Just like that, the King's balls drew up to his belly, and he became a fountain, spending his virility into the air.

This orgasm was so intense that it brought dissatisfaction, an irritation that the pleasure had to end, a hunger for new arousal and further sensation. The King resolved to regain his mastery and his erection, so he took a candle that was narrow at the tip and wide at the base, blew it out, and anointed it with oil. He bid the nervous boy to put it inside himself, rest it on the floor, and rise up and down on it, and continue to nurse upon the royal staff. The King also made the Hostage roll and rub his proud but fledgling cock against his owner's heavy, sandaled foot, yet refrain from reaching satisfaction. Full of sensations he was not used to enduring (the need to evacuate, the need to come), the boy was more humble this time, more urgent, yet more careful. Both of them had expended all their seed now, so it took longer to reach climax, and what little fluid they were able to expel was boiling, thin, and felt as if it took forever to cease coming forth.

By the time the King allowed him to rest, trembling, on the cushions, the Hostage did not know if he hated this man who owned him, but he knew he was valuable property, and would not be tossed aside. Here in the King's court, it was better to bow to Fate and be prized as a jewel or a pet or even a catamite than it was to be a sulky, worthless, stupid infidel boy. More use was made of him (beginning with removing the King's sandals, and cleaning his feet with gentle swoops of the tongue), but it only served to reinforce this teaching and make his mouth swell like a ruined maiden's slit.

When the King was done with the Hostage, he called for the Captain of the Archers (who had heard everything that passed between them while he guarded the King's door) and thrust the boy into his arms. "Here is my falconet," said the King. "Take him to his perch until I wish to go hunting again."

The Captain carried the hostage-turned-peregrine to the chamber set aside for him. The eunuchs put him to bed, cooing over the hand-prints that marked him behind, positioning him carefully upon huge, soft pillows, covering him lightly against the heat, silently drawing the insect-nets together and tying them shut. They imagined that he was one of them now, without the excuse or permission of castration, and pitied him.

The Captain contemplated the beautiful bruised lips. In sleep, the proud look of the eldest son had returned to the Hostage's face. He was so fair, a lamp in this palace of dark and warlike men. In a far corner of the chamber, one of the eunuchs sat cross-legged, stitching the veil that the King had ordered, which the boy would don upon waking so that the Captain would never see that sweet mouth again. The boy was steeped in the mana of the King, he had swallowed the essence of his virility, absorbed a part of the royal man the Captain loved, feared, obeyed, but must never touch. Would the King also have the boy pierced so that chains ran from his earlobes to his nostrils, like reins? Then this Hostage would resemble his predecessor in every aspect. That was a fierce one, lost now forever in funeral fire! No Seif, but no eunuch, no. How many times had he saved the old King's life? The King who ruled now had been drilled in his first set of arms by that solitary, deadly man.

From his niche, the slave boy whose job was to pull rhythmically on a silk cord that made the fan spin lazily, drawing a current of warm languorous air through the room like a caress, saw the Captain stare hard, then shake himself as if waking from a dream. He walked to a desk (for the Hostage's room was large and well-furnished), took up pen and parchment, and wrote. Wide as his eyes were, the fan-boy averted them and sealed his mouth, lest he lose his sight or his tongue for speaking out of turn.

When he had finished writing, the Captain went forward, pinned a poem to the Hostage's pillow, and reluctantly left the room. In this country a man was counted a poor warrior if he did not love his comrades in arms—for who could face battle courageously if he was not standing next to men he loved? And it was a poor sort of lover (or soldier) who was not also a poet.

> Even the Eagle may be hostage
> To an emperor's wrist,
> But in the sky,
> The king of birds is free
> To strike whatever prey he will,
> If it is light enough
> To devour in the air
> Before he hears the whirring lure.
> Seize my heart.
> Though it is full of you,
> It will weigh so little
> In your talons
> That even the wind
> Will be unburdened
> By my love.

Walking down the dim hallway, the Captain thought, *I will go now and prepare a gift for him—a little bow of precious wood inlaid with horn, the kind of thing princes learn to shoot with, and a quiver of arrows, fletched with green and blue feathers. Let me show him how to find a target with a flurry of arrows or slowly sink his spear into a vulnerable body, let me teach him how to keep his seat atop a strong and wild stallion. If he must go to war, let him learn the art of battle from me. I will gladly be the second man that he conquers.*

The Spoiler

He slept in a pile of dirty socks and soiled jockstraps, souvenirs of the men he adored, sometimes acquired without their permission. In winter, for warmth, he pulled a leather hide over this nest and its virile odors. When he woke up, he ran three miles. His spartan breakfast was part of a careful diet supplemented with a bewildering rainbow of vitamins and minerals. Every other afternoon he lifted weights. His body was well-defined and hard, which pleased him, but not because he was narcissistic. It was the value others placed on his physique that gave him pleasure or, rather, made it easier for him to procure what gave him pleasure. The rest of each day, Monday through Friday, he worked diligently at his chosen profession. It brought him a comfortable income but placed no demands on his heart—or his evenings and weekends.

It was the rest of his time that was important, the time when he could prowl and sniff for the men who made him hungry, carefully laying the plans that would allow him to pounce and feast. That was when he became the spoiler.

When he went out he always wore the same set of leathers. These carefully tailored black skins had cost him several times more than some men pay for an entire wardrobe of tanned cowhide. He wore a very tight short-sleeved black leather shirt that laced up the front. This supple, buttery-soft garment clung to him, moved with him as if it were his by birth. He was fair-skinned but very hirsute, so the black fur on his barrel chest sprang up around the laces, and the thick, curly hair on his biceps and forearms made it hard to tell where the sleeves ended and his bare arms began. He wore pants (not chaps) that fit snug across the ass but were not tight enough in the crotch to mimic a hard-on if he was not really erect. His belt was a plain strap of leather, innocent of studs, well-oiled, and as flexible as a whore's tongue, with a massive silver (not chrome, not aluminum) buckle. No keys hung from his belt. He did not wear a cock ring or a wristwatch. He had no epaulets to hang a chain from since he did not own a leather jacket.

A cute clone in Adidas and a "Daddy's Boy" T-shirt who saw him leaving the bar one night asked, trying to pick him up, "Did you forget your jacket?"

"No. I don't have a jacket."

Daddy's Boy thought, *Thank God, he doesn't take all this leather drag seriously, he's not going to get me home and do something ungodly,* and decided to cruise in earnest. "You should. You'd look hot in one."

The spoiler gave his admirer a puzzled frown. "But I don't own a motorcycle," he explained.

Men in full leather are usually conspicuous. But the spoiler's appearance was so neat, his lines so clean, his bearing so modest that he often passed through crowds of the bourgeoisie without changing the topic of their conversation. In the self-consciously masculine bars and rotting piers he frequented, other men relied on flashy, cheap metal to signal their presence in the darkness or a heavy tread that would make their keys and other accoutrements jangle. He, on the other hand, was rarely noticed unless he chose to be. Nearly every leatherman in the city had been elbow to elbow with him in some club or alley, but few recognized him on sight.

Of the elite handful who acknowledged him with a bare nod, the kind of minimal gesture that was harder to get from them than a knighthood, one man wore only cowboy fringes, conchos, and suede; one man wore no leather at all; and one was not a man. But each of these folks have legends of their own.

Only his boots glittered, and that was a mirror-bright shine, the kind that takes months of work to complete. Even a USMC drill instructor can't force someone to get that kind of sheen on a pair of boots. It takes constant caressing. Your brush has to touch the boots as often and as lightly as you touch someone who has just made you fall in love. The spoiler had never been in love, but his boots were perfect. He kept his pants tucked into them. They went up to the knee, glossy as a frozen lake at midnight.

The absence of right/left signals should also have made him conspicuous. Instead, he was often discounted as a tourist or an amateur. Only one youngster, drunk enough to think he was the most attractive boy in the bar and thus immune to snubs, ever had the nerve to accost him and demand, "What are you?"

The spoiler replied (perhaps amused because of what he was planning to turn himself into for the sake of his latest conquest), "A man."

"No, I mean what are you into? Which role do you play?"

"I don't play," the spoiler said. The look in his eye momentarily sobered the curious, intoxicated kid, made him want to ask another, better question. But those eyes were too deep, it was too far to fall—so he chose instead to get drunk enough to fall off his bar stool. Not that the spoiler noticed; taking out the trash was not his job.

Why did he take such care with his dress if he intended to travel incognito? If he did not want to be recognized, groped and drooled over, why was he a regular in all the grimy Mafia firetraps that pandered to compulsive cocksuckers, gay bikers, fetishists, bondage freaks, masochists, expert handballers and other sexually bent, homomasculine men the good Catholic mobsters saw only as a horde of spendthrift drunks and perverts? Every scene attracts a certain number of voyeurs, those too timid, alienated, or unattractive to participate. You might call the spoiler a voyeur since he spent most of his time looking and listening. But he was a watchdog, not a spectator. He paid minute attention to the scene. He knew the names and histories of most of the topmen who shared his specialized tastes. He could predict their behavior better than a seasoned bartender. And he selected some of them to be cut out of the herd.

His selection was made for him by a signal that socked directly through his eyes or ears or nose into his gut. His balls would roll as their pouch shrank, pumping blood into his dick so fast that it started leaking even before he got hard. Any number of things could trigger that signal. It could be the inborn authority in a tone of voice, a certain sure grip that revealed a talent for handling objects and men who wanted to be objects, an offhanded way of revealing esoteric abilities and interests. An expression of the mere need to control or dominate was not enough to throw this punch into his guts; too many people try to act like lifeguards because they are drowning themselves.

One night the stars were in a favorable conjunction for completing a drama the spoiler had been hankering after for months. He found himself being agreeable to a young man who had never been in "this kind of place" before. He was sandy blond, clean-shaven, with a trim body that looked fit because he was moderately active and under 25. He said his name was Curt, and he had borrowed these chaps from his roommate; did they fit? As soon as the spoiler realized this good-looking kid was a complete novice, he realized he was the perfect lure and began to turn him into his pawn. He also forgot his name.

The newcomer did not know why he was telling this plain, unsmiling leatherman about his bizarre secret fantasies, asking him questions, and accepting his suggestions. He did know he was nervous and needed to be patted on the head and pointed in the right direction. It was easy to confess his lack of experience and his longstanding fascination with leather. Like most other raw recruits, he thought leather was synonymous with S/M, and S/M meant being whipped. He did not know how rare this ritual actually is. The grave stranger was knowledgeable and reassuring. He drew verbal thumbnail sketches of the half-dozen tops who were hunting in the bar that night and told him which one he needed to meet—an older man, graying at the temples, with the build of a boxer and sad eyes. He also told him how to do it. The spoiler knew this master very well. His name was Roger, and he had a protective instinct toward novices; it was almost a reflex for him to take a courteous one home.

Before he could say "whips and chains," Curt was leaning his head on the master's chest and whispering, "Sir, may I buy you a beer, sir?" The gesture was too touching, the offer too well-bred to be rejected. When the boy returned with the cold, sweaty bottle, he was ordered to tell his story. It came out easily, since he had rehearsed it in the corner with the sympathetic stranger. He was not surprised when the big man put a hand around his throat and guided him down to the floor until he knelt with his cheek pressed against the worn denim that covered the master's cock. Curt wrapped his arms around the thighs encased in latigo, smelling of motor oil, and felt that he had come home. But he was surprised when the stranger (he had already forgotten exactly what he looked like) loomed near and inquired if he, "the boy," had given offense to the master.

Roger scowled and said he had not known the boy was in anyone else's service. Before the pawn could deny this, the stranger said, "Sir, he is not in my service. But I pointed you out to him and suggested that he introduce himself. I would hold myself responsible if you were not pleased." Placated, the master relaxed, and the upshot of the matter was that all three of them left the bar together, to game in one of the city's better-equipped arenas.

This master's forte was whipping. In his black room he had a large collection of antique English hunting crops, nautical cats, Scottish tawses, monks' flails, and Australian quirts on display under glass. The spoiler gave each one a separate scrutiny and made a quiet comment or two that showed his appreciation of their history and construction. These implements were not for use. But the walls of the master's inner sanctum were hung with enough modern copies to flog the entire mutinous crew of an aircraft carrier.

The room was clean but somber. These walls would never forget what they had witnessed, and they made the visitor feel an obligation to live up to their memories. Wooden beams ran the length of the ceiling, massive enough to support any load hauled into space by the greasy sets of block and tackle that hung here and there. A vertical beam equipped with large iron rings stood alone in the center of the room. In one corner there was a waist-high device that a man could be comfortably bent over and bound to by a strap buckled across his back. It looked like a huge, ancient butcher's block and was authentically stained. In another corner was a waist-high Barkley bench, the width of a human torso, minimally padded, with a hole in the center.

To his credit, the young man stayed, something that is not easy for a novice to do the first time he finds what he is looking for. For a fleeting moment, he hoped that he would be bound face to face with the stranger who was (he finally realized) responsible for his presence here. Surely it would be easier to take what was coming if he had a companion, someone more experienced who would encourage him and share the pain. But the stranger had taken care to keep his relationship to the master ambiguous. He had been respectful but not servile. The master had not laid a hand on him.

Now the boy found that the first direct order of the evening was addressed to him alone. He had wanted his obligations cut in half; instead, he imagined they were doubled. After all, there were two pairs of boots to trample and crush him (which he licked), two pairs of hands to bless and terrify him (which he cringed from and kissed), two wills bent against his own (symbolized by the hard flesh he was briefly allowed to expose and worship). He was too green to understand the hierarchy. Only one of these men was the master, taking the ultimate control and responsibility. The other acted only as his tool, his assistant. Roger was, ironically, too experienced (or jaded) to imagine that the power could be distributed any other way in his own dungeon.

Out of compassion, the master bade the novice stretch out on the table, with his cock and balls dangling through the hole. This would save him the embarrassment of buckling knees. Yielding to panic, the prone boy said, "Please, sir, don't tie my hands."

"All right," the master rumbled, and used three feet of leather lacing to bind his subject's nuts in such a way that he could not take them with him if he wanted to escape.

They began with their hands, one set gloved in thin kid, the other sheathed the old-fashioned way, in tight black silk. The boy was massaged, kneaded, pummeled, then tapped, given a series of slaps that began with light glancing blows and ended with hard smacks that landed deep in his flesh. He was allowed to rest, stroked, made hard until he plunged against the bench trying to fuck empty air, then assaulted by hands that smashed into him, broke him apart, went right through him.

While he cried, the masters broached fresh cans of beer and ordered their thoughts. When the work resumed, the spoiler knelt under the table of his own accord, then captured the pawn's bound and aching parts in his mouth. While he worked the length of the disembodied organ (swollen to the bursting point) within his throat, the spoiler stretched and prodded the well-restrained nuts, choking in their sac, full of fluids they could not release. The master selected a black and red cat-o'-nine-tails from the wall, a standard enough instrument. But this one had been made especially for him by Fred Norman, and the braiding was (of course) superlative. The round tails were tight, thin, and faster than thought.

The pawn thought nothing of it. He had never imagined anything else, other than a belt, perhaps, being used to whip someone. It had never even occurred to him that some whips are made better than others. The master's collection had seemed a bit gimmicky to him, a butch version of his granny's knickknacks. His memories of the only corporal punishment he had ever received—a few hand spankings given to him as a child—were vague. Lucky for him, the spoiler had told him specifically to be very honest with the master about just how much of a beginner he was.

Roger was a laconic man. He spoke freely only to the accompaniment of some object falling on naked flesh. The conversation he addressed to his new victim was carried on for the benefit of the whip, to make sure Curt stayed put long enough to let its nine tails drink enough sweat and pain to keep it well fed until he took it from the wall again. Whips that are not used can become as lonely as kept women on Christmas Eve. So he explained to the young man what he was doing and why, and he urged him to pay attention to it, learn from it, even enjoy it. He paused frequently to allow Curt's body to absorb this new knowledge before his mind could take it away.

Under the table, the spoiler had ceased to suck actively on the pawn's cock and simply kept his throat open around it. The whip cracks made the boy go up and down like a bridegroom, feeding his unseen comforter the whole length of his manhood at every burning, intolerable, indescribable stroke.

Again, to his credit, the young man persisted. He did not beg to be released (though he did beg for a reprieve). He did not lose his temper or revile his tormenters. He struggled with his pain, willing (though not wise enough) to savor it. But he began to see what transcendence might be possible, what god he might someday be fit to serve.

The spoiler suddenly pulled away and stood up. His pawn had almost come, and he would not allow that, even if the boy's cock had not been trussed up and the orgasm would not have damaged it. The master was running his silk-clad hands over the bruised scarlet skin, murmuring like a groom soothing a jumpy horse. He had no more use for the boy, so he was tender. He could tell that Curt couldn't take much more, and he was not interested in continuing at the present level. It would have taken days of this sort of work to make his arm just a little tired, and nowadays, exhaustion was the chief thing he got out of flogging.

Normally, at this point in the scene he would offer the subject's ass to the other master, if one were present. Most bottoms got pissy if there wasn't some kind of sex at the end of a scene, and he personally found it distasteful. There was a limit to pretense after all, a limit to what you could give someone who was not your heart's desire. But the spoiler had anticipated this and deflected the invitation.

"My turn," he said, drawing a whip from his shirt. It had been wrapped around his waist, hidden until now. He had been lucky to wear it on this night's jaunt.

THE SPOILER

This occasioned some alarm on one face, some curiosity on the other. "Be my guest," said the master, and he went to hold up the wall and commune with a small brown cigar. This was the man who had pointed the boy in his direction. Perhaps Curt had capabilities the master had not sensed.

The spoiler shook out a dog quirt. It was a single length of light tan leather, plaited in David Morgan's workshop, 39 inches in length. Of that, 10 inches were the cracker of braided black cord. Sweat had started to darken its handle and the inside of the wrist strap. It was a signal whip, intended to make a rhythmic noise that would set the pace for a dog team. It could also be used to alert the lead dog to change direction, or break up a fight. It was not used to punish huskies, who had such thick fur and hides that they would have simply grinned the way dogs do when people do something foolish and continued about their noisy bad-dog business. But a boy's skin is not nearly as thick as a wolf dog's, as Curt was about to learn.

The spoiler told his pawn all of this because he wanted the master to know that they shared a love for the original context out of which the classic whips—working tools—came, the métier they occupied before being appropriated for sexual purposes. He did not realize that the boy was also listening, hungry for any sort of clue about why he was here and what it all meant. Tops should guard their tongues around bottoms once a scene has begun. An offhand remark can burn like a brand in a receptive mind for years after it is flippantly uttered, and someone can shape his life to obtain a similar piece of praise again or prove that a rebuke was undeserved. A top who is not similarly vulnerable will probably remain a mediocrity. An aroused bottom is an oracle.

"You'll want him standing up, then," the master said in his gravelly bass, and he undid the cock-and-ball bondage with a single tug on a loose end of the lacing. He hustled the boy to his feet and slapped his front up against the smooth wood of the pillar. This time the necessity for bondage was not questioned. The boy had longed for something to pull against while he was on the Barkley bench, some way to express his distress that would not put an end to the scene. He was surprised when the master buckled his discarded chaps around his waist, leaving his ass naked, and zipped up the legs. Curt had not seen the interaction behind his back, when the master had held up a weightlifter's kidney belt, and the spoiler had indicated he needed his target to be protected more completely by taking the boy's borrowed leather from the pile of clothing folded in the corner.

"I'm still getting the hang of this," the spoiler murmured apologetically.

The master inclined his head. He rarely met a top who cared to go to school, and the admission of apprenticeship charmed him. Anybody can pick up a whip and then try to chop wood with it. It's not a very effective way to keep warm in winter, and it rarely heats anybody else up either.

The spoiler did not start by cracking the whip. He trailed it over the tense back, stepped away, grasped it by the middle, and whirled the end of it lightly across the surface, warming it. Gradually he let his hand slip closer to the handle, increasing the force of his strokes. Not until the boy's back was well reddened did he move far enough away to use the entire length of the quirt. It looked like throwing a baseball—he seemed to be hurling something at the boy—but the whip stayed in his hand, and only a fireball of pain flew free and hit like a grenade.

When a whip is cracked, the tip of it is going faster than the speed of sound. So Curt may be excused for feeling that each scream was being torn from his throat and praying that his next breath would be his last.

He could have taken even this if he had not had to take it alone. But the stranger who had been so helpful did not speak to him, and he could not see his face. This pain had no purpose, it was madness. He was being taught things he did not want to know—why men broke under torture, how much you can suffer and still live, the sublime indifference of the sky that covers us and the passage of uncaring time that turns that sky from blue to black and to blue again; finally, that he was alone with this knowledge—alone, alone, alone with pain.

The spoiler did not intend to send the young man spinning through the existential void. True, he felt little or nothing for this piece of bait, but that was not his fault. This novice did not have any of the qualities that aroused him—for example, a good-humored willingness to make others suffer if they would not obey. The category of beginner, virgin, or chicken was erotically neutral and empty for the spoiler. That was why he did not speak to the boy or establish empathy with him. They had nothing to say to one another. Whatever agony or ecstasy fired the boy's synapses was immaterial; no electricity would jump the gap between them.

This performance was for the master, whose eyes were glazing over as he watched Curt's fit young body being painted with red streaks and welts. He did not have to imagine what it felt like. He could remember. More than that, he was experiencing a rare, intense pleasure from watching someone else work. Only at major tribal gatherings like Inferno did he get a chance to see tops whose working style pleased him. Even when he co-topped, he usually found respectful, unobtrusive ways to relegate his partner's activities to his peripheral vision. Not only was he eagerly watching this sober, quiet dude cut the kid to ribbons, he had a roaring hard-on and thought that if it went on much longer he was going to come in his pants like a teenager.

Just before the master's excitement built to that point, Curt broke. They untied the sobbing kid, threw a bucket of cold water on him, gave him his clothes and a Valium, and called a cab to take him home. The master was so put off by this display of cowardice and bad manners (and by his own frustrating sensation of coitus interruptus) that he did not notice that the boy said an effusive goodbye to the other man's boots and ignored his own. This whipped-dog devotion saddened the spoiler, but he was relieved that the ex-novice was leaving. He might get what he really wanted now. It could not take place in front of witnesses.

Curt was too much of a beginner to realize he was being dismissed in disgrace. He felt giddy with joy, thrilled at his own daring, awed by the men who had taken him to this magical place. He told the cab driver to take him back to the bar. Before he walked in, he took off his shirt, and men bought him drinks all night long to hear the history of his stripes. Just before the bar closed, he was taken in tow by a black master who had an easy smile and a bullwhip. He was off on the long road that might lead him to become the kind of person the spoiler would take an interest in again.

The master shut and locked the door after the boy, then turned to see the man he thought of as his junior S standing in his hallway with a friendly grin on his face and two beers in one big hand. The guy certainly made himself at home. But the aborted scene had left a bad taste in Roger's mouth, and it was not hard for the spoiler to lure him back into the basement and entice him into lecturing on the merits and limitations of each of his treasures.

"Why do you think," the spoiler said quietly, "some men can take heavy pain and others cannot?"

"Well, masochists and submissives are not at all the same thing. There are fundamental differences. In my experience, you can't get to a masochist by humiliating him or making him chew on your boots, although he might pretend he likes it if that's the price of a good beating. And a submissive is not going to respond to anything as quickly as a hand around his throat. He understands pain only as punishment; he won't cream in his jeans at the mere thought of you hurting him unless you do it to prove you own him."

The spoiler nodded. This was his own observation, though he would have had to extrapolate from the difference between sadists and dominants. "Why is there such a difference?" he asked to keep Roger talking.

"Damned if I know. Been doing research on this all my life, and it keeps me so busy, the findings will have to be published posthumously. Submission is a deep-seated psychological need. I don't mean to discount it. But masochism is inbred, almost biological. Somebody can be trained to be submissive, but if you want a masochist, you have to just go out and hope you can find one. It's how some people are wired. Like some people can't stand the cold and other people never get cold. It's not just a matter of wanting or liking pain, I believe it literally feels different to the person who can't do without it."

"Which do you think is more common?'

"Oh, submissives, definitely. Of course you do get some overlap. A sadist has to be a bit of a master, a master has to be a bit of a sadist, or he gets no trade."

They both laughed. The master held up his empty can. "You ready for another round?" he asked. The spoiler nodded, even though he had not finished the beer in his hand. He didn't want to say no to anything. It would change the mood, set a bad precedent. "Laundry room is off of the dungeon," Roger said, lumbering over to a door at the end of the room. "Got a fridge back there. Be back in a second." He had forgotten that his guest had already procured drinks for them both. For him, the three brief sentences he had uttered before leaving the black room were the equivalent of a car ride's worth of nervous debutante chatter.

As soon as Roger returned, the spoiler turned the conversation from speculation and theory to something that had actually happened. Evaluating the scene would give him a cue to Roger's emotional status. "I don't feel too good about the way the scene ended," he lied. "Maybe that kid really wanted to be a slave. If he just wanted to be dominated, I shouldn't have pushed his limits."

The master waved a dismissive hand. "You were damn good to that kid, better than he deserved. Nothing wrong with what you gave him. He got exactly what he asked for, with bells on."

"Maybe. I haven't had this whip for very long. I have a lot to learn about how to use it."

"Didn't look that way to me."

"Well, somebody like you ought to know. But I wonder if I was hitting him too hard. Do you think you could help me figure it out? I really like this quirt a lot. Makes my arm feel so good. I want to use it again, but I'm afraid the same thing will happen."

The specter of that brutal length of braid never biting flesh again made the master blanch. "Of course. Of course. But what exactly do you need to know? You don't have much choice about the amount of force it takes to crack it," he said. "Once you flick your wrist the speed is standard."

He was leaning on the pillar. The spoiler put his untasted beer down against the wall and came up to him, carrying the quirt coiled in his right hand. He touched his arm deferentially and said, "You could tell me how you think it feels."

Oh, why the hell not? It was the kind of thing you would do for a friend who wasn't sure he wanted to buy something he'd just spotted at the Noose, let him try out a few licks on your thigh, then take it out of his hand and whack his ass with it. "Sure," the master said, turning around, doffing his jacket and the khaki police shirt underneath it. The spoiler took his clothing, hung it up (there was no shortage of hooks), and returned to run his fingertips across the bare, heavy shoulders. He palpated the skin, gauging its thickness, the ratio of fat to muscle beneath it, the placement of shoulder blades and spine. And since he did not know if he would be allowed to touch this man intimately again, he tried to memorize every pore and freckle.

"If you could watch in the mirror," he suggested, "just to check my form." As soon as the master's face turned toward the reflecting wall, the spoiler cast the quirt once across his shoulders, a tingling and invigorating strike.

"That's fine," the man said, getting a grip on the rings in the pillar. "Do your worst." If he had known how long he would be clinging to those rings, he would have recoiled from them as though they were white-hot.

The work the spoiler did now made his flagellation of the pawn look like a hatchet job. He handled the quirt as if it were a detachable limb of his body, hooked directly into his nervous system, guided by his keen eyesight and even keener need to titillate and hurt. Long, single-tailed, braided whips may be the hardest whip to master. And the spoiler proved that all it took was enough skill to get as much modulation out of them, as much variation in their effect, as a razor strop or a cane.

The first blows were like kisses, kisses for a virgin turning into kisses for a whore, passion kisses, rape kisses, kisses becoming bites. Then the strokes were like a mother cat's tongue on a squirming kitten's pelt. It felt like kissing a man whose mustache and beard gradually became rougher and rougher. When the abrasion stopped, the pelting began, like snow, then like rain, then hail. Denting his back. Cosmic rays, flecks of sand, pellets of iron, then whole meteors fell, pocking his skin like the surface of the moon. The weight of the quirt seemed to increase. Roger could have sworn that the knot at the end of the cracker was embedded in his flesh and had to be yanked out before the whip could land again. Then the direction and speed of the blows changed, and instead of penetrating him, they sliced blade-like across his skin. It was like being slapped by a tiger or seized by an eagle.

It had been so long! The master screwed his eyes shut and pressed his forehead hard against the beam, trying to halt a flood of regret and bitterness. His body shuddered with joy. He prayed that the stranger's arm would not wear out too soon.

How many years ago had he given up? It had been hard to accept the fact that he would never meet a sadist who would greet his masochism with joy, as the stuff of which great art is made. So he had moved to a new city to make it easier to complete his own work of art, creating a living, breathing replica of the man he had always hungered to please, whose hands and eyes he could envision perfectly. Someone (even if it could not be him) should pass under those deft hands, be stripped and dissected by those merciless eyes.

Then he had discovered, to his chagrin, that the true masochist is nearly as rare as the genuine sadist. He was often as alone and disappointed standing behind the whipping post as he had been when he hugged it to his breast and waited for the perfect blow that never came.

But these blows were like balm. Physical pain was so much easier to bear than ennui and self-hatred. When the man behind him stopped, he could not turn around because he was ashamed of his own excitement and did not want anyone else to see it. His cock was up, flushed and eager, the head so sensitive he almost came from feeling it rub against the fly-seam of his jeans. The thought of how obvious his erection was only made it come back against his belly in a full brace instead of merely standing at rigid attention.

"Stop," Roger said faintly, dishonestly, as if the whipping had not stopped already.

"But we aren't finished yet," the spoiler said, taking control in his sweetest, softest, most reasonable voice. *And I never will be,* he thought, as the master kept his broad shoulders level, flexed in front of him, both booted feet flat on the floor. There was no evasion in that body, only attentiveness, receptivity. *I love what you are, beautiful and frustrated, a stallion in a herd of geldings, a sexual athlete surrounded by men too spoiled and lazy to pull their own puds, the last Roman gladiator in a world of puling Christians. I will never break you down or damage you. How could I, when this is exactly what you want and need more than food or sleep or your next deep breath?*

He was there for hours. During the night, the spoiler changed hands, implements, the position of the subject. But by the time he was done, too tired to lift his hand to wipe the sweat from his face, they both knew that the master's expertise at administering pain came from a very deep well of need for it. And the master knew he had to go back to that well as often as possible if he wanted to keep his expertise or just his sanity. We usually don't know how much we need something until it's possible to get it.

The spoiler helped the master up to his bedroom and applied ice to his welted back. He wanted to stay but did not know if he could sleep there, show his face in the morning, and still be forgiven. He said offhandedly, "I wasn't about to let that kid come in my mouth. I wanted to tease him while you were giving it to him, but I didn't want to have sex with him. I don't feel that way about you."

No human being is ever too exhausted to feel curiosity. "Why?"

"Because you deserve it," the spoiler said simply.

"Blow jobs bore me limp," the crusty voice said bluntly. The master was lying on his side. The spoiler slid into bed behind him. He had already located a bottle of lotion on the night table and pumped himself a handful. Now he twirled his hand around the head of his dick, soothed the rest of the cream up the shaft, and eased his hard-on between the master's lightly furred thighs. The leg muscles tightened, and the hard buttocks thrust back at him. He ran his fingers over the bruised shoulders and the master grabbed his own cock and began to pump it.

"You want me to fuck you?" the spoiler asked. He ran his hands over the bruises before he could get a verbal answer, and the master bucked. By reflex, he shoved his hips back into Roger's butt. It felt good to hump the crack of Roger's ass, the cleft between his thighs, to nose the head of his dick into the loose ball-bag that was being jostled up and down by the master's frantic hand. Since Roger hadn't said no, he took the other man's hard cock as permission to keep on pushing. The spoiler continued to pet and press upon the fresh welts and thrust between the close-held thighs until Roger rolled into a more accessible position and gave up his ass.

The spoiler was considerate, assuming that the master was not accustomed to being used this way, but he also assumed that any discomfort might actually help Roger to enjoy what he was doing, since his masochism had been activated. The ass that received him was not experienced, but that didn't mean the spoiler's cock was not welcome. The hunger that radiated from Roger's body was an aphrodisiac to someone with the spoiler's sexual wiring. Sometimes laughing, sometimes swearing, the two men competed to see who could give the other the most pleasure until both of them came, within seconds of each other.

Despite Roger's growing openness and responsiveness, the spoiler was startled and amused by the first thing he said when the lassitude of ejaculation had worn off.

"That would have felt even hotter if my ass had been marked up," the master rumbled.

"True." The spoiler was falling asleep.

"I have some things down there that have never been used."

"They will be, then. Tomorrow." The spoiler took the other man in his arms, made himself a pillow on his near pectoral, and slept.

It actually took more than one tomorrow.

This was the spoiler's avocation and the reason he chose to live like a retired spy or a prince in exile. It had nothing to do with revenge or competition. The men he pursued had committed no crime that should be punished. In his eyes, they were clearly his betters, or he would not have wanted them. Since he had no interest in bottoms, he did not even think of himself as a top. He was more like a trusted servant who would think nothing of knocking his drowning and struggling master unconscious so he could be paddled to safety. Or he was like a radio telescope, one of those huge dishes so sensitive they can hear the stars frying in the vacuum of deep space. Instead, he heard the unvoiced cries for rescue from the yoke of obligation, the exaggerated expectations of others, of minds too weary to concoct another scene and hands too discouraged to show off their unusual skills. He had to work hard, very hard, to get away with this and succeed at it. But it was worth it to him because he went after the only men in the city who could tell him whether he was a virtuoso or a hack.

The spoiler once spent almost six months studying Japanese bondage pornography, which had taken twice that long to obtain. He practiced intricate knots, experimenting with different types of rope, until he could take a man he thought of as his model (who never realized he was not the star of the show) to the bar with him. The spoiler trussed his model in a harness that was a sphinx's riddle—a sonnet to restraint. If he could, the spoiler would have apprenticed himself to the Yakuza. All this to fascinate a man he had had his eye on for two years, a man who was an expert with rope, to make it safe for the two of them to speak to one another and create a pretext for getting together sometime later in the week.

Then there was that bike run—200 mostly drunk and lust-crazed men rutting with each other. He didn't like drugging people, but that time he had slipped a discreet tab of acid into his idol's beer, then led him through the woods to a clearing (prepared that morning) where a leather sling hung from the strongest branches of an old oak tree.

Each of his heroes required a different form of worship. Over the years he had learned how to do tattooing. He had pierced his own tits, perineum, and cock head to teach himself how to run needles through the body. He had spent weeks constructing an apparatus that could hang a man without killing him, and tested it on himself. He had collected, piece by piece, a complete and authentic uniform for an officer of a disbanded and disgraced army that was nevertheless the ultimate fetish of a particularly handsome and worn-out man.

The trunk of his car was specially altered so a victim could be kept bound securely there for hours without smothering. A friend of his who owned a ranch kept one stall vacant for his use, equipped with a saddle and bridle tailored for a human beast of burden. He had a trunk full of diving gear, pieces of firemen's garb, latex garments imported from England and Denmark. He had learned enough kendo to enter a local contest and lose to the appropriate party. Under his bathroom sink he kept the largest collection of catheters and enema nozzles to be found outside a medical museum. One pursuit had required him to give up coffee and asparagus for months and subsist for three days on nothing but fresh strawberries. Somewhere in one of his closets, there was even a suitcase containing a makeup kit, a pair of false eyelashes and another pair of equally false tits, a red spandex minidress, crotchless fishnet hose, a blond wig, and seven-inch patent-leather spike heels. There was nothing, nothing he would not try to learn or concoct or arrange if it would snare a topman, master, sadist, or dominant for a few precious hours.

It never occurred to the spoiler to wonder what impact he had on the lives of the men he ministered to. He assumed that they continued on exactly as they were before they met him. Why shouldn't they? Their reputations were not besmirched or tarnished—he never told anyone about his adventures since he knew no one else would understand them. He was available if they wanted him again, so there was no need for them to submit to someone who was less discreet or kind. Why would they feel reduced or humiliated? If he had thought about it, he would have assumed they felt flattered, since he himself felt only gratitude and admiration for them.

He was obsessed, and that is not the best frame of mind for tracking one's impact on the world. He paid no attention at all to his backwash. In other words, he wasn't watching his ass.

The fact that he did not gossip did not mean that others held their tongues. When Curt arrived at the leather bar spouting tales of his adventure, there were those who were unkind enough to ask why the two lucky topmen had not come with him, and speculate about what had gone on while they were alone together. When the spoiler stood in the middle of the grove and plunged his gloved arm up to the elbow in distended ass lips and Crisco, he was so pleased by the idyllic setting that it did not occur to him that other people were sexing in the woods during the run. Some of them heard the groans and curses of the man he was fucking until the sling made the oak tree creak and sway. Two of those who were interrupted by this racket went to see what all the fuss was about, and what they saw made a story that traveled fast and far.

The spoiler was not always kind in the pursuit of his obsession. He often did the emotional equivalent of picking people up and moving them out of his way as if he were passing the ketchup to a stranger in a diner. The erstwhile tops and persistent bottoms he brushed aside were not pleased to be treated like so much flotsam, and some of them had a taste for revenge. He had made enough enemies to acquire a nickname, and not enough friends to hear what it was.

He also did not think that some of his targets might become, in turn, obsessed with him—too obsessed to risk seeing him again. He never knew that the bondage expert began to tie himself up every morning, putting himself in a complex wire harness that he wore under his business suit. This excited him so much that he repeatedly had to leave his desk to masturbate. Lunch hours often led him into the thickest shrubbery of the cruisy part of the park. Sometimes he did not come back to work. The spoiler could not comfort him when he lost his job, because he did not know about it, but the other man could blame him for it, and did.

We are raised to think that everything in the world occurs naturally as a set of paired opposites. It is almost impossible for us to know what anything is if we cannot locate and define its counterpart. The spoiler was an anomaly. The system of sadomasochistic eroticism that created him found that he threatened its premises. And that system was not known for dealing with irritating matter by making pearls out of it.

There are many reasons why an individual selects one particular role. A man who knows that his need to bottom is much stronger than his need to top, and who persists in presenting himself as a bottom to other people even if he does not get played as often as he would like, may be more stable than a top with a full dance card. A desire that a bottom can take in his stride may horrify a top beyond endurance. The sad truth is that many tops (even good ones) are made out of failed bottoms. To such a man, there is no point in topping if it does not somehow make him a better person than the meat-puppet he is working over. There is dignity in self-control, there is glory in ruling others, but there is none in being a bottom who simply can't get laid.

A man who sees that there is a shortage of his brand of sex objects in the world and turns himself into something that he would want desperately, if only it were possible to encounter this doppelgänger on the wharves, may be doing the best he can with the material available. Performing such a transformation is probably easier (maybe even healthier) than trying to alter the nature of his desire, the face that he sees when he imagines that someone is making him come and watching him do it. But narcissism is a sad kind of love, doomed to be unrequited. We can fall in love with our own legends, but they never love us back.

Tops acquire status not just by doing good work but by taking down other tops. A fairly mild form of this is the verbal competition over who is the best informed, the safest, the most exotic, the most sadistic. Another mild form of competition is comparing your boy to another man's attendant, making sure the bottom-man who accompanies you is going to outshine all the other masters' possessions. A more efficient, albeit nastier, method is to discreetly allow the word to circulate that someone has moved his keys over for you. It is de rigueur to make a disclaimer that this is no disgrace, it is a completely human thing to do…but still, that other top knew who to come to when he wanted someone who was his superior. The speaker then buffs his fingernails and prepares for business to boom.

The spoiler did not engage in verbal jockeying for position because he was not interested in being better than other tops, only in attracting them. Everyone wants to get the stud at the top of the pyramid. That's why enchanted princesses live on top of glass mountains. Need it be said that the spoiler never bottomed in a sense that most leathermen could recognize? He made a perfect icon of the dominant without peer, the unavailable, unattainable beauty who seems ripe for—well, spoiling.

That is why he was surprised, when he finally came home from the master's house, to feel a cold cylinder of metal graze his temple and come to rest behind his ear. He froze, his key not quite inside the lock. The man behind him sounded out of breath. His gasps were so wrenching that it made the gun tremble against the spoiler's head.

"What do you want?" he asked gently. He really wanted to ask who it was. It seemed absurd to die ignorant of who had murdered him, but he was afraid the gunman would be infuriated if he realized the spoiler had not recognized him instantly by the sound of his footsteps or the smell of his sweat. And if he could avoid it, he would much rather not die. He had not learned how to use his new straight razor. His wrestling coach was due at 11 the next morning. The magneto he had found in an Army-Navy store was still sitting on his workbench, waiting to be repaired. What about the lessons in Vietnamese he had planned to start at the community college next month?

"I want—I want—I want everything back that you stole from me!" This was no doubt supposed to be a bold and irrefutable demand; instead, it was a whine full of self-doubt and self-pity.

"If I have anything that belongs to you, I'll be happy to give it back," the spoiler said carefully.

"Damn right you will!"

A long silence followed. What was he supposed to do, the spoiler wondered, start turning out his pockets? It finally occurred to him to simply say, "Can you explain this a little more? What's happening here?"

"Don't play dumb, you sneaking, lying son of a bitch—What do you think this is, a hold-up? I don't want your money, you asshole. I want my self-respect back! I want to be a man again."

"Oh. I see." He thought that over, his brain working with serene rapidity despite the fact that this was a life-or-death situation. "If I hurt you, I'm sorry," he said. "But I would never deprive anyone of his manhood—I love men. All I want to do is give them what they really want. How can anything that two men do together make one of them less than a man? If I did that, I would defeat my own purpose, can't you see?"

"Bastard. You planned it. You plotted against me. I trusted you, and you turned on me. Now I'm going to show you what it feels like to lose control when you think you're in the driver's seat and everything is coming up roses. How do you like it so far, huh?"

"I wish I understood why you are so angry," the spoiler said, deeply saddened by his inability to console this man but a little irritated by his trite metaphors. "Did I do anything to you that you didn't enjoy?"

There was no answer. The gun shook. Would it go off by accident?

"Did I do anything you didn't want me to do?"

Silence.

"Did you really want me to stop? Would it make you happy to

do the exact same thing to me, whatever it was, right now? Come inside with me. I promise I will let you. You can even take pictures." He had no idea how haughty this sounded. One of the things he had never done to get next to someone was beg or plead.

Quiet. Quiet busy as the grave.

"Do you want to be sure no one ever does that to you again? I give you my word I won't ever touch you or notice you. It will be like we never met."

Still no answer. *I'm getting tired of talking to myself,* the spoiler thought. Was that grating sound pent-up weeping about to burst forth, or was it someone gritting his teeth as he cocked a trigger?

"Can you think about anything else when you come?"

Prez Meets His Match

Author's Note: This story is excerpted from a novel, *Doc and Fluff: The Dystopian Tale of a Girl and Her Biker*. Fluff, a young girl who is the prized possession of the leader of a gang of outlaw bikers, has been stolen away by Doc, a big diesel dyke with a motorcycle and a few nasty tricks of her own. Prez has just led his men on a fruitless search for Fluff, whom he had terrorized into doing the terrible things to him that he secretly enjoys. Upon returning to camp, the bikers find that their women have holed up in the house, where they are partying together and venting their disapproval of Prez's exploitation of such a young girl. (Doc has done her best to make herself popular among the bikers' old ladies and girlfriends.) The men are none too pleased about being left to fend for themselves in the barn. But one of them, Anderson, Prez's highest-ranking officer, is about to take advantage of a rare opportunity to spend some time alone with his leader.

A fierce gust of wind and rain scattered everybody, sent them running to get their sleeping bags out of the storm. When they dragged everything into the barn, Anderson was there ahead of them. He was heating up the stew. Prez was in a rage. "Well, you don't seem too surprised," he shouted, getting up in his face. "Did your fucking insubordinate, smart-ass, mouthy old lady Tina have something to do with this?"

Anderson looked at him calmly. "Well, you've known her longer than I have. Why don't you tell me?" He filled a bowl with stew and shoved it into Prez's hands, scorching them. "Just remember, motherfucker, you're talking about something you gave me."

Charisma has its limits, and Prez knew when he had hit his. He sat down and shut up. But he was still so mad, he stuck his fingers into the stew before it was cool enough to eat and burned hell out of them. It almost felt good. But not as good as having Fluff bind his wrists with wire and throw her lithe body on top of him and his bound hands. Her sharp little teeth felt like they were punching holes in his neck, and she had chewed on his tits until they were perpetually sore. He checked them, pinching them surreptitiously. Yes. Still sore. Then she would wind more wire around his balls and more around his wrists so that every time he pulled on his dick it felt like he was going to cut it off. Next time, she said, it would be around his throat. Then she hoisted his legs into the air—

His face went hot and cold, hot and cold. Somebody was looking at him. He jerked his head up and met the cool blue eyes of Anderson, who was offering him a spoon. "Just found a few of these," his sergeant said. Anderson descended to a crouch in front of Prez, close enough to smell. One hand dangled between his legs, cupped his crotch. Prez shut his eyes and took the spoon. Anderson held onto it for just a second, made him pull a little harder to take it away. "Too many bodies down here," Anderson said. "I'm going to sleep in the loft. Want your bag taken up there?"

"Yeah," Prez said.

Anderson touched his face, his lips, so lightly he thought he imagined it, and when Prez opened his eyes, the man was standing in front of him, his hips at eye level. The denim was faded below and to one side of Anderson's fly, where the fat head of his uncut dick had worn it down. Prez closed his mouth.

Anderson had already turned and walked off. The sergeant whistled between his teeth as he gathered up his own bedding and Prez's blanket roll. He didn't catch that look of weakness and lust on Prez's face too often. And he didn't stop to analyze his own response—the strands of adulation and resentment that bound him to Prez had been twisted into a thick cable that would never be broken. Like most of the men here, Anderson lived by the credo that if you wanted something, you took it, and if other people got in your way, you ran over them.

He took one of the Coleman stoves up to the loft and set it up not too far from the sleeping bags. It wouldn't do shit to keep them warm. But Prez was about to generate enough heat for both of them, and he wanted enough light to see Prez sweat. Anderson grinned as he pulled his bone-handled boot knife and laid it on the grill. By the time Prez made the rounds and charmed everybody into forgetting how useless their cold, wet ride had been and got his ass up here, the blade would be cherry-red. There had been something else useful in the cardboard box of utensils and supplies Tina had left the exiled men—a big can of Crisco, half full. He set it down by the head of Prez's sleeping bag, where the man would be sure to see it and equally sure to ignore it.

His own dick started to talk to him, letting him know it needed to sniff the breeze. He got it out and let it dangle. Soon it wanted to stretch, so he helped by pulling it a couple times. He couldn't resist picking up the knife and testing its point on his forearm. His own hair sizzled and curled into nothing. Mmm-hmm. Getting there. He put it back over the flame.

Downstairs, everybody had gathered around Prez and a bottle of whiskey. Mendoza had taken one of the rusty farm implements off the wall and was sharpening it. The curved blade made an irritating noise, rasping against the stone. The sight of Mendoza made Prez's gut knot. Fluff really was gone. She hadn't just taken a little ride with Doc (and on Doc, if Prez knew that raunchy old bulldyke). Mendoza, as the bearer of bad tidings, was the natural focal point for Prez's wrath. It was Mendoza's fault that Fluff had become aware of Doc's sexual prowess and stamina.

Prez genuinely liked Doc, but he had always been afraid that someday she would humiliate him. She knew too much about his weakness, the forbidden drug he needed more than he needed sex or power. Now Doc not only had his secret, she had a living witness to all the kinks in his libido. Fluff was probably singing her head off about all the weird and evil shit he'd made her do. Made her—

come on, he had slapped her a few times, threatened her, but that wasn't deadly force, it was just priming the pump. Prez had been doing this long enough to know that you couldn't make a chick dominate or torture you, she had to be bent that way. All he'd done was point that bitch in the right direction and squeeze the trigger. You never knew what you'd get when you did that. Sometimes it was like cocking your thumb and forefinger at somebody. Sometimes it was like squirting a water pistol. But Fluff was a fuckin' howitzer.

And now somebody else had her. Prez averted his eyes so that Mendoza could not see the hatred percolating inside them.

Every one of the bros in the circle wanted to tell his fucking life story. Prez kept nodding and smiling, nodding and smiling, while his tits ached and his asshole itched, until he wanted to smash their heads together. Finally, Michaels, who had come in from taking a leak, said, "Hey, leave the man alone, he's done in," and hoisted him to his feet.

Michaels pointed Prez in the direction of the ladder and pushed. Prez staggered into it and grabbed blindly for one of the rungs, still feeling Michaels's slap in the middle of his back. He was deeply grateful to the treasurer for replacing him in the circle but wondered if the slap had not been a bit too forceful to be brotherly. And how the hell did Michaels know where he was bedding down?

He climbed the ladder heavily, wondering if this was not a mistake. The first time he had made it with Anderson, he'd gotten him good and drunk. But somewhere in the middle of the sex, he had opened his eyes and met that icy Viking gaze and known it wasn't booze that made Anderson willing to take his ass down. The wolf on Anderson's face was mate to his own beast, and while it would never betray him, it meant to enjoy him completely.

Tonight, Anderson wasn't drunk at all. Prez took the whole scene in—the grease, the Coleman stove with its ominous burden, the big blond man airing his stiff dick—and almost disappeared back down the ladder. But Anderson was quicker and darted over to the trapdoor as soon as he saw the top of Prez's head. "Come and get it," he said, slapping Prez's face with his hard meat. "Cocksucker, come and get it."

He hauled Prez the rest of the way up by his ears, put him on his knees, and kicked the trapdoor shut. He immobilized the dark-haired man by pulling his leather jacket down over his shoulders, trapping his arms in the sleeves. And with the hot knife, he slashed apart the T-shirt underneath it, leaving deep, bloody cuts and angry red burns beneath the ribbons of knit white cotton. Prez didn't scream, but his face was contorted like a gargoyle's. Then Anderson grabbed one of Prez's nipples between the knife and his thumb and bore down. "Suck it," he said, pushing his hips into Prez's face. "Suck my cock, or by God I'll cut this off."

The bearded mouth opened obediently, and Anderson sank into wet, responsive, submissive flesh. "Take off the rest of your clothes," Anderson hissed, "but stay on your knees, and don't stop suckin' my dick."

Prez stripped himself while Anderson wrapped his big hands around his head and face-fucked him. It had been a long time since Prez had sucked cock, and the shame of it, combined with Anderson's brutality, made his own dick as hard as Fluff ever got it.

"I'm not ready to come yet," Anderson told him. "So stop right there." He had to shove Prez off his cock. "Get on your back," he said, giving him another shove to help him get there.

They were pretty much of a size, but desire made Prez's limbs tremble so badly that he could not keep his hands still on the floor or keep his knees from shaking. Anderson laughed at him. "You need this bad," he said, lying full-length on top of Prez. The sergeant bent his head to suck one of his commanding officer's nipples completely into his mouth. The cuts around it began to sting as Anderson's tongue opened them, and he sucked them hard enough to make the blood flow freely. Prez swallowed hard, trying to choke back cries of pain, and each time he swallowed, it seemed that the taste of Anderson's precome and foreskin went down his throat again.

"Don't even need to tie you up," Anderson said. "Do I? *Do I?*"

Prez refused to answer, and Anderson's left hand went between his legs and hoisted his nuts high enough into the air for both of them to see. The knife, which had been laid on the stove again, was in Anderson's right hand. "So help me," Anderson said, "you'll answer to me here in private or to every single man that's sleeping downstairs."

"No, you don't have to tie me up," Prez said. He took a deep breath and let it out slowly, his chest heaving. Blood and shadows highlighted his pectoral muscles, his well-defined abdominals. He was strong, almost young, healthy, arrogant, and completely self-centered but afraid, and Anderson loved the look of him. "Not that I wouldn't like it anyway," Prez added, grinning.

"Oh, I like that smile," Anderson said. He touched the tip of the glowing knife to Prez's cock head. The resulting scream made him grimace with satisfaction. "But I like making you eat it better," he decided, and ran the hot knife all the way up the underside of Prez's rigid shaft. "Like the way you keep it up under pressure, Prez, tells me just what a sick motherfucker you are." His compliment could barely be heard as Prez raged in agony.

Anderson got on his knees and raised the other man's legs. "Hand me that grease. Yeah. You think I'm going to shove my big fat dick in you? You're right. But that ain't all we're gonna do. Play with your tits, you're going to need all the help you can get."

None of Anderson's parts were small. And he liked to have plenty of space to stretch out and make himself comfortable. He made room for himself inside of Prez's body with the same insolence he would display taking his lane on the highway. "Give me these," he grunted, knocking Prez's hands away from the bleeding, throbbing nipples, and bit down on them with jaws like a bear trap. "Make you feel my dick in your throat," he promised, shoving home. "I've had bitches who didn't like to have their tits played with as much as you like it. And I've never had a bitch who took it up the ass as good as you."

Prez's eyes were half-closed, his head turned to the side. His hips responded to Anderson's insults and his cock, but his face did not acknowledge them. He might have been asleep. So Anderson pulled out, grabbed a handful of Crisco, and began to shove his fist up Prez's ass. The man under him came to life, staring and keening. "Grab your legs," Anderson warned him, "and keep 'em up, because nobody's going to stop me from getting into this. And you are going to know I've been there, I promise you. Every time you spread your legs for your Harley you're going to think about me."

Now Prez cried out, whimpered like a lost dog, and stared into Anderson's face as he ground his hips on the sleeping bags, which provided almost no padding between him and the bare wood floor of the hayloft. The fingers pointed within his sphincter belonged to a hand that was three times the size of Fluff's. But so was the muscle in that arm, and Prez knew if he did not open himself, Anderson would rip him apart. This wasn't about sex any mor; maybe it never had been. There was too much blood-smell in the air between them, too much violence locked within them, hoarded for each other.

Then Anderson took Prez's left nut between the knife and his thumb, and Prez gave it up completely The largest part of the sergeant's hand slid within the ring of muscle, and Prez screamed. That was when Anderson bent forward, covered his mouth with his own, and administered the ultimate indignity—a man's tongue, thrust deep enough to make Prez gag. "Swallow my spit," Anderson hissed at him, and hacked a large gob of it into his open mouth. "Pretend it's come, if that makes it taste better. Come out of my hard dick. You gonna scream again when I go in? Don't know if you sound more like a virgin or a butchered pig. But it's all music to my ears."

He tucked more grease inside his fist and gave it one final push. By the time Prez was done screaming, Anderson had his fist lodged securely in his butt and was using it without mercy. "You go ahead, make all the noise you want," the sergeant told him. "We'll sell tickets. I'm beginning to get an inkling of what rings your chimes, Prez, and it ain't normal. Is it? There's a part of you really digs the idea of having your own club piss all over your face while I fist-fuck the shit out of you, just like there was a little part of you loved sticking your tongue up that little girl's asshole while she made you hurt and bleed. Was she the one opened your butt up enough to make room for me? I sure hope you had her using two hands, buddy, because the best is yet to come."

Anderson made Prez tilt his ass until it was pointing at the ceiling. Then he got up on his toes, as if he was doing push-ups, and pushed his cock into his own inserted fist full of grease. Prez groaned like someone giving birth, and his dick shot a thin mixture of piss and come that left a silvery puddle across his belly.

"Yes, that's right," Anderson said, his lean hips forcing his sex into the other man's body. "I'm jerking off in your ass, Prez. While I fist-fuck you I'm jerking myself off inside you. I'm gonna come inside you, make you take my load. Tell me you need it, tell me you want the whole thing, beg me for it or I'll pull out now and ruin you."

Prez's belly ejected another stream of piss and come. His limp dick acted like a garden hose and sprayed it over both men. Anderson slapped him for that with his free hand, and stopped himself from doing it again, harder, only by the greatest effort of will. Prez would forgive this entire evening—reward him, more likely—but he would not forgive having to appear in public with a fat lip. Instead, Anderson went for the knife. "I'm gonna slice you open and your nuts are gonna drop into my hand," he said, and crushed the base of Prez's scrotum with the dull side of the blade. "Beg me to come now, or you'll never come again."

As Prez screamed, "Come! Ple-e-ez!" Anderson drew the wrong side of the knife hard across Prez's ball sac, and they both shot. The convulsions of Prez's asshole trapped Anderson's hand. So he just withdrew his cock and kept fucking the helpless body on the floor, fucking it during, through, and past its climax, and into another one while Prez chewed his own mouth bloody and beat his fists to pulp on the unforgiving planks.

When he finally extracted his hand, Prez had passed out. Anderson wiped himself off with the rags of the demolished and bloody T-shirt, then threw it into a corner. Anybody who found it would wonder what the fuck, but let them wonder. He drew a cover over Prez, stripped, and rolled himself into his own bag.

Sometime toward dawn, he woke up. Someone was moving around, bumping into stuff. "Prez? " he said. "Izzat you? What's the matter?"

"I'm in trouble, " Prez said softly. "I forgot to do something last night."

Anderson got all the blankets off his face (he had a childish habit of wrapping his head up in the covers) and located the unhappy voice. His fearless leader was sitting next to the stove with a belt around his arm.

"Goddamn it," Anderson said sadly. "Not that shit again. Prez, I thought you cleaned up."

"I did, for a long time."

"Yeah, I bet. How long has it been? Months?"

"Yeah, a couple."

"Why can't you shoot speed like everybody else, huh? One of these days you're gonna nod out on your bike and probably take two or three good dudes with you."

"Don't give me a fucking lecture, Anderson. I hate crystal. Things go too fast already. Too much happening." Prez sucked at his arm, where two or three drops of blood showed. "I can't find the damn vein. I can't show tracks, Anderson."

"Oh, come on. A man with your arms?" Anderson went over to him, knelt on one leg, and balanced Prez's arm on his knee. The veins were like fat worms, bulging above and below his elbow. "You just like somebody else to stick it in," Anderson grinned. "Open your mouth." He put the end of Prez's belt between his teeth. "Bite down on that mother and pull, now."

"I'll remember you said that next time you shove your dick down my throat," Prez growled, following his orders.

"Shut up and take your medicine." Anderson hit blood, depressed the plunger. "Would this happen to be another one of Fluff's useful household skills?"

"That chick could find a vein in a turnip," Prez said softly. His eyes were luminous, his face completely relaxed. "Want me to fuck you now? Be quite a ride."

Anderson slammed a foot into his chest, knocking him down. It took a couple of kicks to roll Prez over. By then he had his own belt off, and wound around his hand and forearm. The leather cracked as it came down across Prez's shoulders. He used it again, and again. When a stray stroke hit the back of Prez's neck and his face, he covered his head with his folded arms. He lay quietly while Anderson beat him, only shuddering when the sergeant changed tactics and used the buckle. Then Anderson rolled him over again, dropped over his torso, and fucked his throat with enough careless force to bang the back of Prez's head on the floor and make him dig his fingers bruise-deep into Anderson's thighs in an attempt to throw him off and breathe. But Anderson had both hands wrapped around Prez's neck and was too absorbed in his need to pour come down Prez's gullet to be distracted by a few feeble attempts to break his hold. "You aren't even sucking my dick," he spit at Prez. "I'm just fucking your face the same way I fucked your ass. And you're going to take it because you can't help it, you can't make me stop, you can't do anything except let me use your throat like I'd use some bitch's cunt."

He came like a flamethrower and almost immediately fell asleep. Floating in a high engendered by Anderson's battery and heroin, Prez rolled Anderson onto his side and kept his mouth around the limp cock. He tucked the balls in with it and jacked himself off, didn't come, nodded out, came to, and jacked himself off some more without coming. Anderson began to piss in his sleep, and Prez was swallowing avidly when the sergeant woke up a second time, said, "*You* are a *pervert*," kicked him away, and dragged blankets over them both.

But before he slept, it seemed to Prez that he heard Fluff somewhere behind him in the darkness, and she was laughing.

Unsafe Sex

Malcolm loves me for myself. If I put on 15 pounds, he worries—not because it's unattractive but because it's not good for my health. I'm sure Malcolm doesn't jack off in a frenzy, yanking on his tits while he visualizes isolated parts of my body—my dick quivering to hold itself up, my asshole spread wide with both my palms flat against my cheeks, the little smear of hair that decorates my booth-tanned crack.

In fact, I'm not sure he jacks off at all. But wouldn't it be peculiar if he didn't? Malcolm probably masturbates just often enough to be well-adjusted. Then I bet he gets up and changes the sheets.

No, what we have is a mature, adult, gay relationship. As k.d. lang says, "Sex is an important thing, but it is not *the* thing." It is my whole self that engages Malcolm. He is patient and considerate, thoughtful and kind. He never forgets anniversaries, birthdays, or holidays. He even sends out cards to my parents for Mother's Day and Father's Day.

I am the perfect other half of this perfect relationship. Malcolm and I live in a midtown Manhattan co-op. Every square foot of it cost a few thousand dollars, and we deserve it. We've decided it's OK to take good care of ourselves. We need our home to be a haven, a retreat from the dog-eat-dog, mercenary atmosphere of the business world. We can afford security. That's because we work hard at our respective professions. Malcolm is an attorney; I own a travel agency. We have health insurance, medical powers of attorney, and wills that we update every two years. We are each other's beneficiary on our life insurance policies. Our prosperity counselor has helped us to create a safety net for our old age.

Malcolm and I do not use words like "fabulous." We do not own pets. There is nothing more ludicrous than grown men slobbering over small, fluffy dogs. We do not go disco dancing (although we did when we were dating). Only 10% of our video library is porn. We keep the K-Y and the condoms in the bathroom. Sexual paraphernalia on display in the bedroom is just a little gauche, don't you think? We had our six weeks of mating frenzy, but we're safely past the honeymoon phase now, thank God. Our relationship is held together by much more than just fucking.

We walk with Dignity in the annual Christopher Street march, but we would never be caught dead at one of those poorly planned, inflammatory temper tantrums that the ACT-UP boys with the nose rings and the Doc Martens are so fond of staging. Do they really care about anything besides getting on the evening news? I don't think gaining personal notoriety is necessary to promote social change. Malcolm's family in Connecticut would slit their wrists if we got ourselves on the front page of the *Daily News*.

We make an annual donation to the Gay Men's Health Crisis because we have to take care of our own. Malcolm and I would really love to find some time for volunteer work. But if we had time to volunteer, we wouldn't be able to afford that sizable contribution, would we? Oh, and we don't give handouts to panhandlers. The taxes we pay to provide welfare are quite enough, thank you. I'll grant you, the homeless are a terrible problem. They make it so hard to get into the subway stations. So I give my spare change to cab drivers instead. At least they're working. Although you'd think if they planned to stay in this country, they'd have the courtesy to learn to speak English.

Like so many other hardworking men who just happen to be homosexual, all Malcolm and I want is our little piece of the American dream. We have to take responsibility for proving that the stereotype of the promiscuous, narcissistic clone is false. We are men first, gays second, but we don't want to make a fetish out of our masculinity either (although Malcolm needs to add a few more squats to his routine to build up those flabby calves). Oh, and you should have seen the look on his face when I told him I wanted a diamond ear stud for our last anniversary! I must say, I was more than happy to take this Rolex instead. We don't want to be bitchy, but we deplore those members of our community who continue to live out mainstream America's flamboyant and perverse images of the gay lifestyle—the Queer Nation kids in their kilts and pierced eyebrows, the tattooed leatherboys, the diesel dykes on bikes. I will admit it makes us a wee bit resentful that their freedom to slander the rest of us was won at our expense, through the efforts of decent, ordinary men like ourselves.

But you shouldn't think Malcolm and me dull. We try to keep the playful and spontaneous spirit of our limerence phase alive. We don't want to lose touch with the child within. We have our wild and crazy side. We're even thinking of buying one of the new Volkswagen Beetles.

Malcolm is working late again. I wonder when that new assistant of his is going to get the hang of the firm's filing system. It's too bad Malcolm's not trying to teach him his numbers instead of his letters. They could use Malcolm's dick for a yardstick, then they'd only have to go up to six.

When Malcolm phoned with this news, I told him I might not be in when he gets home. I have to take care of a sick friend. And it's the truth. How could I ever lie to sweet, decent, open, trusting Malcolm? Let's be real. My dick is the sickest friend I've got. If I asked him, I'm sure Malcolm wouldn't dream of trying to isolate me within our relationship. Outside interests enhance a couple's intimacy.

Tonight I want somebody who does not love me for myself. I want somebody who does not love me at all. And I want someone I can adore blindly. Someone to worship. It has to be just the right person. Not everybody can be an icon, even for the 10 minutes it usually takes for me to suck them off. No, it has to be a big man with a hint of brutality, more than a hint of the animal, the bestial. Somebody strong and domineering who will be deaf to my comfort or my history, somebody who doesn't care about my taste in restaurants or the location of my seat at the opera. But he can't be too smart. I don't want to talk to him, for chrissake. And no kissy fags who will ask me for my phone number. I don't want to found a cult, y'know, I just want to throw myself down, grovel, get used, and get up and go home.

I take a cab to the meat-packing district and walk around. They closed the Mineshaft a long time ago. I have no idea what took them so long. But honestly, what do they think went on there that doesn't go on now in the alleys and cul-de-sacs that surround that foul pesthole, that shit-encrusted and semen-drenched toilet, that firetrap that was probably saved from going up in flames only by the hundreds of quarts of piss that were sprayed upon it every night?

Most of the streetlights are busted. The streets are paved with brick and cobblestone and garbage. Mud and less palatable things clog the storm drains and gutters. It isn't dark yet (I'm not that much of a fool), but the hookers are already starting to stake their turf.

I can't help but stare at one whose starved-looking midriff is a moon crater between her metallic silver halter top and a cracked black vinyl skirt. I can tell she's a real girl because she doesn't have any cleavage, just an exposed collarbone and knobby shoulders. The only ones who still have tits are the queens on hormones. Boys or girls, their stockingless feet are crammed into thrift-store high heels. All of them wear a score of rubber bracelets and probably have a tattoo. Some of them come out in tattered lingerie. It makes you wonder what on earth they change into to go to bed—if they ever sleep in a bed.

Why do whores put all of their makeup on their eyelids or their lips and nowhere else? It makes the ornamented part of the face jump out at you. The effect is rather frightening and carniv-

UNSAFE SEX

orous. How can anybody let that into a car with them? I can only believe that the act of paying is much more important to their johns than the indifferent blow jobs they will get from these strung-out crash cases.

I give up trying to figure out which ones are really girls and which ones are boys. They might as well all be fish to me. When I see them, I don't feel that pull in my gut as if somebody were trying to make violin strings out of my intestines. I don't feel my teeth set on edge and grow points. I don't feel my knees tremble and my throat get thick with the sour phlegm I'm about to be forced to cough up.

Still, the hookers glare at me. They fold their arms, plant their feet, and give me looks as sharp as the razors in their ratty wigs. Tricking for free offends their morality. Little do they know what I am willing to pay for this evening's adventure.

Then I see him. It never fails. I have sometimes wondered why the fates always send us out together, me and the object of my desire, and how they manage to guide us so that our paths will cross. He is a big black man wearing boots and leather pants, a police shirt and a Sam Browne belt. No badge. That's good. Phony police badges are such a turnoff. His leather cap is pushed so far back on his head, he must be a little drunk. His face does not move to acknowledge my presence. But he hesitates a split second before stepping off the street into an alley, and once around the corner, he makes enough noise to let me know he has stepped behind the first Dumpster.

I come upon him pissing up the wall. The yellow jet is so fierce, I imagine he will hit the fire escape. It is quite honestly one of the biggest dicks I have ever seen. He smiles at me, obviously expecting me to be impressed. I have a master's degree in sociology from Columbia University. What kind of brainless twinkie does he think I am, to be swept off my feet by that old chestnut, that tired staple of stale pornography, the muscular, mean black hunk with a monster piece of sex meat?

One of my knees lands on something mushy and wet. There is a piece of gravel under the other. I shift to avoid both of these unpleasant trifles and shuffle (crawl, really) onto blessed dry, dirty brick.

"Why, lookee what we got here. We got us a cute little cocksucker, just look at the doggie hang his tongue out and beg. Wanna chase this bone, white boy? Wanna get force-fed some real man stuff? This is gonna make you pant for sure. Open wide and show me you want it, white boy. Beg for me."

While he is saying all this, I am making the appropriate whining noises. I've never done this before, but I discover that I know how. It's a latent ability, sort of like my talent for collecting on delinquent accounts. He reaches into his jacket pocket. The only way out of this narrow back street is the way we came in. I wonder nervously what the hell he has in there. A knife? Tear gas? A stun gun?

Something much, much worse. A condom! I can't believe it. I actually back away half a shuffle.

"What the hell do you think you're doing?" I say. Actually, I'm afraid I snarl. It's not the best way to encourage a topman, but my libidinous dreams are going up in latex-scented smoke.

"Wrappin' my joint," he says matter-of-factly, as if this was a natural part of what we are about to do with one another.

"That's really not necessary," I say.

"Who asked you? You think I want your white-bread fag disease?"

This blatantly homophobic remark from a leather freak who is so obviously queer in his butch drag compared to me in my casual J. Crew clothes makes me choke. I like being called a cocksucker and a fag as well as any other man fortunate enough to be born with a throat like an Accujac, but this is too much. I wonder what he'd do if I called him the *n* word?

He continues to put on the rubber. "Oh, come on, it won't even go all the way up!" I protest. "Look, it only covers a third of your dick."

"Tell you what, if you can get anything besides the head of this big banana in your mouth, I'll peel it for you, baby. Now get over here and do your job."

Before I can tell him this is not safe, sane, and consensual, he is fucking my face. I squirm and twist, but he has me by the hair. All this resistance means that his erection isn't getting enough traction. "Stop that," he says sharply, cuffing me, then grabs me again. "I'm gonna kick your nuts up around your ears if you don't cut that shit out and suck my dick, you pussy-face fag. You know you want it, and I'm gonna make sure you get what you want and a little bit more."

He is wearing heavy boots. Their steel toes can probably do all the damage that he promises. When rape is inevitable, you might as well relax and enjoy it. I try, I really do.

"Don't like the way that tastes, do you, punk? Tell me what you like, you scum-sucking cunt. Do you like uncut dick that's gotten really raunchy, grown itself a real crop of cheese? Or would you rather drink rank bitter piss out of truck drivers' hoses? Or is your thing just plain old spunk, huh, white boy? Seems to me a gourmet like yourself ought to be relieved to have nothing on his breath after he gives a blow job but a clean old condom."

I'm trying to prove that he was wrong about how much of his dick I could get down, but it's hard to point out my success when he's so busy enjoying it. I'm losing my tonsils to the Roto-Rooter man. But nobody wants a piece of rough trade who's using protection!

"I wanna fuck you, baby. You got a cute ass for a white boy. That's a nice little bubble-butt that's restin' on your heels. Bet it's even tighter than your throat, ain't it, cocksucker? Drop your pants, bend over, lemme see that tiny pink hole."

I'm only too happy to oblige. But I make sure I position myself facing the main street so he is not between me and an exit. Surely now, I think, now he will want to plunge all the way into my aching furrow, and he will have to dispense with that ridiculous barrier. But when I hint at this, he says, "I'm getting real tired of your bullshit, princess. Whatchoo want me to do, tear you a new asshole? Let's just go for a ride and you quit your bitchin'."

I make one more attempt to get what I really want, and he slaps my butt. Hard. So hard it takes my breath away. I hate that.

Of course, it also makes my asshole open up like an umbrella. He's a marvelous fuck. It takes a lot of skill to drive something that big. Too many well-hung men think all they have to do is the old in-out. But this man is teasing me, stroking all points of the compass, doing everything inside me except turn cartwheels. I wish it were enough, I really do. But I know he isn't going to lose his stinking, filthy load in me, really use me, soil and despoil me. And without the fillip of that violation and defilement, I can't let go.

"You like come so much, I wanna see yours," he pants. "Get it out and jack it off, boy. Show your master how much you love taking his hard dick."

The stupid thing is hard, of course. It apparently doesn't realize we aren't having a good time. I told you it was my sickest friend. So I dutifully beat my meat, agreeing with everything he says, echoing the names he calls me, swiveling my butt as if I were Catherine the Great and this were the last member of my guard who could still get it up. He is Sir, he is Daddy, he is my Master, and he owns my ass. I am a dirty bitch, a high-pocket slut for hard cock.

"Don't you dare come without permission," he hisses, but it's too late. I flood my palm and the ground below us. He shoves even farther into me, which gets him close enough to grab my wrist. He forces my hand up to my face and smears my sticky fingers across my nose and mustache. "You like jizz so much, lick that off your lips," he sneers. Then he yanks on my hips, bucks three times, and comes.

There isn't even time to say, "I hate you." I see them coming long before he does—a small gang of undernourished urban youths carrying baseball bats, car antennas, and what looks like a brick tied in a pillowcase. I have to get away! I push him and all the disappointment he represents away from me and hear him fetch up against the Dumpster as I bolt out of the alley. I sprint to the corner, whistling and yanking on my trousers. A cab miraculously pulls over. There is no time to look back, only time to throw open its door and escape.

UNSAFE SEX

During the ride home, I brood about how safe I will feel once I am back in my own space with its Persian rugs, Shaker furniture, and David Hockney prints. I mustn't forget to take my Elavil tonight. I will brew a pot of chamomile tea and listen to Debussy. Do you think it's really possible that Malcolm loves me for myself?

The Wolf Is My Shepherd, I Shall Not Want

Ulric awoke. A fever was upon him. He burned with a hunger that made his toes and fingers ache and shriveled his balls. The darkness that beckoned beyond the glossy windowpanes was not enough to hide the heat and light of the glowing embers in his belly. Surely if he walked the streets in this state, people would run for the nearest door and bolt themselves behind it, frightened by his intensity. But this was San Francisco, and a winter fog had wrapped the city, stylish and flirtatious as a drag queen's feather boa. He could walk these damp streets as safely as a phantom, and the fire that drove him would keep off the drizzly cold that ate into other men's bones.

His guardians ringed his sleeping place and came to brush their elegant bodies against his ankles and calves as he sat up and stretched, trying to work the stiffness of eight unmoving hours from his limbs. *Hungry,* they each said, and the word was as substantial in his mind as a goblet of AB-negative in his hand. There had been no intruders, or they would have been plaintive in their demands that he get up and rid the house of what remained of the prowler.

There was Luna, the mystical Abyssinian; Anastasia, the regal Russian Blue; and Charley, the enormous alley cat with long black fur and a white ruff.

It was Luna's turn tonight to watch the house while he hunted. The rest of them Ulric released through the back door, having no fear that these cats would be crumpled by a speeding car or crushed in the jaws of a pit bull. Luna waited gravely until he brought her the puzzle-ball containing her dinner, a half-dozen clever white mice. He reset the combination and placed it on the floor, and as he walked away he could hear her already calculating her strategy for breaking in to the little cage and releasing its tasty bits of animated fur. In the meantime, though, it was important to punch the spherical cage with her right paw and send it rolling. There were some bells in the box along with the mice to make her sport more merry.

Ulric's hunger was cocked within his body like a snake coiled to strike, but he kept it at bay for a little while, puttering about the house, touching this book and that painting, reassuring himself that his treasures were still there. Unlike his sister, Adulfa, who scorned the comfort of mortal trappings and preferred to sleep in crawl spaces and rafters, Ulric always made himself a lavish home. He found that the camouflage of wealth was at least as effective as the feral camouflage Adulfa shared with wild bats, owls, and raccoons.

He went into the bath that adjoined his bedroom and prepared himself for the evening's festivities. He had always been meticulous about his grooming, unlike many men of his era. He bathed and washed his hair and paid especial attention to cleaning his teeth. In the bathroom mirror, he saw another difference between himself and his sister, and he sighed. Adulfa had hair the color of corn silk, and she religiously shaved it every evening, so that by dawn it had grown out only a few inches. Ulric's hair was black as a raven's wing, and he wore it long about his shoulders. It curled a little, as did the edges of his blue-black mustache and beard. Was Adulfa still shaving her head? Was she still living in wild places or abandoned buildings, sneering at his masquerade of antique furniture and Persian rugs? Better, perhaps, to do without an update. Ulric shuddered and went to dress.

The leathers he pulled on were skintight and soft from frequent contact with his body. It's easy to get good tailoring when your weight never alters by so much as half a pound. He still found trousers a little awkward, but one must change with the times or be left behind. Snaps, however, were a great improvement over troublesome lacing or buttons, and practically everything he wore could be doffed or donned with the bright clicks of these handy little metal appliances. What would they think of next? Ulric shook out the fringes along the edges of his shirtsleeves and the outer seams of his leather pants. A man liked to have a little dash, a little panache, a little something that cried *Peacock!* rather than peahen.

His hair seemed to repel water, like the fur of an elk. It was already half-dry. There were a few annoying little cramps in his stomach, threats of what was to come if he did not go courting soon. Ulric opened a window and let the breeze in to complete his toilette. He could feel his hair breaking into additional curls. By the time he hit the street, he would look like a pirate. Then he saw the full moon, shining through fog like a lamp swathed in gauze, and knew why his hunger tonight was especially keen. Was it his imagination, or did he hear a wolf howling somewhere over the green hills of this beautiful city? For the second time that night, Ulric shuddered, and he put the thought of Adulfa firmly from his mind.

He tugged on his boots, hooked keys to the right side of his belt, and left, stopping only to give Luna an encouraging caress. The sand-colored cat flipped onto her stomach, took his hand between her teeth, and gave him an arrogant look that invited him to move. "You are the queen of my home and my heart," Ulric acknowledged, and she graciously released him without breaking the skin.

His motorcycle was waiting in the garage. Ulric started it up and rode toward the door. At the last possible moment, it swung open. He rode away chuckling, hearing the door fall shut behind him. It was not quite the same thing as jumping a high fence on a hot-blooded Arabian, but it was important to avoid boredom even in the little things. Adulfa was such a sourpuss. The world had never been so full of amusing toys, and he had enough money to buy all the amusement he could enjoy. It was good to be alive in 1975.

There was a fisters' bar on Market Street and a brand-new leather bar down on Capp in the Mission. But Ulric was not interested in either of these places. He wanted to surround himself with other stallions and become just another stud in a herd of wild horses. And so he went south of Market to Folsom Street, where half a dozen bars and three times that many sex clubs and bathhouses had men in denim and leather queuing up in lines three deep for blocks and blocks. The thick smell of sex and the acrid scent of poppers almost managed to defeat the faint whiff of sewage from bad drains. Music from the bars and clubs spilled into the streets until it seemed that the entire neighborhood was partying. He supposed other people must live here, people who were not leathermen, but he never saw them. Small wonder that so many of the men did not wait to get indoors before they began to pleasure one another.

It all reminded Ulric of his youth and the sexual frenzy of warriors after a battle. His feral good looks and hard muscles made him an easy sell in this part of the city. Few of the men he cruised had bodies as impressive. But then, they had never trained for eight hours a day in a full set of armor. And that had been Ulric's upbringing, under the harsh eyes of the Germanic Christian knights who had slaughtered most of his pagan people, saving only the most comely of the children. After their ignominious defeat in the Holy Land, the order had been given land between what was now called Germany and Poland, and their Grand Master had almost immediately declared a crusade against the infidels who already lived there. This crusade conveniently doubled the order's holdings.

Thinking of those days still made Ulric's fists clench, and he went down Folsom Street at freeway speed, angry at his own helplessness. He could not save his folk or, for that matter, himself. The knights had tried to tell him that Christ was just like all the other hero gods who had been hung on trees and brought back to life, but the savior of the Grand Master was no savior of Ulric's. One day, he knew, the banners of the Christian armies would be trampled in the mud, and no man would lift a hand to preserve them. It was one of the hopes that kept him alive after so many years.

He hoped that tonight would provide an unusual feast, something savory and out of the ordinary. Ulric's ears were ringing with hunger, and he was sweating despite the chilly wind that bathed his upper body. He brought his bike to a halt in front of the Eagle's Lair and backed it into a parking space as if he was in a dream. His consciousness seemed to be floating slightly outside of the boundaries of his skin, as if he were watching himself perform in a trance.

There was a bar called the Eagle in every city. Ulric should know. It was one of the first things he looked for when he scouted a new territory. Even in this age of the machine, men still remembered their true heritage. The warrior's totem of the eagle lived on and would probably survive after the last living eagle had fallen from the poisoned sky. It had been a long time since Ulric had been drawn to a woman. What he needed now was the direct simplicity of contact with another man's flesh, to slip in among his brothers as a canny black sheep is slipped into the herd to keep its silly white flock mates from straying.

The sweating, oiled bodies that packed the Eagle were indeed as slippery as raw wool that was rich with lanolin. Ulric picked up a beer because it was such a useful social prop. He had to admit that he was also glad to see his favorite bartender, Alain. Alain had six inches of height on Ulric and 20 pounds of muscle. He had shaved his balding head and his beard, but his hair was so thick and black that the outline of it could be clearly seen against his white scalp and ruddy cheeks. His earrings were solid gold, thick hoops of wealth and disdain for heterosexual convention. His oversize ear lobes jutted out rudely as if to say *fuck you*. He wore what he always wore, a leather vest and a dirty pair of 501's. Rings as big as the earrings were shoved through his raspberry-size nipples. The bottom button of the jeans was undone, not because Alain wanted to create the illusion that he had a big dick. He *did* have a big dick, and there was no way his cock and balls were going to fit into those jeans with the fly buttoned all the way down. On the left he wore a hefty bunch of keys and a coiled-up whip. Ulric scented old blood streaking its tip.

THE WOLF IS MY SHEPHERD, I SHALL NOT WANT

Alain was a sadist. His reputation was such that even in this bottom-heavy city, he often went without a weekend tryst. He always looked at Ulric as if he knew secret things about him. Ulric was never sure he would actually get the order he placed with Alain, and he felt sheepish about having such a chieftain wait on him. In another age Alain would have been the leader of a war band or a great king. Ulric supposed he had done the best he could to find his own domain. The part of him that was still a stripling longed to please Alain, dedicate some service to him, obey and perform great deeds for his approving eyes. But the very great danger of walking into Alain's iron chains kept Ulric's troubled eyes down and his tongue civil in his head.

Alain handed him the beer with a little shake of his head, as if he were saying *too bad*, and Ulric almost snatched it out of his hand. He turned his back on the impossible man and rolled the sweating brown glass over his forehead, trying to cool his drenched face. The cramps in his stomach were spreading to other parts of his body so that his hands were making small, involuntary gripping motions and his lip was threatening to curl up and permanently expose his teeth. Ulric handed the beer to someone who had been waiting in line for 20 minutes to get one, gave and accepted the obligatory pat on the crotch, and followed his nose and his memory toward the back room.

The farther you went into the Eagle's Lair, the darker it became. Too dark for video games or pool, too dark to make sure you were hitting what (or who) you were pissing at. Out of the darkness came groans and sighs, bellows and shrieking, as if a horde of men were being slowly roasted. It was this cathexis between pleasure and pain that made human beings seem such ideal victims. And tonight Ulric wanted to approach that state himself, to kneel as close as he could actually come to the flames of true submission. He supposed that anyone who knew about his physical strength and his other powers would have expected him to dominate other men, and sometimes he did. But more often Ulric was compelled to sink into a state of passivity and response.

He wanted to be swept up, carried along, to feel as if he had no choice. The hunger had taught him that. It was a hard master, this pain in his heart and throat, and now he would find the wherewithal to drown his longing.

He went a little way into the room, which was twice as big as the rest of the bar, and dropped to his knees. Now he was in a forest of boots—laced-up lumberjack and combat boots, cowboy boots, engineer boots, and tall riding boots and Dehners. Levi's, leather chaps, jodhpurs, police uniform trousers, and firemen's rubber waders towered above him like the trunks of trees. He ran his hand up the nearest leg and cupped the balls that rested at the bottom of an undone fly. He never saw the man's face. He knew him by the funk of his crotch and the size of his quadriceps and the fur that nested his scrotum and shaft. Ulric's initial touch was permitted, and so he brought his face closer and tongued, then swallowed, both balls. This got him the gift of two hands, clasped behind his head, and a belly-deep groan of surprise.

Ulric managed to bring his tongue into play and turned his head to one side, applying pressure that compressed the testicles and made the skin over them more thin, taut, and sensitive. Stretching and licking, he resisted as long as he could the cues he was receiving to spit out this man's nuts and pay attention to his cock. He got a brief reprieve by reaching up and milking the rampant organ with his hand. The shaft was fat, long, and already half-hard. Ulric didn't mean to pry, but he understood (as precome slicked his palm) that this was a man who liked to play for hours before he came. It would be a real triumph for Ulric to get him to shoot. He had been letting cocksuckers try to make him come ever since the bar opened. The slightly raw skin that slid back from his cock head was probably one of the things that had drawn Ulric to him in the darkness.

Other men, sensing passion, were gathering around them. Ulric could hear other cocks being beaten off nearby, smell the crowd's voyeurism and approval. So he carefully expelled his victim's balls and swallowed—more slowly than any sane man would have per-

THE WOLF IS MY SHEPHERD, I SHALL NOT WANT

mitted—the steadily leaking length of his stud's sex. The hands locked behind his neck could do nothing to speed him up; Ulric was so close to getting what he wanted now that no mortal's strength would avail against him.

Until now, Ulric had not tampered with the other man's mind or his sensory perceptions. He took a perverse pride in being good at what he did on his knees, in the dark, and he never liked to think he had to cheat to attract his prey. But now it was necessary to shift things just a bit, and provide a few distractions as well. So Ulric called the men around them, and they began to unbutton the stud's shirt and suck his armpits and nipples. Someone else was kissing him. Ulric could tell, from the discreet nibbling he had done upon the man's balls, that he was not entirely averse to a little pain. Getting your dick deep-throated for hours was, after all, as much about abrasion as it was about suction.

So Ulric drew his teeth up the length of the cock and delicately dragged them along the cock head too. He fiddled with the way this felt just enough to make it seem more exquisite than damaging. He also encouraged the men who were holding up his victim to begin to explore his furry ass. First tongues, then fingers, and eventually a cock were sent between those square, heavy cheeks. Ulric thought it was a bonus that this man did not normally enjoy getting fucked. All the more reason to give him an excellent suck job and take his mind off his troubles.

When he slid his mouth back down the length of the scored erect cock, he was at last rewarded with the delicious taste of something hotter, saltier, and sweeter than come: the red blood that had enslaved Ulric so long ago, when the Grand Master gave him the unwelcome gift of perpetual darkness. After all these years, each time was as glorious as the first. Ulric had been reborn to do this, to feed and adore this virile, handsome animal who made it possible for him to live.

The cock in his mouth suddenly became even more rigid, and Ulric's eyes flew open with surprise. One, two, three, it pulsed, and filled his throat with bitter jism. There was enough blood mingled with the come to make it palatable, but Ulric could not stifle a cry of disappointment. It would be virtually impossible to feed until he was satisfied now, without the concealing intoxication of arousal.

He got up and took himself to another corner of the room, licking his teeth with frustration and hissing like a wet cat. About the man who had been on the brink of giving him everything, he did not spare a second thought. Somewhere in the back of his mind he could hear the man's confusion and self-hatred as he was forced to all fours on the floor of the bar and a second man began to piston his ass and a third took possession of his head. This was not how the evening was supposed to go, this was not what Ulric's meat wanted or liked, this was not who he was, why wouldn't anyone help him?

Screw you, Ulric thought. *How does it feel to be lost in a crowd?*

He calmed himself enough to look around for a second victim. This time there must be no mistake. In the past this bar had always been so good to him. In fact, Ulric realized, he could not remember exactly how often he had fed here. Was it seven, or was it more? Tomorrow he would find another place to quell his hunger. But it was too late to start all over again. There had to be somebody here, somebody who was a sure bet, an easy score.

The atmosphere in the back room was suddenly stifling. Panicked by claustrophobia, Ulric scooted for the door. To reach the main bar, he had to pass the urinals. A blond boy with a bad haircut that marked him as a recent arrival from the Midwest was staggering to his feet. His hair and chest were rank with piss. But Ulric found those human secretions that were akin to blood to be rather attractive, if a bit of a tease. The kid had been on his knees drinking piss. He was fucked up from the shame and excitement of performing this forbidden act, and he was also flying very high on the acid, cocaine, MDA, and alcohol he had ingested along with the hot jets of piss and clots of come.

Ulric did not even bother to move his keys to the left. He just beckoned to the woozy young man and took him by the arm. He was

THE WOLF IS MY SHEPHERD, I SHALL NOT WANT

not about to go back into the darkness and risk losing this quarry to other hunters with lesser appetites. No, it was into the alley with this one, a quick kill, and then he could spend the rest of the night dawdling on his bike or head for home and listen to music.

The alley was, for a miracle, empty. Of course, until closing time, with a back room available, few of the patrons would be likely to take their tricks out here. Even for a raunch pig, it was an intimidatingly filthy scene. But what did that matter to the boy who had been used as a human toilet?

Ulric had received just enough blood to make his cock swell in a painful imitation of a human erection. Arousal made him rough. He knocked the kid down, and the boy sprawled on the pavement, immune to the garbage, as loose-jointed as an abandoned puppet. Sighing, Ulric hoisted him up to his knees. He nuzzled Ulric's fly and got backhanded away from it. *Easier and safer to take it out myself,* Ulric thought, and fumbled his equipment out into the breeze. His cock didn't have time to get cold, though; the wanton farm boy swallowed it whole, showing an enthusiasm that did not make up for his lack of experience. Ulric was always ambivalent about these situations. Was it worth it to give the kid some coaching when it was hardly likely to benefit him in future encounters?

Ah, well, but that slobbering and gnawing had to stop. Ulric stepped into his victim's mind, not being nice about it, and snapped out some quick orders. The pressure on his cock became more even, the tongue more insistent, the teeth less bothersome. Yes, that was much better. Ulric let his frustration out now and gave the kid a skull-fucking that expressed some of his displeasure at losing his first choice. The young man was sobbing, beating on his own dick, and Ulric snarled, "If you get one drop of your scum on my boots, I'll kill you." Caught between the need to laugh at his own joke and the sudden surprising need to come, he came instead. Ulric did not let the boy register the lack of semen before he picked him up off the ground and raped his carotid artery.

Ulric's teeth went into the boy's throat more quickly than the piss had run down it. Now, this was satisfaction. The blood was thick and rich, a vintage like no other, unfermented but utterly intoxicating. The mad fire that had threatened to capsize Ulric in agony all evening subsided. He could almost feel every cell of his body drinking its fill. Life was grand when you were the one who was going to go on living.

The backdoor of the bar opened, and out came Alain with a double-barreled shotgun. "Put that son of a bitch down," Alain said. Ulric did as he ordered, with hatred in his heart, and hatred of the bittersweet longing he had to fling himself onto the trash that had been quelled by the thick soles of Alain's work boots.

He looked into the perfectly round nostrils of the sawed-off firearm and wondered if this was the last face he would ever see. Ulric had survived some terrible wounds in his time, but he knew a stake through the heart would kill him and thought perhaps a couple of shotgun shells in the chest would do the same thing. There was no way to be sure, and he would much rather not make the experiment.

Then the gun roared, and he flung up his arms, surprised that this idiotic and predictable reflex was his last gesture. It took Ulric long seconds of not falling down to figure out that his own body was intact. Alain had defaced Ulric's victim. Now he took a razor blade from his vest pocket, unwrapped it, and handed it to Ulric. "Wipe off our fingerprints and put it in his hand," Alain said curtly. His Cajun accent made the invitation to engage in a conspiracy seem more believable than such an offer from any other mortal.

Ulric performed the task requested of him, protecting the steel from his fingertips with a corner of the victim's T-shirt. He even thought to wipe his prints from the dead boy's chipped and bitten fingernails.

"Business has been pretty good since you started coming around here," Alain said. Ulric jerked around to stare at him. The gigantic bartender lit a match on the sole of his boot and twirled the tip of a cigar in the blue flame. "Once word got out somebody was murdering guys in the back rooms, practically biting their cocks off, we started getting so many new customers, I do declare there are nights when I thought we might run out of beer before midnight." He pointed the cigar at Ulric, who was hard again after feasting in earnest and weak in the knees from shock and relief.

"You did that, didn't you? You're the bastard who's been turning all this prime beef into dead meat."

"What do you want?" Ulric whispered.

"I just want to hear you admit it."

Ulric put his hands up, showing open palms that held no tricks. "I am the one," he acknowledged.

Alain pursed his brutal lips, and blue cigar smoke shot at Ulric, curled lazily about him. Unlike the fog, however, it refused to hide him. He felt as if Alain had just dressed him up in something sleazy and was wondering whether to dress him up some more or rip the garment off. But the bartender was waiting for something else. Finally Ulric could not bear the silence any more and said, "What are you going to do with me?"

A long parade of conflicting emotions flew across Alain's face. He wanted this dandified long-haired rebel biker with his piratical good looks. He had wanted to chain him up, whip him raw, and ride his narrow ass since the first moment he'd set eyes on him. Now that he knew Ulric was more than he seemed, this desire took on another twist, like the loops of a hangman's noose. The presence of genuine danger was such a challenge. And then there was the other side of Alain, which he had locked screaming into a cell many years ago.

The two men stared at each other, not even aware they were leaning toward each other. Their cocks also strained toward each other, tenting their trousers as if to say, let us out and we'll figure out a solution to this standoff.

Ulric could not stand the suspense. He took a gamble. "What is your pleasure, my lord?" he asked softly, resurrecting the courtly speech of the page boy and squire he had once been.

Alain's face closed up like a Bible being slammed shut by a pastor who was done with his sermon. He had never been more frightened in his life than he was at this moment, confronting this dangerous creature of legend. Why did this hell spawn have to look so damn good as well? It would have to figure that a man he had cruised every time he came into the bar would turn out to be no man, but a demon. On top of that indignity, the evil thing was making fun of him, letting him know that the gun in his hands was no real impediment to its sinister power. "My lord," my ass. If the thing was going to kill him, it probably would have done it already. The only thing Alain thought he could do was to carry on with his bluster and hope that by some undeserved miracle wrought by one of the saints he had neglected (and would, he had to admit, continue to neglect even if he got out of this alive) would save his queer neck from being slit like a pig's.

"Once word gets out about this," he said, nudging the body with his shotgun, "things will go back to normal. Everybody will think I killed the serial killer. If I were you, I'd stay away from South of Market for a while. Give Folsom Street a rest if you want to keep your pretty face intact."

Ulric shrugged and turned to go. It was ever this way between him and humankind. They were natural enemies, after all. His quest for a soul mate among them was pathetic, as mad as a cougar singing love songs to a white-tailed deer. Loneliness was his ordained and proper lot, and if he were half as sane as Adulfa, he would accept it. He was nearly to his bike when something else Alain said made him stop and turn.

The bravado born of years of topping, years of forging ahead despite the performance anxiety that made his knees shake, because he had a man on his knees who expected him to know what came next, stood Alain in good stead. "You might come back in a couple of years," Alain allowed. "Business might need to get jump-started again. I don't mind selling more booze to boys who love to tell each other ghost stories about monsters that stalk them in the night."

My lord. Had that honorific been a joke? He thoughtfully blew more smoke at Ulric, who took it in his face like a kiss. His whole body was erect and trembling with desire. The single word *please* resonated again and again within him, but he could not say it out loud. He bit his own lips until they bled to keep himself from saying it. Alain was handing him back his life. Since vampires did not consort with one another, there was no such thing as a shared history, but Ulric found it difficult to imagine that such a thing had ever taken place before. How very stupid it would be for Ulric to ask for anything else, for a more personal sort of attention. Alain hated him. How could he feel anything else when Ulric fed upon his brothers? It would take him days to unravel Alain's last comment and see anything more in it than a twisted and arrogant desire to profit from yet another titillating wave of rumors of danger.

Alain had no idea that he had just been shown a rare sort of tribute. Ulric, for all his sentimentality, did not often shed his own blood for the sake of a mortal, no matter how handsome he might be. Instead, what Alain saw was indifference, or insolence. Nothing as powerful as a vampire would stoop to traffic in the mundane lusts of human beings. The blood-drinker had somehow been tricked into thinking that they were in a standoff. Best, Alain thought, to take his own life as the only gift he was likely to receive from such a bizarre encounter and make an exit.

The bartender gave a little bark of laughter and waved Ulric away. "Be off with you now," he half-shouted, hand on the blessed door that would let him back into the music and frenzied coupling that heated the bar. How hard it is to break the habit of never having what you really want, the habit of refusing to see what is marvelous in the world. So it was that this time around, the closing of a bar and the impending arrival of dawn came to seem more important than closing the bargain of mutual desire. It would have taken only a little more courage, a little more imagination, on the part of either man to bring them into each other's arms. The dead body between them was only slightly higher than a speed bump, but it might as well have been a castle wall. Neither of them had the wherewithal left to scale the barrier between them, even if it was made of assumptions and suspicion rather than quarried stone.

Shaking his head, Ulric mounted his bike and drifted home. Without turning to look back at Alain, he lifted a hand in a graceful gesture of farewell and surrender. The vibrations from the motorcycle's V-8 engine made his balls ache like a bad tooth. He longed to find a suitable niche for his aching cock before dawn made him impotent and knew it for a futile desire.

The Cop and His Choirboy
(Written With Matt Rice)

I have been following him for weeks.

I noticed him watching us when my friends were shooting up in that alley behind the hotel across from the park. He was skeeving all over us.

We pretended not to notice.

I've been seeing him a lot lately.

I've heard that sometimes the rats he picks up do not come back to the warren. I want to find out more.

I notice him too much. Is watching gutter punks and skate rats some kind of sport for him?

I wonder where he puts all the lost boys he takes in for questioning. I wonder if he is one of those boring middle-class men who just want to blow you. Nah, if that were it, he'd be up on the strip.

I found a knife on the seat of his car. I took it. I want to keep it for a week and see if I can return it. Then maybe he'll know he's not the only one watching…

❖ ❖ ❖

This fuckin' city is coming apart, man. Nothing but whores, dopers, and bums as far as the eye can see. This trash heap tells you what really keeps things running: greed, lust, hatred. The only thing that matters is power. There's no way to clean up this mess or make it better because it is a perfect reflection of what people are and what they really want. It's only tragic if you let yourself slip to the bottom of the food chain. I'm actually quite at home here. Happy, even. Wolves couldn't hunt here, but I can.

Every now and then a face leaps out at me from the parade of losers and misfits. I don't know what it is, a sense of style, maybe. Somebody who isn't completely defeated. Or they know they are doomed but they still keep fighting. It's attractive to me. It makes me want to crush them. The last time it was this black drag queen. She had a low sexy laugh that could turn your bones to water. Taking her down occupied several weeks of my time. Incarceration. Indoctrination. Then marketing. I was sorry to let her go, but the price was right. Sometimes I still think about her. The place where she was going was not exactly easy. But I had done my best to prepare her for that. Nothing better waited for her on the street, just AIDS or an overdose. I was her savior, but I doubt she sees it that way.

Now it's this goddamn kid. Always running with a pack of other hustlers, all of them too skinny, way too fast, and extremely mean. They are sticking needles in their arms and studying the finer points of sexual perversion at an age where they should still be blushing at a copy of *Playboy*. I'm not sure why he stands out from his buddies. Maybe it's those blue eyes; they don't miss much. His friends are always talking big about some score that's going to set them up for life, but he doesn't. He knows there isn't any hope. I think there's something about being on the edge of survival that appeals to him. Makes me want to get him alone in the backseat of my squad car and see if I can't push him far enough to find his will to live. I'm sure he's seen and done some terrible things, but it can always get worse. I wonder if he has any idea how bad it can be just before the lights go out forever.

He has a pretty mouth. And I know where it's been. Still, I do believe I want to kiss him, after I've got my hands wrapped around his throat. Cut off most of his air and then block the rest of it with my tongue.

The thing that pisses me off the most is all these queer T-shirts he wears, those brazen fag slogans about silence and death. What does he know about silence and death? Enough to keep me watching his ass, that's for sure.

A few things have gone missing from my car. Including my favorite folding knife. Serves me right for leaving it out in plain view. But I thought when I saw him the other day there was a flash of something silver in his hand, before him and his friends took off in the other direction. If I find out he's been rummaging through my property, there will be hell to pay.

Meanwhile, it's really nice just circling him slowly. Letting the circles get smaller and smaller, a little at a time. At night before I take off my uniform I think about him blowing middle-aged creeps in their family-man station wagons, running that pierced tongue of his up and down strangers' dicks, trying to avoid swallowing their come. It makes me want to shoot all over his face and slap him hard, slap him for having a pretty mouth and blue eyes that don't miss anything.

Time to meet the wholesaler downtown and pick up my cut of this week's party favors. Maybe get a little extra for myself. I'm going to pass the taqueria on Polk Street; maybe he'll be standing there whittling on a stick, pretending he's just another innocent farm boy lost in the big bad city.

I know his name. His friends call him David, Davy, or D. Eventually I will know a lot more than that. All in good time.

Time to go see how the rats have rearranged their trash heap.

❖ ❖ ❖

I think he's following me. It seems hardly coincidental that he found me in that huge crowd of people. He let me go. I am thankful for that. Puddle and Linus said they thought they'd never see me again. When I showed up at the squat again I felt like I was walking into a ghost town. Most of the rich-kid faux-squatters had run home to Mommy and Daddy. I can't say I blame them this time. I still haven't spoken much. My face is healing, but I've become accustomed to this silence. It is like insulation—cold on the outside; warm on the inside. The little kids still sleep with me, but they have learned to not ask questions. I find that writing in this book is the only thing that helps me sleep. The smack is always there, but I'm saving that for later. Plenty of time to immobilize myself, like Durtball. I don't even know what I look like. I haven't had the guts to look at anything but my chest when that guy from the clinic bandaged it. I told him it was all from a trick…

I just wish I could get the image of his cock out of my mind. It is such a beautiful thing attached to such a wretched soul. It is hot and long and wide—almost pure in its responsiveness to my bloodied mouth. I found myself wondering if a man like that could ever need me. I mean, as long as he just wants me, I'm safe enough. He can have his fun and let me go, continue this game of cat and mouse…but if he ever feels that he needs me, I'm not sure I'll make it. I don't think he could kill me. Would have done it already; chance was there. But if he needs me, finds in me the one thing that he can't get from his other victims…

Can he love? Can I show him how good it can be to bring someone back from that edge, knowing you can take them there again and again? Can he need without destroying? I returned his knife to him today, covered in my pus and blood. Thought he might need it for those long nights. I'm going to try sleeping in the park for a while. Scooter scored a tent from one of those rich white guilt-laden college kids. At least no one will have pissed in it yet. Provided Scooter's not fully gone.

This is stupid; I don't know why that fuckin' guy told me writing about this stuff was supposed to make it better. Nothing can make it better. This is as good as it gets. This is all I will ever know until the day someone comes along to put me in a bag and take me away. I like it here. I know that no one can ever take anything away from me ever again. There is nothing to take but my soul, and I lost that a long time ago. Lost that when I quit trying. Now I just make sure the little ones don't go down too fast. The real ones, the ones who don't have a place to go and parents looking for them. The ones who find no romance in panhandling, who would rather go home than squat another day, only there is no "home." They're the ones I look out for. I watch them. I fix them. I clean their abscesses. I take their shit to exchange so Child Protective Services doesn't come after them. I figure a rapist with $80 is better than a rapist with a foster care license.

POK and Linus are doing real good. They've learned to work fast. Puddle's not doing as well as the other little kids, but he almost broke my heart when he brought me clean water and bandages last night. I was too out of it to notice the infection. Hadn't left my sleeping bag in two days. Kept thinking about…Him. I keep seeing Him, over me, looking like Wolverine in a cop uniform, only with white hair. His muscles are such a contrast to my skinny boy body. I had the biggest dick I'd ever seen till I saw His. He's in my dreams all the time—watching. Always watching. I just hope He leaves me alone for a while. I've got to try to quit following Him. I just feel so drawn to Him. I want to know what He's doing, where He's going, where He sleeps at night…

Even better. Scooter scored me some new fentanyl derivative. I don't know how that kid works those hospitals. Good night, everyone!

❖ ❖ ❖

Goddamn that little shit. Leaving my fucking property in the car in a Ziploc baggie like it was a piece of evidence. Caked with blood and gunk, way past cleaning up unless I stick it in an autoclave. Windows not broken, no holes punched in by the locks, just a nice clean lift with no damage and I'm damn sure no fingerprints. Letting me know he can get in and out of there any time he feels like it. Skillful little motherfucker.

I have to admit it was pretty good. I was not happy about having to show up and join the cordon around the federal building. But every now and then to keep the uniform and badge in good standing I have to actually put in some boring time at the cop shop. All that yelling and screaming and theatrical bullshit. Like there was somebody inside the building who could have fixed the fact that all of their friends and some of them were dying. Like anybody cares. I got distracted by the dykes who were swallowing and spitting out fire. I almost missed him. But he has this belt he wears that has studs on it. I caught the glitter out of the corner of my eye.

We were told not to go into the crowd, but I say fuck that, are we in charge or are they? Just let one of those little sons of bitches put a hand on me, he'll lose it. It wouldn't matter to me if we just shot the whole bunch of them, but the mayor would be peeved. Looks bad on the evening news. Hypocrisy, that's what's wrong with the government in this town. Anyway, I lunged into the crowd just long enough to nab him by the back of the belt and yell something about an outstanding warrant to the big blue dumbbells on either side of me; then we were off to my squad car and a nice easy drive to the crib.

He fought a little when I was putting the cuffs on him. It is a pretty desperate feeling to have your hands held behind your back by circles of cold steel. So I threw him up against the car a few times to remind him that he'd been caught fair and square, then searched him, running the palms of my hands along the outside and inside seams of his clothes. "You got anything sharp in your pocket?" I asked, even though I was wearing Kevlar gloves, and he laughed and turned his hip a little so that his cock touched my fingers. There was plenty of fabric between us, but the insolence of it pissed me off so much that I turned him around and beat his face up good before I stuffed him into the car. Wondering what that cock was going to look like when I got his clothes off. It seemed fairly hefty. Would explain why the kid is still alive after more than a year on the street, a marketable commodity like that.

The crib is in a deteriorating hotel that's run by a Vietnamese guy who never leaves his room. I bring him a lot of opium twice a week and that's my rent. The other residents don't come out of their rooms when I'm in the hall, and they don't complain. It's a good place to take a snitch for a private chat, and if I got caught with this smarmy queer activist, that's exactly what I would say he was, a snitch I pretended to bust so none of his pals would know he had turned on them.

I guess I was a little impatient. I didn't really want to talk. What was there to talk about? I know his story. And there's nothing he needs to know about me except that I will force him to give me what I want. So I taught him the first lesson: Don't resist. But I'm not sure how well it took. Even when he was on his knees, there was still something about that look on his face, remote, as if some part of him was really someplace else, and what I made him do did not matter. I hate that ability to check out.

So I hurt him, to force him to come back to his body. Back to me. I hurt his face. I found my knife in his pocket and cut his chest to ribbons. When his mouth was completely bloody I just had to get my cock in there. But first I uncuffed him and brought his hands around to the front, made him take his own cock out, and cuffed one hand to his balls. It was, as I had suspected, a sizable piece of hustler meat. I couldn't help but wonder how many suburban daddies had slobbered over it, reducing themselves to a submissive frenzy while this mean kid laughed at the top of their bowed heads and broke his promise to not come in their mouths. His big hands locked around the back of their necks. Holding them down, keeping them at their work.

But this was an entirely different situation—he was on his knees, bleeding, afraid, almost crying, almost 100% present and accounted for. I told him he had better get his cock hard because I wanted to be sure he absolutely appreciated the privilege of blowing me. Then I went into his throat, and it was like a dark nirvana, a shadow Shangri-la. He sucks cock like a demented angel of sex, the tongue and throat working together so perfectly that I could have come easily in the first five minutes. But I did not want him to think it was that easy to get around me. I had to keep pulling out and slapping him around some more so I wouldn't lose it. Fucking kid. I hate the way he came so close to making me lose control.

And all the time he never knew what was going on with me, I think; he had too many of his own troubles to worry about. Because when his cock did get hard, I told him he was not to come until he begged me for the privilege. We were locked in quite a competition, me doing my damnedest to fuck his throat hard enough to choke him but not lose it, him determined to keep his cool and not give in to me, despite the fact that everything I was doing to him had hit some deep nerve. He couldn't help but respond to the abuse. Maybe just because it was so much personal attention. All this time I've been watching him I've been hoping he had that masochistic streak because it makes it so much easier to turn people against themselves.

But I was the one who lost. He got to me. I had his head between my hands and I thought I would crush it, I came so hard I thought blood would come out of my eyes and ears. That was just so unacceptable. I stood away from him, watching him try to spit out my come, and I took out my revolver and put it where my cock had been. I told him he had till the count of five to come, and pulled back the hammer.

I'll never know if I would actually have shot him or not. I haven't killed anybody in that room. Cleanup would be awkward. But I didn't have to find out, because the sound of the hammer going back and clicking into place made him spew white ribbons of come all over his own chest and the floor.

Then I felt sick. It was like everything got black and closed down around me. I had to get rid of him. I took off the cuffs, shoved the knife into his pocket, and literally threw him out the door. But before I picked him up to toss him away I told him what I was going to do to him the next time I found him on my streets, that his ass was the forfeit.

He ran and limped away, and I shut and locked the door. I don't think there's enough scotch in this crib to wash me clean. The hunger for him is in me like leprosy. Working to destroy me. I've never been so angry and so hungry.

It's been 10 days since that happened. He's nowhere to be found. Did he skip town? Somehow he didn't strike me as a kid who just had to take the bus back to Marin County. Everybody calls these young men "runaways," but most of them didn't have a choice about leaving home; they got thrown out. Their families don't want them back. I've checked the shelters. SROs. Squats. I've seen a couple of the losers he runs with, but I won't ask them; I don't want one of them looking at me in that appraising way they have and asking me, "What do you want Davy for, officer?"

There has to be some other place, something obvious that I just haven't thought of. Jesus Christ, I'm losing my edge.

❖ ❖ ❖

The voice was shrill with desperation. It was one of the little ones, though I cannot remember which one. I remember being dragged out of the tent, sort of. I mean, I recall the feeling, but I was still stupid from the shit Scooter scored at the hospital. It's like a dream where you're blind but can still see everything from the outside. I remember feeling like I was moving, and lots of screaming, but I don't know if I was really aware of what was happening.

Now I'm in this room. It is almost completely dark, except for the light coming from under the door. All of my stuff is here. I found my books and my pack. That really scares me. I have been in and out of consciousness for what seems like a long time.

The last little while in the park has been good. Scooter has kept me consistently high, and I think I've finally started to heal. I touched my chest and it feels like there are scabs now where the worst weeping wounds were. I can't believe that bastard cut my tattoo off. Fucker has no respect for investments. Why should He? He can own anyone He wants.

There is a small pile of blankets in the corner. They have begun to smell, even to me. I think the small bucket that I've been using for a john is getting dangerously full, though I can't really tell in this light. I don't know how long I've been down here. I can't remember the last time I ate anything. I am light-headed, but I feel like I have this clarity. Must be what Joe talked about when he said his fasting brought him spiritual insight. I thought he was a fuckin' idiot.

This situation has Him written all over it. I guess He finally figured out I had something for Him. Some ability to redeem Him with my mouth and my skin and my blood that He will never get anywhere else. He can fuck me up all He wants, but inside I know He cares about me. That was obvious. The more He has needed me, the more out of control and brutal He has gotten. I knew He loved me when He hit me in the face and then got mad at my nose for breaking. Like He wants to be able to put my head through a wall and have it come out more fucking beautiful than before. Now I think He's gone fucking Gary Heidnik on me, number 12 in my deck of serial killer trading cards. What does He think, I'm one of those cheesy old-school leather fags who gets off on this shit when it's just for pretend? I don't like the pain. I don't know how anyone could when it's real. But I can see through it. I can see Him. I can see Him.

❖ ❖ ❖

I have to think. Got to get ahold of myself. I have him. I have him. He's safe for now; I still can't get over how smoothly it all went down. Down. Ha. That was the whole problem, wasn't it? I had gotten too focused on downtown, forgot there's a whole city full of places where a slender, barely bearded queer skate rat with big blue eyes can hide his mutilated chest and sweet round ass. Where would you go if the city had gotten way too dangerous and you wanted to be someplace a lot less urban but didn't have the means to really escape? The park, of course. That facsimile of the countryside.

Unmarked cars come in handy. What a lucky man I am to have this plum undercover narcotics assignment where I can disappear for weeks at a time, look any way I want to look, and blend into the crowd. Camouflage for the predator. So important, if only as a fashion statement. It only took two days. I had to track one of them from Polk Street to the 38 Geary and then a crosstown bus. Davy himself won't be in much shape for cruising for a few more days yet, I told myself, he will need somebody to shove a roast beef sandwich and a Mountain Dew at him from time to time.

THE COP AND HIS CHOIRBOY

I am guessing this kid is maybe 19, if his fake ID is being flashed under dim light. Can somebody that young be as much of a chicken hawk as I am? I mean, he has these little fuckin' kids clustering around him like he was some kind of mama hen. All of them thin as stilettos and twice as likely to go between your ribs. My experience with Shoshonna stood me in good stead here; the go-between was in drag the first time I spotted him. With this crowd you have to be able to recognize your perps in a variety of genders. I have to admit there's something about a teenage boy's ass in a miniskirt. But I'm not after any of that right now; I have my obsession and it obscures every other desire.

So I followed this kid, and in between one bus and the next she becomes a he; there must have been a pair of bike shorts in that Hello Kitty plastic backpack. I made sure I had plenty of pictures in both guises. I couldn't have been any luckier, found parking right next to the place where he looked over his shoulder and began to crawl through the brush. I stayed on the path and followed the movement of the shrub tops. Carrying a leash, looking like I had lost my fuckin' dog. Which I think I had.

There's this artificial waterfall that attracts a fair number of tourists. But on either side of it are some hollows set back into the hills. Not a lot of people know about them; they're overgrown. Park and rec people don't like to prune there, too afraid of getting stuck with a dirty needle. And I might have lost them or had to alert them to my presence way too soon, except the silly little fuckers had pitched a tent, one of those single-man tubes you crawl inside, just room for one sleeping bag. It muffled my approach and kept them from seeing or hearing me. It was a melon-pink color I could have seen for miles. Why didn't anybody pull some branches down over it or at least splash a little mud on the walls? They're just kids, trying hard to be grown-ups, but they can't think of everything, I guess.

The little tyke I just grabbed by one arm and tossed to one side. He landed crooked and I hope to hell it hurt him because he was in my way and that pissed me off so much. Davy was there too, in his sleeping bag, and there was a smell of sickness in the tent. The infection has gotten worse. He must have been on something, because it was no trick at all to stuff him back into the sleeping bag, zip it over his head, cinch him into it with the leash, and put him over my shoulder. I had no trouble at all carrying him back to my car. The weight of him in my arms brought tears to my eyes. He was so helpless I pitied him. He didn't even struggle. He just moved a little from time to time, the way I imagine a woman moves underneath the cock of a man who loves her. I kissed the place where I thought his mouth might be before I laid him in the back of my vehicle. There's a panel between the driver's seat and the back, and the windows are reinforced, but it looks like an SUV outfitted to carry German shepherds in the back.

Then I went back for his stuff. I'm not sure why, it just seemed better to tidy things up. And it sort of made me smile, the thought of him waking up in a dark place, scared, but with all his belongings around him. The little one was still there, moaning, in the same place where I had thrown him. His shoulder was dislocated. So I put it back into place, that was good for a scream, and gave him Davy's shit to carry. Once in the car, he got cuffed and shoved down into the passenger footwell. Then we all went for a little ride out of town, to the big farmhouse in Marin County where I plan to retire.

The little pup got chained in my upstairs rec room. Davy went into the hole. I got the digital camera and made some educational images of the tyke, under extreme duress, then printed them out as slides. Shoved a handful of glycerin suppositories up the baby bunny and turned him loose with a stern warning, my heartfelt thanks for the nice prezzie, and a big enough bag of dope that he can kill himself quite easily if he feels too bad about betraying his pard. I doubt he makes it as far as the shuttle across the Golden Gate Bridge before he has to fix. Not my problem. If he's going to dress up like a girl, he should be prepared to get beaten up and banged like one.

Maybe I should have killed him. Any witness, no matter how

THE COP AND HIS CHOIRBOY

disreputable, can be dangerous. But I think it's good for him to be alive somewhere. If the kid is dead, he's no longer leverage with Davy. I could just shoot him and lie about it, but I think those blue eyes would know. Davy would smell the death on me.

Now it's been a few days; the water ran out yesterday or the day before. Fortunately, there is a drain in the floor; the place is probably really stinking. I haven't gone down the stairs to check. But I am going to do that now. Put on the slides and show Davy a little entertainment. See how he reacts to my quaint ideas of fun. See if his friend being placed in jeopardy will keep him docile. I bet he has a protective streak, no matter how tough he tries to act.

Then I'm going to give him something to eat and drink. I've got the bowl of dry dog food right here, ready to piss on. If he cleans out the bowl, he can have the roast beef sandwich and the Mountain Dew and something even more important. Antibiotics. Because the boy is dying in there, I can feel it in my heart. Losing his grip on life. Oh, God, I can't let him die before I have a chance to…what?

I don't know. I'm not sure. I have to think. I have to do this right. Every step. Plan it out ahead. Get a grip on myself, get ahold of my viciousness. He has to be made to last a long, long time. I want each bite of him to be a little one, and I want to taste and sample and savor it completely. But I have him. The triumph is exhilarating. And he knows who has him. He knows it's me.

I felt his mouth move inside that sleeping bag. How dare that queer punk try to kiss me. He is going to pay for that. Never mind if I pressed my lips to his first. Never mind. It's not his place to respond to me or try to make me feel anything for him. You can't trust a twisted hustler punk like that. They're all smiles and wiles, always knowing what you want to hear. But this one is going to shut up and listen.

Time to turn on the hidden projector. The images will be the first light he's seen for days. Then I can kick in the door and announce that it's feeding time at the zoo.

❖ ❖ ❖

The concrete leaches what body heat I can muster. The floor is hard, even through the blankets. I lie here on my back, legs Indian style. My journal is propped on my pack, which weighs heavy on my tummy. Joe always made a distinction between bellies and tummies. Mine was too flat to be a belly. He insisted I had a tummy instead and refused to acknowledge the little pooch I was managing to pack on with all the pizza and fast food I could wheedle out of tricks. My lighter is getting really hot…just like I'd been smoking all night and needed to heat up my lighter and scar my arm to remind myself I was still alive. The little ones were doing that the other night. I didn't tell them to stop. They would have resented me for it. I just got out some salve and made them sleep with the fresh wounds covered. Last thing I needed was a bunch of punks with staph infections. I should try to sleep, but all I can see when I close my eyes is what He did to Linus. I mean, I've seen Linus as a girl before, but never like that. I wish I could feel these tears. I'm not sure if they're from the bright light or from—

I keep passing out. What kink is this guy working? What draws Him to me? What dragged me to chase after Him? What does He do with all the little rabbits He picks up? He certainly doesn't send them to church to sing in the choir. I've heard things. Evidently all I'm gonna get from Him is dead. Maybe sold off if I'm lucky. I've heard things. One man on the planet so surely crooked and I have to want Him. Need Him. Need to be consumed by Him, need to belong. Long to see fondness in the contempt in his eyes. Feel the boldness that drives Him to climb up inside of me and imprison my heart. I can feel His eyes on me. Am I just losing it? Is the paranoia taking over for good this time? I think sometimes it has helped me, but here I cannot help myself. I can't help anyone. I think I am starting to fade again…

❖ ❖ ❖

The peephole slides open silently. But I would guess he knew I had some way to watch him. Otherwise, why bother to keep him imprisoned? So perhaps he was just performing for me. When the first image came up, I thought, maybe he will cover his eyes. It was a kicker: boy with running mascara, screaming until his eyes bulged while I twirled the dial on the electrical box. Davy had been in the dark for a long time. But he didn't flinch away from it. Just watched, calmly. In the projector light I could see his chest rising and falling. Maybe he was breathing a little more rapidly than usual. It's hard to tell. He's cold.

It pissed me off, him lying there without responding to the torture, and I had to force myself to unlock the door before I kicked it open. No sense in breaking down all that hardware. I set my props down on a little table and tried not to breathe too heavily; the slop bucket was overflowing. And his wounds stank.

The machine accidentally projected a square of blank light at the end of the show before starting up to automatically repeat the half-a-carousel of images. And in that light I saw something that made my heart leap with triumph. There were tears at the edges of his eyes, silver stains of pity. That settled me down. So I could get to him after all. There was a weakness there, a crack I could set my crowbar into and use to pry him apart.

I didn't speak for a long time. It's better to be silent. Someone who has been alone that long is craving company. There's been so much dread and anticipation that it's a relief when the torturer appears. Not much hurts worse than waiting to suffer. Finally he licked his lips and said, croaking, "Who do I have to fuck to get a drink around here?"

We both laughed, because it was funny, and then I showed him the bowl of kibble. "Too dry for you?" I asked.

He nodded slowly, not taking his eyes off my face until I unzipped my fly and took out my cock. It was already half-hard, sore from the rough handling it has gotten while I left him alone, simmering in the darkness and his own bad dreams. He licked his lips again, and I said, "I can fix that," and pissed all over the dog food. Stirred it up with my cock and put it on the floor, at the foot of a chair, in which I seated myself.

He had been holding his hands above his head, as if he were tied. Now he looked at his wrists, as if reminding himself that there were no bonds. He slid to the floor bonelessly, as if he were a sheet of wet wallpaper, and came to me on all fours, graceful as a cat. With dainty precision, he sucked the moisture out of the bowl first, then ate the meaty nuggets, giving every appearance of relishing it.

I was nonplussed. What do you do with someone who actually enjoys this sort of humiliation? He was defusing my attempt to undercut and degrade him by treating it as a commonplace, and making it a pretty act besides. My cock was completely hard, and I was, as I so often am with him, furious. Working to avoid the feeling that somehow by submitting so perfectly, easily, and completely, Davy had humiliated me.

So I kicked him in the ribs. More than once. And in between kicks he crawled back to his bowl and kept on eating. Determined to draw sustenance from it. "Stop that!" I finally said.

"Why?" he asked me, coming up to his knees. His blue eyes had turned dark gray. "Do you think this is the first time I've had to eat dog food?"

"Or drink piss?" I sneered.

He nodded gravely, like a prince in exile being questioned by ignorant reporters. *I can do anything I must to survive,* his mien told me. Though he held himself hunched a little, trying to ease the pain in his ribs.

"You've earned this," I said, and threw him half a sandwich. He ate that too and drank the whole soda in one long swallow. I thought for a minute he might get sick, putting that much food on a stomach that had been empty for days, but he kept it down. I had to seriously wonder if this kid's life had been so hard that it wasn't going to be possible for me to break him.

I stopped the slide show on the first image. "What do you think of my photography?" I asked.

"The contrast is low," he replied. "What were you using?" and he named the exact brand name and model of my digital camera.

But I saw the tears begin again, slow seeping, internal bleeding that can no longer be contained by the skin so it overflows and shows itself to the outside world. No sobbing, he could keep that under control. Again, I did not speak. Speaking to him was dangerous. He was too good with words. Eventually he had to ask me the question. "Is he—is he still—"

"Alive?" I completed the sentence. "Yes. And quite a bit richer for his trouble. No thanks to you. Being your friend is not going to be much of a badge of honor in the near future, Davy. It's going to become very expensive. Next time I think I'll dispense with the camera and just go live. With you close enough to smell it. What do you think of that?"

"Don't do that," he said, begging without whining. "I will do anything you want."

"Without being tied?" I asked.

He nodded, looking terrified.

"Without trying to get away?"

That stuck in his craw. "Will you ever let me go?" he whispered.

I shook my head. "You knew the answer to that question when you woke up in this room. No one here gets out alive."

He sighed. "Well," he said, stretching, still on his knees, "I never liked the number 21, and I never got as far as even thinking about 30. I'm yours, then."

"Too right, motherfucker," I snarled, and slammed his head into my crotch. He swallowed me as if we had been lovers for a thousand years, with an easy familiarity that was impressive. I could not help but catch my breath at the skillful patterns his tongue traced around the crown of my cock and down to the base. He twisted his head as he sucked me, creating a swirling sensation. When pleasure is the trap, who dares to escape? I pumped into him, finally getting to possess the thing I had wanted for so many weeks. Hating myself for missing him and for taking the chances I had taken to capture and retain him for my own. If I got caught, it would be impossible to explain. My best option would be to eat my own gun.

I didn't care, at that moment. I didn't care what price I had to pay. And I knew I had to make him suffer so much that he would not figure that out. Of the two of us, I was the one who was more helpless. Davy could walk away from this room with nothing but some bad scars and worse memories. If I lost him, I would be bereft.

So I made him stand bent over the foot of his cot and beat him with my belt. Withdrawing from his mouth was agony. I was so close to coming it made tears come to my eyes to force myself to wait. I wanted him to give me that release, that pleasure, but I also wanted to mark him with my spunk. As if throwing my come down his throat, up his ass, would render him my property and chain him to me. I beat him for that impossible desire because I did not think I would ever have him, really. He would always find a place inside himself where he could hide from me. I beat him and cursed him and he never once turned from side to side or covered his ass with his hands. He did what he said he would do. He stood there and took it. To protect his little friend, the child he had taken under his protection. I couldn't bear this evidence of his honor and his courage. I did not want him to be brave or truthful. I wanted him to be like me. Because if he were corrupt, I could find a way to hang on to him, I would know how to manipulate and manage him.

Finally I could not stand it anymore. His blood was in the air between us, beaten out of his buttocks. It was in my nostrils, and I spread them wider, trying to draw his essence into my body. I put on a condom and held his ass cheeks apart.

That was the only time he moved. He reached behind himself and took off the condom. I was too surprised to slap his hands away. "I'm already dead," he said simply, and then opened himself, hands flat on the bruised cheeks, showing me the wrinkled eye of his anus. A little blood had run into his crack and hung from the golden hairs that edged it. I could have said something about the rubber being for my benefit, not his, but in some way I knew that I was already dead as well. Both of us, dead to the sane world of normal and ordinary people who could find enough satisfaction in their 9-to-5 jobs and mortgages and 2.5 children, their weekday commutes and weekend barbecues, to keep from blowing their brains out. I was lonely for the darkness in his body; it was the mate of the darkness inside my chest. So I spread grease on myself and drew him gently back upon me, taking him as slowly as I could, wanting him to feel every quarter of an inch sliding in, spreading and claiming him.

He was so tight, I think it must have hurt him to be penetrated. That surprised me. I expected a wide loose channel that I'd have to order him to tighten. Apparently the boy would rather eat dog food than take on a certain type of john and be able to splurge on a slice of pizza or an egg roll. At first I could not tell which one of us was making that thin high noise, but eventually I realized he had begun it; it was a hum of barely restrained resistance and excitement. He was horrified by himself. And I had joined in; we were making that noise together, a chorus, the two of us made helpless by the need we felt for each other, doing everything we could to hold back yet falling relentlessly toward consummation. The sounds that came from him were a profane music that called me home.

He eventually opened underneath me, began to ripple inside as if he were sucking me with his ass. I fucked him a little faster, making sure I never came completely out, and finally I had to keep myself wedged deep in there, moving just enough to tickle the head of my cock. "Do you want my come?" I asked him, and my voice sounded absurdly grave and fatherly to my own ears.

"Please," he said, and so I gave it to him. Poured into him. Usually when I come I feel three or four separate spurts, but this was one thick sustained burst of fluid coming out of me, as if my cock was a firehose. I saw colors and could not feel my own hands or feet. The only part of my body I could really feel was the part of me that he contained.

I was dizzy. Surely he did not turn around then and help me to sit back down on the edge of the cot. He would not have dared. I must have found my own way there. But I do know he was cleaning me with his tongue when I came to. He was well on the way to getting me hard again. Surely I had put myself in his mouth, put my hand on the back of his neck and urged him to swallow the instrument that had probed him so deeply. But I don't remember. Why don't I remember?

He interrupted me before I could pursue that train of thought. "I taste pretty good," he said, looking up at me with one eyebrow raised, his mouth full and looking rather bruised.

We both laughed. It was, after all, pretty funny.

Then there was long slow torture that culminated in my christening his throat. Jesus. I have had some excellent blow jobs in my day. You'd be surprised how inspired even a straight man can be with a .45 in his ear. For some reason I kept thinking about my partner, Jimmy Iatolli, Giuseppe when he was at home. How he wouldn't take the money that first time we busted a big dealer and could have so easily made a hundred thousand dollars disappear between us without injuring the case against him. He saw me take the money, but he wouldn't take it himself, and he wouldn't tell. But I was afraid he would tell. For a year and a half this went on. The dance, as I got more deeply involved in setting up my own business and tried again and again to cut him in on the profits, find some way to dig under the fence of his Roman Catholic morality. He was proper as only Italian cops can be proper, the ones who see themselves as good guys, who are not going to go the way of the Mafia, not become wiseguys.

Killing him was such a difficult decision to make. I've never regretted it exactly, but I do wish he had been able to come over to my side. I could have spared him so much grief and aggravation. And I pitied him for the conflict he had, torn between his loyalty to the department and to his partner. In his own way he was also trying to get me to come back to what he thought was the light, the good side, the place where we would both be white knights holding back the tide of evil. But evil is too strong. He never understood that the devil has already won. There is no clean ground to stand upon and protect. We are already swamped.

I loved him so fucking much. And he never touched me. After he left me, alone with nothing but his body, I could touch him as much as I liked. But it was cold going, with no cooperation. I knew then that it was a mistake to let him go before he knew everything about how I felt. It's important to give them that knowledge before they are sent away. I need to see myself reflected in their eyes. Those moments of truth keep me sane. And even if he had vomited over my cock or screamed himself hoarse with revulsion when I fucked him, it would have been better than trying to use him when he was no longer at home.

Davy's tongue on my cock and balls was licking at this pain. Licking it away. Each time he caressed me with his spit and sore mouth, he did something to me that made me feel lighter inside. I didn't know if I could stand this. I wanted him to go faster, make me come, leave me alone. But he was deliberate. I could speed him up for a while, but the minute I let go of his head, he was back to the careful work, as if he were sucking poison out of my system. So I finally gave up and let him nurse on me. This time when I came it felt almost like a cramp, my perineum coming up to crush my balls. There was a tingling sensation all down my urethra, as if my come were carbonated, and it felt as if I were losing something other than semen. Maybe a part of my self.

Oh, God, he was pretty with my come all over his face, licking it off as if he liked it, as if it were a reward he had earned instead of a threat or a punishment. I wanted to smack him then, but my arm hurt from using the belt, and I was fucked out. So I made him empty the slop bucket; there's a toilet in the utility closet just outside the cell. I filled the dog bowl full of water. I made him swallow the medicine, and I put him on his back and ripped off the dirty amateurish wad of bandages. Guess they don't teach first aid in runaway school. I have this salve we used to use in 'Nam; it will kill jungle rot and anything else you got growin' in you that shouldn't be there. It smells terrible but works good. So I smeared that on him and pulled a clean T-shirt over his head. But no pants. I wanted his ass and dick bare.

When he figured out that I was about to leave the room he lifted himself up from the mattress just a half an inch or so and said, almost whispering, "Please kiss me."

"Open your mouth," I said.

Those thin sensual lips parted, and I spat down his gullet. Then I stuffed the other half of the sandwich into his abraded palate and left, locking the door behind me.

I was at the top of the stairs before I remembered I should have told him he can't jack off. Next time. We'll take care of that next time. Lesson number 2.

I took a fifth of Jack Daniel's to bed with me, and I didn't plan to wake up with anything other than an empty bottle. He will destroy me. And I do not care. I will destroy him. And he does not care. What is going on in this world, that two people like us can even exist? Let alone find one another. It's beyond me. I never needed a drink so bad in my entire life.

❖ ❖ ❖

He has just gone again. I feel like every time He leaves me alone He is ripping out my heart. How can I feel anything for this pig? I mean, He is a pig, plain and simple. But it's not that simple anymore. I know He cares about me, and I know when I told Him I was already dead that He felt the same way. We are both dead to the rest of the world. No matter what else happens, I will end my life here, at His hands. I will do anything to stay here with Him. I started this dangerous game with Him because something about Him attracted me. I have been pulled through the event horizon of His black heart and emerged on the other side. Alone. Clean. In this world but no longer of it, I will remain prisoner to His heart until mine stops. I need the fact that He needs me. I need to redeem Him. I need to cleanse Him with my blood and my mouth and my soul. I never believed I had a soul until I saw Him, standing over me, holding it. Then, when He took it and shoved it up my ass, I knew I would never be the same. All the time I've spent avoiding that because I knew it was what killed everyone in the Life. Fearing the goodness of it, I settled for making my cash the easy way, blow jobs and degrading

THE COP AND HIS CHOIRBOY

games. I'd gotten quite the reputation as the boy who could deliver for those suburban daddies who needed someone to dress them up and tell them what dirty girls they are. I learned to like it. I learned. Learned well.

So here I am, the one who is supposed to be self-contained and unreachable, craving the next moment of contact from the one man I know will destroy me.

The pain in my ribs draws me back. I still see flashes of Linus, all wired up, crying for real. That boy hasn't cried ever. I don't know where He took him to make him do that, but I know he'll never make it out of that place. I can't even care about him. I know I should, but in this stupor, all I can see is Him.

Officer Patrick Kelly.

Naming Him does not take away his power over me. His name feels like a mantra. Patrick. Officer Patrick. Officer Kelly…Officer Patrick Kelly. I worship Him like a god; I beg Him to allow me to be His consort so that I may receive some of His power, even if it does become weak and distorted by the change in form.

So where do we go from here, lover? Will He kill me when He realizes He loves me? Can a man like Him afford to love anything other than His gun? If I'm going to be His bitch, I want to be up in the kitchen cooking for Him and washing His shorts. Funny, I find it absurd to think that He even does laundry. Doesn't He exist in a plane above the world? Isn't He a manifestation of some spirit that has haunted me my whole life? Have I existed my entire life to meet Him here at this moment?

How many times have I been here? How can something so unnatural seem so right? I am so clear. Even the food has not brought me back to earth. The agony of the infection is priceless. The pain in my ribs when I breathe reminds me that He loves me. It is sweet and decadent, dreamlike as only such physical pain can be…truly existential. I feel as if I have lived my whole life for this moment. Every harsh word, every beating, all of it grooming me for right now. When I have to choose to continue rather than die the death of separation from the one I love, the one I need. I need Him more than food, more than air. He can take away my breath, my life, and I will still have Him. After I am dead, I will see His face.

Or will I? Is this just the easy way out of this pain? Do I really feel anything? Am I just being romantic? Trying to make this easier on both of us? Perhaps my curse in life isn't Him, it's knowing I will never be able to give all of myself to Him. I can't. It's something He can never take from me. That hurts more than any physical pain ever could.

I think I'm gonna throw up.

❖ ❖ ❖

Sometime in between 2 A.M. and dawn, I had a dream. I was fucking Giuseppe's wife, having decided that perhaps she would be more responsive than her recently deceased spouse. I knew she had always had the hots for me, but that didn't mean I wasn't going to lace her drinks with a few little things that would make it easier for her to drown her grief by letting me slap her around and fuck her and tell her she was a shameless whore. So the bed we were in smelled like sex and whiskey and the chemicals I'd given her, and she was covered with tears and her own sweat. She was slick with come, well-greased for me by her fear and guilt. I had my belt around her neck and I was screwing her from behind, asking her pretty personal questions about her dead husband's relationship with her pussy, getting really close to making her tell me that he had never made her feel the things I was making her feel. I was pretty sure that if I got her to actually say that out loud, she would follow him into the darkness, or want to. That was OK. They had two kids. The kids would be left behind.

I was so far from coming myself that it was like watching myself use my body as a tool or a weapon. I was part machine, everything focused on her, taking her apart, making sure that every good thing she felt was twisted into something that would hurt her to think about later. Let her suffer as much as I had suffered, riding in that car with him every day, feeling the judgment of his silence, smarting from the stupidity of his good looks, the fact that he would never in a million years understand what made me tick or imagine what he would have had to do to win my mercy and save his own life. He never knew what a volatile combination of lethality and lust rode beside him. I showed all that to her. Giuseppe was the only man she'd ever had sex with. Let her think that if she ever stepped outside of her marriage bed again, this was what was waiting for her. Offer her up as suttee, a flaming sacrifice to accompany him into the next life. It took everything I had to keep my hands from closing around her throat.

In my dream it seemed I would hover there forever, watching myself drill into her and talk trash. With almost no feeling, just the need to feel her spread out in rubble underneath me, leveled, taken apart, destroyed. Like she was somebody important instead of some juicy Italian bitch Giuseppe had latched onto in high school and married the minute he graduated, as if love could ever be important, as if it could offer any redemption or hope.

I knew he had loved her. That was what I could not stand. But I had taken care of that. I had relieved her of the obligation of loving him. Cherishing his memory. Polishing it. I had told her things about women we had chased together, what he did with them, how he liked it, and she believed me. If they had really been that close, I never would have been able to shake her trust. I was simply pointing out flaws in the relationship that had existed from the very beginning, tearing down an illusion of purity and commitment.

And in the middle of all this commotion, the sweat stinging my eyes, my hands cramping from grabbing her hips so hard, I dreamed that Davy came to me. He walked into the room without bothering to open a door. He walked up to me, and she could not see him because he was there for me, not for her. He put his arms around me and kissed me, and he wrapped one of his hands around my cock and took me out of her. She slid away from me, lay down on her stomach, and I think she went to sleep. In the dream he brushed her back with his hand and she forgot everything about me, the whole evening that I had taken so much trouble to set up. But I did not care because he was running his hands up and down my back, and his mouth was begging for my tongue. And I could feel him. I was no longer a vengeful machine. My skin came to life beneath his hands, and I poured my breath into his mouth as if that would bring me the breath of life in turn.

Kissing him was better than fucking most other people. He played at it, always finding some new thing to do with his lips or his tongue, simultaneously teasing and satisfying me. "I need you," he said, and he repeated that at intervals.

He took me away from that room and the smell of regret and vengeance. He licked my face, my neck, my chest, and I felt as if his mouth was washing me clean. Then he said "I need you" with especial urgency, and I woke up with a hard-on that had no relationship at all to the usual need-to-piss morning erection.

I got up without turning the lights on. It's my house; I know it in the dark. And I went back down to the place where I had sequestered him, still in a state of communion with him, because he had come to me and rescued me, and I knew that he was telling me the truth. He did need me.

I found him half-unconscious with a fever. He had thrown up all over himself and the bed and the floor. I wiped him off a little with the mattress cover, left it on the floor with the rest of the mess to clean up later, and picked him up. He is not a short boy. But he was down to nothing, no mass at all, too many days of being ill and not being given food or water. I had no trouble carrying him up the stairs, just as I had carried him down the stairs, and for some reason it did not bother me at all to find myself weeping over him. "Don't leave me," I said, and took him into the largest bathroom. I put him in the tub and adjusted the spray, took down the shower nozzle, and washed him with soap and hot water. He turned a little, fighting the water, afraid I think that I was going to drown him, and that was when I kissed him. Even in his feverish state he stiffened with shock and surprise, then melted into me as if I were his savior.

I wrapped him in towels and dried him as best I could in the tub, then got him up and wrapped him in a large flannel sheet. He tried to walk but I took him off his feet and carried him into the infirmary. I got him into a hospital gown and the brown-and-white leather restraints. Put the bed at a comfortable angle and pulled up the side rails, made sure there was no way he could roll out accidentally or untie himself. Then I put the tourniquet around his arm and got a butterfly into the big vein that wound up his forearm. It wasn't easy; he was dehydrated so much I had to go after it twice. Started the fluids and the IV antibiotics right away. Twenty minutes of the fluids and he was feeling better. Except he kept forgetting where he was and tried to get away. I made sure he had a little pain medication to help him deal with the fever, nothing that was going to be habit-forming, although it did occur to me. Turning him into an addict would have given me a nice bit of leverage. But I did not want him that way, tied to me by junk. Besides, it's a big world, and a kid like Davy could always keep himself from getting sick. He was no little suburbanite who wouldn't know where else to get his drugs.

Instead I kept kissing him. When he thrashed around too much I would just pull his face around and kiss him. He calmed down immediately when I put my tongue into his mouth. He would breathe deeply and relax and let the medication do its work. When I got a little tired of kissing him I got a glass full of chipped ice and fed that to him, slivers at a time. Then I slid my hands under the blankets and rubbed him gently, all over, knowing there were places where I had bruised him so badly that even a light touch would smart.

My cock had never been so hard. There was nothing I wanted more than to climb on that bed and rape him. But all I could think about was how he had come to me bearing some sort of grace or forgiveness and saved me from doing something ugly twice. Brought me back to himself, to his blue eyes and big gentle hands. But he had almost left me, and I could not allow that. I could not. So I had to monitor the IV very carefully, and I had to get the leg irons and manacle his ankles to the side rails of the bed, but then I covered him completely with a thick blanket and let him sleep for a little while, my hand on his chest.

The next day he was a little better. I made him drink some broth. During one period when he was not so disoriented, he said, "Can I ask you something?"

"Yes," I said, smoothing his hair away from his forehead, wondering if I should shave it. "Ask me something."

"Do you have a bigger bed? Because you look really tired, and I wish you would lie down next to me."

That made me back away from him. I thought then that maybe it would be better to inject some air into the IV. Or get on the phone and see if I had any customers in Saudi Arabia who would like his particular look. But he kept looking at me calmly, like a dog that has no idea its owner is crazy. "I belong to you," he said. "Please let me be with you. Is that OK to ask? You can do anything you want with me, but just let me be with you."

Then he started to cry. And I didn't want him to waste any of the water that we had been at such pains to put back into his body. So I checked his restraints, then went into my bedroom to make a plan. It is a big, very solid bed with square eight-by-eight posts at each corner. I wanted to make sure that the shape of the posts was such that a chain could not be slipped over the top of them. I didn't see any way it could be managed, but I wanted to be sure, so I took the time to put a big eyebolt through one post at the foot of the bed and another at the head.

When I got back to the infirmary he was thrashing around in a panic, and I thought for sure he had pulled that damn needle out of his arm. I walked over to him, not running but hurrying, and slapped him pretty hard. That made him lie still. "No hysterics," I said. "You can't be moved until I'm sure you will leave that line alone. Are you together enough for that, Davy? Got your shit together? Tell me the truth."

He nodded, eyes clear. "I just didn't know where you had gone," he said, still leaking tears. "I was afraid you wouldn't come back."

So I took him out of the restraints and helped him to sit, then stand. He leaned on me, wheeling the IV stand, and I took him down the hallway and across the house to the wing where my bedroom is located. I didn't think I would ever have another person in that room. It has always been the place where I go to get away from everyone else. I suppose I could have put him in a guest room or one of the playrooms or simply ignored his request. But I didn't want to do that. I had gone to a lot of trouble to get him. Now I was going to enjoy him. That made sense, didn't it? If I wanted to, I could keep him beside me. Who was going to tell me no? Who was going to judge me if I let myself have the thing that I wanted? He was mine, he said so, I could do what I wanted with him. *He said so.* And so I flipped back the covers on my bed and let him lie down on sheets that had never been pressed down by anyone's body but mine, and I arranged pillows under his head and shoulders. I put a chain through one of his ankle restraints and locked it to the big bolt through the bedpost. He could get out of bed now, but he would not escape.

"Hold that arm still now," I said, taking off my clothes. Then I got into bed with him and took him. He was still not quite well enough to be used hard. I could sense that fragility in him. His will to live was so strong that it was deceptive. It kept him going. He was the kind who would not look sick at all until he collapsed and died. But I was learning him, the aura around him, the difference between how he looked from the outside and what was happening inside him. And I knew that he wanted me to claim him this way. That if I did not, he would be uneasy in my bed. He needed to be under me as much as I needed to possess him. So I took him with my mouth, my hands, and my cock, and I spilled my seed into him after a fuck that started out slow and considerate but wound up in assault mode. I simply could not control myself with this kid. I wanted him so fucking much that he undid me.

After I slid out of him I realized that I had to sleep. I had been awake…two days? Two and a half? "Three," Davy said, mumbling against my shoulder. I got up and found 15 feet of cotton rope and bound his hands to his sides. Probably with time he could wiggle loose. Probably it was the height of stupidity for me to lose consciousness around this stranger who had made me break so many of my own security policies. But I locked away all the weapons I had on my person, thinking that if we had to struggle hand-to-hand it would be OK, he was restricted enough that I could take him.

Later there would be time for a test. I had to know where his loyalties really fell. But if gangstas had their pit bulls and mafioso had their lieutenants, I could have Davy. He could be very useful to me.

I fell asleep feeling him reaching out with his bound hands, trying to brush my arms or touch me somehow, anywhere. "Hold still and leave that goddamn line alone," I growled at him, and went out quicker than a phone with a cut cord.

❖ ❖ ❖

I woke up to find Him gone again. If I hadn't woken up in His bed, I'd have believed it was all a bad hallucination. I found my stuff here by the bed. The IV rack, cluttered and octopus-like, hangs empty and forlorn in the corner. My heart still pounds in my head. The room spins when I relax. I can't tell if that's because He gave me something, or the fever. I still ache like fever. The sheets seem too heavy…everything hurts. My ribs still take their toll with every breath.

I can't believe He loves me. Without saying a word He can illuminate the dark place where I live. He speaks volumes with one caress. I can feel Him lighten under my touch, as if He knows He can give it all to me and walk out the other side clean.

I fear what His absence means. I am still held to His bed by the one Posey restraint He was so kind as to attach to a long chain. They never did that when I was in the nuthouse. I tried to stand, but it was all I could do to drag my backpack from the other side of the nightstand. These things seem so foreign to me, as if they belong to someone else, someone dead. Once, they could soothe my worst pains. They offer no comfort. Has His moment of redemption signaled my damnation? Should I try to get out? Would anyone even notice I'm gone? Linus knows where I am, but is he even still alive? I hope he played it smart and ran far away, accepting the sanctuary I offered him. I gave myself for him. I always swore I'd give them the love I never got. He changed that.

I am in love with a man who would just as soon stick a gun up my ass as His dick. Not sure there's a difference there...one's just a lot quicker. His plans for me have obviously changed. Oh, the way He tortures me with endless waiting. I was a lifetime in that basement. I died over and over, certain I would not wake again. Now I have been miraculously transported to His bed. At least I think this is His bed. This must be His bed. It is the only room without locks on the outside of the door...

The ringing in my ears won't stop. My mouth feels like it has been badly burned. I try to drink water but I can't even taste it. It does not slake my thirst. It makes me nauseous. I cannot throw up in his bed. My feet swing down and find the soothing cold hardwood floor. The rest of me slides onto the floor. Farther than I thought...but cool. It feels good on my hot face...maybe I'll just rest here awhile.

❖ ❖ ❖

It was good to get out on the bike and clear my head. Hard to believe I had gotten up without touching him, letting him sleep. But I had taken the precaution of removing the IV. He doesn't need it now anyway; the dehydration is under control and so is the infection. Maybe he will find a way to escape. This is, after all, the kid who broke into my car twice. But he promised me he would not run. So this morning is a little experiment, to find out if Davy has any honor. I sincerely hope he does. People with a sense of honor are so much easier to control. Anyway, he can't get far. I know where all the buses stop, and he doesn't have any money anyway. I suppose he could hitchhike, but where is he going to go that I can't find him? If all else fails, there's always the good old all points bulletin. I'd rather not do that, of course; it would be difficult to extricate Davy from the clutches of the system. But I'd rather see him in Vacaville than let him go free. From now on, his life is in my hands.

So I got home feeling pretty good, getting a lot of wind up my nose always does that for me. I came into the house in the same leathers I had worn on the bike and went straight to my room. I was hungry. At first I thought he had run for it—the bed was empty. But then I found him curled up on the floor. "Get up, bitch," I told him, nudging him with the toe of my boot.

In the spirit of leaving him alone in the house, I decided not to manacle his hands and feet. I wanted to see him move around my house. But not naked. So I put him in a pair of cutoffs and locked a chain around his neck. Then I took him down the hallway to the kitchen. He was a little unsteady on his feet, but when I told him to make coffee and breakfast, he pulled it together. Pretty soon I had a plate full of eggs and bacon, a cup of coffee, and a rack of toast, already buttered. He didn't make anything for himself. But there was more on my plate than one person could eat. So I had him sit between my feet, and when I was done, gave him the scraps.

He was graceful without being too flighty, 90% masculine but with that 10% of drag queen potential. I like that about these kids, their ambiguity. It attracts me, moth to the flame, but it also makes me want to hurt them. I think it is their foolish bravery, their misguided hope that the world will actually let them be those people and live like that.

After breakfast it was time for Davy's other chores. I showed him where the laundry room was. While the washing machine filled, I gave him a bucket and a brush and took him back to the room where he had spent so many days and nights alone. This I wanted to see. I stood in the doorway smoking a cigarette and watched him scrub the whole cubicle on his hands and knees. He did a good job. I like that about him too. You can't insult the kid with a dirty piece of work. He just gives it that level blue-eyed stare and puts his back into it. As if it does not matter to him what he does. But I'm not sure I want him to be so fucking good at his chores. Not sure I want to allow him an emotional refuge inside his own pride.

By then it was lunchtime, and we had another meal together, which he cooked and cleaned up. This time I gave him his own bowl and told him to eat from it without using his hands. He managed that very neatly too, without getting anything greasy on his chest. He didn't bug me with a lot of questions or whining, just did what I told him as efficiently as possible and kept out of my way. He didn't look me in the eye very often either, just quick glances when he thought I was not paying attention. Most of the time when he stared at me he was keeping track of my cock. That was OK; let him monitor that along with the other weathervanes that signal my moods.

After the second round of food he seemed to really do a lot better. There was some color in his pale cheeks, and he walked better. I think he was probably afraid I was going to lock him in the dungeon again. I took care of that little anxiety by getting him to go out to the garage and take the big dog bed down from the storage rack. It hasn't been used since Loki died. There is a place for it in my room, at the foot of the bed. I threw a pillow and a blanket in it, then told Davy to get on a pair of overalls and some rubber boots. He was going to get a reward.

That was when I took him out to the barn and introduced him to the horses. They had been in the pasture all day, so they were glad to come back to their stalls for supper and grooming. I could tell by the way he handled them that he had done it before. And they liked him right away. He spoke to them in a nice low tone of voice; moved slowly, let them get his scent. He touched them firmly, didn't tickle or otherwise annoy them. "Put on 10 pounds, and you can exercise them," I told him. He looked at me with joy and hatred. I was giving him something that he wanted too much. "But don't ever think about riding away on one of them. You do that, and I'll shoot the horse. Not you, just the horse."

He turned away from me and began to put away the currying

paraphernalia. I could tell by the slight slump in his shoulders that he knew I had figured out one of his weaknesses. Animals and little kids. Davy Saint Francis.

We went back into the house and he knelt on the floor to fold the laundry while I listened to Sibelius and had a glass of wine. I wondered if he had seen them, hiding in the tall grass just past the corral. If so, you couldn't have told from his demeanor. Without being told, he went to the kitchen and made me a steak, rare, with a Caesar salad. I fed him half of it by hand, getting my fingers into his mouth as often as possible. While I fed him, one of his hands came to rest tentatively on one of my boots, and I slapped him for touching me without permission.

After he recovered from the blow, he came back to me and asked nicely for permission to touch my boots. I had him kneel between my legs and told him to hang on to them while I fed him my cock. We were locked together for a long, long time. I simply would not let him make me come. By now they would have gotten up to the house. But it wasn't quite dark enough yet.

So I dragged him into the dungeon and stood him against one wall. Put him in irons because I liked the look of chain on his slight body. Warmed him up with my hands, first in gloves, then bare. First open hands, then fists. He was still recovering from being kicked in the ribs, but he took it like a trooper, barely grunting. I decided to get out the four-foot dog whip and take a few cracks at his back. He was good about that too, just shaking his hair out of his eyes when the braided fall landed across his shoulder blades. Hissing a little. Only his eyes begging with me. Begging for more, or begging me to stop? I did not think he wanted me to stop, and so I did. Let him understand the fact that he needed me to hurt him. Let him live with that need for a little longer. I had left the window open, hoping to make him scream, hoping those screams would carry on the evening breeze. But he had not screamed.

I should have put him over the horse and fucked him in the dungeon. But I could not. There was something about picking him up that made me get so hard. I used the same knife he had returned to me to cut the shorts off his body. The blade slid between the denim and his skin, parting the fabric like butter. He did not even shiver, but I could tell the cold steel was raising goose bumps on his thighs.

I carried him in my arms back to my bed and put him there, propped up on pillows, so I could look at and stroke the red stripes across his back while I plundered his ass. It was so good to be in him; I had not fucked him for days, holding myself back to give him time to heal. I think he had missed it as much as I had. I couldn't resist slapping his back a few times, opening up the stripes a bit. Smelling his blood on the palm of my hand. Rubbing it onto my cock so I could fuck him with his own blood. We had not spoken much to each other all day, but I could not make myself shut up when I was in him. Finally I said, "Whose bitch are you? Tell me that," and he said, "Yours, your bitch," and came in his own fist. I made him eat his own come, then told him to go to his bed.

He disobeyed me, staying at my side to help me out of my leathers, which he put in the closet, neatly, on padded hangers. I went between the covers and fell asleep then, or pretended to, and he went down to the floor to kiss my hand, hanging outside the blankets, before crawling over to the bed. I held still, breathing slowly and evenly. He was an alert little motherfucker; I wanted him to think I was dead to the world. But it would never be easy to fool him.

Eventually, he got up, just as I had suspected he would. He went tiptoeing downstairs, and I came along behind him, taking refuge in a room off the hallway so I could watch without being seen. I had not locked the front door. An experienced thief like Davy would notice such things without even intending to notice. So I expected him to bolt. It was a little mystifying, the fact that he was still buck-naked and hadn't brought down his backpack. I didn't think I'd given him any time to stash a spare pair of jeans outside.

The little shit was locking the front door for me.

Of course, synchronicity being the fourth dimension, it was just at that moment that his friends came piling into my house uninvited, intent on rescuing their protector. There were three of them. Including the sweet little transvestite I had already introduced to my electrical equipment. He had balls, coming back here after that.

Davy was making shooing motions at them. "Get out of here," he stage-whispered. "My God, what are you doing here? Run! Run away! Don't you know how dangerous this is? You idiots, you stupid little kids, *run*!"

They were clutching at him, trying to drag him out of the house. One of them said something about Stockholm syndrome. Another was saying something about a rich trick who had a room at the Claremont where Davy could hide. A third was saying they would call the police and be witnesses. That was a really good joke. They were crying and pleading with him. He was crying too.

That was when I stepped out of hiding. I told them all to be quiet. They didn't listen. They wouldn't let go of Davy either. One of them kept fingering the chain around his neck, and I could tell he was both impressed and trying to figure out how to get it off of there. Not bloody likely. Why didn't it occur to them that he could not take care of them here, in my house? It really was not wise of them to challenge me, especially not on my own territory.

"A gentleman who's paid a lady for her services and told her to fuck off doesn't like it when she comes back for more of the same," I told the kid I knew the best. He tried to slide behind Davy's back, but I crooked my finger, and Davy put the boy in front of him, crossing his arms protectively around his torso. "What's the matter, angel, was I too easy on you last time? Need a little more sugar in your bowl?"

He said something foul back to me, and Davy cuffed him on the side of his head but could not repress a sliver of a grin at his chutzpah.

"Last time I had one of your crew in my home, I let him walk," I told Davy. I was through talking to the flotsam and jetsam he had once surrounded himself with. "Paid him handsomely for his time. After giving him a night to remember. And immortalizing him on videotape. He'll be the toast of Singapore when that hits the Asian market. They like watching little American boys get hurt real bad, over there. I'm afraid I can't do the same deal twice. I've had to take a lot of time off work to acquire my new slave. But with what I'll get from selling the rest of you, I can make up my losses. Davy, I think you know where the holding tank is?"

He looked at me bleakly, his cheeks literally sunken in. As if my words had undone these days of careful feeding and medication. With his arms still around them he sank to his knees and said just one word: "Please."

I waited. "Do what I told you," I said finally, using my coldest and flattest tone of voice.

"I'll talk to them. I'll make them understand. You'll never see them again. Please. I promised them—"

"And what about your promises to me?" I reminded him.

He looked as if I had hit him full-strength in the stomach.

They were quiet. This had not gone at all the way they had planned. "Davy, we can *take* this asshole," one of them announced. "There are four of us and only one of him. Why are you listening to him?"

"He has a gun," Davy said, not even bothering to look at the one who had spoken. "Don't do anything more stupid than you have already, OK? I'd rather not have your brains splattered across my chest. Or the floor. Because I would just have to clean it up. On my hands and knees."

To me, he said, "I will keep my promise to you. Show some mercy, and I will be grateful to you for the rest of my life."

"I can get everything I want from you without your gratitude," I reminded him. "Still, I suppose three of these feral children would be a lot to take on at once. It's a lot of bother to train stock like this. So I'll tell you what, Davy, you can pick one of them. Pick one, and I will let the other two walk. But if I ever see them on the streets of San Francisco, they will be mine."

He was looking at his friends, wondering if he could do what I had ordered him to do.

"Pick one," I said, "or I take them all, now. Why not pick your favorite, Davy? Because you will be training him. To my specifications."

❖ ❖ ❖

In the end, I did not talk to them. They would never be able to reconcile their savior, tagger, rogue street-rat überfag Davy with the instrument I am now. I just took Puddle's hand to lead him away. He looked like the most frightened 12-year-old I had ever seen. We didn't speak. It was heart-wrenching to see one of my monkey boys so vulnerable. But he had this peace about him, like he'd known all along that he'd sacrifice himself for the others. I knew he had no future on the street. The other two were good; Scooter was too good. It was hard to look him in the face, but I had to let him know that this was meant to be. I knew they wouldn't be back. When my eyes showed how unwilling I was to leave, I could see their hearts leap to their deaths. Nothing would make sense to them for a very long time. Even I quit understanding this what seems like a lifetime ago. I just know the only thing I have ever been, truly been is His.

"Let him go," I heard my Master say. His revolver came up, and I dropped Puddle's hand before I really understood what was happening. My three would-be rescuers vanished into the darkness just as awareness dawned. Word would hit the street about my act of treachery. By allowing my friends to run away, He had erased any hope of returning to my former life.

"Welcome to Patrick Kelly Incorporated, partner," He drawled, and shut the thick wooden front door, cutting me off from the cold night air.

Skinned Alive
This Story Is for Tony Valenzuela

I met him traveling one of the dark conduits, the brave father who loved me enough to pick me up and take me from the cradle. Everybody knows about these unregulated outlets for outlaw desires, although some people think they are an urban legend, like the story about the Martian and the helicopter. Ever since we figured out how to turn the human body into pure information and beam it from one point to another, people have used the bright conduits for business and the dark for pleasure. Some of them are specialized—blonds only, maybe, or four inches and under. On some of them, you get a mix. Usually, the traveler and the host have mutual right of refusal. The conduit shows its charge in focus for a few split seconds, and if either of you hit the "no" button, it's on to the next stop. If you're really daring, you might try an "as-is" line, both host and traveler committed to hit the cradle with whoever pops up. The One Worlders are always trying to get the licentious conduits shut down. But they manage to stay open employing one legal dodge or another. The latest pretext is freedom of religion—these trysts are supposed to be sacrificial acts in honor of Dame Fortune, spinner of the Great Wheel.

I know a little bit about that, about tempting fate. More about bowing to Her. After all, I do choose to stay alive in this crazy time I was born into, even though I have no memory of reading the recipe and saying, "Hey, that's the meal for me, dump a big hot serving right here into my two cupped hands. Hang a big yellow bag of *that* up by the hospital bed of my sick life." If you believe what you read in the history books, there's never been a better time for *Homo sapiens* and *Tersiops truncatus*[i] (may *Pan troglodytes*[ii] and *Eschrichtius robustus*[iii] rest in peace). Thanks to the rainbow discoveries, we have a clean source of energy, which is good, considering that electricity causes cancer. The depopulation that followed the Bio-Wars solved quite a few other ecological problems. For one thing, it made it possible for us to spread out, each of us stewards of our own 50 or 100 square acres, where we must raise or hunt our own food and protect the habitat. The scientists still hive together in city colonies like this one, New Algonquin. They are so smart and have so much goodwill and are the object of such fervent prayer that surely they will soon succeed in cleaning up the terrible mess that we have all inherited.

I am not a scientist, but I live with them, since I am one of the people who make their Gaia-blessed task easier. I do a little of everything—making chamomile tea, rinsing out glassware from the lab, recording the results of certain tedious experiments, sweeping up. If I have any spare time, I am supposed to get one of the antique books out of the library. It really creeps me out to touch those pages made out of dead trees. But there are a lot of things that are not already on comp, so I manually scan things into the system.

These time-consuming menial chores are my raison d'être because I have a rare birth defect that affects the structure of my brain. I am not able to communicate with comp directly. I have to read things, slowly, one letter, word, sentence, paragraph, and page at a time, like Nagasaki Man, off a screen. If I want to talk to comp I have to use a keyboard, actually press the letters and punctuation marks with my fingers. I'm so slow they can't give me anything important to do, even though I'm much brighter than most blue-collar citizens. The work is boring. I guess the fact that a few of the scientists perv on us is supposed to be some sort of compensation. But it just gives me the Korean pox to know somebody is breathing heavily while they watch my fingers crawl up and down the blinking letters, cumbersome as a lobster's claw.

Especially Dr. Oleander. She comes up behind me so quietly

that I can't hear her, and she smiles when I jump to see her so close to my desk. I can't understand why it pleases her so much to scare me, to subtly crowd me like that. You'd think I would at least hear the ventilator going, but she's got it fine-tuned so it makes less noise than all the equipment in my office. Her suit is painted with green vines, purple flowers, yellow birds, and red tree frogs, you know how old people do that, and she's always offering to decorate mine, but I prefer its stark silver, black, and clear surfaces. It's my way of telling her I hate her. She loves to lecture me about quiet brain syndrome, as if I don't already know more about it than I want to know. Her voice gradually gets higher and higher as she talks about it, until the words run together in a mush of data. If she wasn't shrouded, I think she would be spraying me with fine droplets of spittle as she ranted. It's disgusting to even think about such a thing, isn't it?

Quiet brain syndrome. As if it were merely an exercise in serenity or a meditation technique. Have we always dealt with our tragedies by calling them something else? There are dozens of these horrors toting tags that sound like blessings. But the one that hits me where I live is called The Gentling. Those who have been gentled walk among us in lavender-tinted polysuits. They can never take them off. They live in them, work in them, eat and sleep and shit and piss in them. They have sex in them. The rest of us only go suited when we are going to interact with one another. We get to take our armor off in the privacy of our carefully filtered living quarters. For maximum health and safety, everyone lives alone. A gentle who takes off the suit receives a death sentence, even though this world has largely lost its appetite for bloodshed.

The gentles carry a disease that was created by the descendants of Nazi scientists, who had been enslaved by the Russians, then sold to an Islamic dictatorship, and spirited out of that country just before it was nuked back to the Stone Age. Exactly which nation sponsored the experiments that resulted in purp is unknown. Mass destruction is not kind to the bureaucracies that engineer it or to the records that could hold them accountable.

This plague is so deadly that the scientists who built it surely told themselves it would never be released, that its mere presence would serve as a deterrent even more powerful than the atomic bomb or the sirocco. They were not paying attention to the element in human nature which practically forces us, once we have sharpened a stick, to throw it at something to see how it will fly. But I don't mean to come across as a breast-beating member of the Weapon Breakers. Their guilt is too generic for my taste. If I am going to sweat from self-recrimination, let it be for a crime that is mine alone.

A hundred times more infectious than hepatitis B or narcoleprosy, we call it the purple plague because of the strange tint it leaves in the victims' eyes and skin. Hence the lavender suit, color-coded to instantly inform the beholder, regardless of class, caste, sex, education level, or ethnicity, what sort of coyote they are looking at. Oh, we've come a long way in dealing with it. Provided they receive prompt treatment, those who are infected no longer die in 90 days. They can expect half of the normal life span, which today hovers at 45, give or take five years. You can catch purp from someone who has it if they are a block away, unsuited. You don't need to touch them. Or perch on them. Or have them skewer you.

No, I don't know where it came from, this obsession that I have with it. I guess it started when I was a kid, watching newscasts of the Hierophant of the Sacred Androgyne delivering an impassioned speech about hope and solidarity while shim was ringed three-deep by hir pastel bodyguard. Peacekeepers, they call them. Nobody would risk tearing open one of those suits to get at the World Chair or any of the other caretakers and artists they protect. When purp kills you it's slow and nasty, the fragrant acid building up in your blood, burning and dissolving your tissues from within, leaving the central nervous system for last so you feel every precise minute of it. How poignant it is to see these poor victims of our poisoned world protecting the people who are struggling to cleanse us. When I did my Rosary of the Lost and Damaged, I always lingered the longest over the Peacekeepers' prayer, repeating it over and over as if it could somehow make me that pure and special.

It's not the only thing that's catching, just maybe the worst, so everybody knows if you want to have sex, you have to use the cradle. One of you lies down under the polyfilm, the other lies on top. Or you can flip the lattice so you can lie side by side. The only rule is, you never place bare skin on someone else's skin. Have you read one of those romance novels about a perfect couple whose courtship is shattered by an accidental, too-intimate touch? I have, lots of them. The lovers always turn out to be healthy in the end and get back together. Yes, it's predictable. But it tells me I'm not the only cit who gets congested by the thought of forbidden contact. So far, privacy laws have kept monitors out of the citizens' bedrooms. So nobody really knows how many people use the cradles and how many people…don't.

I think I'm allergic to the film. The few times I've tried to have sex under its protective umbrella, I break out into a bumpy, painful rash wherever the screen has touched me. The doctors say no one can be allergic to poly—it's perfectly inert and doesn't interact with human biology. They did give me some antihistamine gum, however. Or maybe it's just a placebo. My suit troubles me too, but I'm afraid to tell them that. Doctors have a mandate to report safety violations, and I don't know if that qualifies or not. I wear a thin cotton single underneath it. I chew the gum. And I hate the cradle.

So that was where I started, wondering if there was anybody like me, somebody who was left completely limp by having his mouth penetrated by a poly-coated tongue, much less a more sensitive orifice. Yeah, you can see through it. So what? You can't brush a lock of hair out of somebody's eyes. You can't feel his sweat slick across his belly or taste his armpits. I can't remember a time when I didn't yank off to thoughts of having my nipples rubbed a little raw by the fur on another man's torso. Look, if this is making you sick, you don't have to listen. Go back to the dark conduit. It will receive you with even less judgment than I have shown.

If you are going to stay, I will continue with my story. I figured if there was a conduit that catered to my taste, it would have to be the sort that you heard only rumors or dirty jokes about. But I had no idea how to find one. There certainly wasn't any clue at my own stainless steel home terminal. Then one day, pushing the mop just got to me so bad I had to purge in a hurry, so I visited a public link, an opaque booth that didn't even have enough room to lie down in it. The safety veil hung on a ceiling roller, waiting to be pulled down and secured for a stand-up encounter. For some reason, the graffiti caught my eye while I was shucking my suit. It didn't say anything, so it confused me. There were just these cryptic assortments of letters and numbers. Most cits simply told comp what they wanted. But all public comps have keypads to accommodate crips like me. What if they kept the dark conduits hidden by allowing access only through the letter board? Somebody had written, in neat block letters, s2s. Could that mean what I thought it meant? Maybe "skin-to-skin"? With shaking fingers, I punched the code.

The screen turned a completely different color and then showed a message that was not in standard conduit script. I anxiously scanned it. I was asked to apply my thumb print as certification that I was of legal age, 13 or over, and 100% healthy. I paused before pressing my flesh to the screen. I did not want my identity on record. Then I came to my senses. It was probably just a formality, like calling the "as-is" conduits "religious experiences." The message beeped at me, letting me know I had three more seconds to agree or lose my chance. I took a wad of gum out of my mouth and pressed it to the screen.

Not only was the warranty bogus, it didn't care if you had a real fingerprint or not. In another two seconds, a woman came through the conduit and into my arms. We didn't speak. We were both so excited that I forgot that I'm a man's man and a bottom besides. I put my nose into her hair, hoping to find a poem there, or at least a metaphor. But she did not smell like anything other than herself. And it occurred to me then that she was not to be compared to flowers or a trick of the weather; she was her own fact of nature. I did not know how two such different bodies would fit together, but she had worked out that puzzle before and taught me quickly. We were joined so briefly, I could not tell you if it was pleasure or pain I felt, keyed to her lock, a frenzied hostage. I had expected to feel like a wild animal, but I had never felt so…human. It was most peculiar. Astonishing yet mundane. She was gone before I could ask her any questions.

In the days that followed I had one panic attack after another, seeing every little hangnail as a harbinger of death. In between panic attacks I flogged my stick so hard I'm lucky I still have it. She had really been with me. She had taken my saliva into her mouth, my other fluids into her—you know. I don't want to name her receptivity. I don't know any name for those organs that wouldn't sound like something from a sermon. She was the only woman I'd ever had sex with, and I encountered her as another mortal, not as a goddess. That was the wonder of it. Perhaps there was a sort of holiness in the way we jostled one another, seeking ecstasy, but what would I know about anything sacred?

The next time I used a public terminal I took a chance and punched s2sm, figuring that might get me a male partner. After declining a series of fierce, lash-toting travelers or decoratively bound supplicants for my attention, I realized I might need to give the terminal more information. So I went for s2sman. That was the key that opened up a whole new world to me.

I was a wanton. I chewed on beards. I put toes in my mouth. Bathed armpits. Gnawed on necks. I let them lick the sides of my chest, slide their fingers down the crack of my ass. For some of them, that was as far as it went. I never forced anybody to risk more than he wanted to gamble. A few of them would let me put my face next to their crotches while they flogged. One of them spattered my face. I rubbed it into my cheeks before he could wipe me clean. I wanted to keep the smell and the texture with me for as long as possible. To me, the thick, salty cream was an emblem of generosity and freedom, nothing to be terrified about. But when I saw that man again, which happens sometimes, even on the dark conduits, he spurned me, and I knew I had gone too far for his notions of safety. No matter—I had other, more compliant partners.

Another—one I saved and replayed over and over again, alone in my bed, this pale golden man with bright red hair put a poly parachute over his piston and bounced me stupid. With the danger of his nipples drilling into my gloriously bare body, I had no problem gushing. Flowers do not mourn the loss of the honeybee more than I mourned the loss of his tongue lancing in and out of my mouth. Through the five days it took the itching and pain to go away, I had not one regret. I had rested in his bare arms. He had actually been deep inside me, in a way the cradle simply won't allow.

I must have been lucky because I never got sick. Not once. Not even a cold. I began to think that perhaps this was to be expected in a population of people who had so carefully protected themselves from contact with one another. Of course we were all healthy. When had we ever been given a chance to be anything else? Our food was organic. Our drinking water was relentlessly purified. We were born through plastic chutes—may we be preserved as Africa was not—to protect us from our own mothers' internal ecology. Breast-feeding is as illegal as making sugar.

But what about *them*, the ones who were not healthy? Why did I stand at the brink of the great canyon between us and yearn to throw myself across it? Well, why are there pale people among us who feel a vocation to become African, who wear the ancient tribal fashions and sometimes even speak those dead languages or practice obscure handicrafts? These people are held in the deepest contempt by the dark-skinned cits whose ancestors were forcibly removed from that doomed continent. Why are the white pretenders drawn to something they cannot have, an identity erased by AIDS and quicksickle? Why are there a few sad men who cannot accept the fact that most women are gender resisters or priestesses who have time and affection only for each other or our planetary mother? The remaining handful of women are in such demand that they are unreachable for anyone who is not very powerful. Why does an ordinary man waste his life in the harshest servitude, hoping in vain for a woman to see something special about him and raise him up so that their hearts can meet as equals?

Maybe we always throw the rope of desire to those we have lost, cast off, tossed overboard. Perhaps it's just the rotten part of my cannibalistic species which fouled its own nest and is guilty of a million other stupid and self-destructive acts. All I know is, as I embraced these naked strangers, in my mind's eye I painted them all a different shade of purple. I closed my eyes, not because I was overwhelmed with bliss or love but because it helped me to visualize them as purps. May Terra cleanse me as she cannot cleanse the silver rain.

I got bolder and whispered a hint of this to some of my partners. And I found a few of them who liked to pretend one of us was a Peacekeeper unsuited. It was such a dangerous fantasy, we could only stammer out a few words of it to one another. Just the mutual confession of this lunacy was enough to flush us out. But nobody had a clue about how I could get closer to the real thing. I didn't dare ask, actually. Maybe because I wasn't ready yet. It's not the kind of trick you can do more than once. Even though the delay made me frantic with frustration, I think it was just a part of the whole thing, a preliminary to savage joy, prolonged until I wanted to scream.

I had discovered by now that the clandestine codes worked just as well at my home terminal as they did in public conveniences, so I embarked upon a campaign to conjure up a sigil for my own damnation. If the gentles had their own dark conduit, surely I would be able to access it, if only by trial and error. PEACE did not work, or any variation on that word. Nor did GENTLE. Both root words put me midstream with vague and tender people who wanted to place crystals as well as the polyfilm of the cradle between our copulating bodies, or sit touching suited knees while we chanted and vibrated together. Not exactly what I was panting for. I began to feel as if I was in a war with the code, a battle I would never win. Maybe that's why I punched in DETENTE.

Three cards, all of them dragons! A lavender suit came into focus. Came into my room, taking all the air out of my laboring lungs. Within it I could make out the features of a man roughly my own age. He would be getting close to the end, then, when the treatments would no longer preserve his life. He seemed startled to see me. When I explained my purpose, he was horrified. This conduit was only for peacekeepers who wanted to get naked with other purps. It had never occurred to me that they might want to unsuit and lather up one another! Only the fact that this too was illegal kept him from turning me in, I'm sure. But one word he said to me stuck in my mind. He called me a bug-chaser.

I had a new code word to try. That ebony river unloaded me the cargo of an indignant herm with a heaving bosom and a delicate penis who seemed completely undone by my pink, unsuited self. "You can't give me the gift!" shim snarled, melting back into the dark matrix that had brought hir to my chambers. Hir face had been tattooed to turn the butterfly pattern of lupus-3 into something more glamorous. The pale yellow and blue wings seemed to linger in the air long after shim had been swept away from the cove of my room.

This was as hard as evacuating Hawaii. But I tried again, ringing the changes on GIFT. Most of the conduits that opened to this sesame were occupied by citizens with an entirely novel fetish. They wanted to pay me or be paid. To pay someone is to compensate them for goods or services with a token which represents value. Yes, it's a difficult concept. But there really was a time when people didn't automatically receive what they needed or routinely agree to do necessary work—before comp made currency obsolete. I didn't mind the squares of plastic or the disks of metal, and some of the beads were lovely. But the paper, printed with arcane symbols of exchange—feh. I don't know where you would get something like that, and I don't want to know. Books are bad enough.

GIFT4U, I think, was the key that opened the door to the palace of my libido. Maybe that's right. It doesn't matter. Even if it worked then, it won't anymore. You know the password is changed every few days. Sometimes every hour. By now I was so desperate that I wouldn't have cared if the matrix gave me a female purp. I was frantic to simply stand next to the tinted suit and look through its visor to find the lonely, longing, elite human being within its isolating embrace. But it turns out there aren't very many women who have this plague. Some animals being more equal than others, the female of our species is even more heavily guarded from contamination than the male. Healthy ova can be cloned, after all.

He was perfect for me. But then, how could he be otherwise? Because I wanted what he carried, invisibly circulating in his body fluids and tissues, I adapted my libido to his visage. He became my type because he was deadly. His black beard, short dark hair, stocky torso, and muscular legs brought me to my knees because they belonged to a Peacekeeper. A blond, a redhead, or the fronds of a Martian hybrid could have done the same.

During that first visit, he would not unsuit for me. In fact, he made me go and find my own carapace and climb into it. He would only talk to me, sit close to me, allow me to bump my shell against his own. But he memorized the address of my cell before he left. And he promised he would return, after I had a chance to think this through.

On his next visit, we stood face to face, both suited, palm to palm, toe to toe, forehead to forehead. I mimicked each of his gestures as he swam in a graceful ballet of self-stimulation. It was his voice in my ear that made my dry stem flower in my fist. He talked about how intense it is to purge when you know that you have only a few more years to live. About how sad it makes you to see the others, the uninfected, walk around in plain suits, suits they can remove once they are alone. How heart-stopping it is to catch a rare glimpse of a child, something that anyone would find memorable, but in his case it brought actual tears to his eyes. He talked about how you know when you've been infected because you can watch your skin changing color as the preprions run like lightning through your system.

In subsequent visits I learned so much from him. How the suit drains the savor from your food, so that everything winds up tasting like murky water. Some of the famous and powerful people he had escorted and kept safe. I never would have guessed that the secretary of our city had a secret penchant for arranging cut flowers. I'd heard rumors about the singer Lucien, but he had actually seen her collection of antique toys, running on batteries. Despite the excitement of a wisp or two of scandal, he found it very boring to be a bodyguard. He described the deep aches and pains in your joints that follow each dose of the medication. The constant physical workout you have to engage in to keep your body from wasting away because the preprions are stealing your vitality. How lusty you are, constantly, yet also filled with lassitude. The temptation to touch someone, just once, before you die. The endless speculation about whether it is safe to caress another purp. The knowledge that it is illegal, fatally illegal. And the choice that always looms—whether to go by euthanasia and chance depriving yourself of a year or month or week of life that you might have had or to wait for acidulation, which is irreversible once it begins, and proof against any narcotic or nerve block.

He also told me that the only way people get purp any more is from someone who already has it. That almost every Peacekeeper had deliberately pursued infection. The infectious agent no longer circulates at random in the environment. I found that more shocking than the ecocrimes you see on that silly but very popular program, *They Made Mother Nature Weep*. You know what I mean—a clandestine greenhouse full of roses or an antique music box running on a cylinder full of toxic chemicals or a poor animal some fool has tried to domesticate. If everyone knew the truth about the Peacekeepers, there would be a huge outcry. The tragic and romantic reputation of the corps would be irretrievably tarnished. I suppose I should have been disillusioned, but this harsh truth just fed the wicked part of me that was determined to have my way with him. I knew for certain now that I was *not* the only seeker on this path. Why should I be forbidden a delight that so many others had not scrupled to taste?

I told him everything about myself as well. How reading had hamstrung my education. The frustrations of my cleanup work.

How ironic it seemed to me to try to keep one small corner of the world pristine when so much of it had been irrevocably sullied. My long search to find him. My obsession. Always my obsession. To have what he had. To be a part of him. To carry him with me, inside of me, forever. I would gladly trade the second half of my life away, if only the time I had left would not be quite so lonely.

It took me months to persuade him to be my midwife. I knew all along that he would eventually agree, I think, and he knew as well. But there were formalities we had to go through first, like the complicated steps of a minuet. The dance would not come out all right at the end unless we followed each twist and turn, dip and kick of the chorus, to confront ourselves when the orchestra fell silent. Besides, we would only have that one opportunity to gratify what had become an unbearable pull toward one another. Think of it as foreplay.

Meanwhile he was getting inexorably nearer to the point of no return, when the disease would eat him one cell at a time. Just how close that was we had no way of knowing.

We did it the old-fashioned way, on my birthday. I lay down on my back upon the cradle. With a sharp, archaic knife, I carefully cut away the polyfilm from its lattice above me. After today I would no longer live in these quarters. I got an erection just sawing the hated thing out of its holder, permanently wrecking it. My savior stood close to me so I could run my hands over the suit that would never stand between us again. He could not undo it himself. He could not see the catches or reach them. It was up to me to figure it out, undo the wisdom of protection and let loose love's folly. Before I pressed the last button and turned the last knob, I looked at him with a question in my eyes. He looked so frightened. His mouth was a red slash in the black curls of his beard, his lips tight and thin. I would have taken pity on him and stopped if he had given me the word. But he gathered his courage, showed me his teeth, and told me to go on. Deprived of energy, our translucent pastel enemy fell about his ankles, and he stepped out of it, then lay on top of me.

Until he made that gesture, I had not known exactly how he intended to give me his gift. If all I wanted was a lethal dose of preprions, we didn't need to do any more than share the same room, unsuited. He had never told me for certain that he was willing to be my stud. I had not dared to hope for this much, naked contact along the entire length of both of our bodies. *I could smell him.* His dark coarse fuzz tangled with my own. I stroked him with trembling hands, feeling exalted and yet shy and uncertain. But he did not have to tell me that he found my touch pleasing. I could tell by the goose bumps that came up along his flanks and the way his stem swelled alongside my own. He let me suckle at his nipples, and I wanted to swoon when we lay face-to-face again and I could feel their wet points against my own crinkled, tiny nubs. My ritualistic fantasy about these four points of contact was a script that we were enacting. But all those years of pounding my own pubes had not prepared me for the matter-of-fact reality of clinging to him, skin to skin. He even let me put his prod into my mouth, and no matter how brief that contact was, I will never forget the raw, real taste of him. A thick, salty water welled up out of the hole in the center of his cock head. Each time I lapped at him, I got more and more excited, thinking about what was coming into my body along with this viscous aperitif. The preprions had seasoned the products of his body the way a chef will alter the taste of a dish until it reaches perfection.

A body gel is issued to enhance rocking in the cradle. We used it for a blasphemous purpose. Without gloves—without gloves!—he inserted the nozzle into me and squeezed, filling me, preparing me, marking me. I wanted him so much that it felt as if every muscle in my body had gone as rigid as my sex. Except for the little mouth that cried out for him. That part of me was trembling with weakness, a silent bell awaiting the clapper that will bring it to life. He slid into me on a slick sheet of euphorics and glycerin. Maybe it was just the knowledge that I would not have to pay for this intimacy with a week of hives. Or maybe it was the fact that this would only happen once in my life that made me open to him as deeply as the woman in the public link had yielded to me. There was a little pain, but it was nothing compared to the huge ache around my heart that was being assuaged. He was with me, he was actually truly *with me*. I felt as if I had never been fed before. If I close my eyes, I can still see his forearms, one on either side of my head, straining to hold up the weight of his rocking body. I can evoke the way my thighs ached, wrapped around his short and powerful legs. I can recapture the puffs of humid, heated air between us, where our sweat had mingled and created a third intoxicating scent.

His timing was exquisite. Just as I noticed the first flush of color gathering under my toenails, he baptized me. He stopped moving while he arrived within me. We both stopped moving and paid homage to our courage and stupidity, which would have been easy to mistake for love. I was born again out of the gushing jets of his desire, being remade in his image. A gentle. A Peacekeeper. A purp. The words of the rosary came to my lips, and as I repeated them, I poured out my gratitude in burning ribbons of sanctity. He had his fist wrapped around my wand and somehow managed to catch every bit of liquid I hurled at him. He put his fingers to his lips and tasted my offering, then smeared the rest across his chest, where our nipples had collided. It was beautifully done.

He did not leave me immediately. But he did reach out and set the timer beside the cradle. One hour. That was all the time I had to make my decision. Would I call the medics for intervention, or would I lie here and let the gift I had received incinerate me? Given how little time he had himself, I was touched when he lingered for a bit of conversation. Even though he had finished the job I had asked him to do, he kissed me anyway. Let me know I was special. I swore I could feel the weight of his presence within me, where I would harbor a part of him forever, to comfort me for his loss.

Then I helped him back into the suit. Its seams had turned bright red, evidence that the seal had been broken. I did not ask him where he would go or what he would do. It was pointless, really. If anybody saw him in public, he would be apprehended. Even if he managed to return to his own quarters unobserved, that was no sanctuary. The medics would take samples of the preprions from my body. They would decipher the genetic signature of the particular strain of purp I had been infected with, and they would trace it to him. "Take care," I thought I heard him whisper as the dark conduit reclaimed him.

I was alone with the delicious dilemma I had worked so hard to be in. If I called for prophylaxis, I doomed my lover. If I did not call for it, I doomed myself. Even though we were both going to die anyway, it was a pretty pickle to be in. Even remembering it now, I have to unclog my pipe. As you will, soon, yes, I won't make you wait forever. But not yet. Not till I say so.

Do as I do. Imagine that the lining of your suit is the lining of my inner recesses, the mysterious cave that you long to flood with neon light. Think what it would feel like. Imagine yourself in that quandary, poised between murder and suicide. Moral equivalents? Perhaps. The One Worlders think so.

I know it's a very pleasurable fantasy. If it didn't scare you rigid, you wouldn't be here with me today. But fulfilling this fantasy means the end of all the pursuit and posturing we indulge in for the sake of an eruption of sludge. What pleasure could possibly be great enough to justify the murder of all future delights? It's only an embrace. One simple, face-to-face, bare-skinned hug.

Be very sure before you ask me to fulfill your last wish. You tempt me so much. I think it is your ignorance that makes you beautiful to me. Your brave vulnerability. You must want me very, very much if you are willing to give up your life simply to see me naked. I can't pretend I'm not terribly flattered.

We're not going to do anything in a hurry, changeling child of mine. If you asked me for advice, I'd tell you to stay in the cradle. Remain a son of the age that orphaned us both. Don't kick and push and yowl to be reborn into my arms. I am no mother wolf, suckling abandoned human cubs. I am Charon, and this is the pole

SKINNED ALIVE

with which I propel my ferry across the river Styx. I am the meathook that pins Inanna to the wall of Ereshkigal's abattoir. I am a wicker man, reaching for a torch.

And it's not too late to save your own skin.

i The bottle-nose dolphin.
ii The chimpanzee.
iii The gray whale.

Parting Is Such Sweet Sorrow

Ulric stood in the living room of his Victorian mansion, using a small crowbar to pry the top and sides off a crate that contained his harpsichord. His long black hair was getting in the way, so he stopped to scrape it back and bind it in a ponytail. If he had been able to sweat, his beard and mustache would have been damp with perspiration. And if water would have done him any good, he would probably be chugging a quart of it by now. Other crates bearing stickers from Europe stood nearby, waiting to be unpacked. It was good to be home, back in San Francisco.

Not that Amsterdam had not been fun. The weather was cool and damp, and social attitudes were so liberal that sometimes, if he kept his eyes and mind out of focus, he could almost believe that he was still in the city of gaudily painted Victorians and buff young men. It seemed as if the whole gay world had fallen in love with San Francisco and tried to imitate its sensual openness, its lascivious pride. Very little distinguished the adult bookstores with their glory hole–riddled booths, the backroom bars, and the bathhouses in Amsterdam, Paris, Berlin, London, and Madrid from the militantly masculine and hopelessly homosexual haunts of Baghdad by the Bay.

But there were always these annoying differences that plucked at Ulric, distracting him even in the middle of a hunt and making him homesick for the city where a very butch bartender had helped him to conceal a kill, then warned him not to return until things had cooled off. He would be flirting with a long-haired beauty in a coffee shop, for example, and the man would say something in Dutch. Although cafés in San Francisco reeked of pot smoke too, they didn't have 13 different brands of hash on a menu posted above the espresso machines. San Francisco had more than its share of erotic entertainment, but nothing like the boy brothels that floated down the canals, barges full of choice meat. Ulric had always been fond of hunting junkies, especially in New York's Alphabet City. He loved their furtiveness and shame. It made any interaction with them seem like espionage. But there was little of that melodrama in Amsterdam, where it was public policy to turn a blind eye to possession of narcotics for personal use. Ulric never visited the heroin quarter of the city unless he had more on his mind than feeding that day. Nothing bored him more than the posturing of addicts who believed their need set them apart from other people and made them special. Or was it just that he resented the similarity between himself and them, the fact that an analogous hunger drove him with crippling intensity?

The flight over had been stressful. Ulric's muscles still made cranky comments about being confined inside a trunk. He needed a safe container to protect himself from harm while he slept the sleep of the dead. But during the dark hours of the night, he was as awake as any other man, and it was tedious beyond belief to have nothing to do but count the studs that held the trunk together. The vampire cats who were his guardians and companions had been irate and refused to entertain him. He might have booked a passenger seat and flown with everyone else, but he was afraid a perky and conscientious stewardess would notice his total lethargy and decide that he was dead. The thought of some self-appointed hero cutting him open with grubby airline cutlery to give him open-heart massage was disgusting.

He had tried flying as a passenger once, but the big dark cloak he had wrapped himself in to sleep had drawn unwanted attention from the other passengers, and they were also startled when he applied duct tape to the window to keep it shut. The controlling powers that normally kept him safe from mortal malice or curiosity didn't function while he was asleep, so he couldn't count on them to make everybody draw their shades and leave him alone.

He could endure daylight, but he didn't like it much, and if his sleep was interrupted by the sun, he would awaken in such hunger that no one would deplane alive.

In a similar predicament, Adulfa, his charming (not!) sister, would no doubt have taken one of the many animal forms that were her forte and simply flown or swum across the ocean under her own steam. Or she would have boarded an ocean liner, stayed on it until she had fed on all the passengers and crew, then sunk the damn thing and taken bird or bat form to wing a few miles to the harbor. With her great power to make people forget what they had seen, Adulfa could afford to be fond of slaughter on a grand scale. But Ulric had only one animal form, and wolves did not take to the sea like pinnipeds. He could compel people to do things they normally would not do, and make them forget what they had seen, but he shrank from intimate contact with their minds. Afterward, Ulric always found his mind cluttered by unwelcome bits and pieces of their lives and personalities. Perhaps Adulfa was able to alter mortals in a more surgical fashion.

But Adulfa was not here now. Ulric knew it because he felt happy and comfortable. There had been one vampire in residence, a young and confused prostitute who had probably been created accidentally. At any rate, she had been abandoned by her maker, and it was no problem for Ulric to dispatch her. He liked killing other vampires when he didn't know them personally. That sort of blood lasted longer than a day. He might have as much as a week in which he woke up without feeling the pulsing in his temples and his gut which told him he had to feed right away.

There were other vampires across the bay, in Oakland, in Berkeley. The natural aversion of their kind for one another made vampires space themselves out, as other sorts of predators do, so that each had an adequate territory to meet his or her needs. In cities, where population density was higher, vampires tended to cluster more closely together than they did in smaller towns or rural areas. But Ulric was famous for forcing other vampires to give him a wide berth. He would tolerate no challenges to his dominance in a city as small and lovely as San Francisco. She belonged to him; her streets were his to caress and her hills were his to embrace. And all her people were under his patronage. The only vampire he could share a city with was his sister. When it pleased her to crowd him, there was nothing he could do to stop her.

One nice thing about cities was that people moved around. Ulric had already checked out his neighbors, and there was only one old man still living there who had seen him during his previous tenancy. It was easy to make him forget someone he had only glimpsed a time or two. So Ulric kept the same house, rejoicing in the shipments of antique furniture, Persian rugs, and first editions that arrived from Europe. Each time a crate arrived and he opened and unpacked it, he felt as if he were coming home again. Soon everything would look just as it had the night when he had been told to leave San Francisco. Well, plus a harpsichord, a set of originals by Aubrey Beardsley, a Tiffany lamp, and several stained-glass windows that would have to be installed somewhere. You couldn't expect him to be gone for six years and stop shopping. That would be inhumane. He wrestled the musical instrument into a corner and dusted off his hands. The rest of the boxes could be dealt with tomorrow. Night had fallen an hour ago, and he wanted to go out.

The cats were also glad to be back. They loved the backyard of Ulric's Victorian, and now that it was overgrown, wild creatures had made their home there. They might catch anything, perhaps even a raccoon. "Just leave the skunks alone," he warned them as he let Anastasia, Luna, and Charley out to forage. Russian Blue, Abyssinian, and black-and-white tomcat sent him identical images, cats licking their butt holes with great absorption, to tell him what they thought of his fussing.

Ulric hoped that no one in his neighborhood let their dog run free. The cats would pack together to hunt an obnoxious canine. Charley was going to be left behind to guard the house while Ulric went out on reconnaissance. Before he left, the vampire opened a vein in his wrist to let the long-haired black-and-white tomcat feed. All the cats could use a tonic after being cooped up for so long at high altitudes. He shook his head to rid himself of the memory of his last kill's welcoming smile. She had been so glad to see one of her own kind at last, someone who could explain the painful metamorphosis that had changed her body and given her needs she did not understand. She had thought that Ulric was going to take care of her. The nasty feel of her fake leather jacket still clung to the palms of his hands.

The purring cat at his wrist brought him back to himself. Life was not fair, was it? Even if he had wanted to become her master, Ulric knew she would have been hopeless as a student. She was not independent enough to endure immortality. And Ulric was not about to burden himself with responsibility for an inferior. A relationship of that sort was slavery for the ostensibly dominant partner.

He had purchased a new motorcycle yesterday. But before he went to straddle it and conquer the night, Ulric picked up Charley and held him. He loved the big white ruff that outlined the male cat's chest. His fluffy fur made his big feet look even larger, and between the ebony toes sprouted tufts of more white fur. The cat had a long spray of thick white whiskers that pricked Ulric's face. Charley went limp in his arms, a sure sign of deep contentment. Ulric sometimes carried him around the house for hours, over his shoulder, while Charley purred and drooled. Ulric hoarded the feeling of Charley's vibrating body against his chest, storing up the animal's deep love for him in his own undying heart. In a mental picture that included smells as well as visuals, Charley told Ulric that he loved him as much as a bowl full of goldfish, though he would love him even more once the fish tank was set up. The amorality and pitiless nature of the cats was a great comfort to Ulric. They took the sort of joy in life eternal that sometimes eluded their formerly human caretaker.

Ulric put Charley down and dusted cat hair off his leathers. The last time he had been here, he had gone in for a lot of fringe, if memory served. Now he was into a sleeker look, and wore an expensive, body-hugging racer's jumpsuit. It was amazing how persistent cat fur was. How often had he interrupted a killing bite so he could brush a cat hair from his victim's neck? Almost reluctantly, he went to the garage to start his brand-new bike. It was strange to travel out into the world without being driven by the great hunger. He almost wanted to stay home and putter with his things, alphabetize his tapes and albums, reshelve the books according to topic, author, and age.

But he knew what he had really come to San Francisco to do. He had come to see Alain, the bartender whose shotgun blast had obliterated the signs of Ulric's feeding on the body of a young man who had been snatched from the urinals and taken into the alley to provide his nightly feast. He still got goose bumps when he remembered the cool tones of Alain's voice, informing him that the kills he had scored in the Eagle's Lair had been good for business. It wasn't like a mortal to see him in a positive light or have such callous feelings toward his own kind.

Unlike a hundred other mortals who panicked or denied his true nature, Alain had seen him. And he had not flinched, not turned away, not denied the truth or tried to run from it. Surely six years was enough time to let the titillating scandal about a South of Market murderer subside. Alain had said he could come back. And Ulric wanted to see him, but he was also afraid. Mortals changed so much in such a short time. Besides, Ulric knew nothing about him except that he was a bartender at the Eagle's Lair. He didn't even know his last name.

Lacking any other place to start, he went back to his old haunts South of Market. The new Harley handled easily, and Ulric realized the BMW he had been driving in Amsterdam had needed its front fork aligned. Oh, well. The student he had tossed the keys and papers to would have to worry about that. Ulric was at the Eagle's Lair before he was aware of much time passing. Unfortunately, the place was now boarded up, the sign faded, the back room no doubt full of ghosts who still hadn't found a trick for the night. Shit. This quest wasn't going to be as smoothly plotted as a Falcon video, was it?

Ulric turned the bike and went down Folsom Street, looking for other places he remembered. Most of them had closed their doors. A few of the bars had simply changed their names. The Combat Zone was the OK Corral now, and Ulric shuddered as he listened to the country music that poured out of its doors as faux cowboys came and went. Appalling stuff, that, the aural equivalent of possum cooked in molasses. The boots were nice, though. Colorful. Ulric liked a bit more of a heel on his boots than this century found appropriate for men.

Finally he spotted another man on the street who was wearing leather. Two men, actually, a well-groomed couple in their 40s. The top was in leather pants, a leather uniform shirt, and a cap with a thin chain about its brim. The bottom was in chaps and a leather vest and had an attack dog's choke-chain draped loosely around his neck. Under the chaps he wore a jockstrap, nothing else. Ulric made a little face. What use was a collar that did not lock? Still, these men were the closest he had seen to brothers in an hour and a half of searching, so he let his bike drift to a crawl beside them and said, "Good evening."

"Evening," the top said, turning to face him. Ulric adored his gray handlebar mustache and big sideburns. The pocket of the uniform shirt bulged with hefty brown cigars, which smelled wonderful but did not compensate for the lack of a big bulge farther down. The bottom turned also and waited a little behind his master, although he leaned over to make sure he got a good look at Ulric's body. *Smack that boy,* Ulric thought impatiently, then focused his attention once more on the older of the two.

"I just got into town," he explained. "Where's the party? Seems like it's been hidden pretty good."

The top chuckled. "Eager for action, huh?"

Ulric gave him a look that would have made him step back if he was any smarter. "Oh, yes," he said finally. "Action."

"Well, you can't do any better than the Bear Cave," the man with the bodacious mustache said. "But it's not on the main drag." He gave Ulric directions to a side street. "We're headed that way ourselves," he said, and put a hand out to drag his boy forward. "Wait for us, and we'll buy you a drink. Welcome you to San Francisco in style."

Ulric did not say yes or no. He just nodded, raised his hand, and sped away. Could it be that in this thriving queer metropolis there was only one leather bar? What had happened to this town? Back in 1975, he had been aware that many of the butch men who stood around in hundreds of dollars worth of cowhide couldn't wait to take all that hot, cumbersome clothing off the minute they got home with a trick. The number of sadomasochists, as opposed to the number of men who simply liked the masculine look of leather, had been small. Could it be that leather was no longer a fashionable fad? Was he going to have to go hunting in preppy sweater bars?

Shuddering at that humiliating thought, Ulric raced to the location the couple on Folsom Street had given him. He parked his bike between a little Suzuki and a good-sized Yamaha that had seen better days and went in, eager to inhale the scent of beer, cigar smoke, piss, and sweat that colored and thickened the air of such places.

There it was in abundance, and Ulric's nostrils drank it in like wine. He took off his gloves, tucked them under the epaulet of his jacket, and went to the bar. There were two men behind it, but neither of them was Alain. He ordered a single-malt scotch that he could not drink, just to enjoy the incense of its fiery aroma. The young man who brought it was pretty in a common way and clearly thought himself a great beauty. The silver bar pinned to his leather vest said "Billy." Ulric scanned the patrons of the bar and was bitterly disappointed to see that Alain was not among them. He got the bartender's attention again by holding out a $50 bill and leaned toward his ear. "I'm looking for somebody," he said, and the upstart laughed.

"You came to the right place," the bartender said, and made a grand gesture that included everyone in the place.

"No," Ulric said emphatically, slamming one hand on the bar.

Billy jumped away. Ulric summoned him closer with a crooked finger. "I am looking for a particular man," Ulric hissed. "An old friend. Someone I lost touch with a few years ago. I need to find him now." He gave the bartender the limited information he had and was delighted to see comprehension dawn in Silly Billy's weakly handsome features.

"Why, that's one of the owners," Billy said. "He doesn't come around much anymore. Sometimes he's here on weekends."

"Where does he live?" Ulric demanded.

"Well, I can't just give you his address," Billy protested. "I mean, I'm not even sure I know it. It would be worth my job to give you his telephone number."

"Then give him mine," Ulric said through clenched teeth. He wrote it down on one of the cards the bar provided its customers. It said, "Here I am falling in love with you and I don't even know your name _____ or telephone number _____." Billy took the card with the tips of his fingers, and Ulric suddenly knew that he was in love with Alain and not about to pass another man's telephone number on to him. As if this puppy could endure what Alain's lust demanded! Furious, Ulric went into the young man's mind and took the information he wanted.

But first he found out that Billy the bartender had about six more months to live. His death would have something to do with the red marks on his chest, marks that looked almost like bruises, except that they were raised. Coming back to himself, Ulric had an ugly moment in which the vapid face behind the bar had turned into a grinning skull. He turned away to escape this macabre vision, and the consciousness he had opened was invaded by information about everyone in the bar.

All of these men were sick. Well, not all of them. Perhaps half a dozen were whole. But the rest would die sometime over the next year, mostly of pneumonia. Ulric turned and almost ran for the door. He collided with the couple who had directed him to the Bear Cave, and he knew for a fact that the master would barely have time to bury his boy before he himself was in the hospital. He would find himself dying of an infection that was not supposed to be fatal, something he caught from the bright, jabbering tropical birds he loved to keep.

It normally took a lot to turn Ulric's stomach, but this onslaught of death in a place where he had hoped to renew his own life was just too much. He muttered an incoherent apology to the master, handed his boy back to him, and darted out the door.

"Daddy, what's wrong with that man?" the boy asked.

"I don't know, son," said the master. "I'd rather know he's crazy now, though, than find out after we took him home. Go get your old man a beer, now, and try to do it without shaking your ass at every big dick in this place."

It took Ulric two tries to start his Harley. Too bad the people who made these things could never get certain details right, like making them start up when you turned the key. Finally he kicked it alive, and the violent gesture calmed him down. Some of the shaking went away as the big bike's vibrations went through his hands, up his arms, and into the rest of his body. He went back to Folsom, got his bearings, and took Howard Street back toward the Eagle's Lair. Alain had bought a building close to the bar. There were three apartments in the building. He lived on the top floor.

Ulric parked outside the somewhat dilapidated facade of the building and went to the front door. There were buzzers for each apartment, but the front door was unlocked, so he simply went in. The stairs were a nuisance, but he bolted up them, more and more angry with himself for staying away so long. Why let Alain send him away in the first place, hmm? Vampire reflexes were so much quicker than mortal ones, it wouldn't have been that risky to take the gun away from him. If only he had dragged Alain out of the alley and taken him home! When you lived forever, it was too easy to lose touch with mortal frailty, the brevity of their lifespans. Ulric cursed himself in the medieval Germanic dialect of his boyhood, a language he used only when he was very upset or surprised.

Then he was at Alain's front door, and he did not know what to do. He wanted to break it down, but that would be crass and might attract unwanted attention. He gently rattled the knob. This door was locked. Ulric shrugged and rapped it hard with his knuckles.

There was no response. But he could feel warmth inside the apartment, the heat of a human body. So he knocked again, more sharply this time, leaning into it. Someone on the other side opened the door abruptly, and Ulric stumbled in.

"What's your goddamn hurry?" Alain snapped, then he saw who had troubled his day off. "Well, speak of the devil," he said in an awed tone of voice, and grinned. Ulric found himself being picked up and vigorously hugged, an embrace that would have cracked a normal man's ribs. Then Alain was kissing him, the black stubble on his cheeks scraping Ulric's face. His tongue was big; his mouth tasted like sex and cigar smoke. Ulric petted his shaved head (more coarse black stubble there) and massaged the big muscles in Alain's broad shoulders. He had not been wearing a shirt, just a pair of dirty 501's, so Ulric could run his hands down the planes of muscle that outlined his back. There were more tattoos than there had been when they last met, and the rings in Alain's nipples were a bigger gauge.

When Alain was done smooching him, he put him down, and Ulric gasped. He had not been able to expand his chest to draw a full breath for several minutes. Alain was talking a mile a minute, and Ulric was having trouble following it all. The phrase "you bastard" appeared frequently. "How the hell did you ever find me?" Alain demanded.

"The Bear Cave—Billy—" he gasped, and Alain nodded.

"I should can his weasly little ass for handing out personal information, but I'm so goddamn glad to see you, it can wait until tomorrow. What can I get you? I know it's early, but let's have a drink. Or would you rather smoke a little bud?"

Ulric gave him a look that said, "Be real."

"Oh, no, I guess you wouldn't." Alain stood three feet away, chewing his full lower lip, trying to think of some other form of hospitality he could offer his strange visitor. Ulric had a few moments to examine the furnishings of the room, which were simple but expensive, all the furniture made of oak and upholstered in brown leather. While he was distracted, Alain advanced upon him, embraced him a little more gently this time, and began to unzip his leathers. "Get your clothes off, man," he said impatiently. "I'm not going to let you get away this time."

If Ulric had been able to weep, he would have been in tears. His sexual encounters with mortals had been brief, controlled affairs. It was hard to let go when you had to keep your true nature a secret. Thank the horned god for the vampire blood he had ingested less than two days ago. It made it possible for him to be erect between Alain's hands without feeding on him first. The experience of being undressed and fondled was terrifying. Ulric found himself hyperventilating, straining to get away and straining to get closer to the big man who had gone straight to the heart of a hunger that was much more difficult to satisfy than a mere need for blood.

Then Alain had picked him up again and was taking him into another room. Ulric once again felt the panicky sensation of wanting to escape and wanting to have this moment last forever. He was being held, comforted, practically abducted by a handsome, brutal man who knew he was a vampire and wanted him anyway. He stared wildly around the room, trying to distract himself. It was a cross between a bedroom and a dungeon. There was equipment hanging on all of the walls, workmanlike stuff that was obviously used frequently. There were a couple of posters, framed, from bars that Ulric remembered, places where he had found sweet young men who tasted of springtime and workouts in the gym. On his way into the room, Alain had punched a button on his tape player, and the big reel had started to turn, surrounding them with the spacy sound effects and insistent beat of queer disco, the kind of raunchy, high-tech music straight people were afraid to dance to.

Alain dumped him on the bed, wound his hands in Ulric's long black hair, and stretched out on top of him. By the way their bodies sank into the mattress, Ulric guessed it was a waterbed. Heated, fortunately. Then Alain was kissing him again, taking the time to do it right, and Ulric almost came from the wonderful feeling of having his mouth explored with so much ruthless tenderness. He dared to put his hand on the buttons of Alain's fly and ease them out of their holes. When he palmed Alain's erection, the bartender groaned and dug his tongue so deeply into Ulric's mouth, he was about to hit his tonsils. Ulric had seen Alain's cock a time or two years before, when he took a piss at the Eagle's Lair. The Prince Albert was still there, the thick ring that went through his piss hole and came out just below the rim of his cock head. But he also had a series of smaller rings that went down the underside of his cock and a couple in his ball sac. Figuring anybody who liked to get pierced this much wouldn't be able to do without a certain classic ornament, Ulric reached a little further back and found the guiche that pierced Alain's perineum. When he tugged on it, Alain's cock jumped and his precome stained Ulric's thighs.

His own cock was painfully rigid. Alain was stroking it with one hand and ran his thumb across the head. Ulric made himself meet Alain's gaze, saw the question that made one of his eyebrows go up. "I don't do that," he explained. "I mean, I come, and I come really hard, but it's dry. No jizz."

Alain shrugged and began to play with Ulric's nipples. His broad thumbs were capable of small, delicate motions, and Ulric felt his pelvis lurching forward, toward Alain, driven by the arousal that was heating up his chest. Alain, sadist that he was, quit toying with Ulric's nipples and stuck his fingers in his mouth. He felt his pointed fangs, then stuck another finger in, and moved them in and out. "Did you ever think of getting your tongue pierced?" Alain asked. "It's already a wild trip, kissing you with those big, sharp canines. But a ball in your tongue would be too much, I'd come just from swapping spit with you."

"I don't know if my body would hold a piercing," Ulric said, trying to sound thoughtful and objective. The truth was that the idea of it frightened him to death (well, not quite that much). "Does it hurt much?" he asked, trying not to sound timid.

Alain wasn't fooled, and he laughed so hard, Ulric thought he might suffer internal damage. "Oh, what a big old chicken you are," Alain guffawed. "Mr. Nightmare, creeping around in shadows, has to catch and kill his own dinner every goddamn day, and he's afraid to get a little old needle stuck through his tongue. What would you do if I made a big fucking hole in the head of your dick, Ulric? Pass out on me?"

Ulric hid his head against Alain's chest and swore he was blushing. "I hate you," he said.

"Well, of course you do," Alain said comfortably. "Everybody I bring into this room comes to hate me sooner or later. Why else do you think I do it? Nothing makes my cock get harder than that cold stare of pure hostility, when I know if a guy could get loose he'd break my neck. Except he can't get away, all he can do is rage against me, and he's so frustrated he's ready to cry. Pure gold, that is pure gold. Better than a case of champagne or a pile of cocaine. So, scaredy-cat, get your nose down there and lick around those big old rings of mine. If you can't stand the thought of getting a few of your own, you better admire the ones that I've got."

Ulric was happy to oblige. He slid the head of Alain's cock into his mouth and down his throat, carefully guiding the shaft so that it ran between his fangs. It wasn't easy to keep from puncturing or scratching it. None of Ulric's teeth were dull. But he wrapped his lips around them, trying to cushion their edges. He didn't care if he cut his own mouth up a little in the process. His tongue was equally problematic; it was thin and raspy, more of a file than a human tongue. But Alain seemed to enjoy the way it felt moving back and forth on the underside of his dick.

If he thought about it, Ulric would have had to admit that he was not protecting Alain from the sensation of having his cock scored. Anybody with this much gold in his equipment would probably love to be nibbled by vampire teeth. He was protecting himself from Alain's blood and from the unwelcome knowledge it might contain.

Alain rapped him on top of his head. "Quit daydreamin' and tend to business," he snapped.

Ulric obeyed. Soon he was rewarded by a dose of hot come that nearly choked him. Alain hauled him up so they were face-to-face and licked off the spit and white stuff that had spattered Ulric's mustache and beard. "I always like to come before I play," Alain murmured in his ear. "It makes me so much meaner if I'm not distracted by a hard dick. Know what I mean?"

Ulric did not know, but he was certainly trying to figure it out now. Alain interrupted this anxious reverie. "So tell me about yourself," he said, tugging on Ulric's hair to force his head back and focus his eyes on Alain's face.

"What do you want to know?" Ulric replied.

"Don't be a smart-ass." Alain tightened his grip on Ulric's hair and slapped him lightly on one cheek.

"I'm honestly not being flippant," Ulric said patiently, relishing the smart along one side of his face. "I don't know what you are planning. I don't know what you need to know. Ask me questions, and I will answer them honestly."

"Stand up," Alain said, and roughly dragged him off the bed and onto his feet. Ulric played along, allowing himself to be manhandled. It was delicious to be able to pretend he was out of control. Alain handed him a piece of chain. "Can you break that?" he demanded.

"Of course not," Ulric said, relishing the way each cool link slid through his hands, like the scales on snakeskin. But he could not look Alain in the eye and say it, and the master sensed his lie. For that, he was kicked to the floor.

"Don't jerk me around; grab that chain and show me just how strong you are," Alain said impatiently.

Ulric shrugged, yanked the chain taut, and snapped it like a piece of string. "I'm sorry," he said when he saw Alain's look of disbelief.

"Bend over the horse," Alain said, not acknowledging his apology. He reinforced the order with a pointing finger.

Ulric went on his knees to the piece of equipment Alain indicated, stood, and bent over it. The padded surface was comfortable and sturdy enough to make him feel quite secure. "I'm going to hit you with something," Alain said. "You tell me how it feels." A braided cat-o'-nine-tails landed hard across his shoulders. Ulric sighed happily. "Well?" Alain said impatiently, poised for another blow.

"It's hard to know what to say," Ulric said sadly. "It's been a long time since I was changed, and there are so many things I've forgotten. And other things I don't know how to describe, since you have never experienced them. I'm not very sensitive to pain. I don't need to be; my body can repair almost any injury. That insensitivity helps me to ignore the risk to myself when I go out to feed. When you hit me, I know it should hurt, but it doesn't exactly. It's more as if it makes me remember what it is to hurt."

"Well, goddamn it, that sucks," Alain said. Ulric knew without looking that he would be chewing his lower lip.

"I want you," Ulric said. "I've wanted you for years. Think of it this way, Alain. You can do your worst with me."

"You've got my attention now," Alain said. "Go on."

"Haven't you ever wanted to go as far as you could? You're a sadist, Alain. But you're smart about it. You don't go around kidnapping and torturing strangers. You ask for permission. You prefer men who don't have a lot of limits, but you stay within those boundaries. But surely you've wondered about it. What are *your* limits, Alain? I'm willing to bet that no bottom has ever been able to give you carte blanche. And I'm hungry for this. Think about how horny you get if you've got to do without sex for two weeks. Then imagine what it would be like to be me. I'm a creature of physical, sensual appetites, Alain. That's all that I am. I live to satisfy the cravings of my body. I manage to get a few other things done from time to time, but mostly I exist to feed, to feel the pleasure that comes from satisfying that hunger. But I have other appetites, just like you do, and this has never happened to me before. I've never had this opportunity. It's been centuries, Alain. If you tell me to stand inside your chains and leave them unbroken, I will do that. I will. You are the only person here who needs to set any limits. Not me."

Alain gave him a sharp look. "That sounds too good to be true. So there's nothing that can permanently damage you or threaten your life? You're just immortal, you live forever, nothing can kill you?"

Ulric had thought he was completely open to this man, and would hold nothing back from him. But he balked at answering this question.

"I thought so. Well, that's OK. We've all got our little secrets. I like secrets. Just promise me you won't hate yourself when I make you give it up. I'm going to take you up on your offer, Ulric. I haven't been this horny for months. Don't know what's been wrong with me—ever since this winter I haven't been myself." Alain shook himself like a wet dog. "Well, nothing's more boring than having to listen to somebody whine about their health like a senile old lady."

He took Ulric by the shoulders and guided him to a wall where chains dangled from heavy eyebolts that were sunk deep into the building's supporting timbers. He wrapped the chains around Ulric's wrists and secured them with large padlocks. "No need to protect your nerves and tendons with a pair of wrist cuffs, is there?" he jeered. "So just to make this official, I'm telling you: Leave those chains alone. If one of them breaks, I'll find a way to make you sorry. It's a tough order to find a way to punish somebody like you, but I've got a few tricks up my sleeve that might surprise you."

Ulric bowed his head and waited while Alain sorted through the whips that hung from a circular cast-iron frame that was probably manufactured for gourmet chefs to hang up their anodized aluminum pans. His sharp hearing caught Alain murmuring under his breath. "Forget that, too light. Too candy-assed. Ha, ha, don't need to bother with that bugger. Well, fuck all. I don't need to warm him up at all, do I? Goddamn. Let's see. What have I got that's really effective? Yes, you, and you, and you. You too. Come to the party, babies, daddy's about to have himself a *good* time."

Alain began with a wire brush that he'd bought at an auto supply store. Ulric supposed it was used to clean machine parts. The brass bristles were sharp and stiff. Alain pulverized the skin over his shoulders, back, butt, and thighs. It felt to Ulric like lying out naked under a hail storm. There was more of a feeling of pressure than anything else, although occasionally a bright thin spatter of pain would penetrate his consciousness.

"Yesss," Alain hissed. "Gonna have myself a *good* time."

A rubber cat was next. The heavy latex cords had been tipped with metal nuts, knotted to hold them in place. This made Ulric grunt a bit. It was a nice deep massage. Then he felt Alain's hands all over his back and butt, smearing thick liquid across his skin. "Baby," Alain said gently, "you're a mess. Let me make it all better," and turned his head to kiss him. The kiss created far more sensation than the beating. Ulric drank it in, giddy with pleasure. Alain was full of fierce joy, and it made Ulric happy to be able to put him in that altered state.

Other implements followed. It made Alain cheerful to show him each one before using it and tell him a little story about where it had come from and how it had been used in the past (if ever). The truck antenna had been set into a steel handle by a tool-and-die worker in Seattle who promised Alain he would make him a new one if it ever broke. Alain had managed to bend it on its maker, but it remained intact. The little flail tipped with hooks was something Alain made himself to frighten away a persistent would-be slave who was not his type. The beautifully shaped wooden club was acquired on a fishing trip. (It was made to knock out big salmon.) Until now, it had mostly been used to fuck boys who wanted something bigger than a dick up their asses.

Ulric's feet slipped. He was apparently standing in a puddle of his own fluids. Alain was growing progressively more and more excited. Finally he left Ulric's side and came back with a blacksnake, six feet long. "If this won't make you dance for me, nothing will," Alain declared, and let it snap.

This was not a massage. This was a slicing caress, with just enough of an edge to it to make Ulric wonder if it was pleasure or pain. The novel sensation made him crazy. He panted, whined for it, and almost forgot his vow to leave the chains unbroken, just because he was so excited. Again and again Alain let him taste the snakebite edge of the long braided whip, until Ulric was biting his own lips and crying, "More, more, more!"

But before he had enough, Alain was at his side, unlocking the padlocks and catching his limp body, turning him around, locking him up again so he faced out from the wall. He drew a Bowie knife from a scabbard that ran down his right thigh. It was a monster knife, Ulric thought. Not quite big enough to be a bayonet or a sword, but definitely longer than the four-inch limit on a legal pocketknife. "Remember," Alain said evenly, "I told you not to break those chains. And you told me you would obey me. Do you have honor?" The point of the knife came to rest between Ulric's nipples, slightly to the left of his breastbone. Ulric whined at the sight of it, but Alain was still talking. "And if you have honor, how far does it go?" he asked thoughtfully. The point of the knife went into Ulric's body a full half-inch. "Far enough to trust me with your precious overextended life?" Alain wondered.

Ulric was shrieking, rattling the chains that he had given his word to leave intact. Alain's face was set in a snarl, the lips drawn back exactly the same way that Ulric's cleared his teeth when he was ready to drink. To the excited vampire's senses, Alain's hand seemed to draw back in slow motion. This was it, the killing stroke, the knife to the heart that could end his life. Ulric found himself howling in his wolf voice, driven by desperation back to the animal part of his nature, and then the knife arced forward—

And lodged in his chest only a quarter of an inch away from his heart. Alain pulled it out, and a spout of blood hit him in the chest. The two men stood facing one another, panting, marked by a nearly identical gout of blood. Then Alain sheathed his knife, laughed a little at both of them, and released the padlocks. Ulric allowed himself to fall into his arms. By the spear of the Sky Father, he had never been so scared.

Alain half-carried, half-threw Ulric face down onto the bed and shoved a big piece of Crisco up his ass. Ulric's ability to feel pleasure was the opposite of his numbness to pain. His predator's body was more sensitive to arousal than mortal flesh. It seemed as if he could feel every vein on Alain's swollen cock, and he could certainly feel the outline of every single ring that pierced his dick. By the time Alain had gone in and out of him a half a dozen times, Ulric swore he could have told you the gauge of each piece of jewelry. Never had he been fucked like this, with so much dedication and determination. Alain reached around in front of him, hauled him to his knees, and wrapped his fingers around Ulric's cock. With the big tool lodged firmly in his guts, Ulric shouted from the intensity of the pleasure he felt as Alain jacked him off again and again.

"Tell me you want it," Alain said, slightly out of breath, the words jerky because of the pounding he was giving Ulric's ass. "Tell me you want my come, cocksucker. Tell me how bad you want it. Beg for it or I'll pull out, I swear I will."

Ulric was surprised by the little speech he made. Who would have guessed he could be that abject, or that poetic? Apparently it was effective, because Alain came hard, and Ulric's thirsty flesh drank up each drop of the white blood.

And now he knew. He had known since Alain came in his mouth, but he had been too impatient, distracted by his own hard cock, to let the information sink in. Alain had it, this new disease, whatever it was. He was doomed.

They snuggled together on the bed, Ulric sticking to the leather bedspread. "We made quite a mess," he said fondly.

"I feel wonderful," Alain exclaimed. "I haven't been so happy since Kip died. He was a hell of a masochist, but nothing like you, baby. My arms are burning like I bench-pressed 300 pounds."

"Kip was your boy?" Ulric asked.

"No, he hated all that role-playing shit. He just liked to turn up at my house once a week, down half a bottle of Jack Daniel's, and get the shit kicked out of him. No games. He was a good man and a good friend."

Ulric didn't want to ask, but found himself voicing a question anyway. "How did he go?"

"Some weird-ass kind of pneumonia that the doctors couldn't cure. Or at least that's what they said. I think they just didn't give a damn. He was just some fag to them. What did they care if he died?"

"So he had it too," Ulric said, then wanted to cut his own throat.

"Huh?" Alain knew he had heard something important, and he would not let Ulric take it back. Eventually he got the whole story out of him: Billy, the skull face, the premature mortality looming over the patrons of the bar. Then, of course, he wanted to know, "What about me?"

Ulric could not answer him directly. "I could make you like me," he said.

Alain studied him coldly. "So you can tell I'm sick, even though I feel fine?"

Ulric nodded.

Alain thought it over. "So what would that mean, to be like you? You have to feed every day, right?"

"Usually," Ulric said. "Unless I've fed on another vampire. Then I can go for a few days without mortal blood."

"So you guys don't hang together? There's no fraternal bond?"

"No, there's not." Ulric's body was still singing from the pleasure this man had given to him, and he could not withhold the information he needed to make a decision. "We can't tolerate each other, in fact. Vampires don't like to be around other hunters. We need to keep a certain zone of space between us."

"So you and I would not be spending eternity playing perverted leather games with one another?"

Ulric shook his head.

"And you say it's bad? Everybody's got it?"

Ulric nodded. "These things happen periodically, Alain. I've seen lots of plagues sweep through the human population and decimate it, about once every hundred years or so. This one is too new to have a name yet, but it's every bit as nasty as the Black Death or cholera. Millions of people will die."

"Including all of my friends. My God. In a few more years, San Francisco will be a ghost town. Do you have any idea what we've built here, Ulric? How many men have sacrificed careers and their families and come here to make this a gay mecca? This is the only place on earth where we can be ourselves and live without fear. We have this city by the balls." He took his arm out from under Ulric's body but stayed close to him, stroking his chest. Ulric waited patiently for him to speak again.

"I killed somebody once," Alain said finally. The confession came out in awkward bits and pieces. "A basher. I was cruising this rest area down on the interstate, and I blew this big trucker. Got up in his cab to do him, just like some kind of Jack Fritscher fantasy. Motherfucker came at me with a tire iron when I was done. If he hadn't gotten himself a really great blow job before he tried to kill me, I probably wouldn't have been so pissed off. I might have just run away. But the nerve of him, to get his dick sucked and then turn all self-righteous and call *me* a queer? Forget that shit. I took that tire iron away from him and beat his head in. Took it home, washed it off, kept it in the trunk of my car. I've still got it. That's weird, huh?"

"How did you feel about it?" Ulric wanted to know.

"Well, that's an interesting question. I guess I had fantasized about it often enough, what it would be like to kill someone. Because, of course, you know that's what I'm supposed to be all about. If I like to hurt people, I must secretly be a killer. But it made me sick. I threw up for about an hour. And then I went to sleep for two days. I don't think I liked it much. Certainly didn't give me a boner. I was just glad to be alive myself. And pissed at him for getting me in a corner."

"It's different when you feel the hunger," Ulric said, yawning. How far away was dawn?

Alain put out his hand and grabbed one of the big canines. Ulric let him, loving the feeling of having this man put his hands in his mouth. "I'll just bet it is," he whispered. "But I don't think I want to find out." Ulric stared at him, stricken. "I know you mean it kindly," Alain said gently, withdrawing his hand. "But my whole life is about fucking other men. I gave up everything in order to have a life where I do whatever gets me hard. My family is the men who come to me to get tied up and spit on and beaten and fucked. I don't want to live long enough to see the end of what we've made here. I can't stand the thought of watching them die and leave me behind. It makes me too sad. And I couldn't do what you've done, Ulric. I couldn't wait a year to get my rocks off, much less a century."

"Feeding is very pleasurable," Ulric argued. "I wish I could show you how it feels, Alain. It's—"

"It's lonely," Alain said flatly, and Ulric knew the verdict was final. For the first time in his immortal life, he felt what might have been tears in the corners of his eyes. Alain reached out and wiped them away, and Ulric saw the bloody traces on his fingers. "I could make you," he said fiercely. "I could force you to drink my blood. And I should do it, I should, I should!"

Alain pinned the clenched fists that were beating on his chest. "No, you shouldn't, baby." Alain gathered him up and patted him on the back, treating him like a mourning child. "I know you love me, and you want to keep me with you, Ulric, but that's just not in the cards." He kissed him on the nose, and the fond gesture made Ulric weep again, painful thin strands of diluted blood.

"There's one thing you can do for me. Two, actually," Alain said.

"What—is it?" Ulric hiccuped.

Alain got a firm grip on his bearded chin. "Let me put a big fuckin' stud in your tongue, honey. Then I want you to fuck me. It's been a long time since I met a man whose dick I wanted up my ass. Then bite me, and let me go when I'm in your arms, doing the stuff I love the best."

"Are you sure?" Ulric demanded.

"Yes, I'm sure. Now let me get up and deal with a couple of things. No, you stay in bed." Ulric watched from the leather-covered waterbed, which was gently rocking from the sudden absence of Alain's bulk. He was moving decisively through his apartment, pulling a few things together: a manila envelope ("my last will and testament"), some keys ("this here's the truck, this here is to the bar, and that's the summer cabin on the Russian River"), a locked strongbox ("somebody oughta get rid of all this primo dope before the cops arrive"), and some jewelry ("won't ever have to pawn my diamonds to get out of the country now"). He sat on the edge of the bed and wrote a note on the manila envelope. "Harvey," it said, "you probably won't believe this, but it was the best time I ever had. Everything in here belongs to you. I love you, man, take care. Throw me a hell of a going away party. P.S. Fire Billy." Alain signed his name, then went away, presumably to leave everything on the kitchen table.

He stuck his head in the door and gestured for Ulric to come out. "The light's better out here," he said. The kitchen was well-lit, furnished with a yellow Formica table and some buttercup-yellow chairs that matched. "Pretty queeny, huh?" Alain said, and got him to sit down in one of the chairs. There was a surgical drape on the table, a needle, and a few different studs. "Stick out your tongue," Alain said, and grabbed it with a pair of forceps. The stick wasn't too bad. Ulric crossed his eyes so he couldn't see it coming. But it made his eyes tingle. The thick post in his tongue was a trip, the stud pressing against the roof of his mouth. He supposed he would get used to it in time.

"Now you belong to me," Alain said, clapping him on the shoulder. "You don't know how many times I've had men beg me to wear my rings and be my property, Ulric. You are the only one who's gotten me to do it. Now a little bit of me will be with you every time you punch open some poor fucker's neck and drink him dry. Feed for my sake, buddy."

Alain just stood there looking at him, and Ulric felt unaccountably shy. "Thanks," he muttered, looking at the toes of his bare feet. Then he looked up at Alain again and marveled at the man's sheer ballsiness. Anybody else who had heard Ulric's bad news would have shrugged it off. They would have preferred denial to a cold confrontation with the certainty of their own death. But Alain faced it the same way he had faced the revelation of Ulric, standing over a bled-white body, fangs out, hunger not quite sated. He saw things as they were, and if they were weird, that simply excited him. His first question about any novel fact seemed to be, What unique sexual opportunities lie in this bizarre event?

Ulric decided that he did not care if dawn was pending. He put away his own sorrow and sealed it in a deep, dark, faraway place. He could mourn later, when it would not taint Alain's last hours. It was the face he had seen bending over the boy's body in the alley that Alain wanted to see now. From somewhere, Ulric found the strength to become his most amoral, ferocious self. He was up off the chair and had Alain by the throat before the big man even saw him coming. "So you like to pick people up, " Ulric sneered, and lifted him with one hand. "You like to make other men think they are helpless." He shook Alain like a woman shakes out a tablecloth. "Let me show you what it's like to be helpless. Let me show you, oh, all kinds of interesting things."

They were back in the bedroom, and Ulric bound him facedown to the bed the way he had been bound to the wall, with chains wrapped around wrists and ankles and padlocked in place. The coroner wouldn't have to think much to figure out where those marks came from. He went to the cast-iron carousel full of whips and picked out a handful. Alain had good taste. There was no junk in his collection. Everything was well-made, the braids tight, the leather well cared for. Ulric had hidden out during the French revolution in a brothel where he dressed as an aristocrat and flogged Parisians, who felt a little guilty about chopping off the king's head. It was pleasant to have such well-made whips in his hands again.

"I don't believe I asked for all this," Alain said menacingly from his spread-eagle position on the bed.

"Like I care," Ulric retorted, and lashed out. "You have wanted this from me since you first laid eyes on me. And you are not leaving this world until you have taken everything that I feel like handing out."

The beating he administered was thorough but tempered with mercy. Alain did not have the experience or the tolerance of a devoted bottom. Still, he took more than Ulric would have gambled on. One of the things he loved about gay men in this city and in this era was their shamelessness. Top or bottom, when they saw or felt something they liked, they went for it wholeheartedly, without apology. Alain liked what he was feeling. Ulric worked him up to a frenzy, then tossed the whips aside, unchained him, and turned him onto his back.

"Are you ready?" Ulric asked, but Alain was already greasing up his cock, which responded as if it had not been milked dozens of times already this evening. Ulric settled on his knees between Alain's spread thighs and rested the other man's feet on his own shoulders. "Just hang on to me," he said. "Don't worry about holding yourself up. I'll hold you up."

Then he picked up Alain's torso and slid him onto his cock. It was hot in there and tight, which pleased Ulric a great deal. Apparently Alain had not been lying about the fact that this was a rare experience. "Does it feel good, baby?" he asked the other man, who had spread his arms out like Jesus on the cross.

'Yeah, oh, yeah," Alain moaned, eyes rolled back in his head.

"Think about this," Ulric warned. "Think about what you're giving up. This beautiful body that feels so good when I touch it here and pinch it here. The feel of my fat dick taking you on a good hard ride. My lips." He kissed the other man, broke off the kiss, fucked him a little harder, a little faster. "Can you say goodbye to all this? Because you don't have to, honestly. You can change your mind. Even now."

"Shut up and fuck me," Alain whispered. "Oh, my God, this feels so good I think I'm going to—"

"Die?" Ulric said.

"Come," Alain corrected. "Yes, baby, just like that, do me just like that. Oh, you are so good, such a stud. Now come on and kiss my neck. Right there, baby. Put your lips right there."

Alain suddenly shoved Ulric's head into his throat with all his might, and Ulric's reflexes took over. He bit deep, and gasped at the wealth that filled his mouth. Then a smack on his ass reminded him to keep his butt moving.

"Harder," Alain said, and Ulric didn't know if he meant the bite or the fuck, so he doubled the force of both, and Alain's come spilled between their bellies as his life ran free and ran out into Ulric's grieving mouth.

He called the bar before he left Alain's apartment and left an urgent message for Harvey. Then he carefully rifled the mind of everybody in the building and made sure they had seen and heard nothing, not even fucking. He got on his bike, and he rode away slowly, deliberately lagging until the sun came up and scorched his worthless hide. By the time he got home, he was burned all over, but he had no more tears. He thought he would never cry again.

He fell asleep clicking the ball in his tongue against the left fang, the right fang, the left fang again, a lonely little ditty that could only be played by someone whose mouth was not being glutted by Alain's voracious tongue.

Pussy Boy

The wet heat of the sauna was almost too much. For a miracle, the small room was empty. But then, not many people came here at midnight. Unlike 95% of the gym's membership, Earl came to pit his muscles against iron, not to cruise. On the far side of 40, he competed with his own achievements, seeking always to better them. What other people were about was none of his business. His workout demanded as much of him as he demanded of those who had pledged fealty to him, so he was covered with a palpable thick layer of sweat. But he knew he needed the steam to leach the toxins from lifting to the point of exhaustion out of his arms, legs, stomach, and buttocks. So he adjusted his towel and took a place on the bench. As he rearranged the soft white terry cloth, he jostled his own cock and was simultaneously relieved to be reminded of its respectable length and girth but also injured and angry about the circumcision scar that ran all the way around it. Once he had been helpless, and because of that, he had been damaged. There was no way to repair his own body, but Lord, it was a lifetime of very rewarding work to find surrogates whose suffering confirmed his own power and freedom.

Earl sighed and settled into the world behind his own closed eyes. Ideas, images, and memories came to him in a quiet and steady flow, and he wandered among them, enjoying the kaleidoscope of his own reactions. In many ways, he was happiest when he was alone. So it was no joy at all to feel a draft as the door opened to let an unwelcome companion intrude upon his meditations. He opened his aluminum-grey eyes a crack to assess the level of risk that another man might or might not bring into the room with him.

But this was no stranger. It was Ross, an effervescent bleached-blond aerobics instructor who also manned the front desk on the graveyard shift. The kid had the most amazing long dark eyelashes and eyes that were bluer than a sunny sky over Malibu's beaches. He also had a tight body—slim hips and a slightly well-defined chest that looked good in spandex. The calves of his long legs bulged with the kind of muscle that you only get from riding a bike. Earl had seen other patrons at the gym pause at the desk to flirt with Ross. He rewarded every paying customer with the same blindingly perky smile. To Earl, it was clearly the inviting grimace of a whore, empty of any promise of real eroticism. But others were apparently not so perceptive. Or picky. Still, he had to admit that Ross was not hard to look at, even though perky people gave him a grinding headache.

"You're breaking the rules," Ross announced breathlessly, shaking his finger at Earl. The insolence of the gesture made Earl open his metallic eyes all the way. He also shifted his posture, awakening his body to a state in which quick movement would be effortless. Ross did not heed this admittedly minor threat display. Instead, he continued on, his eyes dancing with mischief. "Nobody's having sex in here. Can you imagine how bad that is for business?"

The youngster seemed to have no premonition that he might be rejected. He dropped to his knees, practice having made the gesture fluid, and swam toward Earl, his mouth already slightly open and moist. *Didn't Daddy have a nice broad chest, despite the weird way it looked with all that hair?* he thought. Earl allowed Ross to fold back his towel and actually see his cock. But then he planted his foot in the middle of the cute desk clerk's chest and gently but firmly knocked him onto his back.

"You haven't even begun to deserve a reward that big," he said.

Earl's voice was music to Ross's ears. It was deep and bossy. *Ooh, Daddy. Spank me and tell me I'm a dirty girl.* "I've had bigger," he said cheekily.

Earl rewarded him with a dry laugh. "Hasn't anybody ever told you size doesn't matter?"

"I thought they were talking about french fries," Ross quipped. But he had to be content with an amused look on Daddy Earl's face. The other man had a neatly trimmed black beard and mustache. His dark hair had gone silver at the very tips, making him look like a wolf who was changing his summer coat for the argent of winter. (Ross had no idea that wolves actually did not change colors with the turning of the seasons. It would have been unthinkable to compare Earl, a man he intended to become his daddy, with a snowshoe hare, a weasel, or even a fox.)

What a disappointment it was when Earl simply got up and headed for the door, without so much as a let's-have-coffee-here's-my-number-call-me-soon-OK? Hadn't anybody taught this Neanderthal the gay-boy dating protocol? Ross scrambled to his feet and trotted behind him, determined to re-engage. "What's your hurry?" he warbled, trying his best to be nice despite Earl's churlishness.

"Do you think I want to break the rules?" Earl asked him. Ross laughed a lot more loudly than the joke—if it was a joke—deserved.

Ignoring his tagalong, Earl made it to the locker room and opened his unit. Normally he would shower, but he had decided he'd rather clean up at home. So he toweled himself off, not hurrying or lingering just because he had a witness, and reached for his clothing—knitted black boxer briefs, a white T-shirt that looked like it had come straight from a bleach commercial, well-fitted button-fly jeans, and a leather vest. As he turned his back to the kid to shut his locker, Ross read aloud what the studs on the back of the vest spelled out.

"Enough rope," he quoted. "Well, gosh, if you're a daddy, isn't that just your job? I should hope you have enough rope and a whole lot of other things too."

"Do I have enough rope to let somebody hang himself? Why, I think you could say that is indeed my job," Earl said evenly, stepping into his boots. "And, by the way, I do not like to be addressed as Daddy. It is master, or sir. However, you do not have permission to use any title when you address me."

Ross did not respond to the rebuke. His pretty face was as blank as the first page of a flunking student's book report. His eyes were pointed in Earl's direction, but if they were the windows to his soul, somebody had just shut the blinds.

Earl walked away, motorcycle and house keys in his hand, and this time Ross did not come trotting after him. In the garage, putting his helmet on, he shook his head, wondering at the audacity of the pup. Then he forgot about him, just one more twinkie who had been put—kindly, even—in his place. During the ride home, he thought a little about Fernando, the slave who had served him perfectly, and held that office longer than any other man who had entered his dungeon. But Fernando had asked to be released from service some time ago, and Earl had acquiesced, understanding that Fernando did not wish to take the next step that was necessary if he was to be completely owned by this particular master. Earl kept tabs on him through mutual friends, and from what he had heard, Fernando was doing well managing his inheritance, producing charity events. Earl had no patience for the Machiavellian combination of socializing and lobbying that some wealthy gay men in Southern California used to advance the cause of gay rights. Fernando's politics had been his own affair, and Earl was not captivated by temporal power. He had used his own resources to create a private world where he could "do as thou wilt," free from interference by church or state.

Did he miss Fernando? It was a hard question to answer. As Earl parked his bike and walked from the garage into his own spacious house, he pondered it. His dwelling was maintained in good order by a housekeeping service. He had friends who shared his tastes in music and sex. He didn't mind polishing his own boots, and it was easy enough to find a handsome piece of male flesh to hang from the manacles that graced one wall of the black room. He continued to feel love and attraction for Fernando, and yet knew that he had made the right choice. Earl was even able to hope that Fernando might find another master, one who would be satisfied by the level of submission that Fernando was able to give. God knows it was more than most aspiring slaves could actually offer when push came to not shoving back. What he missed, Earl thought as he took meat and vegetables out of the refrigerator and began to slice them for a stir-fry, was the territory within another man's heart and soul. He had everything he could possibly want in the outside world. But to contemplate the mystery of another's sensations, longing, fear, and resistance fulfilled his deepest need. He was a surgeon of the spirit, altering much more than a subject's skin. The deepest bruise will fade in time, but the impression left by the carefully timed whisper of a knowledgeable master lives on and on. Nothing can erase it from the mind of a vulnerable bottom.

Just thinking about it made his dick get hard. Earl laughed at his own reaction and willed it away. It was something he could take care of after lunch. He would work until dawn, poring over his architectural drawings, and then sleep through the hottest part of the day. Though he clothed himself in leather when he left his house, it was the night that was his real garment, a twin to his own thoughts. The caress of darkness on his face was like the kiss of a mother who loved what was evil in him and encouraged him to be the adversary of decency and cheap sentiment. Within its never-cloying embrace, he knew himself to be lethal indeed. Being so, it was easy to keep his claws sheathed in velvet when he had to handle people like Ross. Monarch of men, enthroned by their need to lie beneath another man's boots and whip, he could be lenient with the ignorant.

That is, until he was awakened at 3 o'clock in the afternoon by a phone that was too far from the bed to simply switch off. Excited by finishing the latest set of plans and sending them off to be used to create a model of the building, he had forgotten to patrol the communication devices and make sure they would not yell at him. Awake and irritated, both by the noise and the fact that air conditioning could barely keep the heat outside at bay, Earl allowed the phone to ring itself to death. He settled back in his bed, willing himself back to sleep, but just as he reached the edges of unconsciousness, the phone went off again. The third time this happened, he got out of bed and answered it.

"What do you want?" he said tersely. His clients and friends knew better than to try to reach him at this time of day.

"You, Daddy," a zephyr of a voice confessed. "I can't stop thinking about you, Daddy. Please let me see you. I'll be your good little boy."

"Do not call me Daddy," Earl said automatically, then silently cursed himself for not hanging up at once.

"Isn't there anything I can do to make you want me as much as I want you?"

If this lad ever lost his job at the gym, he could probably make a living selling codpieces to snakes. Perhaps the bittersweet nostalgia about Fernando and the fact that he had not kept his promise to jack off before he slept combined to make Earl ignore his own common sense. Or maybe it was just that Ross had already lost chances one and two and was a sure bet to lose his third chance as well. Earl believed in giving everybody three chances to obey, and three chances only.

"How did you get my number?"

"I was bad and looked up your membership on the computer."

"Those records are supposed to be private. You could get fired for that."

"Oh, I suppose so, but who's going to turn me in?"

What an idiot, Earl thought, and reminded himself to ease the tension in his jaw and stop crushing the phone. He had nothing to say, so he kept silent, which Ross apparently could only tolerate for five seconds, according to Earl's watch.

"You could punish me for it," Ross purred.

All right, you asked for it, Earl told himself, and curtly told the boy the time, date, and place where he was to present himself, in jeans, a tank top, boots, and nothing else. This was one of Earl's IQ tests for new bottoms. If they turned up with a belt on or underwear or, heaven forfend, in running shoes, he knew they were a few clothespins short of a full session.

Having lived up to the slogan on his vest, Earl turned off the phone and went back to his comfortably hard mattress swathed in soft and very expensive brushed cotton sheets. He turned his pillow over so that the cool side was facing up and arranged himself on his side. The meat between his legs came to life and firmed up, moving closer to his fist. Stroking in the syncopated rhythm that built his excitement, Earl gave his body up to a pleasure that was more intense than the average blow job. But as he mentally urged himself to shoot, it was not thoughts of the upcoming scene with Ross that made him rigid within the silky sliding skin of his scarred cock. No, it was thoughts of the more distant future. Ross's future.

The boy showed up 15 minutes late, in leather shorts and a harness, mid-calf engineer boots, and a leather baseball cap, a chapeau that Earl particularly abhorred.

"You are late and out of uniform," he said, in a tone of voice that normally made submissives and masochists cringe into the nearest corner.

"But don't I look hot, Daddy? I can't wait to see how you've fixed up your playroom. You do have one, right?"

Earl put his hand on the back of the obstreperously cheerful smart-ass cutie-pie piece of shit and pushed him where he had said he wanted to go. He kept the boy bent over as they walked, which was quite a trial to Ross's back. This very raw recruit wasn't shy about complaining either.

"You don't know how lucky you are," Earl said, slapping cuffs on the disrespectful chatterbox. "You did not present yourself to me as a novice. But it seems that you have had no training at all, or poor training, which is even worse. I doubt I can correct all of your bad traits in one session, but I expect to make a good start. And for the last time, do not call me Daddy."

When selecting his whips, Earl had to force himself to include one that was not a killer. Out of respect for his own craft rather than any merciful feelings about Ross, the master gave the eager and panting youth a modicum of warm-up. Since even this did not shut him up, Earl ditched the soft short flogger and moved on to a braided cat. At last there was blessed silence in the dungeon. Perhaps Ross was one of those rare birds who was a heavy masochist without a shred of submission. That was fine with Earl, who proceeded to administer a drubbing that would have made a medieval executioner cringe. But just as he was building himself and Ross up to a perfect crescendo of pain—

"You haven't marked me on my legs, have you? I don't want anything to show when I wear my bike shorts."

Ross screamed and did the twist when Earl disdained to answer this very stupid question and laid on with a single-tail, six stripes of fire and ice that continued to ignite Ross's white cupcakes long after the whip had been put away. There were, incidentally, no marks below his tan line.

In a sadistic haze, Earl took Ross down from standing bondage and dragged him over to a padded leather bench. "Oh, it looks like a little tiny picnic table," Ross giggled. Even that inane comment could not cut through Earl's erotic rage. He strapped the pesky blond down, using relentless pressure on the straps, buckling them so tight that the flesh on either side of the leather belts turned red. Ross's muscular thighs were separated and cinched down to the legs of the horse. Earl inserted a 30 cc syringe into a bottle of lubricant, shoved the syringe up Ross's ass, and gave him a tiny enema of lube. (The needle had been removed from the syringe. Perhaps that had been a mistake.) Standing at the side of the horse, the whipmaster took his cock out and rolled a condom over it.

"Oh, Daddy," Ross moaned, "aren't you going to let me feel your sweet bare meat in my pussy? Don't you want to fuck me raw?"

"No," Earl said testily, and slid home, thinking of Fernando's smooth channel consecrated to his use only, milking its tribute of jism out of his desperate tool. Fucking Ross was not the same. But it was a hot, wet ride, fueled by the triumph he felt over Ross losing his third chance. As the gym bunny groaned about getting his pussy stretched and hurt by Daddy's big thing and pleaded to have it taken out, to be spared from being turned into Daddy's dirty little whore, Earl smiled to himself. This was going to be a gratifying treasure hunt indeed. The boy was doomed.

After that, Ross took only a week and a half to move into Earl's house. Earl set aside a room for him and tipped the housekeeper extra for shoveling Ross's crap back into it. He tolerated Ross's demands and tantrums, biding his time. Each fuck-up, taunt, and inappropriate comment got written down on a secret list. He bought Ross a used car, which Ross found inadequate, even though it was a classic convertible. He wrecked it within a month, and Earl replaced it without a rebuke. He set up a joint account for the two of them, and replaced the funds that Ross ran through as if money was just sand you could scoop up and allow to dribble out between your fingers. But he did not introduce Ross to his friends, nor did he appear with him in public. Ross could wear his collar. He could have all the new toys and clothes that he wanted. But no matter how peevish he became, Earl would not take him to a play party or show him off at the bars.

Then Fernando called. He wanted to get together; he wanted Earl back in his life. Fortunately, he did not utter the cliché, "Let's be friends." The master knew he was being perverse when he issued an invitation to dinner. "Do you mind if my new boy is there?" he asked, and Fernando gallantly said not at all. Ross was unbearably excited by this opportunity to strut his stuff in front of an audience, even if it was just one of his daddy's fuddy-duddy old man friends. Earl agreed that his "slave" should be made much of, and put some eyebolts into the dining room wall. Ross would be chained there and eat his dinner out of a dog bowl, rather than dressing up and serving the dinner, which to Earl's way of thinking would have been much more arousing.

So it was only himself and Fernando at the table. Since it was Earl's house and his dinner party, he even served them both from the dishes the caterers had left over warming flames in the kitchen. Fernando made small talk through most of the meal, but after the level of wine in the second bottle dropped to a certain level, the conversation became more personal. Ross for once was dead silent, all ears, awed by Fernando's expensive clothes and jewelry. He knew who this man was, knew what his place was in West Hollywood society. This was somebody who had dinner with the mayor, got invited to cocktails at the White House, was rich rich rich. Ross tried to make himself utterly invisible. He didn't want Fernando to think of him as a dog boy. Nobody has less time for a bottom than another bottom.

"What happened to us?" Fernando asked, his liquid brown eyes full of sorrow and Bordeaux.

"You know the answer to that question," Earl said, taking his sixth careful swallow of wine, patting his beard clean with the snowy white napkin. "You left me."

"But—I—oh, Earl, there will never be anyone like you in my life. Not ever." And Fernando broke down in tears.

It didn't seem odd at all to Earl that he was moving around the table to take a former slave in his arms and comfort him for abandoning that relationship. Their contract had formally ended, but the bond between them continued to be very strong. He calmed Fernando down with soft words and a kiss on the cheek.

"You are very special, you know," he said when he had gotten Fernando settled in his seat again. "Any master worth his spurs would be delighted to have you. And when you are ready to fall that deeply in love again, my dear, I believe that the right man will come for you. But you are still grieving. It would be a poor time to try to learn the ways of another owner. Let your heart take its time and heal. You know that I will always care for you."

"But I failed you," Fernando choked. "I could not—"

"I know," Earl said evenly. "And you made the right decision. That was not your path. A true slave has not failed his owner when he tells him the truth, Fernando. I hope I taught you that."

After a long silence, the conversation turned to easier topics, and it wasn't long after dessert was served that Fernando wanted to go home. Earl dialed his driver's cell phone, surprised that the number was still in his head, and they waited in comfortable chairs in the living room until the limousine pulled up outside. The master walked his former property to the gleaming anthracite car and tucked him inside, then kissed him on the mouth, a kiss that was both proprietary and dismissive. "Don't be a stranger," he said, and closed the door. The limousine pulled away, its engine almost silent, and to Earl it bore a brief resemblance to a hearse.

It was no surprise to him when his next scene with Ross went even more poorly than it usually did. Ross had pestered him with innumerable questions about Fernando, most of which were none of his business. They were in the dungeon, and Ross had been told to kneel on the floor so he could be collared. But as the collar approached, he put out one hand to stop it.

"Daddy, I just can't do this anymore," he said, looking at the floor.

Earl thought cynically, *Well, at least he has the grace to blush. I wonder if he can do that on purpose?* "Why not?" he asked, sure that the answer would be entertaining.

"Your little boy has grown up," Ross said, and then looked at him, tiny crystal tears beading his long eyelashes. In another time, those blue eyes could have driven prelates and princes mad, Earl was sure.

"What are you saying?" he replied.

"I don't think I'm a bottom anymore," Ross said, barely keeping a quaver out of his voice. "And I'm in love, Daddy, wonderfully in love. With another man."

"Oh, my," Earl said, struggling to keep a smile off his face. He walked away and put the collar back on its hook.

Ross was on his feet now, looking a little lost. He had apparently expected a major confrontation and was a little pissed off about not getting a more dramatic response.

"You can put the keys through the mailbox after you leave," Earl said, and went off to do some work in his office.

In the next few days, it did not surprise him to learn that Ross had taken his car, cleaned out the joint account, and also helped himself to one of Earl's credit cards. When friends told him that this strange new wanna-be top had been seen in Fernando's company, he shook his head, knowing how badly Fernando needed somebody in his life to pick up the reins and order him to canter. He thought Ross had probably gotten in touch with him by snooping in his master's address book. Did Fernando know that his ostensible owner was Earl's latest acquisition? And if he did, would that make Ross more or less attractive to him?

The only real question in the master's mind was how long he should wait before laying his trap for the runaway. How long could Ross pretend to be a top before he had to get his oil changed? The timing was crucial. Earl made certain calls to Mexico and also acquired a supply of various medications. Then he notified the manager of one of his more profitable enterprises to prepare a room for its new inhabitant.

The honeymooning couple had taken a trip to Hawaii. Earl waited 10 days after they got back to start monitoring the rutting grounds. If he had spread some cash around, no doubt he could have had some help locating the AWOL poseur, but he wanted to keep this matter sub rosa, just between him and the by now madly frustrated Ross. There were only so many sex clubs in WeHo that were sleazy enough for Ross's feverish butt hole.

Dressed in his trademark vest and other leathers, Earl paid a ridiculously high door charge and sauntered into a grimy labyrinth of glory holes and fuck benches. His eyes adjusted quickly to the darkness. The other men gave him space, warned off by his formal black leather and hostile attitude. This was mostly a suck joint, with a little butt-stuffing thrown in, about as vanilla as you could be and still be queer. The place would have cleared out if anybody had gotten strung up and flogged. Well, what do you know, there was Ross, perched in the club's only sling (made out of crossed pieces of nylon webbing, to Earl's disgust). The small crowd was circulating past him, checking him out. One bearish man with a beer can of a cock was standing at attention, the bare head of his dick grazing Ross's shuddering ring. Mr. Bareback was at it again. Earl didn't know if he cared much about Ross catching something, but he was incensed at the thought of him taking a virus back to Fernando's trusting body.

Earl snarled, and the big man said, "Sheesh, I didn't know it was already taken," and wandered away, his dick bobbing like a fishing lure. Earl walked in between the tan legs that were already in stirrups and simply stood there, regarding his naughty puppy. "Oh, Daddy," Ross crooned, caressing his cock and cradling his tight balls. "I've missed you so much. You must have heard me calling for you. Oh, take me, Daddy, just the way you used to."

"First I think you should take these," Earl said, and offered him three capsules.

"What are they?" Ross asked, swallowing them without any water.

"Just think of them as happiness."

Ross did not ask whose happiness the mysterious pills might contain. Instead he reclined, sighing gently as Earl massaged grease into his aching hole. But what he thought was Earl's cock entering him was actually an extra-large butt plug. "Oh, Daddy," he cried, his head rolling back over the edge of the sling, "use my pussy, Daddy. You're stretching it so much I won't be able to walk. But you made it so wet. You put your cock in me and now I need it all the time. Oh, Daddy, let me be your come slut, I'm nothing but a hot pussy that needs your big load."

"Get your dick hard," Earl ordered, and Ross complied even though Earl had never cared before whether his cock was erect or not. With the pressure on his prostate that he had pined for, it wasn't difficult for the well-filled boy to bring his organ to a prime state of ferocity. The happy pills must have been taking effect, because when Earl pressed two sides of a mold against his cock, making an impression of it, Ross could only giggle at the cold slick feeling of the clay inside the mold.

"Let's get out of here," Earl said, and took Ross's feet out of the stirrups, then tipped him onto his feet. He had an arm ready to keep him upright.

"We're going back to your dungeon to play? Oh, Daddy, I'm so happy," Ross said. "You've made me a very, very, very, happy boy. Do you know that? You are just the best daddy ever."

The butt plug slipped out of his ass, and Earl kicked it into the shadows. Getting Ross into his tight leather shorts was going to be a pain.

The next day, he was driving south. Ross was humming happily to himself in the passenger seat, slipping in and out of a sleep full of happy sexy dreams. Their IDs were scrutinized briefly at the border, then they were in another country where free enterprise had expanded the scope of medical practice. In a few more days they arrived at their destination, a small clinic in a medium-size city. The doctor raised an eyebrow when he saw Ross's befuddled state, but Earl laid a great deal of cash on the table and explained that his friend had been very nervous about the operation. He also laid down a file folder with two letters from psychiatrists. All the required forms were signed already, and he gave those to the doctor as well.

"This is not standard procedure," said the doctor. "Normally this surgery comes at the very end of a long process. Your friend has no idea if he can really live in a new identity."

"The money for the surgery was available now, and I believe there was a concern that it might disappear if it was not used for surgery immediately."

The doctor looked at the stack of bills and shrugged. "Then I suppose everything is in order," he said, acquiescing with a sigh.

Ross came to on his back on a cold steel table. His legs were spread and tied down and his arms were tightly bound to his torso. "Where's my daddy?" he whispered. "Don't you want to kiss me, Daddy?"

Instead, a mask descended on his face, a needle slid into his arm, and he felt intolerable pain as anesthetic was forced into the vein. But before he could scream, he disappeared into oblivion.

Sucking on ice chips. Sips of salty broth. Cubes of slimy fruit-flavored gelatin. Long sleeps. Peaks of agony soothed by pills and shots. Wet abrasive sponges running over his torso. Repeated bouts of panic about Fernando—where was he?—eased by Earl's face, murmuring reassuring nonsense. And always, always, an insistent pressure between his legs, something wrong down there, bandages, his legs splayed apart by ties attached to the bed rails. And that was something so menacing that he would rather throw little fits about calling Fernando than ask what was going on in his crotch.

The pain medication was gradually reduced, administered less often, and some solid food appeared at the end of a fork held by a brown-skinned nurse with an Indian nose and long coarse dark hair. Earl came more into focus, his body as well as his face. He seemed excited about something, but it was a quiet excitement. Ross drew hope from his optimism. If Earl was cheerful, then surely something good was about to happen. Daddy would always take care of his little boy.

At last the excruciating boredom came to an end, and a day arrived when he woke clear-headed. His ankles were free, and he was being helped into a sitting position. The first thing he saw was a framed photo at his bedside. Although he had never seen one of those disgusting objects in the flesh, he recognized it from the porn magazines his high school friends had passed around. A cunt, yuck, a twat, eeeuw, a snatch, barfaroonie. What was a stinky, slimy pussy doing there, staring at him while he slept? Fear and nausea coiled around one another in his stomach, and Earl's appearance in the doorway did not, for a change, calm him down. Ross gathered enough of his cloudy wits together to begin to piece together the past. How long had he been kept doped up, and where was he?

Earl's smile in his silver-tipped, short black beard was a sinister red slash. His lips framed clean sharp teeth. "Today is the first day of the rest of your life," Earl said solemnly.

But Ross was not about to be sidestepped. He picked up the offensive photo. "What is this—this—*cunt* doing in my room?" It never occurred to him to see something ironic about the loathing that infused his pronunciation of that dreadful word compared to the litany of virgin despoilment that emerged from his mouth whenever he abandoned himself to lust.

Earl picked up the photograph and studied it with a little smile. He didn't seem to be put out in the least. "Why, that's the photo I gave the surgeon before he went to work on you. I have no idea if you really look that way or not. But we're about to find out."

Ross opened his mouth to scream, and Earl was on him, pinning him to the bed with one hand, another hand over his mouth. He had somehow found the time to hit the call button on his way to restrain the patient, and the nurse came into the room, accompanied by a man who Ross assumed was a doctor. They ignored the struggles that Earl subdued and proceeded to unwrap the bulky gauze that had kept Ross's legs apart for days or maybe even weeks, he had no way of knowing. It hurt. Some of the white padding came away rust-colored. The sight of his own blood made Ross feel even more sick to his stomach. When the dressings were all gone, the doctor and the nurse disappeared, without ever having met Ross's accusing eyes.

Ross was still so weak from surgery and enforced inactivity that Earl had no trouble binding his wrists and ankles. The fact that he was being tied up with cloth straps with no fetish value whatsoever made it even more humiliating. Ross was seething, and white with terror.

Carrying the hateful photograph, Earl walked to the foot of the bed and studied Ross's crotch. "Not a bad match," he said, and placed it back on the bedside table. He took a Polaroid camera to the foot of the bed, pointed it between Ross's knees, and pushed the button. He continued to study Ross's body while he waved the photograph to and fro, waiting for it to dry. Then he carefully inserted it into the frame, on top of the original inhabitant. He didn't bother showing it to Ross. Would this cute little narcissist be able to ignore a photograph of himself, however terrible his expectations of it might be?

Ross did indeed find the Polaroid difficult to ignore. But Earl was doing something else that quickly caught Ross's attention. He had a big dildo in his hand, and he was rubbing white cream all over it.

"What's that?" Ross demanded, his voice shaking.

"Well, you know that we're going to have to help this medical miracle along, Pussy Boy. Your new cunt is going to have to be dilated. Several times a day. This is a cast of your own dick, bitch. It amuses me to know that you'll be fucking yourself with a replica of a former part of yourself. Oh, and this is estrogen cream, by the way. We want that boy pussy of yours to be nice and slick."

As the horrifying bludgeon parted his newly cleft and mined flesh, Ross began to cry. "I love it when little girls cry," Earl said, sliding it home. "So how does it feel to really have the hole that you love to talk about so much? I'm waiting to hear it, you dirty little whore. Oh, excuse me, that won't be until much later. After you're well-healed. You see, I have this little hobby, a commercial sex establishment that offers the services of boys who have been modified in some creative and unusual ways. You'll make a lovely addition to my collection. How does it make you feel to know there will be thousands and thousands of men yanking on their dicks at the thought of you being castrated and turned into a slutty little cunt when you don't have a dick to yank on anymore yourself? Well, I guess you could pretend to masturbate *this*."

The master twisted the dilating stick and removed it slowly, then housed it again. The new orifice was tested to its limits. Ross could not believe that there was anything erotic about pain like this. But somewhere in there was a faint response, a hunger to be filled that he knew Earl would exploit. It wasn't hard to foresee the day when he would beg to be dilated or do it to himself, desperate for gratification. He had never liked penetrating other men. But a procession of all the butts that he had never plundered paraded through his mind's eye, and the loss of all that opportunity to spread his seed around intensified his weeping.

"Stop blubbering," Earl said sternly. "I know you like it."

"You won't get away with this!" Ross sniveled. "I'll get away—I'll go to the police. I'll tell the newspapers."

"Tell them what?" Earl sneered. "That you're a self-hating homo pervert who got halfway through a sex change and then changed his mind? Because that's what they'll think. Besides, Ross, you've finally become valuable property to me. I really do own you now. You won't be having much time to yourself."

"I hate you!"

"Why, thank you. But you might want to take a more subservient tone with me in the future, Pussy Boy." The slave's stolen dick continued to pump in and out of the medical marvel between his legs, in and out, making Ross red in the face with wonder and the effort of trying to hold back his pleas for more pleasure and abuse. But Earl had not stopped talking. "After all, this isn't the only thing we can have done to make you a more pleasing commodity. I thought about getting a discreet little colostomy bag installed so you couldn't get fucked in the ass any more. But that body modification will be held in reserve. It's the punishment you'll receive if you ever try to escape. Besides, I need that hot little button inside of you to train you to come from getting your tiny squirming box well-raped. But I guess it doesn't make any sense to call it a prostate anymore, does it? Girls don't have prostates. It's your clit now, isn't it, Pussy Boy?"

Earl slid a finger up the bound boy's ass. The cunning digit found his prostate and began massaging it, smugly assured that he would yield. "It's going to be harder to tell if you're turned on now," the master said, "or if you've come. So I guess we're just going to have to turn you into a screamer. Let me hear it, Pussy Boy. Let me hear you beg to have your cunt fucked until you're split wide open. Just think about how that estrogen cream is going to change you, that ought to get your motor running. And you might also think about the fact that I haven't decided yet whether or not to give you birth control pills and make you have tits."

A picture of himself with a big pair of udders, tipped with pink nipples shaped like the stuffed finger of a glove, being roughly milked by a group of men with foul mouths and calloused hands, undid the captive boy. Every ounce of Ross's self-respect or identity as an autonomous male human being went down the drain. The drain between his legs. He was nothing, a hole, nothing but a hole. A girl's hole. At Earl's prompting, Ross repeated—loudly—all of the things that Earl wanted him to say about himself. Eventually his excitement peaked and he shuddered, but it was hard to say if he had orgasmed or not. It was much less intense than an ejaculation, a strange feeling that flowed over his whole body, leaving him limp and exhausted without necessarily appeasing his need.

Earl removed the dilator and wiped it off on Ross's hospital gown. He rang for the nurse to come and pack him full of gauze until it was time to open him up and fuck him again, stretch him wide with the unfortunately large rubber cast of his own beloved, belated hose.

"By the way," Earl whispered, leaning close to his new acquisition's ear, "you can call me Daddy now. As often as you like."

Polar Bear Hunting

I never got used to having such a cute roommate. Lauren was fresh out of college, face like a model and an attitude to match. Since he could have had pretty much anybody he wanted and had no shortage of offers, you'd think our household would have hosted a stream of tricks. What can I tell you? He was a picky bitch. If he wanted to waste his youth by withholding his perfect body from the (according to him) less-than-perfect guys who wanted to get into his pants, it was no skin off my dick. I had issues of my own that provided plenty of neurotic entertainment. But I can tell you that sex after 40 is a hell of a lot easier than all the competitive dressing up, clubbing, and designer drugs that gay guys in their 20s use as foreplay.

Granted, I'm built for comfort, not for speed. But the men who might reject me because I'm not wearing size 28 jeans don't particularly interest me anyway. I want somebody substantial, somebody with hair (pronounced hey-air), a man with a sense of humor and some experience under his belt. Somebody who isn't afraid to settle his boot heels into the floor and take his time smooching, touching, talking dirty, enjoying every step of a whole night of sex, in no hurry to get naked but not afraid of it either. I like a little girth with my mirth, and some snow on top makes me perk right up. I figure that a homosexual gentleman of a certain age has handled enough dicks, nipples, butt holes, and male bodies to be more than a 50-50 chance of a good time.

Sometimes the men who unsuccessfully pursued Lauren stuck around and appointed themselves his friends. Go figure. One of these guys was just my type, medium height, early 50s, stocky, with snowy hair and beard, a kind face, and a steady job. I noticed that whenever Lauren got himself into trouble, Owen was there for him. Lauren was also frequently late for their get-togethers. (Rapunzel had to stay put in her tower, but if you're into rescuing princesses, you can't count on all of them being locked up where they're easy to find.) I wound up giving Owen the occasional cup of coffee and chatting. I had a firm policy of not chasing my roommate's current favorites or castoffs, even though some of them caught my eye and tugged at my crotch. I guess I was proud or something. I didn't want to service some guy who would be thinking about Lauren while he was blowing me.

Owen was one of those masculine gay men who occasionally camps it up a bit. He had a purple backpack (in fact, he had a lot of purple things—a purple key ring on his left belt loop, purple seat covers in his Jeep, purple camouflage fatigues). I noticed a patch on the backpack that was a flag in tasteful earth tones, with a big bear paw print in one corner. Did it mean anything? Owen, it turned out, was a bear, and had been "part of the bear movement for a long time, before it turned into something just as cliquish and snobbish as all the rest of the gay boys, except this time we're all supposed to be competing to be fatter than anybody else." For a while at least, Owen had found a genuine sense of community or brotherhood among bears. He spoke at length and wistfully about promoting values like acceptance of a wide range of body types, practicing kindness instead of maliciousness, and being honest and responsible with your partners. It made me want to bake the man a batch of cookies and then put a pot roast in the oven.

Uh-oh. Whenever I head for the kitchen and start churning out the desserts and dinners, especially the pot roast or the lasagna, I'm about to become the naked cherubic archer's oversized pincushion. I liked Owen a lot, but there was that little matter of bringing him across the imaginary red line I had painted between Lauren's life-slash-bedroom and my own. There was also that little matter of those keys on the left. I keep mine there too, and I didn't get much of a switchable vibe from Owen. The men he talked about dating were all bottoms, and he seemed to be very well established as a daddy in the bear world.

Still, there was no harm in becoming friends, I thought. That meant brunch only, out of the house. Maybe I could make him lunch occasionally, but nothing more complicated than a sandwich. So we started to make a few social dates of our own. We went out to Yellowstone a few times (the bar, not the park—the trouble with camping in the great outdoors is, they keep all the dirt there). He came to my leather AA meeting. And I invited Owen to hang out in my part of the house. Lauren has the upstairs. I have my own bedroom and bathroom downstairs in the garage, where I've also built myself a decent playroom, with space left over to park my motorcycle. We often wound up in the playroom, in fact, drinking one cup of coffee after another and reminiscing about various scenes we'd done, both good and bad. I thought it was a little strange that we did this, but sometimes I have about as much insight as an anvil.

Things probably could have gone on this way for years if Owen had not taken the initiative, albeit a subtle one. I was getting over a terrible case of the flu. He had brought over some chicken soup and orange juice. I was sitting at the kitchen table moping over, ga-a-ak, a mug full of peppermint tea when I glanced at Owen, who was standing calmly at the sink, doing my dishes.

He had moved his keys over to the right.

I haven't been so excited since the Christmas morning when I got my first bicycle. The rush of adrenaline that ran through me swept the last traces of illness out of my system. I was not going to waste this hot man's energy on a sink full of soup bowls. I went downstairs and traded my pajamas and bathrobe for a pair of leather pants, some boots, and my favorite leather vest with the red piping. (Let me tell you, we get wild about our black leather up here in San Francisco!) Then I grabbed a leash and a collar out of the playroom and a pair of handcuffs.

I'm sure he heard me coming up the stairs, but he kept his eyes firmly on the sink as I marched into the kitchen and stood close behind him, so close that my breath moved the little white hairs on his neck. "Don't turn around," I said. "Hold still." He obeyed me, which was a huge turn-on. I have never understood why other men would do what I tell them to do. But this acquiescence, especially the first sign of it, makes my heart beat faster. It's just so sexy. I can't describe it, but I feel as if I'm being given a huge present that is mine to unwrap and enjoy at my leisure.

We hadn't talked or negotiated a scene, but from our conversations, I had a pretty good idea of what Owen liked when he topped. I took a chance that my opening gambit would be within his limits. Once I got him downstairs, we could go into more detail. I had stashed the leash in my pocket, and the handcuffs were in a leather holder on my belt. So I had both hands free to unbuckle the collar and run it across his neck. "I want you to wear this for me," I said, and he signaled his acceptance by bowing his head. I buckled it in place, hoping that my hands didn't shake, I was that excited. I didn't want to look nervous, even though I was. This was a friend of mine, somebody I loved, and I wanted this to be a perfect experience for him.

I attached the leash to the D-ring in the front of the collar, then put the leather end of it between his teeth. He held it in his mouth for me, looking submissively at the floor, then looked up just long enough to give me a seductive little wink. I knew then that things were going to be OK. So I cuffed his hands behind his back, set the hinges so they wouldn't get any tighter, even though I didn't plan to keep him in them very long, and led him downstairs to the game room.

I don't know about you, but I find it very damn difficult to locate a bunch of black leather toys in a room that's also been painted black. So the walls of my dungeon had been painted battleship-gray. Butch, but high-contrast. One wall was a solid mirror, and there was adjustable lighting. I closed the door and told Owen to kneel on the floor and keep his head down. What a handsome sight he was, this big daddy, all mine, a playground of male flesh. I stood close to him once more and put my hands behind his head, encouraging him to rub his bearded face against the leather crotch of my jeans. I wanted him so much, but if I let him suck me off at the beginning of the scene, I wouldn't have much energy to continue. So I teased him by talking about how much I wanted him to suck my dick, and promising him that if he was good, I'd reward him with that later. "Would you like that?" I asked.

"Yes, sir, very much," he replied.

I took the handcuffs off his wrists. "Then strip down for me, and stow your clothes and boots in that cabinet." He undressed quickly but took the time to fold up his things and put them away in a neat pile, on top of his boots. I appreciate that little gesture. It's one of the things that makes me feel that the bottom is going to work as hard as I am to make the scene a good one. And it shows me that they have respect, both for their own belongings and for my space and my authority.

"Get up on the table," I said. "Lie down on your back." I indicated the large bondage table in the center of the room. This padded, leather-covered platform was the piece of bondage equipment that I used most often. There were several different ways to secure a body to it—the classic four-point spread eagle, suspension, spider-web bondage, mummification. I could also drop the foot of it and hang their feet up in stirrups if I wanted that kind of access.

He complied, moving a little awkwardly, and I was reminded that this behavior was new for him. He was taking a big risk by moving his keys over for me. I briefly turned away to make sure the heat was on, and thought about the problem of what to call him, what my attitude should be. He was a daddy, but that didn't necessarily mean that he now wanted me to call him boy. Was he fantasizing about being my slave? He had called me Sir, which I always like. These were just some of the things we should talk about.

But first, I returned to the platform and touched him gently, one hand on his chest and one hand on his thighs. His cock was half-hard, a good sign, and he looked at me with the light of worship in his eyes. He was already blissed out, on a high from being able to go under and relinquish his will to another. I wanted to prolong that high for as long as possible. So I took each of his hands in turn and buckled them into leather bondage cuffs. I also spread his legs apart and secured them. There was a lot of tension in his body as I maneuvered his feet into position, and I wondered if that meant he was afraid I might try to fuck him. He had complained once about a scene he had done with another top who had a masochistic streak. When they were done playing, the guy had wanted to fuck Owen, and he adamantly refused, saying this was something he did not like at all.

"You know," I said, stroking his inner thigh, "I want to stretch you out here so I can look at you and touch you. But nothing is going to happen that you don't like." The room was warming up, which would eventually make me sweat in my leathers, but I wanted his naked body to stay relaxed. Some of the tension left his legs. I put on a pair of leather gloves and massaged his chest and arms, relishing the fact that he was at my mercy.

"So tell me what you want," I suggested. "Why are we here?"

He looked at me with something like panic. "I don't know," he said. "I've never done this before. You're the only man I've ever met that I wanted to bottom for."

Oh. Hoping my face didn't reveal the fact that I felt as if I had been punched in the stomach, I continued to stroke and massage his body. What I had on my hands was a complete novice, as a bottom anyway, who was also a very experienced and competent top. What an intimidating combination. Well, I was experienced and competent too. This was somebody I found very attractive. So I would proceed as if I were working with any beginner, and if our scene was not the most elaborate or intense one I had ever done, who cared? We were not playing for an audience. Just the two of us were there, and what happened in our hearts and minds was at least as important as what went on physically.

"Well," I said, "I'll just try a few different things, then. And you tell me how they feel. If you like something, we'll do more of it, and if you don't like it, we can stop. I want you to just be honest with me. That's all you have to do to please me."

"Yes, sir," he said. (Note the lower-case "s." A capital-s "Sir" is for ongoing relationships only. Just a little free etiquette lesson for ya there.) Then I bent over and kissed him, taking all of his anticipation and fear into my mouth. I love the contrast between soft lips and tongue and the raspy feel of a mustache and beard. Owen was a good kisser, allowing me to take the lead but responding with skill instead of being simply passive. "I wish I could touch you, sir," he said, lifting his body and pulling against the chains.

"But you can't," I said, running my hands down his hairy chest and belly and taking his cock in my gloved fist. "You have to just lie there and let me touch you. I can do anything I want with you, you know. You're helpless. And whatever I make you feel, you have to express, you won't be able to help it. I'm going to make you feel all kinds of things, Owen. Do you like being helpless?"

"Only because I trust you, sir," he whispered. His cock was coming alive in my seductive grasp. I knew that I had to woo not only the man but his dick as well.

"This belongs to me too, you know," I said, tugging on his cock and balls. He gasped. "I want to make sure you remember that." I went to the wall where my ropes hung and opened a drawer in a cabinet below them. There was a reel of parachute cord and a pair of bandage scissors. I cut off a suitable length of the cord and returned to the bondage table. There I bound Owen's balls at the base, then used the rest of the cord to separate them. Blood could flow into his ball sac, but it would be difficult for all of it to leave. "What a nice-looking package," I growled, and roughly fondled his imprisoned nuts. "Do you like knowing I've got your balls all tied up?" I asked.

"I think so, sir," he replied, breathing a little hard. "It feels strange, but it's exciting to know that you've tied me up that way."

"Just let me know if your balls start to feel cold," I said. "I'll keep checking on them to make sure they don't lose circulation." In fact, it was time to check his hands and feet as well, which I did. As I attended to this precaution, I could feel Owen slipping deeper into submission, letting go of another level of control because he knew

I was taking care of him. I got out a pair of currying combs, especially made to provide a variety of different sensations when applied to human skin. Used lightly, they stimulate the circulation and can even tickle. If they are pressed slowly into the skin, they can be used for deep-tissue massage. But if they are swept rapidly across a sensitive area, they feel sharp and leave a burning sensation behind. They don't, however, break the skin. I used the combs on Owen's chest and the exposed skin of his arms and legs, then handled him with my leather gloves. He was breathing slow and deep, eyes partially closed.

His nipples were of average size. Some men's nipples are so small and their chests are so tight that you can't even get them into your mouth. But Owen's protruded just enough for me to be able to circle them with my tongue and apply pressure to them with my teeth. I chewed and licked his nipples for a long time, then kissed him while my fingers flicked them to and fro. "I want to clamp your nipples," I told him, with our mouths just a fraction of an inch apart.

"Yes, sir," he said, his tongue thick. "Oh, please clamp my nipples, sir."

The question was, Which tit clamps should I pick? At least a dozen pairs, connected by various weights of chain, hung from a peg board next to the ropes. Did he play with his own tits while he jacked off? It didn't look to me as if they had seen much use. How mean should I be? Not very, I decided. I wanted Owen to start surfing the edge between pleasure and pain. A gradual introduction to those feelings would be the ideal way to start.

I picked a pair that looked like they would stay on his nipples, and compress them just enough to make him somewhat uncomfortable. When I went back to the table, Owen's eyes were completely closed. I introduced myself into his world by stroking his chest, gradually returning my attention to his nipples. His hips rose and fell as I dragged the chain across his skin, reminding him of what I was going to do. "Here they are," I said, taking hold of one nipple and positioning it within the grip of the clamp. "These are my helpers. They're going to bite you. It might be a little hard to take. But remember that I want them to bite into you, Owen. I want them to hurt your tender tits. And while they are pinching you, I'm going to give you a reward." I let the jaws of the clamp close, and he acknowledged the onset of pain by nodding his head. "You're doing very well," I said, and took hold of his other nipple. "Keep breathing slow and deep," I said, putting it in place. "If it hurts, just give me the pain. Visualize sending it to me, and I'll take it away."

I removed my gloves and squirted a little lube into the palm of one hand. While Owen concentrated on his breathing and moved into a state where he accepted a small amount of pain and integrated it into all of the other things he was feeling, I began to work on his cock and balls. A top's hands are his most valuable tool, in my opinion. You can do a really good scene with no equipment at all as long as you are knowledgeable about where and how to touch the bottom. I let my hands wander over his sex, squeezing, stroking, stretching, rolling. Breathing deep and slow myself, I allowed myself the leisurely pleasure of fondling him at length. I especially liked reinforcing the cords around his balls with pressure from my fingers. At one point I even put his balls in my mouth, teasing the taut skin, moving the oval glands even farther away from his body. He groaned when I stretched his balls, and said, rolling his head from side to side, "Oh, sir, thank you, that feels so good, oh, oh!"

By milking his cock while he wore the tit clamps, I had taken Owen to a place where he might be receptive to a little more challenging game. But first the tit clamps would have to come off. When I told him so, a look of apprehension crossed his face. "Yes," I said. "You know there's going to be a burst of pain when I release these and the blood comes back into your nipples. But remember that it's pain that I'm giving you. I want you to feel this. So I want you to look me in the eyes while I take these off and open your mouth and let your pain come out in a sound. Yes, just like that. I want to see and hear how this feels."

The sound that he made wasn't as loud as a scream or a shout. It was a muffled roar or a harsh sigh, a hissing acknowledgment that small bolts of lightning had gone through the two red-hot points on his chest. After I took the clamps off, I suckled on his nipples again, returning him to the edge between sensation you want to continue and sensation that makes you want to duck. I even reached down and got one hand around his cock so that I could jack him off a bit while I reminded him with my mouth how much his nipples could feel. When my mouth wasn't full, I told him how good he was being. He rolled from side to side, moaning in a dilemma of pain and pleasure. His body language was getting clearer, his hips loosening up, and I loved seeing him really get into our play.

I abruptly left his side, turned off the lights, and left him alone in the darkness. "Sir?" he asked. I could imagine him on the table, lifting his head, trying to find me. But I was behind him, out of the range of his vision, getting the piece of equipment that I wanted ready to use.

Then I returned, feeling a little silly about the drama I was creating, and held my hand above his chest. Purple sparks flew from my hand to his skin. "Focus on your breathing," I reminded him. "Relax and accept what you're feeling. Do this for me. Will you do this for me?"

"I will, sir," he said, and I put the mushroom-shaped glass attachment into my ultraviolet wand. I had been holding onto a metal attachment in order to do the trick with electrifying my hand. Now the current went from the device directly onto Owen's body. He rolled from side to side and grunted as I experimented on different parts of his body. The purple light was a compelling sight in the darkness, and as it cast its eerie spell, I stopped feeling silly. What we were doing was dramatic. It was an act of transformation. Neither Owen nor I would be quite the same people when we finished this scene.

"I love your pain," I told him, giving him a break from the wand's tingling and burning caresses. I stroked his forehead, brushing back his hair. He was sweating, and his eyes were glazed.

"Why, sir?" he pleaded.

"You don't have to know why," I replied. "It's enough for you to know that this is what turns me on. Your job is to just respond."

"It's hard to get all of this attention, sir. I feel like I'm not doing my job."

"What, by not running things?"

"Yes, I guess so."

"But Owen, you don't always have to run things. I'm here to prove that to you. You don't have to do anything, just be here with me in the present. Now, I want you to do something really hard for me."

"What is that, sir?"

"I want to use this ultraviolet wand on your balls."

"Oh, no, sir, please, I don't think I can take it."

I hesitated, not sure if I should take this as his final answer or do a little coaxing. He hadn't spoken with a lot of emphasis. And he didn't seem to be frightened to me. So I put the wand down and kissed him again, let my hands explore his body. He felt warm to the touch, a good sign, but I wanted to roll him over soon, change his position and his perspective. Should I tell him he had a choice between submitting to the purple sparks or some other even more horrendous toy?

My fingers found their way to his nipples, which I proceeded to drag away from his chest, and twist. His cock slowly filled out as I pummeled them. Maybe tit play was part of his jack-off routine after all. If it wasn't before, I had a feeling that it would be. For some reason, I was inspired to say this out loud. Owen agreed that he was not going to be able to leave his nipples alone in the future. "Now, if I had asked you if you liked having your nipples tortured, you wouldn't have said yes, would you?" I asked.

"No, probably not, sir," he admitted.

"Well, this is no different," I said, hoisting the black plastic body of the wand. "You think you won't like it because you are afraid. Sometimes even if something hurts, it's still exciting. But I think you can take it. And I think it's an experience you should have."

"You know I'll try to do anything that you want me to do," he replied at last, melting my heart.

"I promise it won't last a very long time," I said. "Now spread your legs." (I love saying that.)

With a distinctly ambivalent expression on his face, my bound bear did as I said. But I knew if his hands had been free, they would have flown to cover his equipment. "You can make noise if you want to," I reminded him. "Nobody can hear what we do in this room. Maybe there's something you'd like to let go of when you scream, something you want to send out of your life or your body. Can you think of something like that?"

"Yes," he said after a long pause.

"Well, hold that in your mind and send it away in a good big scream for me."

I switched on the wand and took my time bringing it to his body, knowing that the anticipation would jack things up a notch. I touched the glass mushroom to his hip, holding it firmly against the skin to prevent it from discharging. It traveled slowly across his thigh, over to his cock (he gasped), and down to the two imprisoned nuts. "Ready?" I asked sympathetically.

He looked at me, looked down at his balls, and then took a deep breath in. "Ready!" he cried, and I lifted the wand.

What followed was a respectable cry of pain. But I think he was surprised to find, as I played the wand back and forth across his genitals, that he was actually not trapped inside of the pain. He had escaped it and gone to a different place. He was able to feel what was happening to his body, but he didn't care because he was flying in another realm.

I gradually stepped down what I was doing, dialing the strength of the charge to its lowest point and trailing the wave of purple light up his stomach, onto his chest, where it winked out, and was put away.

"You did very well," I said, untying his poor balls and massaging the swollen sac.

He was out of breath, so I went to the head of the table and squirted a little water into his mouth. "Thank you, sir," he said.

"So do you want to tell me what it was that you were throwing off, when you screamed just now?"

He looked quite shy. "Well, sir, I think I was getting rid of my fear of being here with you, my fear that I won't be good enough."

I stroked him all over, letting my hands express my approval. "I won't let you fail," I said. "I'm going to change your position now. I want you to roll over onto your belly."

"OK, sir. But can I have a minute to just kind of collect myself?"

"Sure," I said. "More water?"

"Please, sir."

After he swallowed as much water as he needed, I puttered around the dungeon, making sure I knew where the things I wanted next were located. I was in full scene mode at that point, moving with self-confidence, full of ideas and enthusiasm. It's always nice when performance anxiety departs, but I've found that if I don't have that initially unpleasant feeling of doubt, I go into the scene without much energy. I apparently need to be challenged to do my best as a top. I need to face the fear that I won't be good enough and walk through it. So I empathized completely with Owen's exorcism and told him so as I got ready to do the next half of our session.

Finally he called me back to the table and told me that he was ready. I unhooked his bondage cuffs and let him get off the table and walk around a bit to work out any stiffness that had settled into his muscles from being in one position for so long. I also caught him checking out his cock and balls in the mirror. "No damage," I said, grinning wolfishly. "You might have a bit of a sunburn tomorrow, that's all."

"Do I dare ask what's next, sir?"

"No, you do not," I said briskly. "On your knees."

He went down to the floor with no apparent resistance. So I had not damaged his trust in me by pushing his limits. I wondered what he would have to say to the next challenge. "I want you to wear this," I said, and slipped a hood over his head. It was a close-fitting leather mask that laced up the back. It wouldn't impede his breathing, but it had a built-in blindfold that would prevent him from seeing anything at all.

"Wow" was all I heard before it went into place. "Sir," he added as the mouth of the hood lined up with his own.

"You're so good at remembering to call me sir, I don't have any opportunity to punish you for forgetting," I commented.

"I don't want to be punished, sir."

"I'll remember that. How does it feel to be hooded?"

"Different, sir. I feel...more quiet, somehow."

"Good. You might really enjoy this, then. The hood is a way to eliminate distractions. It can help you to really fly. Now get up and turn around. That's right. Take a few steps forward. Can you feel the edge of the table? Yes, that's the head. Throw your leg over it and up you go. Great." Four clicks, and he was once more my willing prisoner.

I took two whips from the wall and hung one around my neck. The other was much shorter, and I kept that in my right hand. They were both fairly heavy, with unbraided, flat lashes. I'd worked with the whip-maker to make sure they were constructed so that there was very little, if any, sting to them. These were my whips for briefly warming up a heavy masochist before picking up something more cruel or for using all night long to beat the snot out of somebody who wasn't particularly into pain. I could get a really good workout with both of these whips, usually without making somebody levitate off the bondage table and call for their mama. (Though I do sometimes wonder what it would be like to make a smugly misogynist little urban leather fag call me that on purpose. But that's probably a little too radical to get into right here.)

I approached the table loosening up my shoulders by doing figure eights with the short whip. A sound like that will get your blood going if you're tied up. But Owen couldn't hear me. He was hooded. So I spoke up a bit to make sure he heard me.

"I've decided to whip you now," I said.

He said nothing, but he had turned his head to face the direction that my voice was coming from, and the mouth within the leather casing was shaped into an O. As in The Story of. Oh, never mind.

"You don't have to respond unless you disagree with something I'm saying," I instructed. "I'm guessing that you don't want me to hit you on the ass." Once more, I had guessed correctly. His body settled into the table, and a little of the brittle-as-glass feeling went out of the white double curves of his butt. "So I'm going to flog your shoulders," I continued. "But this whipping is not about hurting you, Owen. It's got a different purpose altogether."

A whipping that wasn't supposed to hurt? I could see that I had his full attention. "Sir?" he asked.

I laid the leather ends of the whip across his shoulders and began to stroke him with featherlight circles. "Think of this as me sort of beating the dirt out of a carpet," I said. "I have a pretty good idea of what you're carrying on those big shoulders of yours. You're a good man and a good daddy, Owen, but it's pretty hard to shoulder all the expectations that your boys have of you. You're carrying a lot of other people's hopes and disappointments and some of your own pain as well. So I'm going to whip that shit right off of you. Thump you till it shakes loose and flies away. What do you think of that?"

"I think it sounds pretty crazy, sir."

His candor made me chuckle, but I was actually pretty serious about what I intended to do, so I made him get back on track with me. I gave him a little bit of a hard smack with the whip, a blow that was out of rhythm with what I had been doing. "Do you think that's any way to talk to a man who has a whip in his hand?" I rebuked him.

"Uh—no, sir. I apologize, sir. Permission to explain?"

There it was again, one of those tricks that a bottom can do that makes me shake in my boots with affection and admiration for them. He wanted to talk to me, but he didn't want to interrupt the flow of our scene or fuck up the roles we were playing, so he had found a polite way to insert his request to continue the dialogue. As a British friend of mine would say, what is he like?

"Permission granted," I said. Meanwhile, I continued to prepare his back for what was to follow. I kept the whip moving around, not too fast and not too slow, drawing blood to the surface of his skin. I was familiarizing him with being struck at an easy tempo and depth to allow him to almost take it for granted that it was OK for him to let me hit him. I was going to step things up so gradually that I doubted he would even notice when I switched from junior to big daddy, hanging around my neck.

"I wish it would work," he said, spacing the words out the way men do when there is a lot of emotion behind what they are saying and a strong determination not to cry. "But it's hard for me to believe that it could work."

"When you had my tit clamps on, did it work when I told you to accept the pain and send me whatever you couldn't handle, so I could take it away?"

"Yes."

"Well, we've had a little break, but we can reestablish that channel now. Just start sharing whatever you feel with me. Send it my way. If we can connect on a deep level, inside of ourselves, I can get a contact endorphin high from you. We'll just drive each other crazy till we can't stand it anymore."

"I'm seeing the whip strokes as particles of light, sir. It flows through me and then back to you. As if we were part of an electrical circuit."

"That's exactly what I'm talking about." I slowed my strokes down, spaced them out a little more, and increased the force just a smidge. "You screamed out a desire to get rid of your fear that you wouldn't be good enough. How did you feel after you did that?"

He flexed in his bonds, somehow arranging himself to greet and welcome the whip strokes. "It felt great, sir," he admitted. "I felt really good, totally accepted and safe, as if nothing could ever go wrong."

"Well, that's why we're here, to build the strong walls of such a safe place and stay there for as long as we can. Now breathe the same way that you did when you were wearing the tit clamps. Keep sending me your pain. And let it rock you into a different state of being. A state where all of the trouble that weighs you down will just lift off your shoulders and melt away. Feel me driving it away, driving it out of you."

"Oh—" he exclaimed.

Then we didn't need to talk to each other for a long time. We communicated through touch alone, and yet there was also a connection between us that was not physical. Sometimes I whipped him slowly, sometimes quickly; sometimes I made him cry out and sometimes I almost lulled him to sleep. In between using the whips I stroked him or slapped him with my hands, keeping him in my power. I felt like a daddy eagle with my wing stretched over a nest.

I knew that Owen was completely open to me when he began to cry. I kept on beating him anyway, because I knew there was more to come. And I was right. For a while he raged on the table, blind to my presence, struggling against who knew what ancient demon. (My friend the therapist says, "All childhood is damaging.") Under my supervision, kept in a place where he could not hurt himself or anybody else, Owen released an impressive amount of old garbage.

When he was calm again, I asked him if he wanted me to continue, and he said clearly, in a strong voice, "Yes, sir!"

So I gave him the little bit of energy I had left in me, finding my second wind because I knew this was the really good part. Owen would be feeling clean and whole now, and I wanted him to have a clear memory of feeling free and proud of his ability to please me. Again and again I told him how very special and good he was as I took him through the last part of the whipping, marking him so that he would have a memento of this holiday from the everyday and ordinary and expected.

When I took his hood off, he needed more water but asked for a kiss first when I put the straw up to his mouth. "Oh, God, sir, please let me blow you," he said in a voice that was cracked from expressing so many different emotions.

I made him drink first, then unbuckled the bondage cuffs and led him by his collar over to my throne. This is a chair I found at a garage sale, a bad imitation of Spanish mission–style furniture, tarted up with some black paint and studs. Look, unlike Nancy Sinatra's little white go-go boots, my Doc Martens with their steel toes are not made for walkin'. So I threw myself into that throne and had a few big gulps of water myself. Then I undid the zipper in my leather jeans and told him to make me come.

Cocks are such funny things. Owen's dick had been soft through most of the whipping. But that didn't mean it wasn't sexy for him. I wonder if your nervous system can only handle one thing at a time. If you're involved in a pain trip, those chemicals are zinging around, working their own kind of purple magic. It's a mind thing, sometimes a heart thing, but not necessarily a grab-you-by-your-balls thing. Getting high on pain almost seems to block the root chakra, pig-in-the-mud, lunge-and-fuck, red energy that gets a cock to stand up and look for something to poke.

There are scenes that are all about my cock, about force-feeding the bottom, denying it to him, making him crawl for it. But when I'm using a whip, I lose track of my own dick. So I'm not really sure what happens to me then. Often after I hang the flogger up, I'm surprised to see that I've got a hard-on. And that's what happened when Owen knelt in front of me and took my sex into his mouth. I wanted it to last, but we were both tired and had stars in our eyes besides. We'd never had sex before, but he knew just how to use his tongue and sweet bearded lips to drive me crazy. I think I made more noise while I got that blow job than Owen had made when I was doing my worst. I thought I would die if I didn't come, and I would have sold my soul to the devil to make it go on forever. So he got a little of his own back. Sucking dick is living proof of the complexity of power and sex. I was in his mouth and he was kneeling for me, but I was also the happy subject of everything that he made me feel and helpless to do anything except hang on to his ears and hope he wouldn't stop. When I came, you might say he had mastered me.

So many words and so much ponderous thought over an act that was accomplished effortlessly, instinctively, with silent animal sanity.

"Dude," he said, wiping his beard with the back of his hand. "What got into you?"

I roused myself and looked around for the water bottle, and noticed a big smudge on the toe of one of my boots. Damn. I hate polishing those things. "What do you mean?" I barely had the brains to ask. "You moved your keys over to the right. I was just picking up on your signal."

Owen stared at me and began to laugh. A big belly laugh that made me a twee bit nervous. "I had to put 'em somewhere. The belt loop on the other side was busted."

"Oh." Fuck. Had I just made a royal jackass of myself?

"No—" He struggled to bring his laughter under control. "I'm not complaining. I meant what I said about you being the only man I've ever fantasized about bottoming for. But I never would have had the guts to come right out and ask for it. Hey, don't you dare apologize. It was one of the best 'mistakes' you ever made." He put the quote marks around the word "mistakes" with his index fingers.

"Well, pard, I guess you can get up now." Listen to me. Pard. My father had a right to talk that way, but he was a real cowboy. Me, I just channel him when I get rattled.

Owen looked around. "I guess I can, at that." As he got on his feet and stretched, I noticed that his cock had apparently started receiving sex signals again while he had been working on mine. So I reached out and grabbed it. Wasn't it nice of Mother Nature to give my polar bear such a useful and shapely handle?

"Let's do something really controversial," I stage-whispered.

He looked around the playroom, seeing it in a whole new light. "Like what?" he said apprehensively, furtively trying to catch a glimpse of his back in the mirror.

"Let's go into my bedroom and have raucous sex."
"Well," Owen said, perking up. "All righty!"
I grabbed a bottle of lube on my way to the sack. I may be a top, but I'm not stupid.

Hooked

I was born in the year of the Hunter, and my Signifier is the card of the Unrequited Lover. I quit school as soon as it was legal, at the age of 10, to become a messenger for my city. The hidden rulers of our world do not like anything that is noisy, although it took a century of plague and earthquake for us to understand that quiet was one of their few requirements of us. Now the graceful power of muscle has largely replaced the clamor of the artless machine.

At the age of 14, I burned my family flag and declared myself a devotee of the falling star, which is not a bad cult for the beginner. I was still a runner, and more highly paid. Because the cargo I carried was more valuable, I learned how to defend it. Eventually I found harsher masters who required more dedication. Worship was more taxing and also a great deal more satisfying. By the age of 18 I no longer ferried drugs about. The substance I craved came to me, and hordes of people eager to watch me acquire the right to it. On this world, which humans took from double-sexed aborigines who died because of something we put into their water or their air, control over nova is wielded by the ringmasters, ancestral keepers of the squared circle.

I do not look like a fighter. I have always been small for my age, and my way of life did not put much flesh upon my bones. But I am quick and efficient, although my methods are sometimes unconventional. We must pass through metal and plastic detectors before we enter the ring, but no device exists that will detect weapons made of shell, stone, or bone. My tall siblings of sainted memory taught me well. On occasion it has been said that I am able to anticipate my opponent's every move. It is true that when the bright lights fall upon me, it seems as if everyone else slows down, and I am able to dart in to make my kill unscathed. But there is also the fact that most people do not fight to win. They are in love with losing and fight to be put on their knees. Or out of their misery.

The ringmasters are implacable. In the beginning, you must win only one bout to be well-rewarded. Nova was everything I had heard that it would be—glad obliteration, explosion of all thought, a seemingly endless golden journey into deliciously cold black nothingness. But it was a drug. Unlike the gods of this world, it came to an end. After a score of bouts, I was told that I must win twice to be rewarded again.

All of my needs were provided for. Food. Sex. Luxurious lodging. Expensive clothes. If I wanted more than the ringmasters were willing to provide, there were fans who would sell all that they possessed and think themselves lucky if I accepted it without even giving thanks. Training was also available, of course, but treated as if it were an afterthought.

The sweaty, narcissistic squalor of sex disgusted me. I thought about food as often as I thought about breathing. Possessions were a distraction. I needed only a flat surface to lie upon so I could attend to the celestial machinery of my mind. I wanted only the experience of desire itself, not the disappointment of longing attained. Nova was my banquet, my lover, my true home. I did not go shopping or have affairs with famous citizens or soak my wounds in the adoration of ignorant cowards. I trained hard and constantly, and this asceticism only made me more beloved. Fighters are allowed to take as much time between bouts as they wish (or can endure). I went back to the white floor in 10 short days. And thereafter, I was never able to wait even that long. I never accepted a gift from an admirer, and I never gave an interview. As a result, I am one of the most famous citizens of my world.

The Signifier for today is the card of Eagle Dropping Tortoise From the Sky. Tonight there are 10 people panting for the tenderness of my fists, and their blood can be exchanged for four times as much nova as I received for my first victory. But this courtly brawl will have to proceed without me. I have put away my weights and hung up my silk robe. The bathroom is scrubbed. My quarters are ready for their next inhabitant, incense burned in all four corners. I have tied a flint knife to my upper arm and rubbed my body with copal, because its scent is said to be pleasing to the Preying Mantics who have never asked for our affection or obedience. I will leave this place naked, and everyone who sees me will know where I am going. They will turn away and cover their eyes, then hurry to the temple to be made clean again. There they will pray for my success and curse me for the evil luck I have brought down upon them by being seen.

I do not believe in luck. The choices I have made in my life make no sense at all to the people who dote upon a spouse, a child, a pet, or a job. My career has been to wring ecstasy from each cell of my own body, no matter how much I might suffer for it later. My vocation has been to avoid entanglements, for engaging with others takes precious time that I could spend in pursuit of my true love. One who called himself my friend and tried to dissuade me from entering the death matches exclaimed in disgust, "You must not like yourself very much." This was amusing. For it is other people that I do not like. I am content when I am undistracted and alone with my chemical deities. I am will personified. And now I choose another doom.

Nova causes wasting. It comes on quickly, all at once, and leaves its devotees withered and sere. But this castration does not extinguish craving. It accelerates it. Two of the people I was supposed to confront tonight were ballast on the card, as easy to crush as dead leaves. But the mob enjoys watching the destruction of their former heroes. I am the only fighter who has ever walked away from the ringmasters. There is no cure for addiction to nova. If you have taken enough of the drug to feel its effects at all, you belong to it forever. If you stop taking it, you suffer, world without end. The withdrawal process destroys the receptors for the drug, so at a certain point you could ingest pounds of nova to no avail.

I had chosen the blazing delights in the void of nova. But I had not chosen to die of it. I was not romantically obsessed with death, I was addicted to sensation. If I had to die, it would be in such a manner as I chose.

And so I choose to take this barefoot walk, this long pilgrimage out of the city, into the wilderness, and above the treeline. To the caves that riddle the rocks of our mountains. To the Reticulated Pythia, who I hoped would have me and take me slowly into a nothingness that would please us both.

The Reticulated Pythia is also known as the Preying Mantic (and how many crusades were fought over which of those names was best, until it became clear that the hidden ones did not care?). It feasts upon the volcanic gases that waft through the caves. Perhaps it also samples the molten rock of the volcano's core. Certainly it has some strange affinity with the planet, and seems able to trigger both volcanic eruptions and earthquakes. Perhaps the part of the Pythia which we see is only the tip of the iceberg, and it has the greatest part of its being deep below the ground. Perhaps the many we see are really one, arms of a single organism rather than separate individual faces.

It took me days to make the trip. I walked through the light and the darkness, sleeping wherever exhaustion felled me. I drank from streams if I crossed them and dragged berries and insects off bushes that I walked past. The native vegetation all contains alkaloids that alter human perception, but I did not fly and saw no spirits. To keep up a constant pace, I did not look at what went between my teeth. The lack of nova warmed me, though not comfortably, and I walked on the broken glass of deprivation. Pain had never been my enemy, and that was fortunate.

The Reticulated Pythia was unable to feel pain, but that did not prevent it from having vast storehouses of hurt to give away with a liberal claw. I was going there, however, because agony was not its only gift. I caught myself wondering, once only, who had taken my place in the bloodthirsty gaze of the frenzied bystanders. Did any of them miss me? A scalding shame for my weakness almost made me stumble, but it burned itself out quickly.

On the evening of the seventh day, I passed the last tree. It was a fighter also, but unlike me, it could not take its struggle to a different ground. I gave it the gift of my water, making a circle around its half-exposed roots, and trudged on. The air was thin, and I appreciated the slight ache in my chest. It was like the pain that follows a good workout. I also took note of the effect on my own cognition. It was becoming harder to concentrate. Was this why I had failed to notice the background murmur that was now shockingly loud?

If the Mantic had been a person, I would have said it was talking to itself. But this litany was much more complex than speech. There were loving recitations of chemical formulae, terrifying prayers, whimsical status reports on various parts of its environment, grand music, sarcastic astrological interpretations, sensuous tallies of living beings or objects near and far, appreciative comments on the weather, and other sounds whose purpose I could not determine. As I staggered uphill to the mouth of the cave, it became so loud that I had to cover my ears.

"Why should I modulate my volume?" the Pythia asked. "I did not ask you to come here." The thing that it had to say to me was mingled with everything else and so difficult to ferret out. Each voice differed in pitch and timbre, and some of the music included notes above or below the range of my hearing. But I never expected the Pythia to shut down all of its activities in order to simply deal with me. Its multifaceted intelligence was legendary and dreadful.

"True," I said, almost overcome by the experience of being spoken to by such a powerful and alien creature. I stood on holy ground and thought it best to curb my tongue. It had known I was coming and by now would already have any information about me it wished to possess.

"What is truth?" asked the Pythia. The volume of sound subsided somewhat. "What is your truth?" it amended. "We shall see," it added, answering its own question. "You are interesting," it allowed, and I could feel rather than see its sensory apparatus, focusing a bit more upon me. Withdrawal from nova must be hurting me more than I thought. Combined with hunger, thirst, and exhaustion, that was a cocktail that might lure a Mantic from its lair.

"Does my pain taste good to you?" I asked. "Or is it like a song?"

There was dead silence for three seconds.

"We can exchange a great deal many more words than meanings," it explained to me, sounding as if it meant to be helpful, and then the babble began again.

Was that the end of my audience?

I waited and pretended that holding my place was a battle I must win. The blows were all aimed at my self-love and purpose, not my face or crotch, and this was the first fight I had been in that I could only win by refusing to hit back.

"Why are you here?" the Pythia demanded, and this time it showed enough of itself that I could see why it was called Reticulated. There are no photographs or drawings of the Preying Mantic. It is not permitted. "Our genetic material is not compatible," another voice told me, not unkindly. "The volcanic fumes are harsh for your species," a higher, almost hysterical voice intoned. "You will be damaged," a deep, fond voice admonished me. Again, it was hard to decipher these messages. The Pythia did not wait to end one sentence before beginning another, and at the same time it was reading a star map, counting air molecules, reveling in the stone walls of a cavern I could not see, and telling over the parasites on the back of a badger. At least there were no hymns to viruses. When the Reticulated Pythia sang the praises of microorganisms, you had seen the last card in the pack of your life.

"I came hoping you would hurt me," I said. "And thereby take from me a pain I do not want."

Seventeen kinds of laughter. The echoing sound of a bouncing ball. Music from a child's pop-up toy. The list of prime numbers. The announcer's narrative of a five-year-old balloon race, with annotations. The defining points of the orbit of a comet. Cannons going off at sea.

If a response was made in my own language, I could not hear it. So I took the flint knife from its binding and plunged it into the muscle of my thigh. Many things that are said of the Reticulated Pythia may be guesses or lies. But I believed this one: that you must draw your own blood first.

This new pain was shocking, and so my mouth flew open. Into that delicate gap sailed a tiny hook cast forth by the Pythia, which pierced my tongue from bottom to top. Thus was I encouraged to walk into the cave, on my tiptoes, at the end of a delicate alien filament. Red and yellow lights, flickering although they came from no visible fire, hid and revealed some portions of my host. It was not like us, or any of the animals we had brought with us 3,000 years ago. I was tempted to compare it to lichen or a snake or a large insect or an octopus or an abacus. But metaphors are dangerous; they encourage the illusion of comprehension where no understanding is possible.

"Watch my shadow," hissed the Pythia against a background of competing symphonies. "See it play with your own, then speak to me of pain you do not want, and pain you will choose in its stead."

Even the slightest contact between human and Pythia floods our systems with chemistry evolution has not prepared us to assimilate. What it does to them I do not know. But if they did not like it, they would have no reason to allow it. From the prick in my tongue a web of prickling spread over and under my skin. Even after the hook was withdrawn from my mouth, I could feel the shape of the puncture wound where a sharp touch had opened and changed me. If I ever ate food again, it would not have a human taste.

On the far wall of the cavern reared a monstrous shadow. It bore no relationship to the actual body of the Pythia, being in the shape of an erect hooded serpent with four arms and the bare breasts and erect cock of an aboriginal hierophant. A proxy of my own shadow appeared before it as if I were one of the tall and beautiful. These two dark beings confronted one another though I was seated on the floor of the cavern, several feet away from the closest appendage of the Preying Mantic.

The sacred hermaphrodite grabbed my shadow by its hair and lifted *me* off my feet. Me! No one had hoisted me into the air since

I wore the absorbent clouts of an infant. I could feel the pull in every inch of my scalp and down my shoulders and spine, but my hair held fast. Then s/he snapped me as if I were a ringmaster's lash or an exercise mat being rid of crumbs. Concentric rings of agony ran down my body from the tips of my hair to my toenails.

But…it was my agony as the Pythia experienced it. The wavering ripples of icy colors that were the Northern Lights. The taste of oranges and burning platinum. An off-key trumpet and an electric harp making love to one another. The hopes of a seed opening in the earth.

My navel blossomed beneath the blows of the Pythia, and s/he skillfully extracted my entrails, weaving them around hir upper body until s/he wore them like a garland while s/he danced. I was entertained, confused, and tortured by the formula for predicting the curve along the edge of a lettuce leaf. The beauty of erosion, relentlessly grinding boulders into sand dunes. The death of a red dwarf star millions of light years away. The anatomy of a single fish scale.

And through it all was woven the endless curiosity and delight of the Reticulated Pythia, who exulted in all manner of data. Who knew nothing but happiness, pleasure, bliss, ecstasy beyond my experience or my imagination. This was what I had been trying to achieve when I stepped into the glare of combat, drawn by the rumor of nova's wonders. The Pythia was never lonely or bored or doubtful or anxious. It never slept, and it had no regrets.

And so it was finding things in me that it could not find in itself. When I could detach myself from the horror being played out upon my shadow, I could understand that it was symbolic. I was being sorted through like a basket of produce, sampled like a sphere of musics.

Nor was there any end to the ecstasy that the Pythia offered. This was where it lived. Its joy was as constant as the beating of my heart and more intense than any orgasm. As long as I could bear it, I could be in it, body-slammed by beauty. For the first time in my life, I knew what it was like to relinquish transcendence before it could desert me. I was sated, undone, and yet desperate to be melded once more into that invisible embrace.

"What is lonely?" the Pythia hissed. "What is musics?"

As if it knew I could endure no more delight, the shadow on the wall freed itself from the loops of my intestines, which reeled back into my body so smartly that I grunted from the impact. I felt bruised but could find no real injury with hand or eye, no matter how I twisted about to inspect myself.

"There is another," said the Reticulated Pythia. Was I imagining things, or did it give this remark a little more prominence, to make it easier for me to hear? "Come and see. Is this lonely?"

We went deeper into the cavern and around a bend. The sun had long since gone down, so we did not lose any light, but my back hairs came up as we moved deeper into the Pythia's realm. The sourceless flames on the irregular stone walls changed color, to transparent greens and peacock blues. We entered a space the size of a small room. On the cavern floor, bedded upon a folded portion of the Pythia's shed husk, lay another member of my species. The Preying Mantic had not lied. Our genetic material was not compatible, and the volcanic vapors were toxic to humans. Despite all the damage that had been done, I could find nothing but happiness in that barely breathing frame.

"I am finished with this," the Pythia said. "I have read it all. I am ready for another. But it will not leave."

So I was to be the next volume in the Pythia's encyclopedia of human gestalt. But if I wanted a place on the shelf, I would have to clear one for myself. The Pythia handed me back my flint knife. "Why did you pull it out of your leg?" it asked, then proceeded to give itself a dozen different answers.

It removed one of its eyes (or a musical instrument or a branch or a hammer) and stuck it to the cavern wall. "Do something," it told me. "You decide. I will be watching. Be interesting." Then it withdrew.

It never occurred to me to ask my predecessor questions. That is the problem with assuming you are unique—or doomed. I thought that every turn of the trail I was on had already been made clear to me. And killing had never been personal for me; I always had my eye on the prize, not the ladder that led up to it. How could a creature that did not comprehend pain or fear have any concept of mercy?

But it does, you know. It knows much about compassion, and even more about its opposite—punishment.

Holes

It was a rare Saturday night when I had been able to hold depression at bay—as well as a clingy, neurotic girlfriend who hated it when I went out alone—and put together the right combination of sexual need, adrenaline, and a little stash of MDA to go to the Saturday night party at the Catacombs. It was only three doors down the street from my house, but the prospect of having to take all of my clothes off in front of a hundred or so sweaty, naked men was a challenge I often could not meet. (Even if most of them were too lost in their own white-hot couplings to be aware of anyone but their mate in rut.)

Catacombs parties happened every Saturday night, so it was easy to persuade myself that next week would be a better time to go. I was young and had lost only one friend to suicide, a bitter woman I never expected to live out the full course of her years. To me, this was the apex of tragedy. I had not yet been slapped around enough by death to know that there is no such thing as a friend you can count on seeing again. And I had not lived through enough election-year crackdowns to know that a space for perverts will not necessarily be open next time you need to strut your wicked stuff.

The door to the insular world that called to me with a (butch) siren's voice was below street level. I carefully picked my nearsighted way down a few concrete stairs in the dark, barely touching the wrought iron handrail. The building was a unique dark blue-green, one of the less tarty painted ladies that marked San Francisco as a queer town. A brusque brass plaque on it said, "If you have not called, do not knock or ring now." (These parties were by appointment only.) Since I had duly made my reservation, I rang the bell and was greeted by Steve McEachern, a tall and handsome man in his early 30s. I followed him into a tiny entry room that protected the rest of the space from view if you were standing in the doorway. In three steps, I left the chill of autumn behind, and entered a super-heated and humid world where everything smelled of testosterone, leather, amyl, and Crisco.

Steve had the biggest nipple rings that I'd ever seen, solid gold, and an even bigger one ran through the head of his shapely average-size dick. His chest was nicely muscled without being gym-shaped, built up, I suspected, solely with marathon sessions of whipping and fucking. He had a jaunty, short, but unruly beard and the devil's own twinkle in his eyes. I signed in, handed over my money, bought a new bottle of poppers, and greeted a few regulars whose names I knew. The door was going to be open for another hour, so everyone was pretty much still clustered in the front room, which had a long bar along one wall, and benches along the other walls. There were long sheets of facing mirrors which made the room seem much bigger than it really was, and gave you no escape from yourself. The sound system behind the bar was pumping out one of Steve's excellent party tapes, driving dirty disco music that made me want to get stoned and fuck somebody's lights out. I hoped this was not one of the awful nights when I would stand apart from the feast, unable to connect and embarrassed by my own thwarted longing.

Steve's ex-lover George, a drunken thug with a handlebar mustache and what we then referred to as "the dick of death," was holding down the far end of the bar, and made some obnoxious slurred comment to me that I ignored. Clustered near Steve and his clipboard were his current boy toy and Cynthia Slater, who had introduced said trickette to the Catacombs. This had happened more than once. She knew exactly what kind of men Steve would fall for. Right now she was in a good mood because they were a threesome; her swain had not yet left her and moved in with the twisted, high-octane fag whose gifted hands were her obsession. (And mine, though I was too cool to drool over him in public.) She had become a fixture at the Catacombs in part because she was as sexually outrageous as any guy in the place. Steve was genuinely fond of her and enjoyed playing with her from time to time. He had pierced her nipples because he knew it was something she really wanted, and nobody else would. But he was not the ardent, bisexual lover whom she later described as her ideal master, when he was not around to contradict her.

Having revolted the Castro clones by being a fist-fucker, and then having outraged the fist-fuckers in a previous club by also being into S/M, Steve enjoyed asserting his independence by pissing everybody off again when he included her on the guest list. The gay men who came to these weekly events were amused or impressed by her epic sexual performances and intake of mind-altering substances and sometimes surprised to find themselves attracted to her. A lot of them also just resented and ignored her. They wanted the Catacombs and the rest of their gay world to be a refuge where they would be protected from women and the fucked-up expectations of heterosexuality. Cynthia had first brought me here as her lover, and that had taken some of the tension out of the atmosphere by visibly making her as queer as the guys we jogged elbows with.

I turned my back to the bar to undress and stow the regulation boots, jeans, T-shirt, and flannel shirt that I had thrown on before my stressful five-minute trip down the hill. The men who came to these parties wouldn't be caught dead out of full leather if you saw them in the Brig or the Ambush, but they rarely bothered to wear more than a leather vest or a jockstrap to the Catacombs, because it was a rule that everything got removed within 30 seconds of signing in. "Prissy queens" who tried to keep their clothes on were often relieved of their finery against their will. You might have thought that Cynthia's presence up front, with her gorgeous full bosom and cute little ass and long black hair, would have made it easier for me to be naked there, but we did not feel the same way about our bodies. She had a sexual style that was stereotypically masculine, but she occupied her feminine body completely and boldly. She was there as a woman, and I was there as someone who wished I was not.

Covered up, it was so much easier for me to maintain an illusion of masculinity. I was the only dyke I knew who strapped on a dick to fuck or made my bottoms call me Sir. As much as I enjoyed seducing butch female bottoms, I wanted to be here, with leathermen who locked other men in cages, flogged and insulted and came inside their chosen prey. Too often, I felt more like one of them than I did like a lesbian. I was soothed by the ease with which they slid past one another, somehow being able to read whether a hand on the butt or a tweak to a tit would be welcome. I could not imagine this sensual treatment of strangers being allowed among a group of women. I loved the leathermen's utterly masculine bearing (often interspersed with a few seconds of camping it up that only underscored their maleness) and unabashed homosexuality. Nowhere else but in San Francisco had I seen this unself-conscious and frank desire that was not only gay but deeply perverse.

At leather bars and at more select gatherings like this one, I was a curiosity. There were men who resented my presence and tried to exclude me, men who felt I belonged there because I was also an enthusiastic practitioner of restraint and torture, and only a handful who were able to articulate some confusion about my gender. It's amazing, actually, that any of them mentioned this to me, because I could hardly bring it to the front of my own consciousness.

Naked and therefore doomed to endure whatever was about to happen next, I oddly felt better. I was only one naked person among many, did not have the only imperfect body. The Catacombs was not a place where you had to be thin, white, well-built, or young to get cruised. Sexual skill was valued as much as a handsome face. My party attitude switched on, a shift in values that made bare skin seem like a bold statement, an act of bravery that proved I belonged. I went back to the bar and deliberately slid between George and the person next to him to get a Styrofoam cup of coffee. He was smoking a cigarette and made as if to grab my tits. I fended off his touch, which wasn't very difficult because he just wanted to provoke me, not grope me. George got what he wanted by being such a crappy and belligerent top that eventually somebody who didn't have anything better to do would throw him on his back and fuck him. "Is that a donkey dick," I asked, wrinkling my nose, "or are you just a jackass?" A few men nearby laughed loudly, so George stood up and jiggled his big, floppy meat at them. Like he ever used it for anything other than a handle.

Bob was also at the bar. We were always glad to see one another. He was a slight, middle-aged guy with a bald patch in the middle of his head. Bob was thought to be a little peculiar because he attended the Metropolitan Community Church on a regular basis. But he was always quick with a bawdy jibe, so his Christianity didn't seem to be holding him back much. He was the first balding man I ever had a crush on. Going bald was, after all, something that only happened to men, so it was virile and sexy. He didn't try to hide it, he just kept his hair short and didn't trip about it. I always enjoyed looking at his scrumptious ass, but the magical spark never flew between us, for some reason. I don't know that I ever even saw him play.

Everybody there was already high, and I wanted to catch up. I stirred a drizzle of white powder into the sweet, milky coffee and drank it quickly. While George bobbed and weaved over his stein of beer, I stood beside him, unable to get the size of his cock out of my mind and equally unable to imagine ever touching him. My skin, flesh, bones, and spirit vibrated with tension and ambivalence about his ruined alcoholic craggy face as the MDA took effect. I had brought an empty glass spice bottle with me, and poured just enough poppers into the bottom of it to be absorbed by the cotton ball inside. I had been taught not to leave any surplus liquid to slosh around. It might burn someone who was too high to keep track of the contents of the bottle while they brought it to their mouth and nose.

Just as the music was melding nicely with my heartbeat and the edges of my vision were beginning to acquire a heavenly glimmer,

I saw him. And he saw me. Jim, the deaf bodybuilder. He had just finished a quick sign language conversation with his small, dark-haired lover, who gave him a peck on the cheek and disappeared into one of the back rooms with a prospective bottom. I had seen Jim at parties before and felt a little self-conscious about his disability, but always gave him a smile. He was gorgeous to look at, thick-chested, with heavy strong legs and arms that could crack an ox in half, and yet he carried himself with a cheerful and even humble openness. There was no shred of snotty attitude about him. As he grinned and swam toward me with the slow grace of a muscle queen, I knew that we were going to play. The eye contact that usually sufficed for Catacombs regulars to make their dates had, for once, worked the way it was supposed to work, for me.

I don't know how he did this, but even though Jim towered over me and probably outweighed me by at least 200 pounds, this sweet monster with his shaved head managed to convey a submissive attitude. As he came toward me he flexed his arms, just a little. It wasn't a studied pose, just an anxious reflex, perhaps reminding himself why he might be an acceptable offering. He made a guttural, indecipherable sound that I think was involuntary. It reminded me of the cry of a magpie whose tongue had been cut out. I wondered what it was like to be born without hearing, to never know that sensation. It didn't seem sad to me as much as it seemed an attractive challenge, a difference that I was determined to bridge.

I reached for his face, and he put his arms on either side of the bar, creating a little cave where I could focus on and touch him. I could not see around him and enjoyed being ensconced safely behind the bulk of his well-disciplined meat. We kissed each other for a long time, long enough I think that he was surprised. His lips were as muscular as the rest of him, but his tongue was small and shy. When I stopped kissing him, it was only to put my mouth on his neck and shoulder, to lick the bitter flavored sweat from his sandpapery skin and bite into his muscles.

One of the things I loved about fisting was the way that it

resembled and yet differed from sadomasochistic role-playing. As an S/M top, I was expected to be distant and formal, but fisting tops got extra points for being hands-on, sensually giving and physically involved. I once heard Steve, our sensei in depravity, say, "Why the hell would I fuck somebody I don't want to kiss?"

The attention in the room had shifted subtly in our direction. Any hot scene in the Catacombs drew voyeurs like a sprinkle of fish food on the top of an aquarium. The assembled body of experienced fisters had eyes in the back of their collective heads for other people's pleasure. Perhaps because we were all so loaded, it seemed as if we could experience a portion of one another's bliss. Watching somebody else get expertly plowed was a fine form of foreplay, a rare bit of pornographic eye candy that could never be replayed. This shot of peer attention gave me a burst of confidence and energy. Eighty-five hungry assholes can't be wrong. Getting my hand into Jim was going to be a very good time indeed.

Many pairs and threesomes had already left the front room ahead of us. There were two more rooms (not counting the tiny bathroom, where I often perched on the sink to pee, to the consternation of whoever was douching out in the shower). The very back room contained "sling alley," a half-dozen leather butt-baskets and stirrups hung facing each other on heavy chain, with studded leather holders for cans of Crisco swinging conveniently at the side of each station. I could already tell from the volume of oinking and the resounding chains that all the available slots in this room were taken. There was also a bondage cross there, built out of heavy eight-by-eight timbers, but that was not where my scene with Jim was headed.

The middle room had several platforms around the walls, each containing a thin plastic-covered mattress. A wide waterbed hogged center stage, and a gurney hung from springs and chains at right angles to it. I saw a vacant platform to the left and just inside the doorway, and steered us toward it. Jim was alongside me, making faces of sweet anguish as I toyed roughly with his pecs. We were so in sync with each other that I didn't seem to push him onto the bed; it was as if I had lifted him and placed him there, like a perfect slice of pie on a little white saucer. I had already grabbed a pile of towels, from exactly where I did not remember. We settled into the missionary position of handballing—he was on his back in front of me, I was sitting with my legs under his thighs, tucking a towel underneath his massive ass. He had shaved all over before coming to the party, but his skin was still slightly abrasive. To my ripped hands, his skin felt both downy-soft and yet had a texture that was elusively pleasing to explore. Jim relaxed completely and let me touch him everywhere. He gave me a lazy, trusting smile, in no hurry for me to shake hands with his joy spot.

When people think of getting to know somebody, the image they have is of talking to that person. But there are other ways to acquire knowledge about another person and make yourself known to them. As I took my time to single out and massage each one of Jim's muscles, from the top of his head down to the soles of his feet, his body was reassured and befriended, the same way that a cat comes to accept the comfort of a knowledgeable stranger's lap and fingertips. I was so lost in sampling every inch of him that some of our voyeurs moved on to more ebullient scenes. But men with a similar style of play were taking places near us, creating an invisible temple of silent seduction. With our hands and heaving hips, we were weaving pleasure that filled the air, and each sensation that brought someone joy got the rest of us higher.

A sexual touch can say "I want you," but it can also say "I care for you," and in the long moments that I was enclosed by this man's scent and the visual delight of his body, I was not in love with him, but I *was* loving him. It was something that we didn't have to say out loud; he knew it by the look on my face and the quality of my caress. He put his hands on either side of his cock, showing me how fat it was, and made one of his incoherent cawing sounds. The tendons of his neck popped out with the tension of arousal.

I am not ashamed to say that from time to time the edges of my eyes stung from unshed tears. I was amazed yet again by the power and generosity of an unabashed bottom. I've never understood how someone can do that, simply let go and invite me into their psyche and their orifices. And as much as I want to glory in that gift, I never feel quite worthy of it. But with Jim I was not intimidated. He was letting me know again and again that I was doing everything perfectly, that he wanted exactly what I had for him.

The smooth surface of the freshly opened can of Crisco was cool and creamy, with a comical little peak, the tip of which curled over and nearly touched itself again. The pointed fingers of my left hand dipped into and destroyed that snow-white, virgin plane. The fistful of grease I took away with me left a hole behind, a pit with a rippled edge that was almost as big as Jim's asshole was going to stretch to receive me. I rubbed the Crisco onto his chest, down the six-pack of his abdomen, and smacked on his pectoral muscles a little, making the skin red. He groaned and nodded and lifted his legs. Because he could not say "please" out loud, his entire body was shouting that wish.

Time slowed as I ran my slippery fingers down to his navel, and around his cock. I would have been happy to jack him off or blow him, but Catacombs sexuality was not dickcentric. I rarely even saw a hard cock until after 4 A.M. I wondered if being able to get an erection was adequate compensation for coming down from whatever cocktail had been chosen for this evening's chemical backdrop.

When I closed my fist around Jim's full, heavy nut sac and squeezed, his face twisted with a little pain and a great deal of wonder. *So this is how much I can feel,* he seemed to be saying. *That, yes, and that, yes, more, yes, that.* Wanting to hear his guttural cry again, I dabbled at the outermost rim of his anus, tickling it, and the strange noise pealed out, a permission and a plea. My other hand wandered across his chest, keeping his nipples hard, while my index finger circled a half-inch inside him, the preliminary move to creating a slick funnel that would admit all of me. I wanted to punch into him, and containing these fierce impulses was like being perpetually teased and kept right on the edge of coming.

As we played, my hunky accomplice would sometimes hoist his

own thighs aloft to give me greater access and sometimes allow them to rest upon my legs again, when his arms had tired or he was being sent into some other world as I entered the private world inside of him. I moved around too, sometimes sliding back so that my arm was parallel to his body, scooting to one side to obtain the proper angle, looking for a moment of relief from fatigue so I could keep my forearm moving. Everything that we did was reciprocal, like a dance. There was no force, just an invitation to press on, as he opened for me, trusting me with his pleasure and his life.

And I could not get enough of him; I wanted him to fly and gasp and experience release after release until he had enough. And by that I mean really enough, not the polite excuse that a self-conscious bottom will make when he fears that the top is tired or losing interest, or is ashamed of needing too much. I thought that getting too much of Jim might almost be enough.

I loaded the palm of my right hand with grease and poised both of my hands side by side, trading off, going in and coming out, changing the direction and pressure so that I did not make him sore. Each time he made way, I rewarded him by advancing a bit more. I felt as if I were being drawn into a labyrinth that was flushed dark pink with blood and lined with a material smoother than satin or glass. My hands were only halfway into him when I began to feel the pulse of his heart, resonating even here, governing the rhythm of our coming together. I do not think I could have dawdled any longer without losing the momentum of growing arousal, but still, when his sphincter swallowed me, it was too soon, too much—for me, not for him. I gasped out loud and almost fell on top of him.

I've heard fisting described with horror (or with faux scientific objectivity as "brachiopractic eroticism"). I am at a loss to understand this ignorance and repugnance. We are afraid of holes and their dark secrets, which they might someday tell—contrary holes, holes that will not open when we want them to, demanding holes that cannot be satisfied, dirty holes that no one is supposed to look at or lick or touch (yet they still receive adulation). It occurred to me, however, that sometimes holes are filled with light. Sometimes the things they have to tell us are wonderful. The empty place within Jim was akin to a forest grove or a cathedral. We need such quiet places in order to hear the voices of the forces that made us.

For a man to allow himself to be penetrated is for some people the equivalent of the sky falling. It is a disaster; nothing could be more unnatural or threatening to the social order. The world does not want the spiritual child that is born from the trusting and magical bowel of a man who is not afraid to be a hole, and a very large hole at that. But I wanted that birth, I was Jim's impregnator and midwife. As Donna Summer wailed like a deranged witchy nymphomaniac, we jousted and joked with one another, each small movement of mine inside of him triggering a wealth of thrills. I tapped my forearm, hard, and his abs vibrated. I kept at it, knowing I would have bruises the next day halfway up to my elbow. Jim put his hands behind his head, holding it up with bulging forearms so that he could see what was in him, and urged me on in his own untranslatable language.

His mad, rolling eyes and excited calls made me hard and wet. It was as if my arm was a cock that was long and rigid enough to make him levitate. The need to come built in the pit of my own stomach, and he saw me delay my climax again and again so that I could stay with him and go a little higher toward heaven. I would see a flash of gratitude on his face, then disbelief as we continued, gently but relentlessly, finding new nooks and crannies, new degrees of being utterly stuffed, fucked, had, fondled internally and loved senseless.

His cock had slowly continued to get thicker and thicker, but not longer, and I had glanced occasionally at this partial hard-on, wondering at his ability to manage such a thing when all of his nerve endings were otherwise occupied. He was covered with a visible gel of sweat and Crisco, and the stench of poppers was making me dizzy. He groaned again, a series of bass notes forced from the pit of his gut, and began to piss. I found his prostate and pressed on it, moved back and forth across it, making sure this expulsion of water felt like the weirdest and most intense orgasm on earth. The hot fluid was almost clear and didn't smell like urine. It was distilled from his body in a mysterious way that bypassed all the usual processes that make come or piss. I leaned forward, grinning ear to ear, and he shared it with me so that we were both laughing and tripping in the hot fountain my hand had milked out of him.

Three times we built up to a point where his body was driven to release some balmy, liquid evidence of his extremity. Each time, I let my posture and facial expression indicate that I wanted to share this communion with him. Jim could not tell me how he felt, so he shared his piss with me, a sweet-smelling gift, playing it across my chest while I shivered and laughed and admired his feckless bulk, joined to me like a Siamese twin. These outbursts came at shorter and shorter intervals, and I began to think that we might eventually have to separate. The texture inside of him had changed just a little, but even such a small effect made me nervous. The fragility of the lining of his channel was something I never forgot. And his color had changed too; he had acquired a pale tone that made me think he needed a rest.

Then there was a break in the music, and every bit of action in the club hung fire. The gut-wrenching bellows of "Yeah, you fucker, yeah!" and "You can take it, take it all!" stopped. We had been caught in the music, everyone unaware that they were moving in time with it, and it had created both a feeling of unity and pockets of privacy in our butt-pumping frenzy. After a long silence of five seconds, we heard three sharp slaps, then the extra-loud sound of a baby crying. When the music resumed, it was as if the power had come back on. "Yeah, you fucker. Fuck you!" Creak, creak. "Take it all!" Enough of us started laughing to break the dramatic tension that had kept Jim and me hard at work. He put both of his hands up and touched my face, squeezing it to say thank you, and made a regretful gesture indicating that I had to begin my departure.

Considering how much I love getting inside of someone, I am usually in no hurry to leave that warm and responsive shelter. Even if it would have been safe to quickly slip my hand out of him, I would not have been so rude. I stopped thrusting or turning my hand from side to side or slowly opening it a bit and closing it again. His guts stopped contracting around me, and his heartbeat slowed. As the tunnel ahead of me slowly collapsed, I withdrew, only turning my hand when I had to negotiate a tiny glitch in the passage. There was a final outcry from him as his rectum shrank and shat me out, but there was no disappointment in it, only victory. His asshole looked like a crimson rose in full bloom.

I lay down on top of him and we kissed again, relishing one another's naughtiness and stamina. I told him again and again how hot, handsome, and fun he was, but all of these words sounded trivial. He had taken me along, allowed me to vicariously experience his bliss, and granted my every wish for a man whose need matched my own. That was the hole that I had needed to fill. For a long time after that fuck, I knew that I mattered in the world. I knew I had something good about me, that there was a reason for me to exist, that my counterpart was real and not some insane figment of my damaged sexual fantasies.

We staggered out to the front room to get something to drink and receive quiet congratulations from friends who had enjoyed watching us enjoy one another. I perched on one of the padded benches, which had become so slippery from contact with a series of well-greased buttocks that even a brand-new towel was no guarantee that I wouldn't shoot off my seat like a burlesque banana fired from the cannon of its skin. I had forgotten, while I fisted my bodybuilder bottom god, that there were breasts swinging against my arms and getting in my way, forgotten my cunt, forgotten that I was not a man he would want the way gay men yearn for one another. I knew what my cock looked like, but if I reached down for it, it would never be there.

I don't remember the rest of the party. I only remember what happened afterward, when I had to leave that camaraderie behind and go home. My lover had waited up for me and was impatient to hear the juicy details. She was titillated but jealous. "You let some man piss on you?" she jeered.

I was abruptly plunged into a worldview where the things that I had just done were noxious rather than blessed. Walking home, I felt like a flawless topman who had triumphed over the tight-assed forces of evil. She didn't want me thinking I was a faggot, even if she called herself a daddy's boy in bed. She had to force me to see that Jim and I were on different sides of the gender divide. He was supposed to be the enemy, someone I held at bay lest he gain some toxic advantage over me. The flat chest that I had unconsciously assumed in my imagination as I walked home and the weight of my cock and balls in the left side of the crotch of my jeans were not spoken of but violently exorcised just the same. I made some kind of sarcastic retort, but shame stuck to me and burned, like napalm. It is too easy to take judgments to heart when the people who issue them also say they love us.

Approximately 20 years later, I place a lot less stock in "love" like that. I am no longer willing to be in a relationship where I do all the things that men are supposed to do while I pretend to be something else. I won't take any shit for being a cocksucker and a man who desires other men. My beard is on the outside of my face now. People have accused me of cutting off my tits, but they don't understand that the surgery, for me, was about what I gained, not what I lost. The flat chest that I wanted is mine now, I don't have to imagine it, I can touch my pecs whenever I want and when I embrace someone, I can relax into full-body contact without wincing away. My cock is still hiding, but hey, I could always win the lottery. In the meantime, I have the pleasure of men who want to be fucked the way that I can fuck them to prove that my dick is real enough. If fist-fuckers who wear their red hankies on the right can be big fierce queer studs, I can try to be as proud of my holes as they are of theirs.

The next time I went to the Catacombs and Jim was there, he smiled at me and came over for a hug. I was happy to see him and embraced him in return, but my girlfriend had come with me, and so I deflected his unspoken invitation. The next time we met, I was available, but he was not. We never played again. We both thought, no doubt, that we had lots of time to revisit that mattress or perhaps even grab the waterbed.

He is gone now. He died, I think, in the first wave of men who died, of a disease that had no name. Steve had a heart attack and was spared the ordeal of witnessing that epidemic. Cynthia died many years later, because she was just enough of a faggot to share a virus with the men who never really accepted her. The Catacombs has been closed for decades. And I find that it is pretty difficult for me to go looking for another grinning, good-natured sex pig to wear for a bracelet. Would it be the same without the drugs? Could I work my whole hand in and out of a shivering, gulping sphincter without being cut in half by grief? I feel like a dog who has lost his master, who mourns without understanding. But I also continue to remember, and be grateful. Within me, still, Jim's shameless virtuoso one-person gang bang is an eternal miracle, a seed of joy potent enough to turn the whole world into a bacchanalian garden.

Do you have a furrow worthy of that seed? And if you accept it, where will you sow it in your turn?

Credits

Some of the stories in this book originally appeared elsewhere in a slightly different form, as noted below.

"Belonging" first appeared in *Advocate Men,* August 1986. It was anthologized in *Flesh and the Word,* John Preston, editor, New York: Plume, 1992, and in *The Best American Erotica 1993,* Susie Bright, editor, New York: Macmillan, 1993.

"The Cop and His Choirboy" first appeared in *No Mercy,* Los Angeles: Alyson Publications, 2000.

"Parting Is Such Sweet Sorrow" first appeared in *Sons of Darkness: Tales of Men, Blood and Immortality,* Michael Rowe and Thomas S. Roche, editors, Pittsburgh and San Francisco: Cleis Press, 1996. Excerpted in *Canadian Male,* November-December 1996. And it now appears as a chapter in *Mortal Companion,* San Francisco: Suspect Thoughts, 2004.

"Prez Meets His Match" is excerpted from *Doc and Fluff: The Dystopian Tale of a Girl and Her Biker,* Boston: Alyson Publications, 1990.

"Skinned Alive" first appeared in *No Mercy,* Los Angeles: Alyson Publications, 2000.

"The Spoiler" first appeared in *Advocate Men,* April 1985, and was reprinted in *Macho Sluts,* Boston: Alyson Publications, 1988. It was reprinted again in *The Best of Advocate Men,* February 1992.

CREDITS

"Swimmer's Body" first appeared in *Advocate Men*, April 1987.

"Unsafe Sex" first appeared in *Melting Point*, Boston: Alyson Publications, 1993.

"The Wolf Is My Shepherd, I Shall Not Want" first appeared in *Switch Hitters*, Carol Queen and Lawrence Schimel, editors, Pittsburgh and San Francisco: Cleis Press, 1996. Translated into Dutch and reprinted in *Wilde Jongens*, Kyra Andriese, editor, Amsterdam: Prometheus, 1997. And it now appears as a chapter in *Mortal Companion*, San Francisco: Suspect Thoughts, 2004.